I0818600

AMONTILLADO

Amontillado

KEVIN KOPERSKI

AMONTILLADO

Published in the United States by Streetlamp Press
www.streetlamppress.com

Excerpts from Edgar Allan Poe stories and poems are taken from various public domain sources.

Dust Jacket Excerpt from The Cask of Amontillado by Edgar Allan Poe (1809 - 1849)

Jacket design: Kevin Koperski
Jacket art: Erik Gloor

Printed in the United States of America

ISBN: 978-0-9884516-0-5

First Edition
0 9 8 7 6 5 4 3 2 1

To you, the reader, for offering encouragement
long before you turned the first page...

PART I

"...for the painter had grown wild with the ardor of his work, and turned his eyes from the canvas rarely, even to regard the countenance of his wife. And he would not see that the tints which he spread upon the canvas were drawn from the cheeks of her who sat beside him."

EDGAR ALLAN POE
The Oval Portrait

CHAPTER ONE

Present

Call me Fortunato. You won't be the first.

Point a gun at my face and bury me alive. Again, you won't be the first.

Tonight I'm like a fish caught in the web of a sailor's net, hoisted from the sea to flop and flounder on a cutting board. My only desire is one more plunge into the black depths of a familiar ocean, a return to life as it existed before that particularly treacherous worm arrived for dinner. I smell of whiskey and urine. I'm cold. My skin is wet and shriveled from too many hours in a storm, and my clothes cling like a dying author to his pen, an author eager to scratch out a final epitaph to encapsulate his career for posterity. If I were that author, and if that pen were mine, I know what I'd write:

Death to Marcus McComber.

Are you confused? Offended by my venom? Don't be. My entire world has been upended. At the center of it all is Marcus McComber. He is the source of my torment, the betrayer, the worm, the antagonist in my otherwise uneventful existence. If he were here now, he would laugh and tell me to accept my demise without a fuss, to admit guilt without question, because to do otherwise would only worsen my sins. He would order an ale and toast my life, and he would joke that his poor Fortunato had been most unfortunate indeed. But as I've already proven tonight, I am no Fortunato.

The man seated across from me is Andrew Ruben, a detective, a burly fellow with a thick beard. He hasn't beaten me yet, which, to his credit, is more than I can say for the lanky gentleman behind him. That man's name, I believe, is Burrows, and I'm sure I've exaggerated his manners by using the term gentleman. These detectives are evil. Ruben with his disbelieving stare and Burrows pacing back and forth like a jailer concocting new methods of torture are the absolute definitions of abusive authority. Every word they utter, every upheaval of their lungs, betrays a belief in tyranny and intimidation.

Now Ruben says, "We're not getting anywhere. Let's start over. For the record, please tell us your name."

"Surely," I laugh, "you already know my name."

"This is not the time for games, Mr. Lyons."

"You do know it!" I say. But these men are incapable of smiles, so I answer, "Jacob Moses Lyons."

And while he scratches the name on a pad of paper, please take a moment to look around. Does this dungeon not speak of Fortunato's tomb with flattery? The walls are dull. There are no windows. The chamber is dank and isolated, rank with fear and uncertainty. No one has told me why I'm here. And yet the inescapable nature of my predicament is as near to being buried alive as one may come.

We're seated at a table in the center of an otherwise barren room. A light bulb swings back and forth at eye level, suspended by a frayed wire, casting the room in a shaky light. A crack of thunder echoes from above. When the bulb flickers, the world ceases to exist, and for a moment I lose myself in the shadows.

During that moment of darkness, Ruben asks, "Why did you do it?"

When the light returns, I notice a crucifix hanging in a corner. It is the only wall adornment in the room, a symbol passed from one floor of authoritarian hypocrisy to the next, meant to frighten and tease the souls of captive men. Do not lie before God, it warns. And the thought makes me laugh.

"What's so funny?" Ruben asks.

"Juxtaposition," I answer. "You and me, side by side, sinner and disciplinarian, confessor and forgiver. But who is who?"

"Tell us why you did it."

"I've heard that many times tonight. Perhaps you can tell me why I did it, because you've told me little else."

They won't tip their hand. They've been tightlipped since the moment they hauled me away. I had arrived home, wet and stinky and drunk, with blood on my forehead and pain everywhere, and a shower seemed too much effort, so I found the bed and collapsed. Eventually they broke down my door and dragged me here, offering no hint as to why. But I have a guess.

When Ruben glares at me further without offering more information, I say, "The answer to all your questions, and the cause of every effect, is obvious and indisputable. His name is Marcus McComber."

A crack of thunder plunges the room into the realms of nonexistence. When the recesses in the corners return to shadow, Ruben and Burrows and Jesus all stare at me with blank expressions. Burrows has stopped pacing. Jesus never moves. And a raised eyebrow is the only hint of Ruben's delight.

"What about Marcus McComber?" he asks.

"Everything that has happened," I say, "whatever you think I've done, it is undoubtedly his fault."

"Is that so?"

"How could it not be? He is the scourge of my life, the treacherous worm whose hook I chewed. He is to blame for every atrocity you've assigned to me, and I can hear his laughter now."

"Tell us about him then."

But how can I do that? Marcus McComber defies description. I've sat beside him many a night and shared enough gripes to sadden a shrink, but I've discovered little of his history and even less of his character. One night he simply materialized out of the shadows and sat down beside me. At times, he is friendly enough, in a distant manner wholly unworthy of friendship in most people. But at other times, when the weight of a moment becomes amplified inside his twisted, drunken mind, he is manifestly evil.

"He's a drunk," I say. "And like a drunk he tells drunken stories."

It's true. He spins tales of murder and intrigue, of seduction, of infidelity, adventure, deception. And worst of all, he believes his lies, or at least behaves as if they are true. For all I know, this entire ordeal could be one of his many sordid concoctions, and he might be in another room toasting his detective pals who've frightened and tortured me beyond any accepted standard of practical foolery. Indeed, this could all be the work of Marcus McComber, but I have my doubts.

"Tell us more," Ruben demands.

"He laughs. He laughs a lot, and then he laughs more, as though he alone knows some strangely amusing joke with a punch line no one understands. I've always laughed along, being, as you've pointed out, drunk myself, but tonight was different."

"In what way?"

"He threatened me. He tried to kill me, to place blame where blame was lacking. It was a side of Marcus McComber I hadn't expected, a trait I dismissed as drunken exaggeration. I was wrong."

Do you see the cut on my forehead? Can you see the dried blood? Even these vile detectives failed to inflict such a deep wound. It was Marcus McComber who did that with the blunt end of a revolver.

And now something has changed. Ruben stands from his chair with his furrowed face afire. Burrows screws a fist into an open palm. And Jesus on the wall screams, "I'm tired of hanging on this fucking cross for morons like you."

"Do you mean he tried to kill you?" Ruben asks. "For no reason? With no motive?"

"Of course he had a motive!" I say, laughing. "He accused me of murder!"

And Ruben, with a smile, leans closer and asks, "Is that when you killed him?"

CHAPTER TWO

9:00PM

"Tell me," said Marcus McComber, still quite alive, and with a rather unpleasant demeanor, "From the beginning, from the outset, spin me the tale of your treachery, my dear Fortunato, and then I will kill you."

"I haven't a clue what you mean," said Jacob Lyons.

The two men stood in the bronze light of a street lamp. McComber, with his hood tossed back and his black coat gleaming, let the rain streak down his forehead. Lightning blitzed the rooftops with an intermittent dazzle, and the streets emptied of pedestrians. A tempest had descended upon the city, and these two men were all that remained to define the boundaries of good and evil, however fudged and mislaid those boundaries may have been.

"Do you mock me?" McComber asked. "Do you laugh at my misfortune? I would argue the right is yours, as you've no doubt suffered the same humiliation countless nights at my side, but now is no time for boasting and betterment."

"Honestly, Marcus, you must be kidding. And if you don't mind, I'd rather be on my way than bickering with you in the cold and the rain."

"To where do you run, Jacob?"

"Home. Can you imagine? Such an odd and bewildering possibility, isn't it? That a man abandoned by his friend at a tavern, after a night of drunken revelry and celebration, might actually walk home through this miserable weather. I'm sure it baffles you. And how about this? I need to piss like you can't imagine. So please, if you might, save your accusations for another day and let me go home."

McComber laughed, as he so often did, a vicious cackle that might intimidate the storm itself but which had no effect on the well-accustomed Jacob Lyons. "How long has it been, Jacob? How long have we known each other?"

"At least one night too many."

"Is it four months now? And how long have you been scheming? How long have you sat beside me in contemplation, waiting to unleash your vengeance?"

This time it was Jacob who laughed. "My vengeance? Ha! There is no solution to you. No grand strategy to cleanse you from my life, and believe me when I say I've thought long and hard on the subject. But wasn't it you, Marcus, who claimed we'd never see each other again? Am I mistaken? Did you not say that very thing a short while ago at the tavern? I'm not too drunk to forget such a splendid promise."

McComber's smile vanished. Thunder crashed around them. "Tonight was indeed our last together, Jacob. Of that I am certain."

"Excellent." Jacob made a move to continue walking, but McComber blocked him. Jacob said, "Come now, Marcus. I can whip it out here and piss on the street, though, given my current disfavor with sobriety, I might mistakenly aim at your shoes. Or, and I prefer this option, you can say goodbye and we can both be on our way to warmth and toilets and much improved lives."

"Of all people, Jacob. Of all the wretched inhabitants of this vile city, I never expected you would be our undoing. I thought it doubtful you'd ever learn the truth, leastways not until long after the end, when your world had crumbled and you found yourself drunken on a street curb wondering when your life had fallen apart. At that moment, on the brink of your utter demise, I guessed you might discover the truth. I thought then you might piece the puzzle whole. But you surprise me."

"That borders on a compliment, Marcus."

"Was it all an act? Every night on that barstool, every night drunken and rambling? A demonstration of disguise? Deceit? If so, I congratulate you, because I took you for a fool. Does that make you happy?"

"My friend, it seems your delusions stretch a bit beyond absurdity tonight. Now must we duel it out here, or can I go?"

But instead of an answer, McComber coughed. It was not a throat clearing gesture, but a genuine throat wrenching upheaval, hoarse and guttural and plagued by phlegm. He stumbled backwards. His eyes shut. He bent over slightly, coughing, wobbling, gagging. Perspiration poisoned the rainwater on his brow.

"Are you ill?" asked Jacob. "I mean physically, you know. Obviously your mental whereabouts haven't been anywhere near healthy for ages."

But when McComber stopped coughing, it wasn't a smile on his face that greeted Jacob Lyons. He lifted his chin and glared. A red streak of blood emerged from the corner of his mouth, dull and wet and quickly diluted in the rain.

"She's dead," McComber whispered.

"Who?" Jacob whispered back.

"The time for atonement is now, my friend. No need to waste your language and poetry on a decided mind. No need to mistake me for ignorant or misguided. I am here with a single purpose: to pay retribution to her slayer; to reward her killer with the very prize he lavished upon his victim."

"As always, Marcus, boastful exaggeration is the hallmark of your lunacy. But color me intrigued, as I so often am by your ludicrous tales. Who have I killed?"

"You know quite well."

"Ah! Your mistress, I assume? Your married whore? And why would I do that? Why would I kill a woman I've only met in stories? Why would I murder so poor a lady, whose soul was the hapless victim of a morally deficient miscreant? Tell me, Marcus. Why would I do such a thing?"

"Vengeance."

"There you go again with the vengeance. Did she wrong me? I don't even know her. To be honest, I thought her a fascinating invention of your drunken imagination. And, perhaps you can help here, but why would I destroy someone who never existed?"

McComber suddenly burst into another fit of laughter. "Such questions, my dear Fortunato. Usually it is I who dissembles so, I who pollutes our conversations with innuendo. After all this time, you finally manage to surprise me. But I know the truth, Jacob. I've seen her in death. I've seen her wretched body curled up on bed sheets pooled with blood. I've seen what you've done. And tonight, Jacob, this creepy, gloomy, nefarious eve, so very similar to the first night she and I met, tonight was to be our beginning."

"Have I mentioned I need to urinate? Because really…"

"Enough!" McComber straightened. He was several inches taller than Jacob. His black coat hung open. "Do you remember when I told you every situation has a remedy?"

"As vaguely as I remember anything else you say."

"Tonight, my life has disintegrated into a puddle of blood and vomit, and this…" He paused, reached a pale hand into the pocket of his coat and withdrew something shiny. "This," McComber said, glaring at the revolver he now pointed at Jacob's forehead as raindrops danced and glistened off the weapon's silver barrel, "This is my remedy."

CHAPTER THREE

Four Months Ago

Marcus McComber was not a man fearful of the night. He enjoyed the solitary nature of darkness, the anonymity of shadow. He was also fond of lightning and thunderstorms, and tonight, as he stood sheltered beneath the jutting brick façade of an unmarked building, such miracles of nature filled the evening with their fantastic brilliance. But beyond the rain, beyond the cold, beyond the barren bleakness of a city devoid of humanity, a city indulgent with the necessities of sin and pleasure but generally bereft the beauty one hopes might accompany such necessities, he watched an altogether different miracle of nature saunter down the sidewalk. Though he had never been formally introduced, had never been in her presence more than a few moments, he knew her to be a woman whose character and beauty had seldom been outdone, a woman who, in his always excessive and imaginative thoughts, had no peers in the modern world and no equals in the realms of history or literature. Of course, he also had a fondness for melodrama and exaggeration, and so, in truth, she was no different than any other woman he set his lust upon.

McComber was new to this city, new to the twists and turns of its alleyways, new to the smells and the shadows, new to the history and behaviors of the people he had only begun to discover, but he was not new to beauty. Nor was he unaccustomed to the artful posturing of romantic pursuit. And he was most certainly not unfamiliar with the fulfillment of his most passionate desires. So when he stumbled upon this woman a week earlier, when he heard her voice in conversation, when he stood delighted by her wit and entranced by her beauty, he knew, though he had never spoken a word to her, she would soon be his.

Patiently, he watched her cross the street. Tall and slender, she splashed through puddle after muddy puddle with a long stride until she met the opposite sidewalk. The radiance of her features battled for prominence with the dark mystery of her silhouette each time she passed a candlelit window. Soon she turned to a set of low steps and disappeared into the very corner bookshop where he had accidentally encountered her the previous week. Tonight's encounter, however, was no coincidence.

He stepped away from the building. To passersby, he would seem a handsome gentleman out for an evening stroll. He wore a long overcoat and pants, with a black fedora to shield his eyes from the rain. A short distance brought him to the bookstore and he climbed the steps to the entrance. But before he entered, before he began to work his charm on this unsuspecting woman, he couldn't help but notice a leaflet on the sidewalk. It was a sheet of wet parchment dirtied by the bleeding ink of an artist's pen. "Tonight's Book Club Discussion:" the flyer declared, "*The Cask of Amontillado*, by Edgar Allan Poe."

§

Once inside, he felt heat. Warmth. It was a damp warmth, like huddling close to a bonfire deep in a forest early in the morning, when dew had not quite frozen, when the chill of the body melted away and clung to newly heated garments. The air hung heavy with musk. Light radiated not from overhead but from dozens of candles and lanterns placed randomly throughout the store. McComber felt as if he were standing on a rocky outcropping overlooking the scattered campfires of a gathering army. He would have made a fantastic General. Sending men to their deaths seemed, to him, delightful.

Everywhere he looked, he saw aged antique volumes of fiction on row after row of bookshelves. It was a beautiful sight to a man well-versed in fiction, but his eyes had a different destination.

As he brushed rainwater from his coat, he spotted the woman. She had stopped near the front register to speak a few hushed words to a curmudgeonly fellow behind the counter. She smiled, kissed the old man's forehead, and disappeared behind a row of books. Once she was gone, the clerk blushed noticeably and turned his attention to Marcus.

"Welcome," the man said, his voice raspy but not unpleasant. "Anything I can help you find?"

McComber shook his head and removed his overcoat. The fellow eyed him warily, but McComber guessed the old man greeted all clients with that same unwelcoming fixation.

Then the old man continued, "Are you here for the meeting? Yes? Well, follow her back then. Most of the group's already here, and they'll be waiting for you, so get going."

McComber nodded, and in the wake of the old man's scrutiny, he followed the woman's path toward the rear of the bookstore. He heard chatter and conversation, small talk emanating from a far corner. He had lost sight of his quarry but refused to rush forward, fearing, correctly, that he might stumble into an undesired and potentially embarrassing situation. Conversations begun by embarrassment seldom went well for the embarrassee.

Soon he emerged from a row of hardback volumes and again laid eyes upon the woman. She had removed her damp coat and was digging through her satchel. She stood beside an intricately decorated oak chair, centered amid an informal ring of a dozen bookstore patrons. They sat on oversized sofas or mahogany rocking chairs. They sipped Chai and espresso from a variety of steaming mugs. Many held paperback anthologies of Poe's work. At first, they failed to notice him. Instead, they were enthralled by the woman at their lead, and they offered her greetings and help and even a towel to dry her hair.

"Thanks," she said, her voice soft but confident. "Sorry I'm late. Forgot my book, if you can believe that."

The other members gave a chuckle. "You could've borrowed one of ours," a woman suggested.

"Now, Gladys, I appreciate the offer, but you know I can't read without my copy."

"Of course," laughed Gladys. "Sentimental value. I forgot. You just remember: that piece of sentimentality you call a book is falling apart, and if you keep using it, there won't be much more than a handful of scattered pages to be sentimental over."

"Thanks for the reminder," the woman said. She smiled an exaggerated smile, acknowledging that they've had this conversation before, and the crowd chuckled. She dug into her satchel and pulled out a torn, creased, bent, crooked copy of Edgar Allan Poe's complete works. "I think this one will hold up well enough, at least for tonight."

McComber watched with fascination. The woman's smooth hair fell past her shoulders in the back and swept across her forehead in the front. She brushed it away from her face with long, graceful fingers. Her skin, silky and rich, held a hint of bronze, as though she spent years in the sun but never suffered from wrinkles or aging. He guessed she was in her early thirties, with deeply set eyes holding a knowledge that belied her years. Perhaps those eyes were the cause of her unexplainable aura, the reason behind her shroud of mystery. He had always been fond of mystery, especially the sexy type.

As he inched along the far wall behind the group, she lifted her gaze and settled it squarely on his sneaking form. An expression landed on her face, but whether it was shock or fear or delightful surprise McComber couldn't say. Regardless of the expression, the face was beautiful, and he wanted it for himself.

"Hello," she said.

He nodded.

"Are you here for the meeting?"

He felt the assembled faces swivel toward him, but they were of no concern. He nodded again.

"Great! We don't get many newcomers. Take a seat anywhere. Seems the electricity has failed us tonight, but the candles should be adequate. My name's Bree. You'll learn the others as we go."

He set his coat on the back of a chair, failed to offer his own name, nodded to those who were watching, and seated himself without incident and without letting his eyes wander too far from the black pupils of his prey.

"Since tonight is your first meeting," she said, "I'll assume you haven't read the story. Basically, every couple weeks, we read something new, and we discuss it. Tonight's story..."

"*The Cask of Amontillado*," McComber interrupted. "I've read it."

"Really? Well, perhaps you'd like to start us off with a summary."

The faces swiveled again in disquieting, disturbing unison. McComber was unperturbed. "Certainly, but please understand, it's been many years, so mistakes should be forgiven."

Coffee sippers and pastry munchers waited anxiously. The woman, Bree, held her head cocked to the side, her brows raised, instantly ready to correct any of his predicted blunders. If she weren't so wretchedly beautiful he might have been annoyed.

"*The Cask of Amontillado*," he began, his voice deep and somber. "It is a dark tale. One of death and betrayal. Drinking, deception, a pipe of Amontillado. Shall I continue?"

She nodded.

"The story's narrator, an unreliable chap named Montressor, is a connoisseur of wines and liquors and, being of unspecified but certainly fabulous wealth, possesses vaults of wine stored deep in the catacombs beneath his palazzo. One evening he brings a man named Fortunato to these vast caverns. We learn quickly that he despises this fellow named Fortunato, and he plots revenge for previous insults. 'I must not only punish,' he says, if I remember correctly, 'but punish with impunity.' Is that correct?"

So entranced was Bree, the woman, his prey, so seduced was she that for many moments no words were forthcoming. She gazed at Marcus, her lips parted, her eyes unblinking. The bookstore patrons chuckled, amused by their leader's sudden and unmistakable infatuation. After a hushed moment filled with schoolyard giggling, she blinked away the trance and nodded. "Please continue," she whispered, swallowing audibly.

McComber failed to conceal his delight. "So, with a bit of feigned nicety," he continued, "Montressor convinces a sick Fortunato to venture with him deep into the catacombs, to sample a pipe of Amontillado he has recently purchased. Ever the dissembler, Montressor claims to fear the cask may contain something less fair than Amontillado, and only the true tastes and skills of Fortunato, he says, can validate the purchase."

He watched her finger the pages of her book, and he continued, making his voice louder, more commanding, and, he knew, more enchanting. "Deep in the dark dampness below ground, lost among the twists and turns of the vast cellar, Montressor lures Fortunato to a hidden recess, a blackened shadowy crevice. He binds the man tightly with heavy rings and iron staples to the far wall of the hidden niche. Then, amid Fortunato's intoxicated musings and cries of terror, Montressor builds a new wall at the front of the recess with bricks and mortar to seal Fortunato inside. He buries the man alive, tucks him away to rot behind an eternally camouflaged mausoleum. To offer my own bit of commentary, I'd say it was a perfect plan. And with his final words to the reader, Montressor casually reveals that for half a century no mortal had yet disturbed the remains of his dear Fortunato. And such is the pleasure of reading Mr. Poe."

McComber grinned.

"Very impressive," said Bree. "You seem pleased by Fortunato's death."

"And why not? He deserved it, I'm sure."

Bree puckered her lips, no doubt scheming to devise a particularly witty response. Instead, she ignored McComber and addressed the group, "What is the first thing to strike you after reading this story?"

Eyes roamed. Fingers scratched chins. Someone blew a nose.

"Fortunato's name," McComber said, smiling, happy to return the focus to himself.

Bree frowned ever so slightly. “You know I nearly forgot to ask, begging your pardon, but we don’t even know your name. Do you mind?”

“McComber. Marcus McComber.”

“Thank you. Now, what it is about his name that interests you, Mr. McComber?”

“It is a true paradox. A marvel of literature.” He noticed her eyes widen. He could feel her pulse quicken. “Fortunato is, obviously, a most unfortunate character, led so unceremoniously to his death. The irony of his name is fabulous.”

“And the paradox?”

“The paradox, my dear, is that Fortunato is also fortunate. He is ignorant of his impending doom, unaware of death’s silent, stealthy approach. He is fortunate not to know it is coming.”

“I see,” she said. “But is it truly fortunate to be ignorant of the inevitable?”

“Not always, I suppose.”

“But it is here?”

“I believe so.”

“Why?”

“Because death will come soon for our dear Fortunato. Montressor knows it. We know it. Such knowledge lends suspense to the story, but it would gain Fortunato nothing.”

“He might escape, or attempt to.”

“He is drunken and ill. He would fail.”

“So ignorance of impending death is fortunate when death is unpreventable?”

McComber nodded.

“Very well.”

They waged war with their eyes, neither willing to break ranks. McComber sensed his victory. He had intrigued her, and as each moment passed, she grew more interested. He knew it. It was the typical pattern in events like these. Surprisingly, her dainty frame held more strength than seemed possible, and her will was unyielding. She surprised him with a new formation.

"Do you remember what Fortunato was wearing, Mr. McComber?"

An odd question. One he would expect from a woman. "Motley, was it not? And a cap of some sort."

"With bells on it," she said. "Yes. And traditionally, who wears motley?"

"Court jesters. Clowns."

"Fools, Mr. McComber. In the plays of Shakespeare and the courts of England, jesters and clowns were often called fools. Fortunato was overconfident and naïve. And he may have deserved to wear motley."

McComber knew she'd broken his lines. Her cavalry came bounding over his spears, charging with the might of a thousand swords. Before she spoke again, he knew the tide had turned, the battle was lost.

"As you must see," she said, glaring at him with the tiniest smirk, "He was a fool." But was she still speaking of Fortunato?

CHAPTER FOUR

Four Months Ago

That same night, at a tavern not a dozen blocks from the bookstore, Jacob Lyons twisted on a barstool in drunken pursuit of comfort. The night was cold and damp, but so, too, was the ale, and always, it seemed, the latter could somehow negate the effects of the former. So he raised his glass and enjoyed the conversation.

"Nay, my dear chaps," said Angus Ferley, the rotund bartender and owner, in response to a criticism of the tavern's outward appearance, "I think you misunderstand the historic nature of our tavern." Ferley's two most noticeable attributes were his aforementioned rotundity and his endless need to bloviate on the merits, both factual and fictitious, of his beloved tavern. "The façade you see street side, unadorned as it may be, consists entirely of original brick. Twenty years ago, just after I bought this place, some chancer on the town board, a Frenchman, I'll wager, rammed through a statute or law or some such miserable piece of legislative skullduggery that, though intended to prevent the sale, resulted in our tavern being named a landmark of historical significance. A wretched curse, if you ask me."

As it happened, on this particular night, two random newcomers, a banker and his son, had taken up their barstools and made the unfortunate comment about the building's exterior, which set Angus to ranting. For the tavern's regular patrons, Jacob included, the tale was routine but entertaining, as Angus had a natural gift for storytelling. He also had a gift for lying.

"You see, lads," Angus began, "this place in which you sit, this tavern, this shrine to the gods of drink and merriment, this place is a century and a half older than yesterday's newborns. Obviously I've made some improvements to the interior, but, as I said, that Frenchman's landmark legislative arse whipping keeps the masses from marveling at the handiwork I might impose upon the outward facing structure. Still, there's a fair bit of honor to be had sticking with the original foundation. You see that door?" All heads turned to the front door. Its shades were pulled and wooden boards had been nailed over the windows. "Let me tell you about that door."

As Angus was about to begin his history lesson, a man took a seat on the empty stool beside Jacob.

"Ah, Mr. Jefferson," Angus said, "you've returned from the cock manger just in time for a tale."

"Wonderful," said Mr. Jefferson, in a long sarcastic moan. "A cock manger? Really?"

"Cheer up, Daniel," said Jacob, "it promises to be a splendid retelling."

"Isn't it always?"

"But there's fresh blood tonight."

Here, at the tavern, Jacob sat among friends, if indeed friends can be counted by the number of drinks two people share or by how many nights a man might endure the drudgery of listening to meaningless tales and whining without a snicker or complaint. These men were friends by circumstance, acquaintances who, by chance and nothing more, shared stools in a local haunt. And when he wasn't kidding himself, when he hadn't poured too much ale down his eternally parched throat, he knew most of them for what they were: a hapless collection of drunks. Like himself.

The exception, in a place with few exceptions, was Daniel Jefferson. Jacob had come to rely on his friend's observations and temperament, both as targets for comedy and as gentle fields in which to retreat during desperate times.

"The legend of that door," began Angus, "dates to the earliest reckoning of our tavern. Ireland, my home, before she sent me off to my destiny, had some one hundred fifty years earlier sent off another of her sons to make his fortune across the sea. Owen McBraidy was his name, and on this very spot, right where you sit, he came upon a Frenchman who stood overlooking the plot of land in obvious dismay."

"'Might I ask what's wrong,' McBraidy said.

"'And what do you care?' answered the Frenchman. I swear they are all cafflers, those wealthy young Frenchmen. But that's what he said, 'And what do you care? Since when does a poor Irish lad give a damn what I worry about?'

"'To be honest, I was hoping you might be the unhappy owner of this little plot.'

"'What if I am?'

"'I would offer to buy it.'

"'To buy it? What a joke. With what money?'

"'I haven't any money, really,' said McBraidy. The Frenchman laughed, as arseholes are apt to do when presented with intelligent ideas they don't understand.

"'How then did you hope to buy it?' the Frenchman asked.

"'An exchange. My two donkeys and a mule.'

"'For a plot of land? Are you crazy?'

"'Seems to me you aren't fond of it. And it seems to me you don't know what to do with it. Why not let me solve those problems for you?'

"'And what would you do with it?'

"McBraidy leapt onto a rock, and by doing so he could now look down upon the Frenchman, as they all deserve to be so looked upon, and he said, 'I shall build a tavern of such magnificent nature it will rival the architects of Paris with its romanticism, it will surpass the grandiosity of Versailles with its ingenuity, and its luster will outlive the empires of Britain and France combined. That's what I shall do for two donkeys and a mule.'

"The Frenchman had little to say. He laughed and snarled. Must have been an atrocious site for our dear Owen. But, seeing as how the Frenchman had no plans for the land and no suitors for its sale, he took the offer. 'All you Irish fellows do is drink,' he said. 'Can't think a thought without a bit of whiskey in your gullet. I dare say you'll be too drunk to ever finish this tavern of yours.' At which time, he took the reins of the donkeys and mule, spat at the feet of McBraidy and walked off. I dare say, in all the years our Father has watched over this world, never had a man seen such a sorry site as a mule and three asses vanishing into the sunset."

The banker and his son laughed, and the banker said, "But what has that do with the front door?"

"Nothing!" shouted Jacob. "But give him time. Old Angus comes around eventually."

"Indeed I do," Angus said, filling himself a pint of beer.

"Well, gentleman," said Daniel Jefferson, standing, "I'm afraid I can't remain for the entire telling tonight."

"Why not?" asked Jacob, feigning offense in support of the bartender. "Must you get up early to ogle at women again?"

"I don't ogle, but yes, Jacob, I have appointments in the morning. And some of us have real jobs, believe it or not, and we must work even when we're not feeling especially inspired."

Angus roared. Jacob recoiled in mock astonishment. "How dare you! I write at all hours, and I haven't felt especially inspired for years!"

"That explains your output, I suppose."

"Are we to duel now?"

"As fun as it might be to shoot you, Jacob, I'm afraid I just want to go to bed."

"First you should tell Angus about the lovely woman you met at the office last week."

Angus' eyebrows raised. "But hold on a minute, Mr. Jefferson. You're a doctor, right?"

"I am."

"What kind of doctor, if you don't mind my asking."

"The wealthy kind," said Jacob.

"Really?"

"I was," Daniel said, "until the alimony kicked in. The ex got the house and half the practice, if you can believe that."

"As I always say," said Angus, "sleep with a woman, and she'll screw you every time."

"Actually, Danny boy here is a ladies doctor. The most revered. Obstetrics and gynecology. Has his own practice. Half of one, anyway."

Concern quickly overtook Angus' puffy face. "And you're 'examining' your patients? Isn't that wrong?"

"It is indeed. That's why I don't do it. This woman was the sister of a patient. Not someone I had to examine."

"Not for work, anyway!" laughed Jacob, patting his friend on the back. "Though, since the divorce, I wouldn't put anything past you."

"Please pardon my friend," Daniel said to the bartender. "He's been married ten years to a gorgeous woman, and it's been eleven years since she made love to him. Poor chap."

"Ah," Jacob shouted, "but at least she still sleeps in my bed. Occasionally." He laughed and stood and shoved his friend toward the door. "Now be gone with you!"

Daniel, however, walked not to the front door, but to the side door, which opened to a dark alley between the tavern and another building.

"See that building?" Angus said to the banker as Daniel disappeared into the night, "That there's a brothel, a superbly clean brothel I might add, should you, or your son, feel the need to unburden yourselves with something other than drink. Of course, an evening with a woman is never as good as a mug of ale and a bit of my storytelling, I'll wager."

The men seated around the bar laughed, and the banker asked, "But what about the front door? And the Frenchman. You haven't finished your story."

"Ah, the door. Well McBraidy did what he set out to do. He raised money and built the tavern in which you sit. In those days it was of a grand scale indeed, and it quickly had a frequent and wealthy clientele. And it was sturdy. Well built. It›s survived civil war, prohibition, you name it. I›m rather astounded the place hasn›t sunken into the ground with all the tunnels beneath the cellar.

"Anyway, many years later, that same arrogant Frenchman took a stool at the bar of our dear McBraidy Tavern, and upon catching the eye of the bartender he lowered his head. The bartender, being a much older, much wealthier Owen McBraidy, leaned across the marble countertop and asked, 'Whatever became of my donkeys and mule?'

"'I sold them to a glue factory,' the Frenchman answered, but his arrogance had long since abandoned him, and his words echoed not with insolence, but with sad and simple truth. 'Seems I got the worse end of the bargain.' And that he did," said Angus. "But Owen McBraidy, being a good son of the island, never let a man weep in his tavern, and so he bought the Frenchman a draught of Irish whiskey, and the two men chatted into the morning. When at last the Frenchman stood to leave and made his way to the front entrance, McBraidy took his arm and said, 'My friends always use the side door.' And so he showed the man the proper exit.

"To this day, gentleman," Angus said, leaning close and whispering. "To this day the front door of McBraidy Tavern has never been opened. Or so the legend tells."

The banker and his son leaned back wide eyed in their chairs and turned to marvel at the doorway. Angus winked at Jacob, an indication the bartender knew he had garnered their lifelong patronage. And at that moment, as though fate itself had instigated the telling of Angus' tale, the front doors to McBraidy Tavern burst open.

Men leapt from the seats, startled. Angus' mouth hung open half way to his belly. The banker's son raised his mug in the air to celebrate the unexpected event. And Jacob Lyons turned slowly on his stool, already certain something wasn't right.

A figure stood in the doorway, its silhouette backlit by a flash of lightning and a thunderous downpour. When Jacob's eyes adjusted, he saw a man dressed in black with a fedora pulled low over his brow. The man's face lifted.

"Good evening!" said Marcus McComber for all to hear. The crowd moaned. McComber laughed. "Bartender!" he shouted. "'Tis a marvelous night. A round for everyone. My treat."

In an unsurprising turn, the patrons altered their allegiances and cheered the presence of their surprise benefactor.

Jacob, however, felt an ominous pang of foreboding deep in his bones. His paunches went queasy, and it had nothing to do with drink. His mind cast black floaters upon his vision: tiny, wriggling, crawling slugs, as though a plague of worms had infested the tavern. He felt vomit pool in his throat, felt his tongue swell and his lungs constrict.

A moment later the sensation lessened, but it would never be forgotten. As McComber brushed rainwater from his greatcoat and slipped a billfold from its lining into the pocket of his trousers, Jacob stared at him. Beneath the coat, he wore a black sweater and scarf with black pants and shoes. The man was an oddity. An anomaly. And many heads were taking notice. Not that McComber seemed to care. He bounded across the expanse between entrance and bar with the grace of nobility and the jubilance of a recently bedded man, but something in his eyes disturbed Jacob. They held a wayward expression that refused to commingle with the outward appearance. The conflicting features made Jacob feel as though this man's mere presence had instigated the onset of his illness. But surely that was absurd.

"What's your name, stranger?" bellowed Angus as McComber seated himself on Daniel's vacated barstool.

"Marcus McComber. And might I add a thousand taverns from here to the shore would be envious of a stout mass of joviality and vigor such as yourself tending bar."

Angus turned a quizzical look at the gentleman, wondering if he'd been complimented or insulted. "A round on the house," he hollered, "Courtesy of Mr. McComber."

Cheers of thanks emanated from the insignificant crowd. At a back table, hiding in the shadows, a whore shouted, "I've got one on the house for you, too, sexy! Any time!" McComber waved his hand in acknowledgement.

"What's your pleasure, friend?" he said to Jacob.

"Another ale would be splendid. Thank you. Having a fine evening tonight?"

"Fabulous."

"Care to divulge your good fortunes?"

"Fate, my friend. Fate. It is a splendid thing to be cherished by so omnipotent a power. I was standing on a street corner, lost beneath the rain, when I saw a vision of perfection."

"Found God, eh?"

McComber laughed. "God? No. But a goddess. Yes, by God, a goddess, if indeed the title is worthy of her beauty."

"That's a bit much, don't you think?"

"You haven't seen her bosom!"

"Ha!" blurted Jacob. "True enough. True enough." He extended his hand. "The name's Jacob."

"A pleasure to meet you, Jacob."

"So what did you do?"

"When?

"When you encountered your goddess? Don't tell me you let her keep walking."

"And what sort of grand romantic would I be if I had? No. I did what Fate required. I did what every man must when tempted by the sweet aroma of lust. I followed her. I greeted her. And I staked my claim. Not quite 'Veni, Vidi, Vici,' but close enough."

"I see."

"I doubt you do," said McComber. "But hear me now, dear Jacob: that woman will be mine."

"If Fate demands…"

"No. She will be my goddess. Fate has nothing to do with it."

Jacob laughed. "Well I wish you the best of luck. Should you ever happen to see her again, what's your lofty plan?"

"When it comes to women, Jacob, one needs no lofty plan. They are predictable and easily manipulated. A touch of romance. Mystery. The promise of excitement. Deliver those things, and eventually she's yours."

"Mystery, excitement and romance? That's all you've got?"

McComber laughed. His was a charming cackle with a tinge of menace. "That's more than I'll ever need, my new friend. You'll see."

CHAPTER FIVE

Not Quite Four Months Ago

Breeana had led discussions of Poe's *The Fall of the House of Usher* on numerous occasions, but tonight was different. Tonight she had a distraction. Tonight the ruin of Roderick Usher's gloomy, desolate mansion bore a hint of amusement and exhilaration. The cause?

Marcus McComber.

He sat in the back of the room and never spoke. His goal, it seemed, was to distract her, and he did so with a smug, handsome grin that begged her to laugh. Once or twice she almost chuckled. McComber was dressed, as before, all in black, but across his broad shoulders he wore a patched, motley cape of many colors and fabrics. There were purples and greens, yellows and reds, with wool, fleece, and cotton squares. It was the garb of a fool, and it made her smile.

Rarely did she find such good reasons to smile.

Quietly nestled into her chair at the center of the bookstore's discussion room, she let her attention drift from the conversation around her, feeling far too much like a giddy school girl. She had begun the meeting by quoting large chunks of text, reading directly from her battered, broken Poe anthology, but she spent little time examining the gothic house of Usher or its gaunt namesake. Part of her felt guilty. After all, it was her job to perform critical readings and offer critiques as conversation topics. That's what these people deserved. But tonight her mind fell squarely on the fool in the back row.

When the meeting finally ended, she sat quietly in her chair. Those gathered around her sorted through their belongings, donning coats and hats, chatting about poetry and books and weather. Like Marcus McComber's odd raiment, these people made her smile. The book club had been her idea, and most nights she found immense pleasure sharing and discussing stories with likeminded souls. Literature had always played an important role in her life. Recently, it was her only escape from an otherwise frustrating predicament.

She pressed her hand against the cover of the ragged Poe anthology in her lap, as she did each week, with a measure of care and unconditional sorrow. The volume itself, so worn and dingy and saddening, was a gift from long ago, undoubtedly forgotten by the giver but forever treasured by the receiver as a relic of happier times. She ran her fingers along the pages. She knew, from breathing near it in bed whenever she read at night, it held the same musty scent as the bookstore, a marvelous aroma that never failed to send her olfactory senses spinning into memory. She often toyed with the idea of buying a newer, more sturdy volume, one capable of suffering the torture she inflicted by repetitive reading, but always she forced the urge away, not yet ready to retire such a meaningful gift. In so many ways, that book was the perfect metaphor to describe her life. A very disturbing metaphor.

Yet, thankfully, here in the bookstore she was almost happy. Here, with books and tales and fantasies lurking in every direction, reality took on a new meaning. Here she could ignore the frustrations of her life and be her happy, proud confident self. Here she was the woman she had been before life became her book. And here, she knew, a handsome, confident fool was about to flirt with her, and that was always a reason to smile.

Once everyone had departed, McComber stood from his seat in the back row and strode casually toward her. She tried not to stare, hoped not to encourage, but she failed, to his obvious delight.

"You play the fool well, Mr. McComber," she said.

"Call me Marcus."

"Marcus the Fool?"

"Seems better than Fortunato."

"Why? Do you fear the inevitable?"

"I fear many things. Death, if that is your question, frightens me only by the possibility of a premature encounter. I still have much to accomplish."

"Like what?" she asked. "Hoping to seduce women wearing that cape? Good luck."

McComber grinned. "Thank you for the encouragement. As for the cape, you seemed rather focused on making your point last week. Thought I might help bring your accusations to life."

"I don't know what you mean."

"You called me a fool."

"Not you," she said. "I spoke of Fortunato."

"Even if that's true, there's a bit of a flaw in your reasoning."

"And what is that?"

"You labeled him a fool simply because he wore the conical cap and motley of a Shakespearean character. But if such garb is what dictates a character's merit, could we not say Fortunato was a wise and observant man?"

"I don't follow."

"Think about it. Feste and Touchstone and Falstaff. All Shakespearean fools. But each was a brilliant and witty observer, each was capable of rooting out the truth of human existence, and each did so with charm and intellect. It would seem fools, in the manner you associate with Fortunato, at least in a literary sense, were some of England's greatest geniuses, even if their roles kept them at a disadvantage."

"So you don't think Fortunato was a fool?"

"Of course he was. That's not my point."

"I assume you'll correct me, then?"

"My point is that I, the ever charming and literary Marcus McComber, am thrilled to play the part of the fool if it is you to whom I offer my insight. And I should therefore like to act foolish." At this he bowed, grabbed the lining of his cape and whipped it around his body in a grand gesture of pride. It reminded her of a vampire about to feed. "Thus," McComber added, "I would be honored if you would join me for coffee at the café down the street. Seems the least you could do after insinuating I was something less than brilliant."

"Hmm."

"Have I stolen the lady's wit?"

"How can I say yes?"

"You needn't say anything. Simply take the hand of a fool, and understand that until you agree, I shall only continue to try harder."

She laughed. "I think you mean that."

"I assure you…"

Bree stared at him, hoping to judge his intent. She wasn't practiced in the art of seduction. At least not recently. It had been quite some time since a fascinating man had asked her for a drink. Her mind, filled with a strange combination of excitement and guilt, warned her to be overly cautious. Still, with a life much like her book, so worn and dusty, the temptation for adventure was a powerful foe.

"I'm afraid you'll just have to prove it," she said with a slight hint of relief.

McComber bowed. "You shall marvel at my persistence. "

"Is that so?"

"Without doubt. As is the certainty you and I will spend our lives together gallivanting across the globe."

"Well, well, Mr. McComber. We've gone from coffee to eternity. You move quickly. But I'd caution you to not get so far ahead of yourself."

"Do you think it won't happen?"

"I'd wager quite a bit. At the very least, you'll need to lose the cape…"

McComber bowed. "For you, I'd wager my life, though I'll keep the cape for now." And with a nod of his head, he flung his cape as deftly as any Shakespearean bard, twisted on his heel, and exited the stage.

She watched him go, astonished by two things: his idiotic confidence, and the uncontrollable smile dancing on her face.

§

Three nights later, the wooing would begin in earnest. The hour was late. She stood in a bright supermarket aisle. A storm approached. There was lightning and thunder and wind, but as of yet no rain. She had been reading at the bookstore until it closed, and on her way home she had stopped at the store to fetch bread and juice for the next morning's breakfast. Into her basket she dropped a fresh barley and wheat loaf plus a package of raisin bagels she would bring to the office to appease her afternoon cravings.

At that moment, a crack of thunder echoed outside and plunged the market into darkness. As happens so often in this city, the electricity had failed. She ignored the instant onset of panic and waited for light to return. Within a few seconds, the aisle grew brighter. Emergency lights flared, but they offered only a sick, dull luminance half as bright as the fluorescent bulbs overhead. Not caring to be in the store if the emergency lights failed, she decided to forgo the juice and make her way to the checkout.

As she turned toward the entrance, she saw her own worried reflection in the market's storefront windows, and the power failed again. The aisle fell away into blackness. She stopped, imagining her other self watching her from beyond the windows. Somewhere in the distance she heard two men and a woman shouting about a generator.

Several timeless moments later, when light returned, Marcus McComber stood three feet away. In his hand, he held a long-stemmed rose. He invited her to take it. Confused and startled and speechless, she did. McComber said nothing. He bowed, his smile wide and handsome and not the least bit sinister. Then, as before at the bookstore, he nodded, spun away and vanished into the night.

She stared at the rose in her hand as though she'd awoken from a dream and discovered a relic of that dream still impossibly clutched in her fingers. Instinct forced her to chuckle. Sanity warned her to be wary. But something very different aroused a tickle of pleasure deep inside and allowed a bit of excitement to infiltrate a life void of such fanciful imaginings. The entire scene might have been stolen from the pages of the most farfetched romance novel, and the reality of the supermarket aisle made it no more believable. Yet there she was, and there he had been, and the rose in her hand was not the invention of a confused mind. Her face flushed at the possibilities. Then she began to laugh, for she had only now realized Marcus had wisely lost the cape.

§

The very next evening, as her literature group dispersed after a lively, passionate discussion of Rushdie's *The Satanic Verses* and the constant metamorphosis of Western civilization's attitude toward Muslims, Breeana shrieked with startled delight as two hands covered her eyes and an alluring voice whispered, "Guess who?" She already knew.

She turned to see him, tried to speak, but Marcus McComber put a finger to her lips. "Not a word," he whispered. "Come with me." She barely had time to pull on her coat and grab her satchel, let alone to protest, before he took her hand and whisked her out to the sidewalk.

"I never agreed to this," she finally blurted. The effort was obviously halfhearted.

"Not a word now."

They turned twice down narrow, cobblestone streets, eventually arriving at a dirt path on the outskirts of City Park. McComber led her down the leaf-littered track, beneath Victorian lamp posts and romantic outlooks, to a cold, wrought iron bench bathing in the glow of the full moon's light.

"I come bearing gifts," McComber said. He maneuvered her onto the bench. Then he reached beneath it and produced two wrapped boxes.

"Marcus..."

He stopped her with a finger to her lips. "Not a word." With a nod, he urged her to open the first gift. After a second of hesitation, she decided to forego caution.

The box's lid detached easily. She lifted out a dark amber bottle of sherry. Her eyes strained across its gold label until the script became clear. "Amontillado," she read, laughing.

"To always remind you of a fool," he said.

The next box had ribbon tied across its corners, and she trembled with such anticipation that she almost couldn't untie it.

With the ribbon untied and the lid open, she reached careful fingers into the box and pulled out a heavy, leather bound anthology of Edgar Allan Poe's short stories and poems. She gazed admiringly, forgetting everything, even, for a moment, Marcus McComber, whose face brimmed with anticipation and delight. She ran her hand across the moist, rich texture of the leather. She fingered the hefty pages. All at once, it felt new and old, as perfectly worn as any collectible but as tightly bound as anything on a bookstore shelf. The pages were many. The font was gothic and crisp. The volume might very well be the most beautiful book she had ever seen.

"Thank you," she said. "But I can't."

The familiar finger touched her lips. "You can, and I beg that you will. That old rag you've got stashed in your satchel is sickening."

"It has significance," she tried to say, but he silenced her again.

"Not a word now."

He set the tome back in its box and replaced the lid. Then he took her hand and pulled her to her feet. She was unsteady. Overwhelmed. "Don't be nervous," he said. "And stop your brooding. Allow yourself to forget the world and enjoy the moment."

"How can I do that?" she asked, staring off into the distance.

"I'm certain you haven't forgotten. Let yourself be swept away and feel what it means to live."

He pulled her close and they began to dance. She wanted to laugh at the absurdity of two strangers dancing near a park bench beneath the moonlight. It was foolish romance. And yet here she was again, her limbs shaking, her mind spinning at the dizzying, mystifying Marcus McComber. She might have feared him. She might have panicked. But she did neither. Had they not met on the venerated sofas of her bookstore, had he not so quickly plunged with her into an amusing and witty debate centered around the stories of her favorite author, she might have dismissed him as seedy or troublesome. Instead, she had drifted beneath his shadow, had been enticed by his allure, and, for the moment at least, felt it to be the most perfect place in all the world.

They danced for an eternity, for what might have been hours but was probably a few minutes. Time became irrelevant as his arms guided her and his hands caressed her back. It had been years since she knew this degree of affection. She began to let her mind wander. She stopped fretting about the life waiting at home and dreamt instead of the new places and adventures to which Marcus McComber might lead her if she allowed him.

It was then that he pulled her close. Their feet stopped. Their bodies pressed together. She felt his breath on her lips, felt his hands slip below her waist. She didn't resist, but she feared what came next and what it might mean.

Then Marcus McComber kissed her.

Later, when she tried to remember how it felt, she would be unable. Instead of focusing on the moment, as he had suggested, she thought only about the future and the repercussions. What did it mean to be kissed by Marcus McComber? What did it mean to enjoy it?

With as much effort as she could muster, she pushed him away. There was no anger in his expression. Only a smile.

"That was inappropriate," she said.

"My apologies," he answered. "I'm sorry if I've offended you."

As much as she tried, her mind refused to formulate a coherent thought. "I've got to get home," she said.

"I'll walk with you."

"Not tonight, Mr. McComber. But thank you. "

He nodded. She felt weak and confused, and that infuriated her. She grabbed her bag from the bench and started to walk away.

"You forgot these!" He grabbed the gifts from the bench and carried them over to her. He slipped the bottle of Amontillado into her satchel and handed her the box containing the leather bound Poe anthology.

"Thank you, Marcus," she said. Without thinking, she added, "Perhaps the next time you ask me out for coffee, I won't call you a fool."

"We'll see," he laughed.

And she hurried away without a backwards glance.

§

And so it was that she found herself, several days later, at a café down the street from her bookstore, seated across from Marcus McComber. The atmosphere was sumptuous, dark but trendy, replete with thick aromas and tantalizing tastes that filled the damp, warm air with a mixture of high society class and yuppie arrogance. Every table was occupied, every booth home to conversation or study. Far from the entrance, nestled deep into a shadowy niche beside a roaring fire, she did her best to act uninterested.

"How's the coffee?" he asked.

She said nothing.

"Come on now," he said, "You asked for it black. Even a fool can't mess that up."

"And you didn't. Congratulate yourself."

"Might I say that sarcasm fits you better than your sweater."

"No," she said. "You may not say that." She grinned despite herself, then turned to stare out the window. Rain slapped the glass and pooled on the sidewalk. "When will it end?" she asked.

"If you mean our little excursion," he answered, "it can end whenever you wish, though I hope not soon. But if you speak of the rain, I'm somewhat surprised. Do you dislike it?"

"I didn't say that."

"Good. Because like the sarcasm, the rain fits you well. As does this city."

"What does that mean?"

"Only an observation. You have a bitterness about you. I noticed it immediately."

"Bitterness?" she asked.

"Maybe sorrow is the better word. Something dark inside. Brooding. Suppressed. Your eyes hint at it, but your voice, your words, they give it away. Sarcasm, by nature, requires a darker view of the world. Or at least a more jaded one."

Breeana continued to watch the window. Outside, pedestrians rushed from place to place, cloaked beneath hoods and umbrellas and an air of mystery. Where were they going, she wondered. What adventures carried them beyond their doorways in such foul weather? It was a question she asked herself often, a question that now took her mind off Marcus McComber and the feelings he invoked. Best to appear aloof, she thought.

McComber continued, "So you are responsible for the book club then?"

"I am."

"But you don't own the bookstore?"

"Correct."

She watched him sigh in the corner of her periphery. She saw frustration in his eyes. Frustration at her sullenness. Frustration at her lack of exposition. He said, "If you'd rather we sit here in silence, I can certainly oblige. But then I might just as well be sitting alone, and I came here to gain a bit of your affection, an aim that suffers your silence poorly. Besides, I think I'm at least a trifle interesting, and I expect you'll delight in our conversation. That is, assuming you choose to participate."

She couldn't stop herself from laughing this time. For some reason, she had hoped to frustrate him. After all, he constantly frustrated her, leaping into her thoughts at inopportune times.

"Very well," she said, turning towards him, "what shall we discuss?"

"How about the bookstore? Who is the old man behind the counter?"

"Why do you care?"

"I watched you kiss him."

"I kiss a lot of people."

"I'm a curious fellow."

"If you must know," she said, "he is, or was, a friend of my mother's."

"A close friend?"

"Perhaps."

"But no longer? Why is that? What did he do wrong?"

"Nothing."

"What did your mother do?"

"She died."

"Good explanation," he said.

"I thought so."

He tilted his head as if pondering his next question or maybe hoping to guess her reaction to it. "Were they lovers?" he asked.

"That's none of your business, I'm afraid."

"Does your father know?"

"I don't imagine he does."

"And why is that?"

"Because he's dead, too."

McComber let his chin fall and admitted defeat. "Does this grim reaper of yours own the bookstore?"

"He's not the grim reaper. He's a very nice man and so very passionate about his books. And yes, he owns the store. And he's kind enough to let us share it for our meetings."

McComber changed gears. "So you're a Poe fanatic then?"

She wouldn't take his bait. She nodded.

"Fits the brooding image of yours," he said as he sipped his coffee. His eyes surveyed her face, her shoulders, her hair, her breasts. He's not subtle, she thought. "And what do you do when you're not at the bookstore?" he asked.

"I work."

"I see." He paused and stared off into the distance, the frustration mounting. "You know, your answers aren't quite as elegant as your arguments tend to be. They're certainly not as elaborate. Perhaps we should try arguing?"

She found his inquisitiveness charming and his frustration amusing. He hadn't lied about being persistent. "Very well," she said, "I'm a copyeditor for a small literary publishing firm."

"Do you enjoy it?" he asked.

"In a way, yes." Truthfully, the answer was a wholehearted No, but the rules didn't say she had to be completely honest.

"If you don't enjoy it," he said, seeing through her lie, "why do it?"

"It pays well enough."

"Of course. The casual answer. The safe answer. It'd expect it from half-wits at the local tavern, but not from you. Life is not about money, and I know by the passion you have for books and stories you crave more than monetary sustenance. Life is about living. Life is exploration and adventure. I bet you crave those things each and every day. So don't lie to me."

"I'm happy enough, Mr. McComber. You needn't worry."

"Why does Poe intrigue you?" he asked.

"I'm sorry?"

"The darkness, the gloom. These are not things for happy souls."

"For one," she said, taken by surprise, "he is a brilliant author. Fascinating and mysterious and enjoyable. Two, I love how he plays with language and manipulates his reader. I read a lot of crap in my job."

"He led a troubled life, you know."

"Is that why you like him?" she asked.

"Don't you find it fascinating that, despite his troubles and torments, he could imagine such tales? He wasn't bogged down by life's vicissitude. He conjured his imagery and emotion from the aching emptiness of depression and suffering."

"The tone of his life no doubt colored his stories. It darkened his words. Each sentence hints at his torment. I do find that fascinating, yes."

"Because your torment, unlike his, is bottled up and unable to escape?"

"Excuse me?"

"I'm only trying to understand you," McComber said. "To get acquainted."

"Acquainted?" she asked. "Then what about yourself? You've said little, asked an unending string of questions, and answered any questions I ask with vagaries and even more questions. Why don't you tell me about yourself? Who is Marcus McComber?"

"Ah," he said, "If only I could tell you. That very question has baffled women for ages."

She glared at him.

"Okay, okay," he said. "Truthfully, I am but a lonely heart searching for companionship."

"That's a bit sappy, don't you think?"

"Is it working?"

"No."

He fell into laughter, and she soon followed.

§

For the better part of an hour, she deflected McComber's intrusiveness with meaningless answers and shrewd rebuttals, until at length their conversation drifted to playful banter over two more cups of coffee.

"How about I walk you home?" he said after finding his mug empty one last time.

"That's not really necessary or possible," she answered. "I'm heading back to the bookstore."

"Is it still open?"

"I have a key."

"Then may I walk you there? If you say no, I will follow you anyway. To ensure your safety, of course."

After two failed attempts to dissuade him, she consented to his escort and they set off down the empty street. The pedestrians had vanished.

The unyielding autumn rain had strengthened during the evening, and she found it necessary to hide beneath an umbrella. McComber let the rain fall on his uncovered head.

"We could share the umbrella," she said

"It's only water." To emphasize, he leaped with a playful skip step and clicked his heels together.

"Aren't you cold?" she asked.

"Not at all."

"Well don't blame me when you take ill."

"Fair enough."

Briskly and without much conversation, they strode past dark storefronts and empty alleys. A tension began to build as their separation neared. Midnight had passed an hour earlier and the shop doors were bolted. A row of street lamps illuminated the walkway and made the puddles of standing water glisten beneath their feet. Even had she wanted to, she couldn't have imagined a more romantic end to their night. And the thought terrified her.

After several minutes of silence, McComber managed to read her thoughts, and he said, "Why did you agree to this?"

"To what?"

"Tonight. Coffee. A drink with a fool."

"To shut you up, of course. And, obviously, I thought it might be interesting."

"Has it been?"

"Beyond my most ridiculous expectations. You're quite a character, Mr. McComber. You wear many faces."

He feigned shock.

"At first," she said, "you were the fool. Then you were an ass in a cape. And then you were the mysterious romantic. And here, after everything, you decide to be a gentleman."

"Ah, a gentleman," he laughed. "I prefer that title. Is that what I was tonight?"

"No."

"No?"

"Tonight," she said, thinking, "Tonight you were the Inquisitor." She couldn't resist a smile at the thought.

"You find yourself funny, don't you?" he asked. But his voice became strangely serious. Too critical almost. The way he looked at her with a raised eyebrow and wrinkled forehead brought with it the slightest sensation of panic.

"At times," she answered.

"Like now?"

"Oh, I'm very funny right now."

McComber stopped. He wasn't laughing. He said, "Does your husband find you funny?"

She halted and turned to him. "What did you say?" she asked.

"Oh, I believe you heard me. But I'll ask again to be polite." His wicked grin emerged. "Your husband. Does he find you funny?"

"Why would you say that?"

"I saw the indentation on your finger the first night we met. So I decided you're married, or divorced, or recently widowed. Which is it?"

"How is that any of your business?"

"I generally find that it's good practice to know the marital status of the woman I fancy. Wouldn't you agree?"

She had no answer. He had caught her, not in a lie exactly, but no doubt she had misled him. And now all the guilt she had forgotten as the night progressed poured down upon her heart.

McComber asked, "Do you love him?"

"Of course I love him."

"Does he bore you?"

And again she had no answer. So she picked up her pace, almost running toward the bookstore. So much for romance.

"That's it," he said. "It fits now. All of it. You are bored. Miserable. You crave the life in your stories while real life drags you down." He matched her pace, grinning at his own intellect. "Such is your torment."

"That's enough, Marcus."

"Very well," he said. "I'm sorry. To be honest, I couldn't care less if you're married. But I would very much like to see you again."

"We'll have to see," she said coldly. She was angry at herself and wanted to dismiss the possibility entirely. But she remembered that kiss in the park, and she realized how excited she felt simply standing near to this strange man.

"Well I beg you not to run and hide," he said. "I'm really not that scary."

"It takes far scarier things than you, Marcus McComber, to send me into hiding."

"That's good," he said. "But there is one other thing we might need to discuss. Something we'll have to do."

"And what is that?"

He pulled the hood of his coat up over his head. His face disappeared into shadow. He said, "We must kill your husband, of course."

The words hung awkwardly in the air. She stopped and glared at him, transfixed. Was he serious? But then he burst into laughter.

"See," he said, "I can be funny, too."

CHAPTER SIX

Three and a Half Months Ago

"Would you kill him?" Jacob asked. "Were you serious?"

"Of course not," McComber answered, but his laughter was not reassuring.

The two men sat side by side at the bar. The normally subdued McBraidy Tavern had been infested with rowdiness. One night each month a local plumbers union would assemble and celebrate its collective skills with all things long, hard and cylindrical, and tonight was that night. They were loud and boisterous, annoying to most of the nightly patrons, but Jacob had learned to envy their gaiety. He watched as Angus filled a legion of pitchers and mugs and traipsed from table to table like an overweight and unbalanced fairy – or an unusually nimble troll – clearing empty pilsners, decanters, and tumblers, smiling as he did so, no doubt thrilled by the fortune he reaped with each raised glass. Surrounded by so much merrymaking, Jacob wondered if happiness would ever return to his own life.

"They're not happy, you know," McComber said. "Don't be confused. Or misled. At least, not by their smiles."

Jacob shrugged, annoyed by McComber's intuition. "What do I care?"

"Every man occasionally wants to be ravaged by a plague of happiness. Don't deny it. Sometimes we search long and through many graveyards hoping to unearth just such a plague. But these men are no happier than you or I. Many are probably worse off. What you see is only the magic of coin and drink, my friend."

Angus roared from behind the bar as he swept a handful of shiny coins into the register, "Indeed, Mr. McComber! The magic of drink!"

"This plague," Jacob said, "has found its way into my life often enough and with some frequency. I needn't go hunting for it. But thank you for the unsolicited advice."

McComber laughed. "Solicitation is only a requirement for those who lack confidence in their ideas. Besides, my advice is brilliant, and I caution all men to take heed whenever I speak."

"I take a drink every time you speak."

"You're wiser than you know."

Jacob ignored the compliment and its sarcastic bent. As with all things to spew from McComber's mouth, he doubted its sincerity. Two weeks had passed since the lying, scheming, outrageous and bizarre Marcus McComber had entered his humdrum existence. Yes, humdrum. That was a fitting word to describe it. He spent all day alone with a pen that refused to spout ideas and all night sipping drinks with drunken lunatics. What word but humdrum would fit? Perhaps bothersome. Or tiresome. He was lonely and, as of late, unsuccessful. His optimism came and went with the storm clouds in the sky, but his own doubts festered. Success, he knew, would return with time. Not that it had ever been rampant. But loneliness was another matter.

In Marcus McComber, however, he had found something of a muse to tease his otherwise uninspired emotions. To be fair, this muse was darker and creepier and uglier than his typical muse. But he enjoyed McComber's tales and lies. He anticipated them each day with the anxiety and excitement of a child before a party, and he often found himself waiting impatiently for the sun to set as though daytime and living had become unpleasant chores standing between visits to the tavern. Jacob, of course, possessed his own penchant for exaggeration and melodrama, which may have explained how he immediately recognized the trait in McComber, but he rarely had opportunities to challenge his skills with an equal foe. Their conversations had become, in some ways, verbal bouts of imagination warfare. To spin marvelous tales, McComber manipulated the spoken word as Jacob did the written word, and McComber's tales, however encumbered by fictions or marred by drunken revelry, motivated Jacob to improve his craft. Given that his recent writing output flowed like a dry river bed, any source of motivation was worth pursuing. He knew Marcus McComber should not be taken seriously, but conversing with the man certainly seemed beneficial and entertaining.

"So how would you do it?" Jacob asked, returning to the original conversation topic. "How would you kill your Goddess' husband?" Hypotheticals were his favorite barstool game.

"A bullet, maybe."

"Bullets are good."

"But messy."

"Very messy."

"Poison then," McComber said. "For tidiness. Or maybe something worse."

Jacob laughed. "Yes. Worse! The rack, perhaps. Or a guillotine. That would be fantastic."

But McComber became distant. Lost. He lifted his mug and guzzled until the glass came down empty. He said, "Definitely something worse. Something far worse."

Jacob wondered what might be worse than the rack or the guillotine. Hanging? Dismemberment? Occasionally he stole a glimpse of his drinking partner. He imagined the invisible strings of a giant puppeteer had been tied to the man's eyelashes, because his eyes were opened impossibly wide, darting side to side and up and down, never pausing to focus in any one direction. If Jacob were to gauge McComber's thoughts just then, he'd say they were under the influence of a substance composed primarily of gunpowder or dynamite. And why not? Filled with farcical delusions of murder, McComber's brain seemed poised to explode like colliding comets atop an erupting volcano. Jacob wondered if there might be a bit of truth in McComber's words, a shot glass full of beer-soaked intent loitering behind the ideas. The view was nerve-wracking, and so Jacob kept to himself, content to parley with an empty ale mug.

"I'll tell you something," McComber said after a lengthy silence, rather composed for a man atop an erupting volcano. "All this talk of retribution…"

"Retribution isn't the right word," Jacob interjected.

"Excuse me?"

"Retribution is like vengeance. But your Goddess' husband hasn't faulted you. Not yet anyway. Obviously then we're talking about unprovoked murder. When you kill him, it will be simple violence and death, not retribution. Go on…"

McComber glared at him. Jacob sipped his ale.

"It was a long time ago," McComber said. "A time when, much like yourself, I felt complacent and knowledgeable in the world. Complacency is not happiness. Never forget that. Complacency closed my eyes. It dulled my senses. I failed to see the world and all its machinations as clearly as I might have. As a result, I was betrayed. Do you know how that feels, Jacob? Betrayal?"

Jacob nodded but then shook his head.

"At the very least it's gut-wrenching. When the people around you, people in whom you trust and confide, when they turn traitor and suddenly seek to benefit from your demise, it's as though life decided to punish you for existing."

Jacob thought he heard actual suffering in McComber's voice. "Who betrayed you?" he asked.

"It's not important. But it taught me to always keep my eyes open, to always be the betrayer instead of the betrayee. Life is much safer that way. Never stop observing the people around you. Never stop listening. People are selfish. If you stop watching, if you stop observing, undesired surprises await. That's my advice to you."

"More advice," Jacob laughed. "And here I thought you were saying something important. But I am thankful. I shall try to keep your words in mind the next time I meet someone who plans to betray me." He raised his glass to let Angus know it was empty. "On a similar note, do you know what I've observed of you?

"Do tell."

"You're rather depressing at times. And positively psychotic. Cheers!"

The two men burst into the laughter of liars feigning amusement. After a few moments, the conversation returned to less dramatic topics than betrayal. Assuming murder is less dramatic than anything…

"So you shall use poison, then?" Jacob asked.

"No," McComber said, his eyes piercing the dark amber of the ale. "Something worse."

§

As taverns are notorious for their ability to warp the very passage of hours and to send patrons home far later than they might have intended, Jacob had no idea how long he and McComber had been sitting in silence when Daniel Jefferson arrived.

"Daniel!" Jacob said, "I advise you to order a drink before Angus puts a wash rag in your empty hand and forces you to dance behind the counter."

"Things do seem a bit hectic," Daniel said, "but have you forgotten? We have plans tonight."

Jacob tried to recall what those plans might entail, but, after failing to do so, he smiled and shouted, "Daniel! Meet Marcus McComber!"

McComber spun on his chair and put out his hand. "A pleasure to meet you, sir."

"I don't believe I've seen you around here before, Mr. McComber."

"I've had better places to be."

"He's new in town," Jacob acknowledged. "Hasn't been privy to Angus' best stories."

"Lucky fellow. Where are you from, Mr. McComber?"

"If you call me Marcus, I will gladly tell you I am from the Eastern Shore, where the descendants of York built their first homes and were promptly massacred by the natives. Call me anything else and there's no telling what I might do."

"And what brings you here, Marcus?"

McComber thought for a moment before raising his mug in salute to Angus, "Why, the beer, of course!" And the bartender returned the compliment with a nod.

"No," said Daniel, "not the tavern. What brings you here? To this city?"

"I'm afraid it's simply another stop along the wayward path, my fellow. Another port in an endless storm. I don't imagine I'll be staying long." And McComber's voice grew louder as he played to the crowd. "Unless of course my stay helps me *get* long, in which case I might desire to *ride* it out!" Laughter abounded.

"You speak in riddles."

"Of course I speak in riddles. Are they not the essence of life? Is not every twist and turn of a day a riddle to solve? The oddities of existence, the happenstances of living. They are but the pieces of a larger puzzle we haven't yet found a way to fit together."

"Daniel," said Jacob, "I forgot to tell you that Marcus is a lunatic."

"Perhaps," Marcus added. "But let's get back to riddles, Jacob, for they are the essence of life. I know you disagree, but do not fret. Riddles, by their very nature, have solutions. Even the most challenging puzzle can be fit together after several of its pieces go missing. Correction, I suppose it can't be assembled completely, given the absence of those pieces, but the overall image will be clear nonetheless. All it takes is a bit of scrutiny. However elusive the answers might be, if one can decipher the patterns and currents that carry us from one year to the next, from one dwelling to the next, one lover to the next, he is well on his way to understanding life. He may be happier for it, or he may be eternally damned."

"You speak of Fate," Jacob said, turning back to his mug. "Of nonsense."

"Not of Fate, but of divine will. Fate would imply a predetermined future. And that's absurd. God has not made his plans yet. He'll decide what must become of each of us as time passes. It is his will that governs the world. And if you pay careful attention, you can find the tools, the cues, the secrets that may affect his judgment or alter his plans. Unfortunately, I must have pissed him off somewhere down the line, because he's been rather unfair lately."

"I never took you for a religious man," Jacob said. "How does your goddess fit into all this? Is she copulating with the Creator? Maybe he's pissed at you for making moves on his woman!"

"Any wrongs I've committed," McComber said, "have been repaid in agony and my own blood. I've told you before of betrayal, Jacob. And I've paid far worse than I deserved. So now I'm claiming recourse. This woman's affection, and her bountiful bosom, shall be my first reward."

"Betrayal?" asked Daniel. "By whom?"

"A woman."

"But why?"

"Does it matter? The whims of a woman's mind are best left to the psychiatrists and the fortune tellers. I care only for their more tangible attributes."

"She gave you no reason?"

"Of course she gave a reason. Believe it or not, she claimed it had something to do with my unwillingness to perpetuate my line."

"To have children?"

"Indeed."

"What did she do?"

"Ha! I haven't the time to detail her derangement. Let's just say she wanted to have me killed, and she herself took up the contract for my killing. I've learned to accept it as comical and ironic. And we shall leave it at that."

"Was this recently?"

"No."

"When?"

"Long enough in the past to have little relevance in the present.

I've since been searching for a better woman. And though, during my travels, I've bedded many and cherished a few, I have otherwise failed in my endeavors. That is, until now." McComber finished off his ale and wobbled a bit on his stool.

Jacob and Daniel shared clandestine smiles, hiding their amusement from McComber, who they now understood to be wildly inebriated.

"Well then," said Daniel, "I wish you luck in your latest undertaking. Sadly, Jacob and I must be going."

Jacob lifted his mug. "To your future," he said. "May all your bastard children be blessed."

"Ah," said Marcus, "thank you. But your blessings are unnecessary. There will be no children in my future, bastards or not."

"A bit out of character, don't you think? Surely you haven't given up on your goddess so soon."

"You misunderstand. My lust will be fed and my patience rewarded. Of that I am certain. But I have never desired children, and I don't intend to have any."

"Such things are often beyond our control. Passion run amuck."

"My passion has never run amuck. And if it did, so be it. There are remedies to every situation."

"Okay," interrupted Daniel. "We need to go."

Marcus ignored him. "And what about you, Jacob? Do you have children?"

"No."

"Has your passion never run amuck then? How very sad for your wife."

Jacob stared at McComber with no response. Marcus, meanwhile, grinned wide like a fool.

"It was a pleasure to meet you," Daniel said to end the silence. He extended his hand.

"Likewise," McComber answered, but he spun on his seat without shaking hands. "See you both very soon.".

Daniel pulled Jacob toward the exit. "A lunatic, indeed," he whispered, but Jacob remained silent well beyond the tavern's doorway.

§

Marcus McComber laughed on his stool. Those two men were idiots. Why, he wondered, are there so few thinkers in the world? Why are there so few challenges? Perhaps, he knew, because he only ever sought worthy foes here in the slums of civilization, here among society's rabble. If he desired a challenge, why not roam the halls of a university or battle with the barons of business? The answer, of course, was because such things held no interest for him. He was content to dominate the rabble, to play his games, to toy with their minds and twist the threads of their worthless lives all for his own entertainment. He had no delusions of grandeur, of course. Great men, he believed, ought to be humble, and so he was humble.

He lifted his glass, feeling wonderful, and not suffering the ale's effects as severely as others might think. "How about another?" he shouted to Angus.

The bartender ignored him. Angus, it seemed, busied himself with a separate and frustrating dilemma. The tap behind the bar, the lifeblood of the tavern, hissed and shrieked and whistled. It spat a great amount of foamy amber spray into a bucket, and it vomited an even greater amount onto Angus' belly and face. After a few last throes and sputters, the barrel ran dry, and the hissing stopped.

"She's empty," Angus said, wiping his face with his hands. "I need to run to the cellar to nab another barrel. Might I interest you in an adventure, Mr. McComber?"

McComber slid his mug across the bar. "If you'll fill me up gratis upon our successful return."

"Follow me."

They left through the side entrance, emerging into the decrepit, waste strewn alley between the tavern and the brothel. With the help of Autumn's endless rain, which, for whatever reason, had stopped tonight, the river below the Clarkston Bridge had overflowed its banks. Though blocks away, the raging water filled the alley with its grainy, incessant noise, and under its cover a bitter cold had snuck in and settled for a stay. Marcus McComber rarely let foul weather bother him, but tonight he felt a chill and longed for the coat strung across his stool at the bar.

Angus' plump cheeks had gone red. The bartender huffed in short breaths, lumbering into the alley as nimbly as a man of his stature may lumber. They reached two heavy plank doors set low against the tavern's brick foundation. Angus lifted them open, and they fell hard against their hinges with a thud that sent dozens of slumbering rodents scurrying for safer beds. Disappearing into the blackness was a steep, narrow set of stairs.

"Cellar," Angus said, to which McComber nodded.

They descended. McComber immediately lost sight of Angus' hefty shadow. The walls to either side of him were cold. The emptiness ahead of him was complete. He expected at any moment to crash into the bartender or slam into a wall. A light flared up ahead, and he soon saw Angus thumbing the wheel of a kerosene lamp. "No electricity down here," the bartender said.

The room in which Marcus found himself was cramped and stagnant, decorated with an intricate pattern of cobwebs and rat feces. Along one wall sat their treasure: a double layered rack of girders housing a dozen large barrels. Angus maneuvered toward the bottom rack and bent to lift one end of a barrel.

"You take the other end," Angus said, hunched over and waiting.

McComber, determined to satiate his curiosity, moved slowly as he inspected the room. He saw nothing of immediate interest. No fascinating artifacts lay among the rodent droppings, no easily identifiable historical relics lost beneath a blanket of dust or webbing. The room, though ancient and captivating, was nothing but a seldom used storage closet for the bartender's meager possessions.

As he bent to lift his end of the barrel, however, something caught his attention. "Where does that lead?" he asked, nodding toward what appeared to be a heavy door set into the back wall. It was mostly hidden by stacks of boxes and several piles of moth infested encyclopedias.

"Bah," huffed Angus. "The tunnels," he said. "Catacombs, the people call 'em. Might as well be nowhere. Now, you got your side? Lift when I tell you to so neither of us ends up a pancake."

"Catacombs?"

"Dug during some war, I'm told. There are only so many places to bury a body in this city, what with the constant rain and all. So they dug into the rock. I hear they go as deep as a whore's honeypot."

"Have you explored them?"

"Not far. It's awful dark in there. And damp. Nothing to make for a good story. I don't imagine those hinges would open if you try, anyway, so don't bother." He grunted, securing his grip on the barrel, forgoing subtlety. "You ready?"

But McComber continued to stare at the doorway. The inklings of an idea stirred in his mind, the sketching of a plan. After all, didn't he have a woman's husband to kill, and wouldn't a string of tunnels prove the perfect device for such a murder, one fit for the literary nature of his goddess? It would not be, as Jacob suggested, a bullet, or poison. But something worse. Something wonderfully worse. The excitement spread. The anticipation grew. The brainstorming swept across the fields of his imagination and—

"Uh, Marcus?" Angus' face had gone bright red on the other side of the barrel.

"Sorry!"

Together they lifted the barrel and spent fifteen minutes maneuvering it up the stairwell and into the bar. Angus returned to the alley to button down the cellar doors. And Marcus, adrift in a daydream of delighted speculation, eagerly guzzled the bartender's complimentary round. It was but one of many rewards for his adventures underground.

§

Daniel and Jacob arrived at the Lyons household a short while later. The walk through the city streets had been pleasant enough. The air was cool. Even better, it was dry. Without its wet partner, the autumn chill lacked its usual ferocious demeanor. Or maybe the two men were simply in good spirits.

The house, modest and ancient as it was, fit snugly among the other homes in the prosperous — though not especially upscale or gaudy — neighborhood. There were paved roads and sidewalks, Victorian street lamps with gas flames, and, unlike the city proper, curbside trash collection instead of alleyway garbage stacking. Given the stench of the city, the perk was no small benefit. Jacob enjoyed the prestige that came with living in a well-respected neighborhood, but it was also a biting slap in the face of his ego. After all, his meager monetary contributions to the household expenses would buy him a dwelling no larger than the trash bins on the curb. But tonight was not a night for such thoughts. Tonight, three friends would dine and converse, and the problems of the world would vanish. Or so he hoped.

"That McComber is an odd one," Daniel said. They had walked mostly in silence to that point.

"That he is."

"Prone to drunkenness and fable making," Daniel added. "Not to mention, and I say this as a medical professional, he's a bit deranged."

"You have no idea." Jacob searched his pockets for the house keys as they approached the front door. "He's infatuated with a married woman now and is quite literally stalking the poor soul. That's assuming his stories are not all fabrications, an assumption of which I'm not entirely convinced."

Jacob found his keys, but the front door was unlocked and the two men entered laughing. They were greeted by the unmistakable aroma of a roast broiling in the oven.

"Smells fantastic," Daniel said. "You're spoiled."

"Only when we have visitors. We're not getting on too well recently."

"Why is that? You don't see each other enough to fight regularly."

"I would have thought you already knew. Hasn't she discussed our difficulties?"

"You mean in the bedroom? No."

"Not exactly, but related."

"Ah, yes! I mean, no, she hasn't discussed anything with me, but I know what you're referring to."

Jacob wondered if that were true. After all, Daniel was her doctor, and he had to know. Still, it was something he didn't like to think about lest he imagine things best left unimagined.

They heard her speaking from the kitchen, "Go ahead and sit down, everything will be ready in a minute."

"Spoiled!" Daniel laughed.

They went straight to the dining room. Jacob saw the fancy china and silver set on the table. Wedding gifts from a decade earlier.

"Been a while since you had a home cooked meal?" Jacob asked.

"Before the divorce. Alicia and I both worked, as you know, and we were always busy, so we didn't often sit together for dinner. Every Sunday she prepared a magnificent feast, and I'd dally around the kitchen helping out wherever possible. They were good times, Jacob. And now, well, let's just say the scraps I cook for myself and eat out of the pan don't quite measure up."

Jacob smiled as they sat down. "This promises to be the best meal I've had since your divorce, too, so don't feel bad."

"Don't complain, buddy. Troubles or no, you've got a fantastic wife. You do anything to piss her off and I'll be waiting in line with all the other men who would be thrilled to steal her. You hear me?"

"Yes. But you're easily ignored."

As they waited for the feast to begin, Daniel peered around the room. "Is that new?" he asked, eyeing an oak curio in the corner filled with antique books.

"She bought that a few months back. I suggested we might already have enough bookshelves. I've got three empty ones in my office. You can see how well the suggestion was received."

"Well, the breadwinner does make the rules."

"Funny."

"How's the latest book coming?"

"Not well. The ideas are there, but the motivation is lacking. And the proper words are entirely absent."

"And the earlier books?"

"Still awful. Each one needs a rewrite. But I'm excited about the next one. That'll be the one. I'm due for a good story. Next one might be the masterpiece."

"You say that every time."

"I published an article last week."

"And how much did that pay?"

"Hundred dollars."

"Supplemental income then," Daniel said.

"Perhaps you'd like to leave now," he joked. "You can take your sarcasm with you and remember this meal by its smell instead of its taste."

"I wouldn't dream of it, Master Dickens!"

From the kitchen, the appetizing aromas leaked out to engulf the entire house. The men heard cabinets closing, footsteps shuffling from counter to sink to stovetop. Jacob felt a sting. Should he offer to help? But before the thought became a gesture, the noise stopped. With his back turned, he could not see his wife emerge with a pot of meat and vegetables. He saw only Daniel Jefferson's eyes as they lifted toward the doorway. Daniel had always adored her.

His friend stood, grinning like a fool, and said, "Hello, Bree."

CHAPTER SEVEN

Three and a Half Months Ago

Breeana Lyons offered her best smile. Daniel was a trusted friend, an old friend, and it had been too long since she and Jacob had shared their table with a visitor. She wanted his experience to be welcoming and happy and more reminiscent of their first meal together than the reality of the current situation sought to allow. She remembered the day when Jacob first met Daniel and invited him to dinner. To think it had been nine years earlier, only a year after their own wedding. Daniel and Alicia were dating then, not yet engaged, and the evening had proven splendid. So splendid she still remembered it well. How the cruelties of the world had led them astray in the years since.

"You look fabulous," Daniel said.

"Thank you. You look wonderful yourself. How are you?"

"As well as one can hope to be," he answered, "given the circumstances."

"I'm so sorry about Alicia."

"Don't be. Please. We had our troubles. What's important is that you and Jacob aren't destined to share our fate. That makes me smile." She forced herself to meet his gaze without turning away. After all, Alicia had left Daniel for another man. It took a conscious effort to push all thoughts of Marcus McComber out of her mind.

"Hello, Bree," Jacob said without standing. Two years earlier he might have used any number of imaginative and doting monikers, but affection had all but vanished from their lives. He had been a different man then. He had been the man she loved, endearing in all ways. But no longer. The constant stench of drunkenness has a way of eradicating sincerity.

"Hello, Jacob," she said, setting the roast at the center of the table and settling into her seat. The chair beside her, where Alicia once sat, was empty, and she knew she wouldn't be the only person to notice.

"The meal looks delicious," Daniel offered.

"Thank you."

"Let's eat!" Jacob said, grabbing a slice of bread and tearing off a chunk with his teeth. "Guests first," he then added, his mouth already full.

As Daniel poked a piece of roast with his fork and dropped it onto his plate, as graceful as a gentlemen, he said, "Tell me, Jacob. Does it not disgust you to know that, while you wasted your afternoon at the tavern, your beautiful wife labored to prepare this fine meal? You ought to be ashamed."

"It wasn't a problem, really," Bree said.

Jacob chewed his bread.

"Please. I take every opportunity to poke fun at your husband."

"He does deserve it."

Bree and Daniel smiled at each other, and Jacob said, "I shall only accept your attacks because the food is as delicious as an apple from the garden of Eden."

"Thank you," Bree said, surprised.

Daniel added, "She's right though, Jacob, you did deserve it."

"That's enough out of you, Doctor."

They ate in silence for a few moments, smiling. Daniel appeared to enjoy his food. Jacob ate everything on his plate. Though she doubted it was his intention, Bree felt his ravished sighs implied unhappiness at the rarity of such a meal. The noises were so unpleasant she wanted to stand and leave, to escape the implication of guilt, the psychological abuse. But at the same time, she knew Jacob loved her, and she doubted he intended any harm. He was too kind and gentle a soul, too easily intimidated or too sentimental to harm another person, especially her. That made her crazy. In any case, Daniel need not know the details of their struggling marriage. He had enough to worry about. But still the torment grew.

Perhaps it was guilt. True, she and Jacob had lost touch, and true, neither was at fault unless both were, but all day every day her thoughts were consumed by someone else. Was that fair? Was that right? She and Jacob were married. Married! For ten years. And though he showed it less than he once did, she knew he loved her. And she loved him, though she often wondered if by love she meant something else.

Nevertheless, she felt a bit of rage stirring as she watched Jacob stuff his face. She began to perspire, to sense flashes of heat. Could she excuse herself? What would poor Daniel think? But she had to leave, to retreat back to the kitchen or to her bedroom, if only for a few moments to regain her composure. Could they see how uncomfortable she was? No, they weren't looking. If they looked at her, if they cared enough to glance in her direction, would they then see her torment? Would they know that her thoughts, when free from the anger invoked by her husband, always drifted to the mysterious man in black who had given her a bottle of sherry and a gorgeous book on a bench beneath the moonlight? How could she leave? The meal had just begun. What excuse would they believe? She knew the answer was none, and that calmed her down somehow. No. She would restrain herself. She had been infatuated at other times during their marriage. Isn't everyone at some point? She could hide it. Couldn't she? Why was Marcus McComber so different?

"So," Daniel said, "I delivered twins yesterday. The Pickelsons, and what a fitting name. Seven times I warned them. You're having twins. I said it over and over. But Mrs. Pickelson, she's given birth to five kids, and she tells me, 'Sorry, ain't no way I've got two in there.' They won't look at the ultrasound. Won't let me reveal anything. They like to do things the old fashioned way. So, I find out they're only planning for one kid. They've had all girls and expect to pass the hand-me-downs to yet another girl, but the twins are boys. Pickle is the best word to describe their situation now. A Pickle for the Pickelsons. And the woman asks me, in the delivery room, when I tell them we're not quite done, another baby's coming, she asks me, 'Why didn't you tell us we we're having twins?'"

To be polite, Breeana grinned. Jacob munched away. The moment was awkward, and, a minute later, it became worse.

"Are you two making plans?" Daniel asked. "Can we expect some cubs around here soon?"

"Cubs?" Jacob asked.

"Baby Lyonses."

"Funny."

Bree stared at her food, fiddled with her silverware. Both men watched her. "I'd rather not talk about it," she said.

"Can't say I blame you. Last thing I'd want around here are tiny Jacobs. He's worse than five children."

"Aren't you a riot tonight?" Jacob chided.

"I don't want to talk about it." Bree said.

Jacob attempted to explain. "We were trying. Had some difficulties. I thought you knew this."

Bree wondered if he would reach for her then, to console her, to take her hand and squeeze it if only to demonstrate his sensitivity to the subject. Instead, he ate another piece of bread. "I haven't mentioned it to him," she told Jacob.

"If you're having difficulties," Daniel said, and she could see he wanted to be helpful. There was no malice in his voice, no mocking undertones. He was a genuine friend. "If you're having difficulties, you could certainly try some new things. I've got pamphlets and books at the office, plenty of recommendations."

"Please, I really don't want to talk about it."

She knew by the look on Daniel's face that he suddenly understood, or thought he did. "I'm sorry," he said.

But Jacob found an interest. "What types of things?"

"Procedures," Daniel offered, eyeing Bree. "But I won't go into them if you don't want me to."

Jacob became inquisitive. "What types of procedures?"

"Now doesn't appear to be the time," Daniel said.

"Tell me," Jacob demanded, mouth full. "We could use the help."

Daniel's sympathetic gaze fell on her again. Jacob sat beside her munching his bread, as eager to hear about all these miracle reproductive cures as he was to hurry back to the tavern after dinner. Finally, now, beneath Daniel's apologetic gaze, the frustration unleashed itself. Not only was she suffering, but Daniel was uncomfortable, and Jacob was either indifferent to their emotions or ignorant of them.

"C'mon, Doc. Tell me," Jacob said again.

And Bree jumped to her feet. She bumped the table. A glass of Zinfandel spilled across the white tablecloth. "I must go," she said. Infuriated, and frustrated, she ignored their stares and retreated to the kitchen. Daniel apologized from the other room. She heard Jacob explain that all was well, that everything would be fine, that he'd attend to the spilled wine after the meal. He never came to see her. And she waited.

For five minutes, then ten, she stood beside the stove fuming, wondering why she felt any guilt at all for betraying a man with no apparent concern for her emotions. Could he not see how rotten their marriage had become? Could he not see that children were the last thing they needed at this point? Was he so absorbed in his failure and his self-doubt that he no longer noticed the tears of his lover? She laughed at herself. Lover? How long had it been since they'd been lovers?

She remembered days past. Jacob had been the most amazing man she knew, the most kind and caring and giving and utterly selfless man in her life. He was a writer, a poet with an imagination unbounded and grand. She had fallen in love with him, with his words, with his emotions, but all that remained of what she loved was a drunken shell that no longer resembled the man she knew. He was broken. He was lost. And though occasionally she encouraged him with hopeless attempts to return his confidence, she knew the man she loved might be gone forever.

Writing, she knew, might help him overcome the sorrows he imposed upon himself. The problem, however, was that he spent very little time writing because he was often hung over from the previous night's visit to the tavern. The spiral continued ever downward, and she had long ago lost hope, and she hated Jacob for his inability to see what was happening.

At that moment, she wanted to abandon everything. She grabbed her satchel and her coat and she left through the back door, leaving the two men alone with their meal. She heard Daniel trying to apologize for a situation over which he had no knowledge and no control. He was a good friend. Tonight, her heart ached for so many reasons.

§

The night was still new, and the waning sliver of moon visible in the darkening sky shone only faintly. She walked with no particular destination in mind, content to spend the evening alone. Already her anger had begun to subside, though the pain continued to fester. She let herself be lost to a world of speculation, searching for relief in the visage of a man about whom she knew so little. Marcus McComber invaded her thoughts like a virus, but this virus brought excitement along with misery.

The sidewalk was cold beneath her feet, and it stretched forever into the distance like a barren road to oblivion. Or maybe Hell. It was as good a destination as any. Several times she encountered other pedestrians, but they passed like apparitions with their heads down, heedless of her and her troubles. She knew the situation was foolish. How could she let her world be pulled apart by affection or devotion or any other silly emotion provoked by men who cared so little for her happiness? Jacob had been passionate once, but everything he had been vanished with his descent into self-pity and mourning. Marcus McComber might be different, but then he might as easily be a womanizing brute who achieved his sexual goals through feigned sincerity and gentlemanliness. How could she know for sure? How could anyone know anyone? Hadn't she once thought Jacob was different than most men?

They met at the university during the short and cool summer before senior year. She was a business major, practical and profit driven, a trait instilled by her tireless, successful parents. But her parents had instilled other traits as well, namely a fascination with literature. Her family was well read, and growing up her father read to her every night. He would read anything and everything, from Dr. Seuss to a biography of Winston Churchill to the aesthetic miracles of modern architecture. Though much of it was dull to a child of five or seven, her father had a voice and a presence that could turn even the mundane laws of relativity into a grand play enacted by the world's most gifted player. He read Shakespeare and Frost, Marlowe and Poe. He read Wells and Tolkien and Shelley and Dickens. As a child, she understood little of the drama and the humanity, but she was fascinated by the adventure and the mystery of imagined worlds, frightened by the gothic horror of her favorite Edgar Allan. As she grew older, she understood more, and she marveled at the beauty of Yeats and the wastelands of Elliot. It was this love and admiration of literature that had been her father's greatest gift, and it was the one thing most responsible for introducing her to a boy named Jacob Lyons.

They met under a massive Cypress tree shadowed by the red brick of the Student Union building. She had found a flyer posted on campus that advertised open poetry readings in the yard beneath the tree, and so at the proper time she lurked beside a nearby oak and listened as a dozen or so students chatted and read poetry and critiqued each other's work. They commented on everything, from the selection of individual syllables to the grandest concepts of existentialism and isolation. They were all brilliant, she had thought, and they were all imaginative. This was not the high school poetry club she despised. These people were not dark and depressing. They were literature fanatics, and true authors, intellectuals who sought truth and idealism and understanding through words and emotions. As they read their poetry aloud, she moved closer, always eager for the next poem, always afraid she'd be sent away if this close-knit group caught her loitering nearby.

Soon she stood among them and would have been mistaken as a member by any casual observer, but she was a trespasser. It was a girl who noticed her first, brown eyes glaring behind tortoise-shell eyeglasses.

"Do you have a poem to read?" the girl asked, to which Bree shook her head no. "Then please come back when you have something to share. I don't mean to be rude, but, like, you know, it's a rule."

With regret, and a bit of anger, Bree turned to go. Before she reached the sidewalk, a boy jogged up beside her. He introduced himself as Jacob and explained that he didn't have a poem to read either, but he had lied so they let him stay. "I'll have one tomorrow," he said, "just for you."

They chatted for an hour. Jacob Lyons escorted her to her apartment and past it, around the block and past it again. They talked about literature and politics and family. They denounced silly little private poetry groups and they complained about early morning classes. The conversation was light hearted and fun. The next day when they met for lunch, Jacob had a poem. It was short and it was clumsy, hastily written, and she had since forgotten the words, but it was also cute and endearing and written especially for her. Though her father's play acting and readings were performed for her alone, none of the stories or poems had been written exclusively with her in mind. That made Jacob's poem special.

She remembered the glow in his eyes, the strength in his fingers. His pen glided across a sheet of notebook paper like Shakespeare's quill on blank parchment, smooth and effortless and utterly romantic. They spent every moment together. Every night as well. Never mind that he was an English major. Never mind that his only prospect in life was the random luck of publication and the even luckier hope of finding a readership. Those thoughts might have mattered to her parents, though she doubted they would, but, to her, Jacob was a man of dreams and adventure. If they were to be married and penniless and starving, his imagination could whisk them off to other realms and wealthier circumstances, to daydreams and pots of gold. He was a mythmaker, a storyteller. He made dreams come alive. And her life, she knew, would never be boring.

How wrong she had been.

A brisk wind sent a chill down her fingertips and up her neck. Clouds swirled in the nighttime sky, pirouetting directly overhead and veiling the crescent moon in shadow. She wondered if Jacob and Daniel had noticed her absence. And if so, what had they done about it? The answer was too obvious. Daniel might have felt sorry at first, but since Alicia left, even the kindhearted doctor fell victim to the tavern's draw and the liquor's allure. At the moment, she could not really blame them. She herself craved a concoction with which to drink away her confusion and misery. For a moment, she began to wonder if she had stumbled down the same path of self-pity as her husband.

It was then she noticed the building beside her. With its lofty arches and stained glass and towering steeple, the church rose up in beckoning radiance with its doors agape and its altar exposed, daring any tortured souls to venture inside and discover God. But despite the awesome image before her, despite the beauty and the majesty and the overwhelming sense of insignificance, what she really saw was a man seated up the burgundy carpeted aisle several pews from the altar. There, in the most unlikely of places, in an empty church, in a Catholic church with its emaciated Christ towering high above the small congregation like a slain, immovable, suffering god, she saw the anomaly. She saw Marcus McComber. And he was praying.

CHAPTER EIGHT

Three and a Half Months Ago

"Seems you're the one hiding now," Bree said, somewhat jokingly. "In a church, no less. Are the townsfolk hunting you with pitchforks and fiery stakes?"

McComber blinked out of a trance. He knelt on a padded board, his elbows resting on the forward pew. His fingers, long and delicate and soft, intertwined with those on his other hand. "Hello, Breeana."

"Hello? That's all you've got? For me? I suppose you go around offering to knock off the husband of every girl you meet then. Is that why the townsfolk want your head? Are you once again unaware of your peril, dear Fortunato?" But her humor seemed lost on him. She thought maybe he might have grinned, but in the dim lighting she couldn't be sure. "Am I interrupting?" she said, but without any real conviction. She was in no mood to care. Behind her, near the polished railings at the rear of the nave where two arched doors stood open, a priest appeared. Maybe she had been too loud. The church, after all, was eerily quiet, as such places often were. "Sorry," she added, a touch quieter. "But it's nice to see you. I expected it to be sooner, but you skipped last week's meeting."

McComber lifted himself off the kneeler. He stared at her with those devilish eyes. "I thought perhaps you needed some time," he said, "to consider your situation."

"Trust me, I consider it every moment of every day." She wondered if the frustration was evident on her face.

McComber looked skyward, to the lofty church peaks where wooden beams came together with perfect symmetry above the Christ's thorny crown. "Now," he said, "when storms of Fate o'ercast / Darkly my Present and my Past, / Let my Future radiant shine / With sweet hopes of thee and thine. Do you know those words?"

"Edgar Allan Poe," she said.

"A hymn to Mary, mother of God. I always think of them when I'm here."

"And I thought you were talking about me. Did you kill Mary's husband, too?" Bree laughed at Marcus' unusual behavior. This was not the same swagger with which he carried himself beyond the pew. When he failed to return the chuckle, she asked, "Why are you here?"

"Where else should I be?"

"I mean, you're not exactly… You're not…" She hated herself for babbling. "I just didn't expect this from you."

"Expect what? Faith? Devotion? What have I done to imply something different?"

You talked about killing my husband, she thought.

Marcus said, "Passion does not lend itself solely to romantic pursuit, my dear. What we may feel for another human must surely pale in comparison to the emotions a god might invoke."

"I don't think Mary's a god."

"A goddess, perhaps. At least in my mind."

"Have you tried to seduce her with a cape?"

"You seem eager to swing the conversation to more personal matters," he said. "Do you have issues with religion?"

"To be honest, Marcus, right now I have issues with everything. And I don't give a damn about religion."

A pipe organ suddenly blared to life, groaning with a deep, aching melancholic chord. She turned to see the priest glaring at her from behind the organ keys. "To be honest, I don't give a damn about anything at all. And I learned long ago that turning to religion to solve my problems was no better than pretending they didn't exist. Prayer and indifference usually produce the same outcome."

"Your problems are not religion's to solve. That's your mistake. God will not help you. Too many fools fall victim to that belief. God is but an experimenter, a tinkerer, an inventor. Imagine he were a binder of books. Occasionally he will mix a new type of glue, and maybe all the pages will pull apart from the binding. The book is ruined. That won't stop him the next time from creating a new type of glue. He makes mistakes. He fails. We are made in his image and we work the same way, trial and error, so we ought to better understand his mechanics. He's tinkering with the world, and our own problems are nothing but grains of sawdust in a pile near his workbench. He has more important things to consider than our petty issues."

"What's your point?"

"That he must work within the confines of this world. He cannot create resolutions out of thin air. Deus ex machina, they call it in literature. When the resolution is too perfect for the world of the story, when insurmountable obstacles are conquered out of nothing as though by the hands of a god. The author gets lazy and wants to suddenly wrap up his story, and so he conjures some miraculous new character or ending from the ink bottle beside him. He does not build up to it. He offers no clues. Contrivance is the only outcome."

Marcus shifted in the pew, excitement evident. "Think about the mystery novels you read. The good ones. Stories, by definition, are contrived, but the good authors know how to disguise the contrivance. How quickly do you know who is dead? You meet a cast of characters, and without doubt one of them, at least, is the murderer. Sometimes there are murderers, plural, but you don't know who they are or how they did it.

"When you finish the story, how often do you look back in amazement and realize you were introduced to the murder weapon, in some form or another, perhaps cleverly disguised, almost immediately? With few exceptions, most clever mysteries reveal the necessary pieces as early as possible, so as to prevent the accusation of contrivance.

"God works in the same way. The clues are there. The pieces with which he must work are evident all around us. It is his mastery of the elements that keeps us guessing. No matter how hard we search, no matter how long we examine, he is the smartest among us, and he is the one setting the course. So instead of looking to religion for answers, you should use it as inspiration. Search out the clues he will manipulate, and use them to make your own solutions. Speak to God not because you need help, but because you want to learn, and perhaps at some point you will learn something relevant, some random lesson that will ultimately prove useful. That is the point of religion."

"I liked you better when you wore the cape," she said. "What about you? What do you seek?"

"Salvation" Marcus whispered.

"From what?"

"Myself. My wrongdoings. My betrayers."

"I don't understand."

"Good. Such things are not for you to understand."

"And why is that?"

"Because there is something you first need to do."

"What would that be?" she sighed, growing tired of the games.

Suddenly his face changed. His wicked grin emerged. "Come," he said, "I'll tell you." And he pulled her to her feet, and they ran out of the church, forgetting thoughts of gods and authors and other such trivialities, leaving poor Jesus alone with the priest to hang on his crucifix, jealous of their departure, forced to contemplate his eternal immobility.

§

They ran through the streets hand-in-hand like lovers traipsing along a sandy beach. The air was sweet and cool, refreshing, and Bree felt a tide of excitement building again. It was a sensation Marcus McComber seemed capable of producing at will.

Before long they passed the familiar façade of the bookstore. She wondered how this dark, secretive man could turn into a boyish, playful fool. Hadn't he been lost in religious devotion a few moments earlier? Hadn't he done a skip and a leap in the rain a few nights ago? How much of it was pretend? How many of his actions were sincere, and how many were meant to confuse and fascinate? He was a mystery of dichotomous personas, and, though she guessed that not everything he said was truthful, his words and behavior intrigued her beyond anything she had known for years. Still, she knew it was wise to be wary.

He led her to Café Noir, where, on a rainy night not long ago, they had first stopped for coffee and conversation. She felt her heart thumping against her ribs, but Marcus was cool and controlled, as if no amount of exertion could steal his breath. From the depths of her mind, a thought emerged, and she imagined a certain activity that might do the trick, a particular form of exertion that might leave him panting and breathless. Her face flushed at the idea, and she forced the thought back into the hidden depths out of which it had emerged.

They took a booth near the fireplace. She didn't remove her coat, and neither did Marcus, though he set his fedora on the seat beside him and fluffed his hair. He ordered two coffees, black, and once the waitress had delivered them, Bree lost patience and asked the question: "What must I do?"

He stared at her. He sipped his coffee, and he proved once again why he was annoying and infuriating and fascinating. "Tell me about your husband," he said.

"What about him?" she asked.

"What does he do?"

"He's an author."

"A failure, you mean."

"I didn't say that."

"You needn't. The truth was evident in your tone. Why do you stay with him?"

"Because he loves me."

"Do you love him?"

She blinked. "Yes."

"Do you love who he has become, or do you love who he once was?"

Perhaps, she thought, Marcus McComber was the devil. Or a god. His omniscience had as many evil qualities as good ones. Was her pain so obvious? And if so, why hadn't Jacob seen it? Why hadn't Jacob been there for her instead of drunk every night at that forsaken tavern? "I don't know," was all she could muster.

"Then here is what you must do," he said. "Your husband binds you to an unhappy existence. Forget his intentions. They don't matter. Perhaps he has reasons, and perhaps he is free of fault. Such things are irrelevant. You are weighted down by complacency and responsibility, suffering a life of boredom and torment. As I told you before, life is about adventure and learning. Life, as they say, is about living. You mustn't allow the world to constrain you. You must seek the adventure and mystery you crave, or you'll be eternally miserable. You," he said, "must leave your husband."

She looked away in disgust. "I'm not going to leave my husband, Marcus. He's done nothing wrong."

"Denial, my dear, is the cornerstone of wrongdoing. It is the blind witness to persecution. Can you not see the truth? Can you not see your own misery? I know you can. You work all day and spend your nights away from home, lonely, desiring more than he can offer. I know what you crave. And I can give it to you."

She felt the many layers of meaning implicit in his words wash over her. His thumbs twirled. His fists rested on the table so casually as to imply boredom. But he had spoken with conviction and determination. He had spoken with energy and passion. His eyes, though black and deep, burned with a fire she had never seen before, and she couldn't force herself to look away. Perhaps he was the devil! During their first conversation at the bookstore, she had overrun his position with wit and knowledge. Now he had taken a stand, using logic and passion as the boundaries of his battlefield. In a matter of seconds she had run head first into the ambush. Her heart had already lost the battle, though her mind was determined to fight.

"You must understand," Marcus said, "I have only your best interests at heart."

"Oh? And what of your interests, Mr. McComber? Do you think you stand to benefit from the demise of my marriage?"

"No," he answered. "Not directly."

"How do you mean?"

"You may leave your husband, but where you go from there is your choice."

"Suppose I went to your apartment," she said, choosing her words carefully. "Where would we go from there?"

McComber laughed. "To the bedroom, of course."

She wanted to scold him, to drench his face with coffee, but instead she found herself in the midst of unexpected laughter. "Charming, mysterious, and now," she said, "facetious. You never fail to surprise me."

"I work long and hard at it."

"But will you offer a serious response? Even the wildest adventures in the bedroom must end at some point. What then?"

He lifted his fedora from the seat beside him and dropped it on his head. With the brim low, his collar high, his face narrow and sporting a black shadow of hair beneath the chin, he was devilishly handsome, and she imagined pressing those features against her own skin. This time she did not blush.

"Together," Marcus said, "we could scavenge the Heavens for splendor and traverse the oceans of ecstasy. Anywhere would be our destination. Anywhere would be our Heaven."

"That's a bit much, don't you think?"

"Not for my goddess."

"So much for serious." She grabbed her satchel and stood. "I should go."

"Finish your coffee, at least," he begged.

"No. I have an empty home to return to." Jacob and Daniel had likely returned to their tavern.

McComber leapt to his feet, blocking her exit. "Just do me one favor," he said.

"What is that?"

"Leave him."

A chuckle escaped her lips. If nothing else, he was persistent. "Good night, Marcus."

Before she could escape, just as he had beneath the moonlit park bench, he pulled her close and kissed her. She forced him away instinctively, but her hand remained on the grainy texture of his cheek. She held it there, feeling his warmth, scanning his eyes for something more than lust. Betrayal and love and guilt and longing clouded her thoughts. She was frozen in a mesmerizing moment of pain, until she realized, with less fear than apprehension, that her will had long since abandoned her to the fancy of Marcus McComber. No amount of denial or logic would matter.

In that instant of acceptance, she banished the voice of reason from her cluttered mind. She slipped her hand behind his neck and pulled his lips to hers. She felt the piercing glances of café patrons, savored the excitement of their smiles, tasted the rage and power and passion of a stranger for the first time in years, and escaped to the sensual timelessness of passion, if only for the eternity of a moment.

When at last they separated, she licked her lips and grinned up at his hungry eyes. Without a word, she walked past him toward the exit. She never looked over her shoulder, but she knew Marcus would watch her leave with that sinister grin playing on his face. The idea stoked the embers of her passion into flames of their own, and at that moment she didn't care if the entire world knew.

CHAPTER NINE

Three Months Ago

Jacob found Bree in the kitchen. Tonight was not a special occasion, although a casual observer could be forgiven for mistaking it as such. On Sunday nights, he and his wife were home together, sharing their abode the way lovers ought, passing each other in the halls, brushing shoulders and smiling with half-hearted familiarity. Okay, he admitted, maybe it wasn't exactly the way lovers would do it, but it was their routine. They had been lovers once, if not recently, and though they often passed their evenings in separate rooms, dancing with the ghosts of their distinct imaginations, at least she was near. Still, the routine had long ago run its course, and he was tired of it. Tonight, he would try something new.

Part of the problem involved those ghosts. Bree had her love of books and stories, as did he, but words had become torture to him. Whenever he picked up a book, he felt guilty that he wasn't writing more, and that guilt in turn instigated his anger, which in turn instigated a disdain for reading. The self-sustaining cycle allowed him to avoid guilt over his failures as an author as long as he never picked up anything to read. And when you don't want to read, a bookstore is your enemy. But what do you do when your wife wants to spend every night of the week cavorting in the enemy's lair? Naturally, you let her frolic in those pages of imagination while you seek camaraderie and shelter with your allies. Of course, his allies were drunks and their drinks. Not exactly dependable companions, and not the best soldiers with whom to race into battle.

But Bree had her passions, and she was nothing without those passions. If not for her love of literature, he would never have met her under that Cyprus tree. So he indulged those passions as often as she desired. If only her desires could be satiated, or focused. In recent years she seemed to desire the bookstore and her book club friends more than she desired him, but who could blame her? What grand peaks of literary accomplishment had he scaled in recent years? Or ever, for that matter? But her passions had not changed. Instead, her focus had blurred. All he had to do was shift her attentions in the proper direction, refocus them on more important matters.

He had tried before. Over the years, he bought her gifts, made her dinners, sometimes took her to the theater. No matter what he tried, she would smile and thank him, but her smile was laced with pity, and her thanks felt insincere. As time wore on, whenever he showed his affection, she would ridicule his drinking and his nights at the tavern. Her anger intensified with each passing season. She could never grasp what seemed so obvious to him, that he spent his nights at the tavern because she spent her nights at the bookstore. Was he to sit alone on the sofa at night while she pursued her passions? Nonsense! But whenever he attempted to make his point she would dismiss it as the hypothetical concoction of an inebriated mind, spat from lips soaked too long in beer and liquors.

He was the author, but she possessed a far more lethal mastery of language.

In any case, tonight he did not carry the stench of liquor. Instead, he carried a dozen white and yellow Calla Lilies, her favorite, and dark chocolates drizzled with white chocolate swirls. Ever the optimist, he would dream the two of them seated shoulder-to-shoulder at the kitchen table, nibbling candies and bantering like young lovers anxious to taste the lingering sweetness on the other's moistened tongue. Once upon a time, they had enjoyed such intimacy daily. Back then his mind was sharper and his imagination boundless. He conjured romantic vignettes out of thin air and improvised the tragic sonnets that tickled her most lustful fancies. The disappearance of those moments invited a simple question: had his abilities grown lax because she had lost interest, or did she lose interest when his abilities grew lax? Perhaps both factors contributed to their relationship's current maladies. More importantly, perhaps both could be overcome.

In the kitchen, he walked up behind her and wrapped his arms around her waist. Her body tensed. He pulled the hair away from her neck and whispered, "Hello, Mrs. Lyons." The complementing scents of perfume and shampoo wafted upwards. His lips tickled her neck, and he kissed her repeatedly, inching playfully up to her ear and along her cheek. She cringed. He took it as flirtatious maneuvering. He swung his head around and kissed her other ear. She cringed again, and this time she stepped away from him.

"These are for you," he said, offering the lilies. "And these," he added, holding out the box of chocolates, "are for us."

She bowed her head, ran her fingers through her hair, massaged her own neck, and stared at the ground. He knew her well enough to know she was searching for the right words. For any words. But it was too late to stop now. He dropped the flowers and chocolates on the counter and reached for her lips, touching them with his fingers. He stepped in close and kissed her.

"Don't," she said, backing away.

"What's wrong?"

"Just don't."

"Why?"

"You don't want to do this, Jacob. Please. Not now."

"It's a kiss. I don't understand."

"Please, Jacob. I'm not in the mood right now."

"Not in the mood for a kiss? That's ridiculous."

"It's not ridiculous. You can't just walk up and kiss me as though nothing's wrong."

"Am I supposed to shake your hand?"

Anger darkened her expression. "Why not? You don't know me any better these days than the strangers you meet at your tavern."

"Oh come on, Bree. Not again with that. I thought you might enjoy a bit of affection."

"Affection? You show more affection to your storytelling bartender than you ever show to me. And do you think affection means a hug here and there or a kiss every Sunday?"

"At least I try. At least I make an effort. You don't talk to me, except when you're angry. You certainly don't touch me. You run out every night to your bookstore, and I'm stuck looking for something to do."

"Oh no, Jacob. No. Don't blame this on me. I go out every night because you're never here. You're off getting drunk and spouting nonsense at a saloon."

"Why do you think I go there?"

"Does it matter anymore?"

"Of course it matters." He stepped towards her and took her hand. "I go because you're not here, and I spend all day alone trying to write. Why be alone at night as well? At least there's someone to talk to while I'm there."

She stared hard at him. Her lips hung open, disbelieving.

"I miss you, Bree."

She spun and walked out of the kitchen.

"Don't you miss me?" he asked, following closely.

She whirled around. "I miss the man you once were. Absolutely I do. The man who cared more about his life than his liquor. You don't miss me, Jacob. You think you do, but you don't show it. You never ask about my day. You never ask about work, or about the books I read. You never ask about the things I want to do with my life, about the places I want to go. You don't listen when I speak, and when I'm done, you don't console me. You whine about your writing or you run off to drink away your insecurities."

"How can you say that?"

"Because it's true. You can't even see it, Jacob. This isn't working anymore. You and I, us, we, we're nothing anymore. And you can't even acknowledge the reason."

"Of course I can."

"Then tell me, Jacob. Tell me what we have now. Tell me what's left of us. Tell me why the answer is nothing."

Jacob's head spun. He had no idea what to say. "We don't see each other enough," he sighed. "We don't spend time together."

"We do nothing together, Jacob. Nothing. Tell me why."

"I don't know."

"Last month, the Greer book reading, do you remember? I asked you to go with me. You said you had to write. When I suggested we see a musical, you said you promised Daniel you'd spend the evening with him."

"His divorce was finalized that day."

"You see him every night, Jacob. Every night! You do nothing with me. Tell me my feelings no longer matter to you?

"They do."

"They haven't for a long time."

"Bree…"

"Don't you get it?" Her voice took on a sympathetic tone. "Of course I love you. I've always loved you. But you're not the man you once were. You're not the man you want to be, and you let that keep you from being the man you really are. There's nothing left of us, Jacob. We live in this house together, but in every other way we live apart. I hope one day soon you're sober long enough to see it."

Then he noticed a new resolve in her posture. She took a deep breath, walked to the front closet, found a coat, and started to put it on.

"What are you doing?" he asked.

"We can't go on like this, Jacob."

"You can't leave."

"Yes, I can."

Jacob followed her to the study where she paused to stare at two books on the desk. After a moment of hesitation, she grabbed one of the two volumes and dropped it in her satchel. She headed back toward the front door. "I don't want you here when I return," she said.

Jacob felt the weight of bewilderment and heartbreak pressing down from some lofty height. "Excuse me?"

"Take some clothes, Jacob. Please take some things and go. We can't do this anymore."

All he could manage was, "I don't understand."

"I know," she said. "Maybe if you did, this wouldn't be necessary."

"I'm not leaving, Bree. We need to talk about—"

"No. Be gone when I leave."

"You can't make me leave my own house."

She paused in the doorway and turned to him. Her eyes held no tears, no sadness, but they were not without emotion. "We need to be apart for a time, Jacob. If there's anything left of us, anything salvageable, anything that could ever equate to happiness, the only way we'll discover it is to be apart. If you feel as strongly as you say, if you love me, please be gone tonight."

Longing to say something, wanting desperately to counter her argument with substance, he stared as she stood in the doorway, but he had no insights with which to argue. "Where will you go?" he asked.

She turned her eyes to the floor, refusing now for some reason to meet his gaze. "I don't know," she said and disappeared. Somehow, the familiar sound of the door closing was louder, harsher, and more final than ever before.

Jacob spun on his heels, spinning randomly, searching for an explanation, an answer, searching on every surface that twisted through his vision. He panicked, he paced, without breathing, without thinking, but for how long he could never determine. Eventually, his mind settled. His breathing slowed. His head ached. His thoughts sputtered.

What had just happened? What had he done? It was a kiss. That was all. A kiss and some flowers and some candies, but it might as well have been a gun firing randomly at angry, confused bystanders. Where was he? The den? He felt dizzy. He paused at the desk where his wife's fingers had been and saw a book resting alone beneath a lamp. It was worn, well-used, but covered with a thin layer of dust. He knew that book. The collected stories of Edgar Allan Poe. To her he had given it as a gift years ago. He didn't know she still had it. He couldn't have known she still used it. And then he realized, far too late, that she no longer used it. It had been replaced with a newer volume, one she had stuffed into her bag, and that new book had gone with her out the door, off with her on a new adventure that didn't include him or his old, torn, ragged book.

For countless moments, he stared at it, lost somewhere between memory and pain.

§

The splintered, faux wood of an inconspicuous apartment door represented so many things to Breeana Lyons. She stared at the brown veneer and contemplated her options. To open the door was to step willingly into another life. To knock on the door, a more subtle tactic, was to be invited into that life. Lastly, to turn away, to walk away and deny her lust for that life, was the one option that was no option at all.

She had plodded through wind and rain for ninety minutes, walking here and there and circling back upon her random route, arriving at this second floor landing to stare at the gates of opportunity. Her hair was wild and wind-blown, her cheeks chafed, her eyes watery and red for so many reasons. A lifetime of thought and emotion had spent itself into indifference during those ninety minutes. Had she acted rashly? Had she treated Jacob unfairly? The questions were endless, answerless, and meaningless. For once, she would not linger on faded snapshots or forgotten words. She would not imagine Jacob alone, drifting down the streets on a dejected journey to his hallowed tavern. She may have regretted the accusations, but they were prompted by her anger, and she would not regret that.

This, after all, was what she wanted. Was it not? Excitement and adventure? Her fingers tingled. Tiny explosions ripped through her veins, just beneath her skin, and her entire body shook with the sensation. Standing there on the creaking floorboards of a dank, dilapidated apartment building, haunted by demons of the past and expectations of the future, she felt like a character in a book, fleeing one man for the stronger, handsomer arms of another, on a journey to discover the requited passion she craved. There was no doubt everything she needed could be found beyond this door. She knew the angles and positions and throes of desire that would manifest themselves in that passion, and the euphoria was greater because of it.

And so she reached for the doorknob, turned it, and pushed.

Marcus McComber stood waiting for her in the hallway. Perhaps he had heard her tromping up the staircase, or maybe he noticed her heavy breathing as she deliberated outside his door. Or perhaps, as seemed possible with Marcus McComber, he simply knew she would come and had been waiting for her, frozen in the hallway, smiling, since the last time she'd seen him. It didn't really matter.

"Come in," he said, and she entered her new life.

"I did it," she breathed. "I left him. I told him to leave, to be gone when I return. I did it, Marcus."

"And how do you feel?"

"Just as I should, I think. Sad, uncertain, anxious, excited. There are no perfect words."

"And now what?"

"I don't know."

"Well congratulations," he said, stepping closer. "You were caged, and now you are free. Now you can live. Now you will have everything you've ever desired." He reached her and kissed her. His lips were gentle and warm yet demanding. She felt passion in those lips, vivacity. She did not pull away, and when their lips parted, she yanked him closer and kissed him harder. Thoughts drifted and senses heightened. She smelled the stale odor of wall paint, but it was masked by the masculinity of his cologne, the sweetness of his breath. She tasted adventure and mystery, felt angst wetting her soul, felt the demons of ecstasy mingling with angels of excitement. And finally, after a night of events she hadn't yet begun to absorb, as they danced the dance of new lovers, bumping into walls, mumbling and giggling through busy lips, destined for a world she once considered lost beyond the realm of discovery, Breeana Lyons found that for which she had so long been searching, and she refused to consider what the dawn may bring.

§

A new life had befallen Jacob, as well. Not a life of passion or desire. Not a life even worth living. As Marcus and Breeana consummated their affair in that dank apartment across town, Jacob Lyons stuffed old clothes and books into a suitcase on a bed in which he was no longer welcome. His throes were of agony, not lust, and his head filled with dread and fear instead of breathless anticipation.

He wondered where he would go, but he knew there was only one option. He wondered what he would do, but he knew he would do what he had always done. He would drink and write and vomit and cry, in no particular order. Daniel had an extra room. Daniel would take him in. Daniel, of all people, would understand. Daniel Jefferson, his only friend.

As Marcus and Breeana undressed themselves, as they cast off garments and insecurities and clawed each other's skin, Jacob dragged his suitcase downstairs to the foyer, where he took one last glance at a disappearing world.

As Marcus and Breeana sucked and licked and penetrated, as they groped and massaged and moaned and shrilled, Jacob left his home and lost himself to the repetitive clicking of suitcase wheels rolling over each new section of sidewalk. Rain had begun to fall, wet and cold, and the wind froze the dampness to his skin. He let it numb his senses.

As a distant headboard rattled above a creaking mattress, as lovers panted and explored, Jacob knocked on Daniel's door. He was sullen and wet without a coat, a dreadful apparition floating in his own haze of disbelief and regret. Daniel opened the door, confused when he spotted Jacob's suitcase. Soon enough, he realized what must have occurred, and he pulled Jacob inside. Daniel forced his friend into a warm shower, and listened over coffee while his own sad story was repeated back to him.

As Marcus and Breeana sighed and sweated and screamed and climaxed, as they showered and smoked and fornicated again, Daniel and Jacob realized they shared a new bond, one of rejection and humiliation, one both undesired and unbreakable. Daniel made the spare bed and retired to his own room, leaving Jacob alone to battle despair. Several hours later, both men lay awake in their beds adrift in separate oceans of lost love.

Across town, Marcus and Breeana lay in each other's arms, breathing deeply, fast asleep.

Part II

"I have been happy -- tho' but in a dream.
I have been happy -- and I love the theme --
Dreams! in their vivid colouring of life --
As in that fleeting, shadowy, misty strife
Of semblance with reality which brings
To the delirious eye more lovely things
Of Paradise and Love -- and all our own!
Than young Hope in his sunniest hour
hath known."

Edgar Allan Poe
Dreams

CHAPTER TEN

Present

Andrew Ruben does not scare me. After all, I have nothing to hide. He's just another violent, vindictive man who laughs behind a shield of apparent authority. We've been at this interrogation for too many hours, trapped here in this drab room, locked away beneath an indifferent world. Do they even have a right to hold me? I don't know the laws well enough to say, but perhaps that's because I never expected to be in this situation.

I still know nothing, except that Marcus McComber is dead, and though I desire to gloat at my victorious survival, I can garner neither the will nor the energy. Ruben has remained calm, but I fear his patience is short lived. He asks the same question a dozen different ways, and he scowls or shouts when my answer remains consistent. The repetition is painful and pointless. His insinuations will not help him learn the truth. His subtle tactics and psychological games, though disconcerting, cannot force me to reveal knowledge I don't possess.

What was it I thought before? That I am like a fish trapped in the web of a sailor's net? Well perhaps I've managed to escape, and he's fishing again. But ten worms will not hook a fish any faster than one. Fancy lures and well-practiced techniques are still subject to the overall degree of the beast's hunger. I doubt he cares. Besides, I've not truly escaped at all. My surroundings, with Jesus staring at me from a corner and two detectives hurling accusations from the other side of a wobbly table, indicate that I'm as trapped as ever in their net of lies. The only worms I see are those two nasty ones seated across from me.

"Mister Lyons," Ruben begins, scowling, after several minutes of silence. "May I call you Jacob?" The room is dark, lit only by the dangling bulb above the table. It shorts out with every crash of thunder. The tempests, both literal and figurative, both inside and out, have not abated.

"You can let me go," I answer.

"Well now isn't that an unfriendly tone? I thought you meant to cooperate."

"You don't believe me, regardless of what I say, so why should I bother?"

"Making my life easier will make your life easier. That is, unless you plan to stay here forever. And by here, I mean the jail beneath your feet."

I want to scream, or to sigh, or to slam my forehead into the tabletop, but delving deeper into the basements of police headquarters holds no allure. I have ventured below ground tonight too many times already, always accompanied by men bearing arms. I have faced the barrel of a gun, suffered the fright of being buried alive, fallen victim to the whims of a madman, and been cuffed and beaten by the despicable despots of corrupt law. As a result, I do not fear Ruben's threats, but I do long to roam the streets and let the tempest cleanse my wounds. That cannot happen if I am buried deeper underground. At a minimum, I'd still like to scream.

Burrows, the other detective, has stopped pacing. Now, he idles in a chair, perhaps contemplating my innocence, or, more likely, devising clever ways to frame my guilt.

Searching for a confession in each shift of my eyes or wiggle of my ears, Ruben twirls a pen between his fingers, and I wonder how long before he caves to frustration and heaves it at my head. "So," he says, "you and your wife are separated?"

I nod.

"Who initiated it?"

"Why does that matter? Why does any of this matter?" When he doesn't answer, I relent. "She did."

"And how did it make you feel?"

"Why?"

"Did it anger you? Were you furious, frantic, livid?"

"I was upset."

"Angry?"

"Sad," I say, "but if you'd like to consult a thesaurus, I'm sure we can think of even more adjectives."

"Did you feel the need to harm her?"

"Of course not."

"Out of rage? Out of pure, instinctive jealously?"

"What are you talking about?"

"Murder, Mr. Lyons. I want to know what state of mind you were in tonight. Could you have killed someone?"

I could kill Andrew Ruben. Of that I am certain. And after I kill him, maybe I can plunge that pen into Burrows' forehead. What frightful opinions they have of me. Two men I've never met. Two men who judge me on speculation, on my answers to horribly suggestive questioning. How can they believe I would hurt her? How can they believe I would wish anything but happiness on the woman I've loved so long? Her decision to leave was the single most painful event of my life.

That night has haunted my dreams and made every waking moment an exercise in managing depression. I may never know her reasons. I may never understand why, on that day, she so suddenly took offense to my advances, but there can be no doubt I loved her then as I always had. As I always have. I never questioned her long nights at the bookstore, but it's true they made me sad. I longed for her every moment we were apart. Instead of sitting home alone, I went to the tavern. The mistake was mine, but I had found ways to justify it. Alcohol, I have learned on too many occasions, including tonight, has a way of breeding misperceptions, and I failed to perceive the world as it was.

But I've always known the pleasure she finds in books. That pleasure introduced us, and so I've always encouraged it. I only wish I could have written a tale to woo her back. I have tried since that night. I have nearly succeeded. Time alone will determine the extent of my achievement or the grandness of my failure. Ten long years ago, she was my muse. And now, as I have struggled to get her back, she is my muse once more. If only I can escape this cursed net and reach her.

"Did you hear me?" Ruben asks.

Perhaps I could borrow McComber's gun and shoot Ruben between the eyes. Unfortunately, I think Marcus may need it where he's gone. The minions of Hell are a powerful bunch, or so he once told me.

"My wife and I separated months ago," I say, hoping to end this line of interrogation.

"How many?" he asks.

"Three. And though it may pain you to hear, I haven't been rampaging through town bent on retribution."

"I wonder," he says.

And now Ruben and Burrows and Detective Christ, who still clings to his fancy little crucifix hanging on the far wall, glare at me with determined eyes. Suddenly I feel concern creeping into my bones. Do they see me dissembling? Do they hear the panic? I answered the question honestly, but it reminded me of something else. Yes, I had sought retribution for a time, but not against Bree. Do they know it? Does it matter? If I so much as blink, I will surely have confessed to one of their imagined atrocities. Thankfully, Ruben changes the subject.

"What was her name?" he asks.

"Whose?"

"McComber's goddess."

"I don't know. He never said."

"You mean to tell me, after all the conversations, after all the stories and babble and hobnobbing, you still don't know her name? I find that hard to believe."

"You find everything hard to believe."

But it's true. I remember that night McComber first arrived at the tavern. There was a storm, not unlike the tempest I can feel reverberating through these concrete walls. He sat beside me and spun his yarn about a goddess and her beauty. Despite all his admiration, despite their endless banter and flirtation, not once did he mention her name. In all the days since, in all the conversations, I recall no description of anything but her bosom. No face. No hair. Certainly no name.

"How is it then," asks Ruben, "given your obvious ignorance, that he accused you of her murder?"

"As I told him, I haven't a clue. I didn't even think she was real."

"Oh, she's real, Mr. Lyons. This lover of Marcus McComber's, this goddess you know so much about and yet so little. She's real. And she's quite dead."

CHAPTER ELEVEN

9:00PM

The world beyond the street lamp had vanished. There were no sounds but rain and thunder. Except for Jacob Lyons and Marcus McComber, two distinct silhouettes beneath a bright cone of radiance, the city had fallen into a void, emerging only in brief glimpses whenever the sky erupted with light. That empty intersection became a world unto itself, with accusations of murder reverberating between the raindrops, and even the stormy night feared to encroach too far. McComber's silhouette stood tall and straight, tense, and it held a revolver in its outstretched hand. Jacob's silhouette should have been shaky, nervous, cowering and leaning backward given the gun pointed at its head, but silhouettes can't be expected to behave when the mind behind the shadow is drunk and stupid.

"This is a poor remedy," Jacob said. His hands hid in his pockets and he wore his hat low to shield his face against rain that pelted him from all sides, whipped into a fury by an indecisive wind. "Killing me won't help you, Marcus. My death, at your hands, will only implicate you in your lover's murder."

"Nonsense." Rain danced on McComber's exposed forehead, but he no longer noticed. "If I were to kill you here, now, with this gun, jurors would excuse it as a murder of passion. I would walk free and she would be avenged."

"Really? You think that's true? Shoot me then, if you mean to murder me. I am drunk, weak, alone, stumbling through town searching for a place to piss. Am I not a wretched figure? End my misery, oh savior of lost souls, if you'd be so kind."

McComber barked with laughter. "Do not tempt me, dear Fortunato, for haste is one of my grandest faults."

Jacob weighed his options. He didn't think McComber would kill him, but he would not wager on the possibility. He shifted his feet to the side, and McComber mimicked the movement. Soon they began to dance, circling each other. Lightning erupted, Jacob stumbled, and the odd dance ended as quickly as it had begun. McComber smiled. Jacob feared his options were few. How could he run? How could he fight? If given the opportunity for either, would he take it? Could he risk it? Or should he simply follow McComber and let the madman prove whatever point he was trying to prove?

"What happens next?" he asked. "I'm too drunk to fight you. If I run, I'll fall. You, obviously, have a gun, which further complicates my predicament. If you're not going to shoot me, and you're not going to let me go, what happens next? A return to the Tavern? I'll buy you a drink. After I relieve my bladder, of course."

"I think you'll be impressed with what comes next, Jacob. You, after all, helped me cement the idea."

"What idea was that?"

"An ending to fit the story. An end to end the end of a beginning."

"Riddles again, Marcus. You know how much I love them."

"It is an ending you helped devise, my friend. An ending she would admire. An ending of which she'd be proud."

"Who?"

Before he could answer, McComber arched his back and coughed. He vomited a grotesque medley of inhuman, throaty utterances. He almost seemed to gargle phlegm, to choke on the imploded membrane of a lung. Coughs echoed through the night. He grimaced, bent over, struggled for air between painful spasms, and fell to his knees.

Jacob glanced down the empty streets, still contemplating which way to flee should the opportunity arise. Was McComber really sick? Could that be blood on the man's chin, spraying onto the stone with each convulsion? The man gasped and coughed. The gun lay trapped between his palm and the cobblestones.

Jacob felt drowsy and drunk. His head ached and his bladder cramped, but was this his only chance? Was McComber seriously insane? How sick and maddened had the lunatic become? Was escape an option worthy of his risking his life?

McComber shook once more before the coughing subsided. He rocked on his hands and knees, struggling to compose himself. He lifted his hand to wipe spit from his mouth with the sleeve of his coat. The shiny sparkle of the exposed gun teased Jacob in the rain and dared him to act. The window of opportunity dwindled with each passing moment. Jacob tensed. Was he crazy? Could it work? Was it worthwhile? Was he acting rationally, or was liquor making him stupid? It wouldn't be the first time, but Time would not give him pause for answers. He waited for McComber's eyes to close.

When they did, he lunged, kicking at the weapon. It slid only a few feet. He tripped over McComber's leg. The world spun around him. He felt a jarring thud as he crashed to the concrete. Dazed, he jumped to his feet and tried to dart blindly in whichever direction his body would move. A hand grabbed his ankle. He kicked at it, but he slipped again and felt his shoulder blades crash into the sidewalk. When he inhaled and opened his eyes, Marcus stood above him, the revolver in his hand pointed at Jacob's head.

"A foolish gesture," McComber croaked. "Foolish and hopeless. But I applaud your effort. The Jacob I once knew would never have been so daring. He was a dimwitted, drunken coward. I commend the transformation, but I miss my old friend. Now get up."

Jacob inched away, scraping his coat against the rough stone beneath him. A wretched figure, indeed, he thought.

"Get up," McComber yelled. "Get up, and I shall show you the path to Hell. Your descent will not be as swift as you might desire."

"I don't understand," Jacob said, clambering to his feet. "I didn't kill anyone. You must know that. And surely your descent into Hell will be far swifter than mine, if your god has even a lick of sense."

With a quickness Jacob hadn't expected, McComber struck at Jacob's gut, using the weapon's weight to heighten the blow. He doubled over, gasped, and stumbled sideways. His brain twisted him into nausea.

"Blasphemy," McComber said, "can never be justified or forgiven, especially by so great a sinner. Now let's go."

Jacob felt blood dripping down his back. His stomach wrenched and heaved. Still, he went where McComber directed. He didn't have the strength to do anything else, and the bastard had a gun.

"Where are we going?" he asked.

"To Hell, my dear Fortunato. To Hell. I have received a pipe of what passes for Amontillado."

"Amontillado?"

"I have my doubts."

"Are you quoting a story?"

McComber laughed and dug the revolver into Jacob's back, urging him down the street.

CHAPTER TWELVE

Two and a Half Months Ago

Living with Daniel Jefferson did little to lessen Jacob's melancholy. Though he was a dear friend, Daniel had his own demons with which to contend, plus an occupation that demanded long and often irregular hours. How very many children come into the world beneath the pallid light of a full moon, beginning their lives during the darkest hours of night. Daniel came and went unannounced, sometimes while Jacob slept, sometimes while they sat together at the breakfast table sharing their misery in mutual silence. A phone would ring, Daniel would answer, and within moments he would vanish like a cloak of fog when the morning sun rises. At such moments as these, when Jacob suddenly found himself alone in a familiar but foreign home, surrounded by the symbols and collected invaluables of another man's life, he was reminded of his own situation, his lack of possessions, his lack of success, but most of all, his lack of companionship.

He spent much of the past two weeks in mourning. It was a shallow mourning, filled with self-pity. He could not be angry with Bree, as much as he tried. Times were rough, and her frustration was understandable. Surely, he knew, she spent her days at work wondering how he managed without her, perhaps wondering if her lesson had been received and understood. Surely, he told himself, she missed him as much as he missed her, and that uncertain knowledge helped to keep him sane. Of course, his sanity was aided always by a bottomless mug of beer at Angus' tavern.

His nighttime sessions on a barstool lengthened rapidly. Though he arrived at roughly the same hour on the first few nights, after tiresome days of staring at blank paper without typing a coherent sentence, he soon found the morning light brighter on his walks home. Within a week, he bypassed the laborious but unproductive writing process entirely, choosing instead to spend all day in a drunken, mindless stupor that kept his conversations jovial and his depression at bay. He wanted more than anything to return home, to see Bree again, and to hold her, but he dared not initiate the contact, afraid of a negative reaction, fearing the finality of another rejection. Best to let the situation resolve itself in its own time. Not to mention, he would need several days to get sober after this current bout of therapeutic boozing.

Tonight, Daniel had disappeared again, presumably to the delivery room. Jacob sat at his usual stool near the bar, finishing his fourth pint of beer in two hours. Marcus McComber sat beside him, reveling in the conquest of his Goddess' bosom. Jacob listened without interest. Marcus had been absent most of the past two weeks, apparently claiming victory in a bedroom, and had not been privy to Jacob's early, drunken rants about women and marriage. He saw no reason now to reveal them.

"You wouldn't believe it," McComber said, mostly to himself but loud enough for all to hear. "In every room. On every surface. Two solid weeks of lust and orgasm. Three, four times a night. I'm almost ashamed to admit I grow tired." He sighed at his own masculinity. "We fit, Jacob. Perfectly. Our bodies, they flow, they dance. Her touch is as soft as the skin of her thigh, of the curve of her hip, the nape of her neck. Truly marvelous. And her bosom, Jacob, have I mentioned her bosom?"

"Repeatedly."

"You couldn't even dream of such perfect symmetry, of such rounded firmness. Ah, but I knew what she had the moment I saw her on that street corner. And I got her, as I said I would. You doubted me."

"I still do."

McComber laughed. "Alcohol brings out your honesty, my friend. But that is good. Why are you so abnormally abysmal this evening?"

"So many reasons, Marcus, not the least of which is your endless babbling. You've had more passion in two weeks than I've had in eight years, and it makes me sick. I don't get sex like that even in my sleep."

McComber patted him on the shoulder. "Perhaps when I'm spent, I shall loan her to you for a night."

"Isn't she already on loan?"

"You mean her husband? I'm working on that."

"What foul end have you concocted now?"

"If I tell you," McComber said, grinning, "you won't enjoy it as much later."

"True enough, I suppose."

The two men retreated to their mugs. Worriless and drunk, Jacob gave little credit to McComber's assassination plans. How real was this Goddess of his anyway? Not very, he guessed. And how dangerous could it be to murder the fictitious husband of an imagined nymph? Let McComber plot his murder, let him poison or bleed or shoot or decapitate. The death of some stranger made little difference, especially when that stranger was make-believe.

Behind the bar, Angus cursed. The ale tap sputtered, coughed, and sprayed a foamy mist on his pants and shoes. "Bloody thing," he said, wiping ale from the floor with a dirty rag.

"Has it gone empty again?" asked McComber with an intense interest.

"Thought I had enough in her to last the night," Angus said. "Of course, Jacob's been through half a barrel on his own today, which I should have expected but didn't."

Jacob raised his mug in a mock salute.

"You need help?" McComber asked.

"I can't carry a barrel up the stairs myself."

"Indeed." Marcus scanned the tavern's peopled tables. "But you've got your hands full up here. Why don't you let Jacob and I get one for you?"

Angus puckered his lips, arched his back, sighed, and rubbed his round belly as he contemplated. "Very well," he said after a moment. "You know where to go."

Marcus sprung to his feet, pulling Jacob with him. Uncertain of their destination or their duty, Jacob followed, stumbling out the tavern's side entrance and shivering in the damp alley as McComber threw open the cellar doors. The descent appeared dark and dangerous. Steep and narrow staircases are hazardous to one with a drunken step. Nevertheless, Jacob chased Marcus into oblivion, falling as much as walking, until both men were lost in the blackness of the underground chamber. The only light Jacob saw was the rectangle of moonshine behind him on the stairs.

"Marcus?" he said, wishing, at least for the moment, he was sober. But then, sobriety could only have heightened his claustrophobic impulses, not to mention the paranoia. "Marcus?" he said again. Somewhere ahead, he heard footsteps glide across the dusty, sandy cement floor. "Marcus, where are you?" He began to retreat toward the stairs, but even as he lifted his foot, a kerosene lantern ignited in the emptiness, and his new surroundings emerged out of shadow. McComber stood beneath the lamp grinning. "Boo," he said, but Jacob failed to see the humor.

"Why did you drag me down here?" he asked.

"Angus needs a new barrel for the tap." McComber pointed toward the racks.

Jacob slid across the cluttered room. "Are they heavy? They look heavy. I'm a slight bit inebriated, if you care to know, and I may very well be a liability to the plan." No reply came. Jacob twirled, far too quickly to avoid dizziness, and saw McComber maneuvering through the cobwebbed chamber. "What are you doing?"

"Exploring."

Covered in dust, untouched for ages, a stack of bound encyclopedias rested on the floor beside three similarly undisturbed cardboard boxes. Behind the obstructions stood a wooden door that seemed, with its solid construction and rusted hinges, almost unmovable. McComber kicked the encyclopedias out of his way, careless of any potential worth such old volumes may possess, and pushed the boxes aside.

"Where does it lead?" Jacob asked.

"Care to discover?"

"Not particularly."

"Our dimwitted bartender claims it will lead us to tunnels and catacombs beneath the city."

"That's nice."

"Come now, my drunken fellow, where's your sense of adventure?"

"Not behind that door." He returned to the girders housing the barrels.

A loud creaking suddenly filled the stale room, followed by a rush of air as McComber pushed open the door. The wooden slats of the cellar entrance at the top of the staircase slammed closed. "Let's get the barrel," Jacob pleaded.

"Don't be a coward. Exploration is a necessity. It is our best source of information, and we must know the world to understand it. Think of what may lie beyond this door. The history, the knowledge. You're a writer. Think of what may be observed in a world so undisturbed. Think of the marvels we may discover. The secrets..."

"Are you going to help me with this barrel?"

McComber grabbed the hanging lantern. "Very well," he said. "If you don't wish to explore, you can stay here. Suit yourself. You're not afraid of the dark, are you?" And Marcus disappeared, carrying the chamber's only light, into the tunnel beyond the doorway.

As the lantern's glow faded, as the tunnel passage twisted and turned and led McComber into its secret depths, Jacob felt like a tiny fish lost in a grand ocean, carried out with the tide and drifting in a current he could neither escape nor control. It was a humorous comparison, he knew, himself and a fish, but the parallels justified it. Tossed from his home, drowning in a sea of misery, not to mention a barrel of ale. He no longer navigated a charted path, no longer sailed a calm sea. He swam the rough and churning waters of the unknown, with no sign of a welcoming port, no indication of a familiar landmark. So why not follow McComber into the maze of history? Why not be that fish and dive down out of the current, into unfamiliar waters but away from a path of another's choosing? Why be led? Why not choose? It was his first coherent thought, his first concrete idea in two weeks.

In the darkness, crashing into boxes and tripping over the dusty encyclopedias, he plunged into the tunnels, tracing the cold walls with his fingertips, stumbling blindly through the unknown, in search of McComber and the lantern, in search of the light.

§

Marcus McComber knew Jacob would follow. The man was drunk and curious. At times, Jacob was slow witted and unobservant, but always curious. Writers often are, even the worst ones.

The footsteps approached with an echo like a hundred soldiers marching slightly out of sync. Then came the breathing, the shortened pants of a man racing toward the unknown. Marcus decided that if silence had been a necessity Jacob would have been a casualty. But here, beneath the surface of a noisy, clamorous city, the need for quiet to hide one's activities was minimal. Here, silence was abundant and oppressive. He welcomed the disturbance.

"There you are," Jacob whined, breathing heavily. "How far must we go?"

"Not far."

"Good, because I don't think we should be here."

"Stop your worrying."

In truth, Marcus had no idea how far they would go, no clue as to what might be discovered. The stone walls, once rough and jagged from digging, were smooth to the touch and damp. Years of water draining from the surface had eroded the sharper edges and formed a glassy layer over the stone. The air, too, was damp, heavy, unlike the dry, undisturbed cellar. Behind him, Jacob coughed, his heavy breathing worsened by dampness. At that moment, McComber was reminded of a story, and of a woman.

They progressed further. Jacob, wheezy and weary, begged that they should return, that Angus expected a barrel, and if they were not to provide one, the rotund bartender might come looking for them, discover their whereabouts, and angrily evict them from the tavern. Jacob seemed terrified by the possibility.

The tunnel was easy to navigate. There were no divergent paths, no unexpected turns. It seemed they drilled downward at a steady pace, in a directionless manner, twisting and turning at random, propelled forward to whatever awaited them at the end. McComber's only fear was that the end might be just that: an end, a blank wall, an unnavigable obstacle.

"How much further?" Jacob asked.

"Tell me," McComber said, "do you ever read Edgar Allan Poe?"

"Of course."

He wasn't certain, but he thought a hint of sadness touched the other man's voice. "*The Cask of Amontillado*?"

"What if we run short of air?" Jacob asked.

"That end I've concocted, the one you asked about, I will tell it to you if you're still curious."

"Now is hardly the time, Marcus. We should get back."

"I could arrange to meet her husband. Offer him a drink. A bottle of sherry, perhaps. And I could lead him into these tunnels. 'Where I keep the stash,' I'll tell him."

"And what do you intend?" Jacob asked. "To bury him alive?"

At that moment they rounded a blind curve into a vast space. The lantern's light faded in all directions to blackness. On the far wall they discovered writing and arrows. According to the signs, a tunnel to the left would take them to the catacombs, while the passage to the right would lead them toward the outskirts of the city. Marcus veered left.

"Is it so farfetched?" he asked.

"Everything you say is farfetched, my friend."

They emerged, at last, into a tremendous vault. The peak of the arched ceiling vanished into shadow. Recesses ran along each wall, dark holes that housed the decomposed remains of past lives. McComber found the place entirely disturbing, and perfectly practical. He led Jacob toward a side wall, where a tunnel began. It reached only a pace deep, the foundations of a passage left incomplete for reasons lost to history.

"Let's go back," Jacob said.

"Can't you be patient? Can't you look around and marvel? We stand in another world? An underworld, exactly as one would expect an underworld to be. There is life to it. Life in the death it houses. Shadows and bones, damp and glorious. Is it not perfect, Jacob? I can see Mr. Poe at his desk, staring at a candle as he wrote, imagining exactly what we see now."

"But there were no catacombs in that story, Marcus."

"Crypts, then."

"No," Jacob laughed. "Wine cellars and vaults beneath an Italian palazzo, if I remember correctly."

But McComber had no concern for memories or accuracy. He grabbed Jacob by the neck and shoved him into the crevice, pinning him, with an elbow to the throat, against the back wall of the unfinished tunnel.

"What are you doing?" Jacob asked.

"How farfetched does it seem now? Hmm? I could bring her husband here, into these tunnels." He turned his head so that Jacob would follow his gaze. A pile of bricks intended for tunnel construction lay several feet away. "The necessary tools are already here. I could lead him into this crevice, wall him up, bury him alive, hide him where no one will ever look. He'll rot in solitude, Jacob, eaten by the cockroaches. Just like the story. Call it a wine cellar if you wish, but the end will be the same. And a fitting end it will be."

Jacob struggled against the elbow at his throat. "Marcus!"

"How would it feel, Jacob? How would you feel, if it were you? Frightened? Terrified?"

"Marcus, let me go."

McComber saw fear in the man's eyes, heard the panic in his words. He let the idea of murder filter through his limbs until his entire body pulsed with pleasure. It had been so long since he felt that pleasure.

Perhaps he missed it more than he knew.

After a moment, he released Jacob, who bent over grasping at his throat. McComber spun in a delighted circle, examining every direction of the vaulted chamber. "Be happy you're not my Fortunato," he said. "Now, let's get that barrel."

§

Across town, and after a moment of hesitation, Daniel Jefferson knocked on the front door of Jacob's home. He could see no lights through the windows, no signs of habitation. Come to think of it, could he still call it Jacob's home?

The hour was late, but Breeana Lyons had never been one to retire early. When he first met her, ten years earlier, her vivacity astonished him. She had been gifted with limitless energy. As too often happens, though, stress and years had depleted much of it, or veiled it behind bitterness and depression, but he knew it hadn't vanished entirely. Every time he looked at her, every time he admired the mind behind the beauty, every time he wondered why he hadn't been the lucky one to meet her under some tall damn tree in college, he knew the old energy lurked inside that depressed soul, inside that beautiful body...

He knocked again. A cold wind swirled past the overhang of the door and a funnel of dead maple leaves sprung up around him. The whirlwinds of life, he thought, come to destroy us all. He laughed, knowing he, too, spent much of his time mired in depression, cast about by the same careless winds. He and Alecia and Jacob and Bree had all shared happy moments in this house, on this very porch. Alecia had always kissed him quickly before every visit, a stolen second in the moments before the door opened. Those days had given way to chaos and turmoil, and the wind's ferocity continued to grow. How long, he wondered, before the calm returned? Would it ever?

A light popped on inside the house. Footsteps approached the doorway. When the door swung open, Breeana faced him. Her robe dangled off her shoulders. A white cotton nightshirt clung to her skin all the way to her bare thighs. They stared at each other, stunned. With the porch light shining on her, Daniel could see the erect discoloration of her nipples through the cloth, and if he let his eyes roam downward…

"Daniel!" she said. "What are you doing here? What's wrong? I was expecting…"

"Nothing's wrong," he muttered, pulling his eyes up to meet hers. "Well, not nothing, exactly. It's… It's about Jacob." Yes, Jacob. His friend. Remember him? This woman's husband. This beautiful, scantily-clad, gorgeous siren of the night, this— Maybe coming here was a bad idea…

"Come in," Bree said, cinching her robe.

"You're expecting visitors?" he asked, stepping past her.

"No one important. A friend from my book club. How can I help you, Daniel?"

"We need to talk about Jacob."

She grimaced. "No we do not."

Daniel followed her to the kitchen. "He's in bad shape, Bree."

"How do you think I am? Do you think it was easy?"

"I don't know."

"That's right. You don't know." Anger flared, but she quickly softened. "I'm sorry, Daniel. I don't mean to be rude, but these aren't the happy times we remember."

"If you'll hear me out?"

She consented with silence.

"I know," he said, "first hand, how you both feel right now. I've been through it, remember? And what I have to say is not meant to imply fault. It's not meant to pry. I'm not asking you to take Jacob back. What you do is none of my business. But as a friend, I need to tell you what I've seen, and I'll trust you to take the observations to heart. The truth is that he's falling apart without you."

"Is that so?"

"He spends all day at the tavern. All day. Every day."

"That's nothing new," she said bitterly.

"He sits on a barstool, drunk, drinking, all hours of the day and night. He doesn't write. He's too drunk. I came home yesterday at lunch, and he was passed out on the floor of the kitchen. He needs help, but he won't let me help him. I'm afraid the only person who can is you."

She went to the cabinets and found a glass she filled with water. She set it down without taking a sip. "I can't help him, Daniel."

"But you can. He'll listen to you."

"If I say what? That he can come home? That I want everything back the way it was? I can't say that. I can't. Because I don't want him here." She sat down at the kitchen table, moving slowly. "The past few years have been miserable. We weren't happy. He wasn't happy. I certainly wasn't. We entertained the foolish notion that children might help, might bring us closer, the way we once were, but we failed even at that."

"It wasn't always so bad, Bree."

"Yes it was."

"He loves you."

"I know. But that doesn't fix anything. You love Alecia, but can that make everything better?"

"That's different. She left me for another man. That's not the case here, correct?"

She fixed him with a scowl. "No. It is not." But she took longer to answer than she should have.

"Are you sure?"

"Absolutely."

He felt his bones shiver for a heartbeat. That denial. That certitude. He had seen it all before. What had he asked Alecia? "Is there someone else?" Those were the words. She responded with the same demeanor and denial. He had believed her, but she had proven him foolish. Was he still a fool?

"He needs your help, Bree."

"I can't help him. Not now. I'm sorry." If she had been a smoker, he knew, this would be the perfect time for a cigarette. She leaned back in her chair. Her robe fell open. Her legs were crossed, head down.

She hadn't sounded remorseless, but she offered, at best, a sincere indifference. Did she care at all for Jacob? Had she already moved on? Who was she waiting for when he knocked on the door? Why had her nipples, so clear beneath that sexy white undershirt, been as long as a wooden boy's nose? As a doctor, he strived for objectivity. He sought to analytically approach any situation. But the clues here were dangerous, and he saw too many behavioral parallels between Bree and Alecia. He didn't want to be a fool again.

"You can't help him?" he said, "or you won't? Which is it?"

She jumped to her feet. "Don't start with me, Daniel. You don't understand. You don't know what I've been through. Do you think this is painless? This isn't what anyone wanted, but I had to do what I had to do, and I'm sorry if you don't get it." She stormed out of the kitchen, stopping at the front door. "If you don't mind, I must get to bed."

"I thought you were expecting a visitor."

She pulled open the door and waited.

He paused before leaving, close enough to smell her. The scent was lovely. "Please understand," he said. "I didn't come here to make you mad. You and Jacob are my closest friends, and he was there for me when life got ugly. I want what's best for each of you. And if you think this is what's best, who am I to argue? But I thought you needed to know. I had to tell you. It's killing him. Literally."

"Thank you, Daniel." He heard pain in her words. Conflict. "I appreciate your concern. And thank you for giving Jacob a place to stay. If the time comes when I feel things might be worked out, I'll be sure to let you know."

To his surprise, she embraced him. He felt a sudden guilty pleasure as her breasts pushed against his coat. How long had it been since he'd felt a woman's flesh? How nice must her skin feel? Would she mind if he removed his coat and shirt and hugged her again?

It was moments later, while walking the empty streets, when he considered how strong the embrace had been, how emotional. She was battling her own demons, he knew, but of what sort were they? Demons, after all, come in many forms. Some are more deceitful than others.

CHAPTER THIRTEEN

Two Months Ago

Breeana Lyons felt sick for the first time at home, alone, reading on her sofa beneath the soft light of a table lamp. Curled up beneath a blanket to keep warm, she sipped tea and listened to the pattering of rain on the windows and roof. A new storm had blown in before the previous one departed, and the wooden beams of the house's aging skeleton creaked as each gale crashed against the siding. A pain in her stomach interrupted the novel, if indeed a novel can be interrupted. She cringed, sensing the slightest bit of nausea. She set the book aside and closed her eyes, knowing the sickness would pass. And it did, for a while.

Later that night, alone in bed, drifting in and out of restless, haunted sleep, she felt it again. She had been dreaming of Marcus, wishing he was beside her. With Marcus near, touching her, inside her, she felt alive. His absence was a type of withdrawal, an itch she couldn't scratch, a smell she couldn't taste. His absence was insufferable. But at the same time, in a frustrating way, it reminded her of what had come before. And her thoughts turned toward Jacob.

Could Daniel be right? And if he was, so what? So what if Jacob destroyed himself? So what if Daniel wanted them back together. How badly could he have wanted it? She had watched Daniel that night he came to see her, almost two weeks ago, and during each successive visit, when his eyes had examined her in a way no doctor ought to examine a patient. Always he came on Jacob's behalf, but she knew what he was thinking. What all men think. Surprisingly, the idea excited her. Marcus McComber had ignited a passion in her veins that revealed the world in a rich new splendor, and that splendor, in so many forms, sent waves of pleasure deep into her soul. Everything came alive to tease and taunt her lustful cravings. A dandelion, a kitten, the shapely plastic handle of an umbrella, the innocuous glances from the janitor at work. The entire world had become one sensuous lover that tickled and licked and nibbled at the most inopportune times or the most absurd places. Marcus had given her that, and she had thanked him many times and in many ways, and she would again. But right now she felt ill.

Daniel had returned again and again, always to discuss Jacob. She had no intentions of seducing Daniel Jefferson. He was a dear friend, and she couldn't hurt him. And yet, new to this world of passion, she toyed with him, with his desires, because she was tired of hearing about Jacob. She touched and she massaged. She sighed in his ear. It was all a game she felt terrible about playing, but something more than logic seemed to be at work, some greater impulse than reason. After all, she told herself, what did Jacob matter? His actions were his own. She would accept a fair deal of blame for hurting him, but he had hurt her worse and over a longer period of time. Just once in life she would ignore her thoughts and let something else dictate her actions.

A moment later, she knelt on the icy ceramic tiles of the bathroom floor, perched above the swirling stench of diluted vomit, flushing away the odor but not the lingering taste of illness. She felt drunk. Sick. Perhaps someone, somehow, somewhere, had kicked her in the gut. Perhaps the chicken at dinner had been undercooked or poorly prepared. Perhaps it hadn't been chicken at all.

Still queasy, but able to crawl into bed, she spent most of the night tugging her knees into her chest, suffering the throes of restless, anguished sleep. She perspired. She ached. Determined to avoid another top down view of the toilet bowl, she resisted the urge to eat. Water stayed down if she sipped it. The night was long and agonizing, and she swore, if only the queasiness would subside, never to eat chicken again.

Next morning, though exhausted, she felt well enough to eat breakfast. Toast and butter. Grape juice. Her stomach spent an hour churning and tossing the crumbs and oil and acid, then rejected it all in one massive convulsion that, because she was unable to reach the bathroom, splattered into a messy puddle on the hallway tiles.

That was enough to get her back in bed, where she stayed all day, except for frequent sessions on the bathroom floor. She called in sick to work. She slept. She began to consider a vegetarian diet, but the mere pondering of food reinforced her nausea.

Finally, late at night, the sickness subsided. Her stomach handled butterless toast and ginger ale well enough. At noon the next day, in her office at work, the sensation returned, and an alarm of panic wailed inside her head. On the way home she visited a drug store, made the necessary purchase, and went straight home to learn her fate.

Fifteen minutes later, she sat alone in a candle-lit bathroom, knees to her chest, curled up on the cold floor, crying tears of panic, disbelief, and, despite her fear, a modicum of joy. It was not nausea that kept her there.

§

Daniel Jefferson felt confused. He had tried repeatedly to understand Bree's motives, but his prodding had failed to produce informed results, and the constant attention he'd given her had fueled the fires of his lust. He had visited her twice more since that first night. Behind her distant, stilted answers, he sensed excitement in her blood. Her mannerisms were flirtatious: her fingers touching his forearm while they spoke, her hand grasping his shoulder as he came through the door. And when he complained of a headache, being so worried about Jacob, she massaged his shoulders. Her hands caressed his neck, her fingernails dug into his skin. At one point, as she massaged him from behind, her hands slipped down to his chest, and he swore he felt a sigh of pleasure touch his ear.

Something was different about her. Something that made him crazy and infested his thoughts with visions of uncontrolled, uninhibited sex. Something, also, that screamed betrayal.

Jacob. His friend and confidant. His drinking companion. It was a simple rule that kept him vigilantly pursuing the truth. No man should stand idly by as his best friend's wife pursues an affair. Daniel had first-hand experience with cheating spouses. If nothing else, his pursuit had originated out of a pure desire for vengeance. Still, he could not immediately warn Jacob of the danger, because his friend's current state was erratic and unpredictable, and revealing his concerns could unleash catastrophe. Never mind that Bree's behavior had resuscitated long dormant sensations in his own mind. Yes, she was a beautiful woman, but that's where it had to end, even if she threw herself at him with greater vigor. She was his best friend's wife. She would not be Daniel's lover, and he was determined to ensure that she would not be Marcus McComber's, either.

On his last visit, when he was still a block from the house, he saw McComber on Bree's doorstep, holding her hand. The man had bowed, kissed her fingers, and departed. Bree had watched him go with a smile on her face. When Daniel knocked on her door, she said nothing of the visitor, but every instinct warned him that something wasn't right.

As a result, he had taken to following McComber. With no experience as an investigator or spy, it surprised him to learn he was rather good at it. He waited outside the bar, or on a street corner near McComber's apartment, until the stranger emerged, clad always in black, sometimes wearing a fedora, sometimes a hood. Spying gave him a purpose. So many nights had been wasted on a barstool, and for what? To watch his life pass by uneventfully? To watch his business suffer? How many women crave the smell of alcohol on their doctor's breath? How many would willingly entrust the life of their unborn child to a man who, the night before, vomited in an alley outside a tavern while contemplating a trip to the brothel next door? His lifestyle made for bad business. Part of him realized, but was not disgusted, that the failure of his business meant less money for Alecia. He had once called her a traitorous whore while vomiting on the sidewalk. The truth always seems so clear while you're inebriated.

But spying got him off the barstool, for which he was thankful. That he spied to benefit two friends further justified the entire enterprise.

For several nights, McComber and Bree never crossed paths. After a week, Daniel had been ready to give up, but tonight he decided to try again. He was half-asleep on a curbside bench a block from McComber's apartment. He had been drinking. Some things were difficult to give up entirely. A flask of what had been top notch bourbon lie empty in his lap, and in the twilight of his mock slumber he occasionally lifted it to his mouth, gulped down air, and whispered a curse when he realized what he'd done. In some ways, he enjoyed this half-delirious state, letting it ease his pain, almost forgetting why he sat on the bench at all. Then McComber stepped out of the apartment building and headed down the street.

Daniel stared after him, blinking away the delirium, deciding what to do. The bourbon flask fell from his lap and clanked on the ground as he leapt up and rushed to follow.

McComber slithered through the winding streets, silent as a shadow, his outline an emptiness drilled through the drab foundations of city buildings, darting in and out of light, in and out of visibility, like a moonlit reflection on the wavy surface of a pond, leaping magically from one watery facet to another. McComber strode confidently, uncaring, almost content, a magician delighting in the perceived mystery of his illusion.

A dog yelped in the distance. An alley cat squealed nearby. Somewhere above, in the black void of the nighttime sky, the early rumbles of thunder hinted at what must surely be an approaching doom. When a door slammed somewhere nearby, when Daniel's feet froze to the concrete underfoot, startled into paralysis by the unexpected noise, he realized the absurdity of his behavior. Here he was, a grown man, fearing the night. He figured it must be the spying. Adrenaline could do weird things. But part of him, a part he might not even admit to himself, wondered if Marcus McComber was responsible. He knew it was another silly thought, but he continued to think it nevertheless.

He followed McComber for a dozen city blocks. He followed him past the bookstore where Bree held her meetings. Jacob always talked about it, about how someday her little book club would be discussing a book he had written. Fate hadn't been kind to his friend.

Soon, as McComber's pace quickened, Daniel grew fearful. Though McComber took odd turns and indirect paths, his destination became quite clear. He was heading toward Jacob's home. Bree's home.

Five minutes later Daniel stood hidden behind a neighbor's hedge, watching McComber knock on that familiar front door. The moon had vanished behind a curtain of clouds. Wind gusted through the yards. Maple leaves fell from their branches, twisting and tumbling through the air, landing at McComber's feet. Daniel's breath came slowly, painfully. This was the very moment he had feared.

The door opened. Framed in the doorway, backlit by a faint glow from inside, front lit by the soft orange touch of the porch light, Bree stood smiling at Marcus McComber. Her features were welcoming, inviting, enticing. Briefly, as she appeared to survey the neighborhood, her eyes paused in Daniel's direction, and he ducked behind the thicket, fearing she had spotted him. She couldn't have seen him at that distance, at that hour, but maybe she sensed him there, spying. When he lifted his head above the thicket, he saw McComber disappear inside, and the door closed.

Daniel drifted then through the night. He and his thoughts. The hour was late. He had to work in the morning and knew he would be tired. But better tired than drunk, he admitted. If only he could convince Jacob of the same.

Ah, Jacob. His friend. His poor, wretched friend. Betrayed by his wife. Betrayed by the stranger who so often sat beside him on a barstool. Jacob had no idea what was happening, no idea of the events transpiring in the darkness of night.

But did Jacob care anymore? Was there enough of the old Jacob still alive behind that constant drunkenness to worry about his wife? There must be, but he could think of no way to coax it out of hiding. The man had been locked in his room recently. Whenever Daniel arrived home, Jacob's door was closed. It often meant Jacob had gone to the tavern, but lately he heard noises behind the door. Perhaps Jacob's sleep had grown restless. Perhaps even alcohol failed to rid his dreams of heartache. What further anguish might this news unleash?

He told himself he didn't know for sure that Bree and Marcus were having an affair. It was entirely possible that Marcus had invented many of the stories he so boisterously related at the tavern. But if that were true, what might be transpiring beyond her front door?

§

"I'm pregnant, Marcus," she said. It was difficult to predict his reaction. How would most men respond? Not well, she guessed.

"Pregnant?"

She nodded.

They sat on her sofa. Shadows danced around them like marionettes, with a dozen spiral candles playing puppeteers. When Marcus had first arrived and noticed the lights dim, the candles burning, he must have expected romance. Could he have expected this?

To his credit, he had yet to bolt for the door. His muscles tensed visibly, and he fidgeted, which was something she'd never seen him do. He leaned back, crossed his legs, sighed, uncrossed his legs, leaned forward, and stared past her toward a candle burning on a shelf.

"I'm sorry," she said. It seemed like the right thing to say, but did she mean it? For so many years, she had wanted a child but failed to conceive. Now she bore the fruit of a passion that had swept in and altered her entire perception of the world. Yes, this was unexpected. Yes, it would thrust their relationship into unexplored territory. But she still felt happy with her decisions, and this would not affect her desires.

If only Marcus would face the challenge with equal vigor.

"Will you say something?" she asked.

"Are you certain it's mine?"

"It can be no one else's."

Her body tensed as she watched his reaction. She feared the fury that might lurk behind his eyes. She had never sensed a hint of anger in him, but she hadn't known him very long. He was mysterious, which intrigued her, but mystery is inherently secretive, and his calculating manner, while playful at times, could hide so many emotions.

He stood and paced around the room. The curtains shifted with his movement. The candle flames danced and their puppet shadows kicked and jumped with excited anxiety. She couldn't guess his thoughts. She wasn't even sure of her own. Yes, this is partly what she desired, but these circumstances were not at all what she imagined. She had dreamt of pregnancy as a joyful experience. Since childhood, she had imagined telling her family and her friends and having everyone smile and be happy. What would she tell them now?

"Very well," he said. He tossed her one of those wicked grins and knelt beside her.

"I thought you might be angry," she said.

"Of course not. This is fantastic."

She exhaled, realizing how tense she had been. "You didn't seem to think so a minute ago."

"I was surprised."

"So was I."

"But don't you see?" he said. "This is spectacular. This is our real beginning. Our relationship has been consummated by His approval."

"Whose approval?"

McComber pointed to the ceiling then leapt to his feet. "We must go away," he said.

"What?"

"We must leave. This place, you're not happy here. Too many memories. We need to start over, you and me."

"I don't know about that," she said.

"You and I, we're not meant to be caged in this dark, wet, wretched city. We shall see the world, and so shall our child."

The words hit her with more force than if the maple trees in the yard had crashed through the roof. Our child. Out of Marcus' lips. An image of Jacob passed through her thoughts, but she wiped it away. This child was not Jacob's. But what if it had been?

"And where exactly would we go?" she asked.

"Anywhere."

She stared at him. What was he talking about? Why did she suddenly feel so confused? Who was Marcus McComber? It seemed such a silly question to ask. Especially now. After all, she'd spent a month naked in his bed, and as impossible as it seemed she was pregnant with his child. Shouldn't she know him by now? At least a little?

"I don't know," she said.

"Don't you crave adventure? Intrigue?"

"I have them. I have you."

"I am nothing," he said.

She knew him well enough to know he wasn't humble. Not Marcus McComber. So he was trying to be persuasive. It was endearing, actually, if a bit frightening. "Marcus, you need to give me time. What if there's a problem? What if it's a mistake? Slow down a bit, just this once."

"So be it," he said, twirling as he once had while wearing the motley cape of a fool.

"Give me a little time. I'll think about it. Leaving… It's not something I had considered. My life has always been here."

"And you hated it."

"Not every aspect."

"My dear, you can start a book club wherever we go."

"Let me think about it."

He stared, then nodded. "Very well."

He kissed her forehead and they sat quietly together, holding hands, for almost an hour. He claimed he must return home to accomplish any one of many nameless tasks, and he departed.

Bree was left anxious, uncertain, and alone – almost alone – with a hand pressed against her belly.

CHAPTER FOURTEEN

Two Months Ago

"The whore!" McComber slammed his fist against the table.

Seated not far away, three ladies from the brothel glared like sirens preparing to sing for their prey, ready to wreak havoc and destruction upon the man who had uttered profanity in their presence, even if that man was the black clad stranger they all adored. Jacob laughed. And why not? Marcus was due for a bit of strife, as far as he was concerned.

"What was she thinking?" McComber said, ignoring the glares.

Jacob lifted his ale mug in a mock toast. "To your bastard children!"

"That's even less funny now than it was a few minutes ago when you said it."

"Nevertheless." He took a long, slow gulp, tasting McComber's anger like it was a drug. It was only fair, after all, that such trouble would befall the instigator. Only fair that good luck be repaid with bad.

"It matters not," said McComber. "She won't ruin this for me. I've searched too long, too hard, to fail now."

"Searched for what?"

"You ought to listen better, Jacob."

"You shouldn't speak in riddles."

"Riddles are obvious to anyone clever enough to decipher them. Or anyone who isn't drunk."

"My word," laughed Jacob. "You are, without doubt, the most amusing fellow in the bar tonight. And I'm not drunk. I simply don't care."

McComber raised his brow. "You seem oddly jovial. And coherent. How is that?"

"I have a new purpose."

"And it doesn't involve being a stooped, slobbering drunkard, I guess?"

"Hardly. " He wouldn't tell Marcus their foray into the catacombs had been the cause of his transformation, that the fear had shaken him out of insobriety. That night taught him a thing or two about drunkenness, and a thing or two about second chances, and a thing or two about life. Let the world take you where it will, and you may end up dead at the hands of the drunkard beside you. Jacob didn't want to be guided any longer. He wanted to be that fish, swimming down out of the current, charting his own path through the ocean. "I realized sitting here all day would not solve my problems. They must be solved with action."

"And did you then discover your mistake? That action only causes more problems?"

"No."

"Why then are you back on the barstool?"

"Reward for a long day's work. I started writing again."

"Really?"

"Indeed. And my muse has returned. Or, well, actually, she is farther away than ever before, but she is once again my muse."

"It seems you've adopted my gift for riddles. Though, out of your mouth, they sound like simple nonsense."

Jacob would not allow his mood to be sullied. It had taken four days of sleep and vomit to recuperate from his binge. Lying in bed, miserable, dejected, knowing he couldn't survive without Bree, that he had no desire to do so, he had resolved to get her back. At first, he planned to meet her, to speak with her, but as he sobered up, he recognized his own insecurity and scrapped the plan. In person, with words, there was no guarantee he could say the right thing or convey the proper emotion.

His mouth, when it opened to speak, was as dangerous as a gun pointed at his own head, capable of inflicting much more damage.

So the idea soon came to him that, if he could not succeed with speech, he would succeed with writing. He overcame the vomiting, the misery, and he cast aside depression. His new goal was focus. He had begun a novel. It would deal with love lost, with fancy forgotten. It would delve into the innermost workings of a dejected soul, revealing the foundations of life, the confusion of marriage, the resentment of aging and passing of time. It would be a memoir. His memoir. It would be a way to describe to Bree how thoroughly he loved her and how desperately he wanted her back. She was his muse again, and she would inspire the ending. How would the lovelorn protagonist win back his lover? He knew, through the process of writing, the resolution would come to him. All he had to do was write it. His productivity over the past week had amazed him, and tonight was indeed a celebration of his output. That McComber was here and experiencing difficulties added a delightful bit of sweetness to the merriment.

Marcus continued whining, unaware Jacob had been distracted. "She will not ruin this for me. That I swear."

"And what will you do about it?"

"As I've told you before, there are remedies to any situation."

Jacob felt a pang of concern, but the sensation was short-lived. He didn't believe Marcus' clever plots, so why should he care about their resolutions? In some ways, his newfound sobriety had turned the formidable Marcus McComber into something of an inconsequential joke. The man inspired Jacob's creativity, and a bit of his pity, but beyond the barstool the man added no redeeming value to Jacob's life. That realization had made dealing with the man an entirely new bit of sport.

With a comic nod, meant to demonstrate drunkenness that wasn't present, if only to confuse and antagonize the antagonist, Jacob stood to leave. With his celebratory drink consumed, he would return to work. "My friend," he said, "it's been a pleasure. As always."

"You're leaving?"

"Indeed. As much as I would love to continue our little celebration of the announcement of your bastard offspring, I must depart. I have a goal, and a muse, and a heart to win."

"You'll be back."

"Not tonight, I promise. You have a fine evening, Marcus. Enjoy the time with your pregnant mistress."

Before he turned to go, Jacob caught the beginnings of a scowl slip across McComber's face, and it prompted a grin on his own.

§

When Jacob arrived home, as was often the case, Daniel was gone. Perhaps his friend was at the hospital, or perhaps the tavern, or perhaps the market for a late night snack. On most nights, or on most mornings, or whatever time Jacob happened to return from the tavern, he returned to an empty house.

Tonight, he worked through his novel, lost to the mechanical click of his typewriter keys, to the hum of his desk lamp, to the whistling of wind beyond the apartment walls. At the desk, with his manuscript growing thicker by the hour, he was alone in a world of imagination, a world of hope, where anything was possible, where the torn pages of existence could be mended, where the plot of his life could be reworked and reshaped. It was not necessarily a happy place, nor a fun place, but he knew it was where he must be.

At an unknown hour, he fell asleep. Not intentionally. The first inkling he had of the accident came when he felt the keys of his typewriter drilling into his cheekbone. When he opened his eyes, Daniel Jefferson stared at him from the bedroom doorway.

"Daniel," he whispered, half-expecting the stoic form to dissipate into the air like the ghost he seemed. But the ghost didn't vanish. "What is it Daniel?"

"We need to talk."

Jacob lifted his head, blinked the sleep from his eyes. He felt strangely cold. The wall clock's ticking pendulum caught his attention. Night had morphed into early morning. The sun would rise soon, but the shade on his window was heavy and would keep the room safely buried in shadow.

"What's wrong?" he asked.

His friend let out an exhausted laugh. "Everything is wrong, Jacob. I suppose that's the point, the way our world exists. That's our purpose, isn't it? To spend life in a hopeless effort to right the wrongs?"

"You need sleep."

"No. I don't." He checked the wall clock for himself. "I've spent a lot of time thinking during the past couple weeks. About you, about me. About Bree. You know I've been to talk to her on several occasions. You asked me to talk to her. I need to tell you a few things. Get some things off my chest. Things you need to hear before you drink yourself to death. "

"Like?"

But Daniel suddenly raised his eyes, surveyed the room, the desk, the typewriter. "What's going on here?" he asked.

"I don't understand the question."

"Are you writing?"

"I am."

Daniel reached across the desk and lifted the hefty manuscript. "You've written all this?"

Jacob nodded.

"When?"

"The past few days."

"But the tavern? Two weeks ago you were a slobbering drunk."

"You should pay more attention."

"When your door was closed I assumed you weren't home."

"I was asleep. I must have forgotten to close the door tonight."

"But how many pages is this? You wrote it all in a week?"

"Why are you so surprised? I'm am author extraordinaire, or have you forgotten?"

"By the look of it, you've written more this week than you have the past three years. Why?"

Jacob wanted to laugh at Daniel's astonishment but could not. During the long hours of work this week, he himself had paused to admire the stack of pages in his manuscript. He usually paid scant notice to quantity. All the words in the world were meaningless if not used properly. But in this case he felt the writing was strong, the story meaningful, and so he allowed himself to marvel again at his own productivity. That was one of the reasons he had gone to the tavern earlier for a drink. "I have found my muse," he said.

"Who?"

"Who else? My wife."

And Daniel's face twisted into a new expression, one of disbelief, of sadness, of worry.

"What is it?" Jacob asked. "What's wrong?"

"Nothing," came the reply, but it was unconvincing. Daniel went to the door.

"Wait," Jacob said. "I thought you had something to tell me."

"It was nothing."

"You're worried. Why?"

Daniel paused, eyeing the typewriter and manuscript. "Not yet."

"When have we have kept secrets from each other, my friend?"

"We've kept many, and you know it."

"Tell me. "

"No," Daniel said. "Now is not the time. I'm sorry. I thought maybe it was more important than it is. Keep writing, Jacob. Keep writing."

"Damn it, Daniel. What could be so important?" He felt an idea emerging, felt its creepy tentacles twisting their way into his brain, mangling and shaping his thoughts. What secret could Daniel be hiding? And did Jacob really want to know it?

"Just do me one favor," Daniel said.

"What is that?"

"Stay away from Marcus McComber."

"That's not what you were going to tell me."

Daniel disappeared down the hallway.

Jacob found him near the front door. "Tell me what you wanted to say."

Daniel grabbed his keys and a coat as a way to ignore Jacob, or because he needed both in order to leave.

"Where are you going?"

"I'm sorry," Daniel said. And the door closed softly behind him.

Jacob stared unblinking, curious, and infuriated. What had Daniel been about to say? And why was he sorry? Could it really have something to do with Bree? The foundations of his fear strengthened. The tentacles of his idea spread more profusely. Daniel was hiding something. Hadn't Daniel always been fond of her? Could she have told him something different than what he relayed to Jacob? Or worse… Might it have to do with Bree and Daniel? The idea seemed impossible, implausible. Repulsive. And so he dismissed it, for now.

He returned to his room to write. At the moment, nothing was more important.

CHAPTER FIFTEEN

One and a Half Months Ago

Not for the first time, Breeana Lyons approached the building that housed Daniel Jefferson's medical practice with an anxious hitch in her step. Two tall glass doors waited for her. Those doors were a bit foreboding, a bit sinister, and a bit angelic. She feared what might happen beyond them. She also knew that what lay beyond them was her best option. Clouds filled the sky above her and trees swayed in a cold wind, but a distant break in the cover let brilliant rays of sunlight escape confinement and brighten the world. She considered them a sign of hope. And at least the rain had stopped for a time.

As often as the moon appears and disappears on a cloudy night, she had waivered on the decision to visit this place, unsure whether to search for a new doctor or return to Daniel. Could she trust any other doctor with her body? With her child? Daniel was a friend who had been her doctor for years, and there had never been awkward moments. Here, Daniel treated her in that polite but stale manner necessary between doctors and patients. Here, he was not a family friend, but a trusted expert. Of course, he would ask about the baby's father. Should she tell him the truth? Would he tell Jacob? Did she care? After a week of deliberation, and with a fair bit of shame surfacing to torment her at night and rob her of sleep, she came to the only reasonable conclusion.

She would go to Daniel. And she would lie to him. She wouldn't feel good about it. Daniel had always been kind to her, and she already felt a bit of guilt for confusing him and leading him on and, well, lying to him about Marcus. But right now she was nervous about everything. A familiar face would be helpful, even if that familiar face had too often sided with her estranged husband, and even if the man behind that familiar face would never forgive her if he discovered the truth.

Inside the building, an unpleasant wave of nostalgia crashed over her. To every wall clung a hideous yellow wallpaper that had always made her sad. Now it felt confining. Constricting. It squeezed her and wrung her insides until they dripped with shame, but she would not let shame linger. Instead, she felt a hint of regret trickle through her veins. How many years had she arrived here with Jacob eager for news? How many times had she come here begging, pleading, hoping for a bit of luck?

"Hello, Mrs. Lyons," said a receptionist at the front desk. Bree knew the smile, but she never remembered the girl's name. "You don't have an appointment today, do you? Is something wrong?"

"I need to see Dr. Jefferson."

"He's booked full today. How about next week?"

"It needs to be today. And it needs to be him. I'm sorry. Please tell him it's me."

With a grin that said she didn't think it would matter, the girl disappeared into the back offices. Bree took a moment to admire a painting on the waiting room wall. Thick oils on canvas sent horses galloping across a prairie, their black manes reaching to the sky. A moment later, the receptionist returned. "Okay, Mrs. Lyons, come on back. He'll see you."

Bree followed the girl to a secluded room down one of the office's many yellow hallways. In college, she had read a short story about yellow wallpaper, about a woman and how that yellow wallpaper made her crazy, how in a world of undiagnosed depression, where a husband and doctor forced that woman to spend her days in a single lonely room, the intricate patterns of the wallpaper served as her only distraction. Eventually, it became impossible to know if the woman had gone crazy because of the wallpaper or if she had become enthralled by the wallpaper because she had gone crazy. Every time Bree came to this office, she remembered that story. She understood now, as she watched the paper's patterns repeat and shift and come alive, how they might transform fear and depression into anger or insanity. Thankfully, she told herself, she did not suffer from depression any longer. At least, none she could diagnose. Insanity was a different matter.

The receptionist guided her into a sterile room. The walls were painted a light gray, which pleased her. Two chairs lingered beside a desk, and in the corner a foldable bed stood sentry over the minds of waiting patients. "The doctor will be in shortly," Bree heard as the door closed.

When the door opened again, Doctor Daniel Jefferson entered holding her chart. Bree swallowed hard. Then she went to work.

Daniel's concern seemed immediately genuine, as did his confusion. "Is everything okay?"

She smiled. "Not even a good morning, Doctor?"

"Amy said it was an emergency."

She shook her head. "No emergencies. Problems perhaps. Sticky messiness maybe. But no emergencies."

"Okay." He accepted her answer and examined the clipboard in his hands. "Sorry. I'm just a bit shocked. I didn't expect you here. Forgive my manners. How are you?"

"I'm good, Daniel. Thank you."

"Why are you here?"

"Well, that's a bit of a story, and you're busy."

"I'll make time."

She gave him a smile but kept her eyes downcast. It wasn't difficult. She felt terrible. Why, when so much of what she desired had finally fallen into her lap, could she never escape the guilt? Why could she never simply enjoy it all? Lies wouldn't help, she knew, but she had no choice. And it wasn't all guilt. Part of her was perfectly happy. "I'm pregnant," she said, hoping the happiness overpowered the guilt.

He nearly dropped her chart. "Are you sure?"

"I think so. But that's why I'm here, right? To find out for sure."

His eyes watched her. They drifted to her belly. They carried that noticeable longing, but only a trace. In this office, she expected Daniel to be all business, and he was. "Well, congratulations, Bree."

"Thanks, I suppose. Given the situation, I'm sure you see the complexities."

"Of course." He grabbed his pen and started scribbling on her chart. He asked typical questions about health, menstruation, sexual patterns. She was honest about the first two. Finally, he asked, "And the father?"

"Daniel!"

"What? It's one of the questions on the form."

"How can you not know?"

"Is it Jacob? You're sure?"

"Daniel!" She tried to appear offended, and it wasn't too difficult. Why would he even suspect someone else? "Of course I'm sure."

"It's just that you and Jacob have been apart for what? Almost two months?"

"Yes, well, sex isn't exclusive to people living together."

"Are you telling me you and Jacob have been together recently?"

"About a month ago."

"He never mentioned it."

"I'm not surprised."

"Why wouldn't he mention it? How did it happen?"

"You're old enough to understand the birds and the bees, Doctor." She smiled, but it seemed he wasn't in the mood for playfulness. "I don't know, Daniel. How do any of these things happen? Life is so rotten and confusing right now. He was drunk. We both were. Too much wine for me. Too much everything for him. I thought we could talk over dinner. After you begged me to see him, I thought maybe it would be the right thing to do. He showed up smelling like beer. I should have walked out right away, but I didn't. I don't know why. The next thing I knew, we were passed out and naked in my bed. I called him a cab and shoved him out the door. Not very kindly, either. He was still drunk. If I'm honest, I should say I'm surprised he made it home, and I felt bad for not checking up on him later. It doesn't surprise me that he can't remember."

She almost laughed at his blank stare, at his open mouth. She could see him calculating, processing, wondering. "Well," he said, "we'll run the tests." He set the chart down. "And congratulations again, Bree. I know this can't be easy."

"Thank you, Daniel."

Then he added, "Jacob will be ecstatic."

She had prepared for this moment, but her stomach turned over in any case. "Please don't tell him."

His expression held half surprise and half suspicion. "Why not?"

"What if something's wrong? What if I'm not pregnant? What if… What if the baby is sick or I lose it?"

"I'm sure everything is fine."

"What if it's not? I need time, Daniel. I need to think everything through. I need to figure out how I want to tell him. We're not even speaking right now. We're living apart. This needs to be handled carefully so we both have the opportunity to make the right decisions. Please don't tell him."

"Okay, okay," he answered, a bit too reluctantly. "But this is all a bit crazy."

She almost blurted out that if he didn't like crazy he should replace that yellow wallpaper. "I know. And thank you, Daniel. It means a lot."

A short while later, standing on the street outside the office, she inhaled deeply and tried to relax enough to enjoy the moment. She could be happy, she realized. It was possible. Maybe this was the beginning. Maybe she could start over, with Marcus, and a child. Maybe they could go away and leave the old sadness behind. Maybe she could leave Jacob behind. Anything seemed possible. If a few insignificant lies were all that was needed, she could excuse herself for making them. They were surely a small price to pay for happiness.

CHAPTER SIXTEEN

One and a Half Months Ago

Jacob didn't think he trusted his old friend. It was that simple. He listened politely to everything Daniel said, but by now he was as likely to believe McComber's stories as Daniel's. As a writer, he had put himself in the minds of other men often enough, and he thought he understood how a character would behave when concealing a truth. The smiles that never touch the eyes, the unwillingness to meet a gaze, the vague comments and non-answers. Daniel had demonstrated all of them the past few weeks, and the absurdity of it had just peaked anew.

"It is good news," Daniel said, emptying his mug with a long swallow. "The very best news, I believe. And things will improve soon enough. Trust me."

No matter how many times Daniel said it, Jacob would not trust him.

They sat together, hidden in the shadows at the far end of the bar. Autumn rains fell most of the day, keeping all but the Tavern's most devout patrons home in their beds. Winter was fast approaching, and Angus the Bartender had already begun making preparations for the Tavern's busiest season. He had cleaned the floors, lacquered the bar top and tables, reinsulated the shabbier sections of the outside walls, and replaced several windows for better insulation against the cold. The place had an air of cleanliness, a reinvigorated atmosphere, and it evoked a sense of newness and potential usually associated with springtime. Unfortunately, Jacob liked none of it.

"Tell me then," he said, eyeing Daniel distastefully. "Tell me this good news."

"I can't. But my reluctance makes it no less true."

Jacob did not mask his disgust. He grunted. "Why should I believe you?"

"Because I am your friend."

"Friends can lie."

"I suppose they can. But this one is not. "

"Prove it."

"Jacob!" Daniel's spirits soared well above his stool. Secretly, Jacob hoped those spirits flattened themselves against the roof and crashed back to earth. "What has put you in so foul a mood?"

He answered with only a grunt. How could he do more? After that night Daniel had acted strangely, Jacob had inquired often about the secrets Daniel kept. The man never answered. One night, therefore, he stopped writing and began to follow Daniel, only to watch the man spend several hours sitting on a bench staring at an apartment building. Another night, he followed Daniel home from the tavern, and twice he had followed Daniel to work. He had seen Bree visit Daniel's office. Why hadn't his friend told him about it? What might be going on between them? Anything so secretive had to be more purposeful than accidental, more sinister than good. But how could he bring it up? How could he mention something discovered while spying on his friend? It all seemed so silly, and all he wanted to do was write. "Have you seen Bree recently?" he asked.

A pause. Fidgeting. And then the calm voice, "Yes."

"When?"

"Yesterday. She came to the office."

Jacob silently thanked Daniel for his honesty, but his distrust would not falter. The man had become too secretive.

Daniel added, "She's doing well, if you care to know. No illness."

"Depression?"

"A little."

That made two of them. His anger slipped aside temporarily as he pondered Bree's emotional welfare. If she suffered, even slightly, she must still be thinking of him. And so long as he entered her thoughts regularly, so long as she hadn't moved on or found someone else to console her, Jacob had a chance to win back her affection. It was not too late. At least, not if he trusted Daniel, which he didn't.

"Did she say anything?" he asked.

"Like what?"

"I don't know. Did she tell you something important? Is that the good news?"

"I'll tell you what," Daniel said. "When the time comes, when you learn the truth, if you don't feel I had every right to keep it from you, I give you permission to pummel me once or twice. My guess, however, is that you'll be too thrilled to take up my offer."

"Don't count on it."

Bree hadn't spoken to him for a month. They hadn't seen each other at all. Why would she go to Daniel? Why not to her husband? Why avoid him? He could think of only one answer, and that answer was enough to make him want to introduce the mug in his hand to Daniel's forehead.

Despite the anger, his plan to win back his wife progressed. His novel's first draft neared completion. The last words of the final chapter should be written within a couple weeks. He was at the crucial point of the story, the climax, the scene where his protagonist overcomes all obstacles and steals the heart of his beloved back from the vile antagonist. He had finally decided how the story would end. It had taken hours of late night thought, more hours of daydreamed speculation with a mug of coffee, and even more hours of personal ridicule as each new idea proved silly or contrived or lacking enough passion and excitement to capture the importance of his idea. The ending must demonstrate to Bree how willing he was to love her again, to fight for her, to prove his feelings in whatever way he could. It must be majestic, inspiring, worthy of her admiration.

And it was. At least, he hoped it was.

Embattled, enamored, his protagonist fights through a stormy night, trampling through puddles and mud and a pit of doubt to reach his love. He finds her wrapped in the arms of the villain, trapped, struggling to break free. A fight ensues. The two men wage war in the ocean of night, as rain falls, as lightning flares, as thunder booms. They battle for hours, like two ancient gods fighting for the salvation of the world. Oscillating light and dark. Good and evil. One begins to prevail, only to be overtaken by the other. The street floods. They are swept away with the rushing current, locked in eternal battle for the heart of one woman, and all the world waits to hail the victor, if indeed there is a victor.

In the end, the protagonist prevails, as he must, and he is reunited with his love.

That's where it will end. The rest, he hoped, he would write with Bree beside him, many years from now. When they are together... When they are happy…

"Why are you smiling?" Daniel asked him.

"I don't know."

"You will smile more soon. Trust me."

Jacob hoped so, but he still couldn't trust his friend, and he wouldn't stop following him.

§

Daniel slipped out of the tavern a short while later. Tonight, he was returning home. No clandestine activities planned. His fears had subsided quite a bit once Bree visited his office. Her news had caught him by surprise, and at first he doubted her story. The more he considered it, however, the more plausible it seemed. Perhaps McComber had simply been someone for her to talk to. Or perhaps they had been potential lovers whose affair would never materialize now that complications had interfered. He didn't know for sure. Maybe he just wanted to believe something good had come about.

He was twenty feet away from the tavern door when he heard muffled noises behind him. He turned back to the alley, facing the side entrance of McBraidy Tavern. A rat scurried past him through deep puddles. The stench of garbage, though dulled by frequent rains, made him wince. Not for the first time, he wondered why people continued using this stinky, wet side entrance instead of the cleaner, sturdier front entrance, especially now that Marcus McComber had destroyed the ending of Angus' favorite tale.

The noise came again, this time louder, like wood thudding against concrete. Wet, decayed wood. Wet, cold concrete. He stared into the alley, having just stepped from the warm light of the Tavern into this unusually black darkness, still waiting for his eyes to adjust.

When they did, he saw Marcus McComber rising out of the ground like a ghost. A moment later he realized McComber climbed a hidden stairwell. When the man had fully emerged from whatever underworld he had departed– Daniel guessed it was a cellar of some sort –McComber slammed shut and barred the entrance doors. Then he saw Daniel.

It was a chance Daniel had sought for quite some time. He had wanted to get McComber alone, away from Bree, away from Jacob, certainly away from the omnipresent ears of Angus Ferley, for weeks. He'd followed the man everywhere, but the situation never presented itself. Now an accidental and innocent encounter here in an empty alley would give him that chance. Rarely did such opportunistic coincidences play in his world.

"What are you doing here?" Daniel asked.

McComber quickly traversed the distance between them, stopping less than a foot away, wiping his hands and eyeing Daniel with the raised eyebrow of a man caught hiding a bit of mischief. "I might ask you the same," he said, "if I cared."

"How gentlemanly of you."

"Fine then, dear Doctor. What are you doing here?"

"Leaving the Tavern. On my way home. Undoubtedly, a much better excuse than any you might concoct. But I'll ask anyway. Yourself?"

"Fetching beer for Angus." McComber wiped his hands again. "Actually, no. I fetched the barrel earlier. Just now I was returning the empty barrel to the cellar."

"There's a cellar down there?"

"Didn't they teach you that in medical school?"

"Funny." Daniel peered around Marcus toward the cellar. He hadn't seen the man all night, and the tavern was too empty for the loud, boisterous McComber to have entered unnoticed. Strange that he would be here now, lurking in the alley, or in the cellar. What could be so interesting down there? It didn't seem to matter at the moment. He had more important questions. "Tell me," he said, "how do you know Bree?"

"Better yet, why don't you tell me how you know her?"

"She is a friend. And I don't like my friends associating with you."

"But Doctor, you hardly know me. Why so venomous?"

"I know more than you think. And it's not flattering. So tell me how you know her?"

"We met at a book club meeting, if you must know. We discussed Edgar Allan Poe, and we laughed, and we shared a drink. She is a truly magnificent woman."

"She's married."

"I don't care."

"Her husband cares."

Marcus laughed. "Her husband is worthless. She has already left him. Soon, I suspect, she will leave you as well."

"What does that mean?"

"Guess you don't know everything, Doc."

McComber pushed past him, driving a shoulder into Daniel's collarbone.

Daniel shouted after him as his chance to act quickly evaporated. "Stay away from her!"

"I do what I wish."

"Leave her alone."

"Sorry, Doc."

And Marcus disappeared into the night.

Daniel didn't move for a while. His gaze wandered between the tavern door, the cellar door, the black sky, and the emptiness into which McComber had walked. The moment had been too brief. He accomplished nothing. But then, what had been his goal? After all the spying, was there really any purpose? Frustration squeezed from all sides. When it eased, it was only to allow helplessness to replace it for a while. Life had to return to normal eventually. This crazy ride since Alecia abandoned him couldn't go on forever. Or could it? And how many more people would get swept up in the craziness?

Here he had Marcus McComber in front of him, alone, and he'd been unable to learn anything. No doubt Marcus pursued Bree. No doubt Bree enjoyed his companionship. But how close were they? Enough to threaten Bree and Jacob getting back together? He doubted that. She was, after all, pregnant with Jacob's child, and surely she would make the right choice in that regard. But Marcus McComber was a force with which to be reckoned. He couldn't be allowed to interfere, and the only way to prevent it was to warn Bree of McComber's intentions. The question then became, Would she believe him? He had no answer. At least it gave him something to do. Somewhere to direct his thoughts.

Alone in the rain, he walked home, wondering how many other bizarre turns he might encounter on this ride. He also wondered, fearfully, if he could overcome them. All rides end eventually. It's the manner of their ending that counts. Did he not hold some sway over the direction? Of course, given his lack of recent control, he wasn't as hopeful as he might otherwise be.

CHAPTER SEVENTEEN

One Month Ago

Jacob was angry. Again. He was not a man often prone to anger, but tonight he no longer felt like the person he had been a few days earlier. Tonight, he was a ghost. An angry ghost.

Daniel's good news had been premature. In fact, the situation had gotten worse. Much worse. And Daniel, he knew, had betrayed him.

Jacob inched along the street, gliding in the shadows, following his quarry with the eyes of a hunter. But this hunter felt no joy in the act, no pleasure. This hunter felt only anger, and he craved revenge, knowing too well revenge was unattainable. There could be no doubt about his quarry's destination. Jacob knew these streets, and he knew where they led. He had lived here many years. But he was no hunter, and he knew that, too. He was simply a lover scorned, and it pained him to know he could no more prevent his quarry from reaching its destination than he could soar like a raven into the clouds and swoop down to periodically peck at the pale flesh of his prey.

In the distance, ahead and to his right, Daniel Jefferson hurried through the empty streets, intent on speed. Daniel wore a long brown coat, a cap, and carried a black weathered satchel in his left hand. Daniel Jefferson, his roommate, his friend, his accomplice in the lonely wastelands of marital estrangement…

Jacob clenched his hands into fists, grinded his teeth, inhaled hard laborious breaths, and wanted to scream. Time and again, during the previous days, Daniel had proven disloyal. Tonight would surely be the pinnacle of that disloyalty. Unable to wait for Daniel's good news, or to believe it existed, Jacob had continued to follow his friend. Twice more, both times at Daniel's office, Bree had come for an appointment. Daniel never mentioned the visits. Daniel had smiled when asked if Bree was ill, dismissing the idea without hesitation. So why then did she need so many visits to the doctor? So many visits to Daniel?

The answer was obvious. And tonight would prove it.

The writer in him noticed everything. The wind, as it always had, gusted between the city buildings, scraping invisibly against the concrete and brick facades, wearing them down in an imperceptible but certain manner, so that the buildings were like tiny rocks on a beach that would, someday, unavoidably, erode into insignificant grains of sand. Occasional traffic drifted down the street, lights bright and blinding. His footsteps, normally soft, echoed each time he passed an alley. Tonight, his senses were sharp, his muscles taut. The adrenaline coursing through him created a shiver in his outer limbs that shook up through his spine and into his brain. It was the sensation his main character would feel seconds before the story's climax, just before the ultimate battle when life and love would finally be decided. Jacob, however, knew the difference between fact and fiction. He would earn no victorious release, and the tension might very well drive him mad.

Daniel made two more predictable turns. Soon they were in a familiar residential area. Jacob's heartbeat quickened. He hadn't been back on this street since the night Bree asked him to leave. That night felt as though it could have happened years ago, but the memory was vivid enough and the emotions raw enough that it might have happened the day before. A moment later, they were within sight of his house.

The lights inside shone through the front window. Bree was home. Jacob stopped in a neighbor's yard, hidden behind a thicket of leafless bushes. Cold winds and more rain had stripped the trees of foliage earlier than normal, but the hedge provided enough cover to hide from stray eyes.

How could everything have come to this? How could his friend betray him this way? The same man who had taken him in, who had consoled him during an especially difficult period. Daniel had eaten at his house, with his wife, had conversed with the two of them as innocently as a child while harboring the wickedest thoughts of betrayal and lust. Jacob didn't want to believe it, didn't want to indulge in more foolish speculation. But now, he knew, it was not speculation. Now, it was real.

The front door of the house didn't open. Daniel knocked and knocked again. Finally, his hand drifted quickly to the latch, and when he pressed it, the unlocked door pushed inward. A moment later, Daniel vanished inside, and the door closed behind him.

From his hiding spot behind the hedge, Jacob imagined he was his own protagonist. He would barrel toward that front door, crash into it with a lowered shoulder, burst upon the surprised conspirators, and challenge his foe to a battle for his beloved. In defeat, Daniel would admit his betrayal, and Bree, eyes tearful and cheeks aglow, would rush into Jacob's arms eternally happy. Such a good story. Such a fantastic finish.

But just as he was no hunter, Jacob also was no hero. Barreling toward that door would lead to nothing more than an embarrassing rejection by an iron deadbolt. And probably a broken collarbone to emphasize his failure. In the past months, he had been a husband, a friend, a writer, a drunk. But he had never been a hero. Alone in the night, cowering behind a stand of bushes, paralyzed by anger, fearful of revenge, he wasn't one now. That, he knew, was the most unfortunate of his many flaws.

§

Bree clutched her belly. She cringed as another wave of pain crashed against her insides, foaming with whitecaps of nausea and exhaustion. This may have been her first pregnancy, but she had read enough to know something was wrong. At that moment, she couldn't move from the couch, but the intensity came in bursts, and she simply had to weather the onslaught of the tide.

Until a few minutes earlier, Marcus had been with her, at her side, holding her hand. When she had called Daniel and asked him to come as quickly as possible, Marcus leapt to his feet.

"I'll get you some bread," he told her, "or some crackers. Can you keep those down?"

She shook her head. Nothing would stay down. Nothing had stayed down for two days. And everything hurt. Her stomach, her bladder, her scalp, her muscles, her eyes. Everything. Over the past two weeks, the spasms had intensified every day. Some days she tolerated them. Tonight she wanted to die. At least Marcus had been with her most of the time.

She had watched him go a short while earlier, wishing he would stay, unable to ask because of the pain. He was so supportive, so helpful, so excited about their future. He had surprised her repeatedly, both with his tenderness and his anticipation. Instead of fearing their future, he savored every moment together and told her tales of the many places they would go with their child. No longer simply adventure and mystery, he became a storyteller, and in him she continued to find every trait she ever desired in a man. Plus, they had passion. A week earlier, they had spent all day and all night wrapped in each other's arms, making love in bed, on the sofa, on the floor, in the closet. The sex was imaginative, uninhibited, overwhelming. The man was insatiable but gifted with enough skill to create the same desire in her. And when they paused for a break, for a breath, panting in a chair or in the shower or on the uncomfortable marble of the bathroom vanity, always he would tell her stories or recite quotations from her favorite authors.

And every day, he reminded her more of Jacob. Not Jacob as he was now, but Jacob as he once had been. Jacob the storyteller, Jacob the dreamer. Jacob the lover. The differences were less apparent than before. She and Jacob had never had sex on the bathroom vanity, or in the closet for that matter, but they had been young and inexperienced, too timid, perhaps, for such adventures, but passionate in their own way.

They always dreamed of the future and what it would hold and where it would take them. They were in love, and they played the parts of young lovers, and they were happy and content. They were everything she and Marcus now were, except for one obvious exception.

Without a child, they had drifted apart. Jacob wanted children but couldn't have them. Was that so bad a flaw? Had something so far out of their control been the ultimate cause of Jacob's downfall, of their marriage's failure? She could finally admit that perhaps she had been too harsh on him, too cruel.

She had said so to Marcus. They were naked on the carpet of the living room, side by side, on their backs holding hands, and she told him she had wrongly criticized her husband. She told Marcus not all their problems had been Jacob's fault, that his drunkenness had been fueled by their inability to have children and not by his failed career. She had been wrong and harsh, and she recognized that now.

"He was a drunk," Marcus said. "A lousy, miserable drunk who savored a pint of ale more than your happiness. If he loved you, he would've fought for you. Instead, he did nothing."

"You're right," she whispered in his ear, but she didn't believe it. "Besides, it no longer matters. We're together now, and we're happy, and we're going to have a baby."

Marcus closed his eyes, smiling.

Now he was gone, off to the market, and Bree was ill, clutching her knees to her chest and wishing someone would rip out her intestines so they wouldn't hurt anymore.

Through the pain and nausea she heard knocking on the front door. She grunted but knew no one would hear. A moment later the door opened and closed and footsteps drifted down the hall. When Daniel came around the corner, his face etched with concern, she offered her best smile.

§

Daniel saw the pain in that half-smile, that twisting of the lips intended to hide the sensations beneath. He saw it often, especially from pregnant women suffering through early contractions. Don't worry, the look said, I can handle it, it's not so bad, but really it hurts like holy hell.

"Came as fast as I could," he said, returning the smile, "How are you?"

"Not well."

Her face, that beautiful, delicate face, appeared pale and rubbery. Perspiration beaded into drops at her temples. Matted, frayed, and unkempt, the few strands of hair that had escaped the pony tail fell across her face and stuck to the sweat on her cheek.

"What's wrong, exactly?" he asked.

"I'm nauseated. Can't eat or drink. Throw it up when I do."

"Any pain?"

"Everywhere."

"Is one area more intense than another?"

"My stomach, my bladder."

"Any bleeding?"

"Not that I've noticed."

"Let me see." He set his bag down. Inside were several pairs of white latex gloves, but he didn't want those. He knelt beside the sofa, pulling her knees away from her chest so she lay outstretched on her back. "Tell me if this hurts."

His hands touched the wool of her sweater and he gently, firmly pressed down on the upper portion of her belly. She closed her eyes and twitched, smiling.

"Tickles a little," she said. "And itches."

"That's the wool. Sorry."

Bree's hand reached down, grabbed the sweater and slid the material upward, baring the smooth, golden skin of her stomach from just above her pubic bone to somewhere near the fourth rib. The round underside of her breasts was exposed. Daniel swallowed hard. He enjoyed this immensely, but reminded himself once again that she was his best friend's wife. And a patient.

He touched her skin with his bare fingers and glided his hands down her belly.

"Still tickles," she said, managing a smile.

"Sorry."

But by now he had forgotten himself. He could smell the sweat on her skin, could see the soft wrinkles of her navel, could almost taste her dry, chapped lips. He pressed on her abdomen, just over her appendix, then near her bladder, then up toward her lowest rib, around the sides toward the back near her kidneys. He had to look away, to detach himself, fearing he might uncontrollably lay his head against her stomach or lift the sweater to expose more skin. The urges were overwhelming. Too many nights alone, too many months of celibacy. And here was this beautiful woman. Here was ecstasy. No, he reminded himself. Here was his best friend's wife. Here was a patient. Nothing more.

A noise near the window, something hitting the house or falling outside, yanked him from his thoughts. They both turned toward the sound, which must have been a shutter blowing in the wind, slamming against the siding, but they could see nothing beyond the dark window. Bree suddenly bent in half, groaning. She leapt from the couch and disappeared into the bathroom.

The excitement passed and she vomited. Alone on the floor near the sofa, Daniel laughed. Vomit was the ultimate anaphrodisiac. He walked to the window and peered outside. He might have seen a tree or a bush swaying in the wind, but mostly he saw his own guilty expression reflected back at him.

When Bree returned, face washed, belly covered, she patted his shoulder and lay down.

"What's the word, Doctor?"

"To be honest, I think you've got a common case of morning sickness. The normal trials of pregnancy. Unfortunately, there's not much we can do except wait for it to pass. And it will, I promise."

"What about the pain?"

"You didn't seem especially sensitive anywhere, so the pain you feel is likely a side effect of the nausea and vomiting. Does your back hurt?"

"Yes."

"That's from the spasms. Uncomfortable, but normal. You're taking the vitamins?"

"Every day."

"Good. You didn't have any problems, right?"

"None. Why?"

"Too much iron can cause stomach irritation. But I don't think that's the problem. Might also be ulcers, but we'll check for them in a few weeks. If the pain continues, maybe we'll check sooner."

"Ulcers? Is something wrong?"

"They're common, and they're treatable. Never you worry. We'll make sure that baby stays healthy."

Bree closed her eyes and nodded. "Thank you, Daniel."

"It's my pleasure. If the pain continues to be a problem, we'll examine further." He watched her expression and wondered if now was a good time to mention his fears about her relationships. Probably not, but he went ahead anyway. "Can I ask you something?"

"What is it?"

"What's the deal with you and Marcus McComber?" He tried to be subtle, to mask his disapproval, but the look on her face proved he failed.

"What about him?"

"How do you know him?"

All her pain seemed to vanish. "You already know how I know him. We met at the bookstore. He's in one of my groups."

"Do you see him often?"

"That's none of your business, Daniel, you know that." She tensed, and he wondered if it was because of the nausea or because she felt guilty.

"I'm sorry. I was just curious. You two seem awfully friendly."

"What does that mean?"

"Nothing. I simply don't want someone to..." He stopped. What had he been about to say? He didn't want someone to come between her and Jacob? What would that imply? She might catch on that he'd been paying especially close attention to her life.

"Someone to what?" she demanded.

"I want to make sure you're alright. He's dangerous, Bree. Don't trust him. Don't even speak with him."

"How is he dangerous?"

"I don't know. But please be careful."

"Wait," she said. Her face twisted, puzzled. "How do you know Marcus McComber?"

"From the tavern."

"The tavern?"

"Angus's Tavern, over on Whiskey Road, past the Clarkston Bridge." He knew she knew it.

"He was there?"

"He's there all the time, talking to Jacob."

"He knows Jacob?" she asked.

And the fury evident in her scowl froze him. There were no more signs of nausea. "You didn't know?"

§

Jacob sat curled up in the dirt, his back plastered against the house. An oblong square of light from the window colored the grass two feet away. Breathing was difficult, whether from fear of being discovered or from what he had seen inside. All his worst fears had come true. Daniel Jefferson, his old friend, with his hands on his wife's stomach. He lifted her sweater to rub her skin. She was on the couch with her eyes closed, and when Daniel spoke she smiled and sighed. How long before he slid that sweater up further and massaged her breasts, until he kissed her and she kissed him? How long before the unthinkable happened?

Rage blistered to the surface until his entire body felt ready to explode. He had slammed his fist against the window, furious and disbelieving. Half a moment later he realized his mistake and dropped to the ground. He sat there, unmoving, and watched Daniel's silhouette appear on that oblong square of illuminated grass before vanishing.

He couldn't bring himself to watch further. He knew what was happening beyond that window. Disgust and anger and hatred and sadness all came to a point, and again he chided himself for not being the hero, for not storming into that house, his house, and ending their traitorous affair. At that moment, he hated himself.

Thankfully, he had a weapon. His novel. And maybe when she read it everything would return to normal. It was his only chance. He renewed his vow to finish it quickly and present it to her in its roughest form. Forget rewrites. Forget polishing. He no longer had a choice. If he delayed, he might lose her forever, and that would make for a terrible ending.

CHAPTER EIGHTEEN

One Month Ago

"Something amiss?" McComber's grin lacked its normal mischievousness.

Bree barged into his apartment, too angry to marvel at his feigned ignorance. "You know him?"

"Who?"

"Don't play games."

He laughed and closed the door. "Perhaps I know him, perhaps not. Who is he?"

She glared, wondering what he would admit, and wondering further if what he admitted would be true or false. "Jacob, you fool."

"Jacob?"

"Why didn't you tell me?"

"Tell you what?"

"That you knew him?"

"What does Jacob have to do with anything?"

And then she saw understanding in his eyes, in the way his brows arched and his lips folded into that familiar grin. "He's my husband, damn it. Didn't you know that? You're off talking to him at the bar every night? That's what I hear. What are you saying? Are you talking about us? Are you the one driving him mad?"

She grew more infuriated when he laughed.

"What's so funny?"

"All this time," he said, "and I never knew. How marvelous."

"Why didn't you tell me?"

But at that moment, Bree felt a stabbing pain through her stomach and she doubled over, clutching her waist. She fell to her knees. McComber lunged and caught her by the waist to slow her fall.

"You okay?" he asked.

But she didn't hear. Her head throbbed. Her stomach felt ready to explode. Her hips ached, as did her back and neck and kidneys. The pain was immense, as though all the vomiting and spasms of the past week had been but the rumblings of a volcano before this, the final eruption. Frightening black dots danced and spun in the air around her. Her ears popped. Her sinuses threatened to blow holes through her pupils. She looked up to Marcus, who ran off inexplicably. This couldn't be morning sickness. She put a hand on her forehead, fighting the pain, but when she pulled it away it was red with blood. Where did Marcus go? She wiped her other hand across her nose and it, too, came away bloody. She coughed, and the blood ran across her lips, and she could taste it, could see it dripping onto the gray carpet, coagulating into a puddle of gore. "Marcus!" She felt dizzy, light-headed. A loud, steady whine barraged her eardrums. She cupped her hands over them to no avail, but they, too, came away bloody. The whine grew into a roar and her equilibrium failed. She felt herself falling, unable to prevent it, unable to care, and soon she stared up through a long tunnel toward the white painted ceiling. Life seemed to be vanishing, but the pain stayed nearby, urging her to succumb. She felt bile battling blood in her throat.

She saw a face then. Marcus' face. He knelt over her, wiped away blood with a towel. She never felt his hands, but she knew he lifted her into the air. Now he ran with her through the apartment, and to ignore the pain she focused all her energy on his determined face. He appeared amazingly calm, as if he knew exactly what to do, as if this was but another act in some grand play. Soon she heard the lock of a door and felt the cold night air and stared upward into a rare, cloudless sky where twinkling stars mingled with the spiraling floaters until everything faded to black. She felt consciousness and all the world slipping away, and all she desired was a release from the pain.

§

When she woke up, she felt lighter. Perhaps the weight of agony had been lifted.

"Bree?" The voice was soft, familiar. She had no true sense of body but knew that wherever her body was, it hurt. The pain was agonizingly dull, as if muted, but strong enough that she knew something had gone wrong.

When she opened her eyes, she saw Daniel. He stood over her, clad in a white lab coat with a clipboard in one hand. Soon she felt his other hand on her fingers, squeezing them. He set the clipboard somewhere out of view and leaned closer.

"Bree?" Though his face was inches away, his voice came from another world. "Can you hear me?"

It hurt to nod.

He said something more, but she heard only fragments. "Medication… morphine… antitoxins." Though it was painful, she swiveled her eyes around the room enough to realize she was in a hospital. Daniel continued. "Blood loss… clotting… liver… kidney failure."

None of it meant anything in her bizarre state of indifference. Something had gone wrong, she knew. She had been ill, pained, and had been bleeding. And wasn't there another problem, a bigger problem? Shouldn't she have remembered? But then she had relaxed and it all went away.

Moving her eyes across the room, searching for answers, she grew light-headed and lackadaisical.

"Can you hear me?" Daniel asked again.

But the world once more turned black.

§

When again she grew aware of herself, she heard Daniel speaking. To another doctor, she thought. The ringing in her ears had lessened, but she found it difficult to maintain focus or understand the words.

"Black discharge. Transfused two pints of A positive. Ten cc's of insulin. Antitoxins for kidneys and liver." Silliness and nonsense.

"My papers show increased hormone levels. Was she pregnant?"

"Yes."

Pregnant? She remembered now! A wave of euphoria swept over her and shoved the pain aside. At least one part of her life was in order. How could she have forgotten.? She was pregnant. With Jacob's child.

But that wasn't right and she knew it wasn't right. Not Jacob's child. That had been a lie. A lie for Daniel. But why?

She opened her eyes and blurted, "Marcus!"

The doctors jumped to her side.

"It's okay," Daniel whispered. "Everything's fine. Marcus went home to rest."

She stared at him, forcing herself to remember what he knew.

"He stayed all night," Daniel added. "Do you remember? He brought you here. Do you remember why you were with him?"

"He's my friend," she said, slowly understanding.

"He saved your life."

She remembered the pain and the bleeding and Marcus lifting her into the air, but that was all. "What happened?"

"You were very sick, Bree. Dangerously sick."

"How?"

"We don't know yet, but we'll find out. I promise. You'll need to stay a few more days." His frown, however, did not support his pledge.

"What is it, Daniel? What's wrong?"

He asked the other doctor to leave. He sat beside her on the bed, holding her hand.

"I did all I could, Bree. But by the time you were here, it was just too late. If we'd have diagnosed it earlier, we might have done something, but there was no way to know."

"I don't understand."

He squeezed her hand tighter. She knew she had lied to him, and now, as his eyes teared up, she wished she hadn't. This man she had known for so long, who she had watched suffer the embarrassment and pain of divorce, who had come to her with adoring eyes to beg that she take Jacob back, may have saved her life. Look at his agony. She knew what he was going to say before he said it. Her heart cracked in three different ways.

"Your baby…" he whispered. "We couldn't save it."

Part III

"Now each visitor shall confess
The sad valley's restlessness.
Nothing there is motionless --
Nothing save the airs that brood
Over the magic solitude."

Edgar Allan Poe
The Valley of Unrest

CHAPTER NINETEEN

Present

Recollection is a vile and bitter thing. Indeed, it seems the most wretched and painful memories are often the easiest to recall. Or perhaps it is circumstance that dictates our thought. Perhaps, while adrift in a world of daydream, on a blanket in the grass beneath an old poplar in the park, when a gentle wind rustles the branches and the aromas of burning autumn leaves or spiced cider cloud our senses, our minds might conjure happier images of childhood friendships, of playgrounds, of box kites or racing derbies or cotton candy at a ball game. But here, in this cold chamber, confronted by men who label me a criminal and a murderer, here I remember only the worst days, the worst occasions. Here I remember guns and babies and rejections, tombs and taverns and arguments. Here I remember all the things I wish to forget. And I remember because they demand it.

"Tell us," says Andrew Ruben, "Tell us why you followed Marcus McComber into those tunnels tonight?"

"I was drunk. It was dark. And I didn't follow him. He forced me there."

"Did you intend to murder him?"

"Never."

"Are you saying it was an accident?"

"I'm saying I never killed him. We've discussed this."

Ruben slams his fist on the table. Burrows has vanished. Without my glasses, I can't be certain, but I think Jesus Christ may be asleep on that cross. Or dead. "If we have to sit here all night," Ruben adds, "we will. If I have to ask you this question every minute for the next two days, I will."

"And I will answer just as I have. Because it is the only answer I can give."

"That's not good enough, Mr. Lyons. You've told us how you met Marcus McComber. You've told us when. You've told us he lied, but that you didn't care because you found it… What's the word you used? Entertaining? You've told us he threatened you, in the tunnels, and though frightened, you believed it a harmless threat, more of an illustration. Is that correct?"

"I have."

"So when do we come to it?"

"To what?"

"Your motive."

"I have none."

"Except that tonight, he threatened you again. Was that all the motive you needed? You've not told us everything about that encounter. You've not explained how, in the end, you escaped. But I have a guess, a very logical guess. You killed him, and you ran away. And then you killed again. And again."

"Who? Who did I kill? You say three people are dead. But you don't tell me who? I didn't kill Marcus McComber. I didn't kill anyone else."

"After you killed McComber, you took his gun, and not far from his apartment, you encountered Daniel Jefferson, your supposed friend."

"What does Daniel have to do with this?"

"You tell us. Was he, perhaps, romantically involved with your wife after you separated?"

And again, they force me to remember. How could they know? How could anyone know? I believe Daniel did have relations with Bree. I'm certain of it. And I have accused him of it, though he denies it as absurd.

But he told me everything would be fine, that good news was coming, that Bree and I would be back together. And then how horrible it was when I discovered the truth. How miserable I felt that day, and on subsequent days when I asked him about it, when he denied it, when Bree, in so many words, confirmed it. All my worst fears, all the emotional anguish. I was certain, for a time, that they had both betrayed me.

Now, all I can say to Ruben, however, is, "I don't know."

"I think you do. Imagine it, your best friend and your wife. Man to man, that's enough to justify murder, but the law disagrees."

"I don't understand what you're hinting at.

"I'm not hinting, but maybe this is more direct. Was your wife having an affair with Daniel Jefferson?"

"I don't know."

"Yes you do."

"No."

"You do know. And you confronted him. Is that correct?"

"No. Yes. Well… He was gone, all the time, and I wondered where he had gotten to, so I followed him. Several times, actually. Most of the time, he went to work. But another time, I followed him to my house. To Bree's house."

"How did that make you feel?"

"Confused. Upset."

"Did you confront him?"

"Not immediately."

"Instead, you let it simmer, you let the pain build inside your head. Didn't you? You waited until you could no longer stand it, and then you confronted him."

"Yes."

"Because he was fucking your wife. Because the man you thought was your friend had deceived you. The man who took you in, comforted you, had all along intended to take advantage of your loss."

"That's what I thought."

And Ruben stands, glaring down at me. can feel another accusation coming. He says, as though the question has already been answered, "Is that why you killed Daniel Jefferson?"

CHAPTER TWENTY

9:00PM

Through the darkness of a stormy night, two figures inched along the cobblestone street in search of a warmer, drier place to quarrel. The taller one was hunched over, sweating, coughing, aiming a pistol with an unsteady hand at the back of the shorter, straighter figure. The man with the gun to his back wore a downtrodden expression alleviated by liquor but exacerbated by fear and anger. Each time the taller man coughed or stumbled, each time the gun wavered or fell, the shorter, straighter Jacob Lyons searched for a place to run or cursed his own inability to do so.

"You can stop entertaining foolish thoughts," Marcus McComber whispered between coughs. The gun trembled in his hand. "There's nowhere to go. And I'll not hesitate to kill you."

"You're sick and you're mad, Marcus. I've done nothing wrong."

"And if I believed you? Do you think that would matter at this point?"

"I guess not."

"You are wise, Fortunato."

They came eventually to McBraidy Tavern. McComber urged Jacob into the alley between tavern and brothel.

"Had I been prepared," McComber said, "I would have bought you a woman as a parting gift. The wildest, craziest whore in town. Too bad you had to be spontaneous."

He shoved Jacob further into the alley, past the tavern entrance. The odor of mold and decomposing refuse defied the weather and permeated their senses. Even their clothes began to reek. McComber coughed and wheezed and prodded Jacob with the gun barrel.

"Open the cellar doors," he said.

"Why?"

"Don't waste my time with questions."

Jacob did as he was told. A gust of dry, stale air rushed up from the cellar and slapped his face. "Now what?"

"Down."

They stumbled blindly into the cellar. Eventually, McComber produced the lantern and the stagnant space brightened with yellow, flickering light. Jacob cursed himself again for not running, for not attempting some method of escape. But what chance did he have? There was nowhere to run, nowhere to hide, nowhere to kick and pinch and slap himself until he woke from this terrible dream.

McComber forced him to the back of the cellar. The heavy wooden door on the far wall was closed. "Open it."

Jacob knew what lay on the other side. "No."

"Open it."

"I didn't kill anyone," Jacob pleaded. "You must believe me."

McComber didn't answer. He slammed the pistol into Jacob's spine and pinned him to the wall. "Open it."

He did.

The air beyond the doorway chilled his skin and the dampness infiltrated his lungs.

"Move." McComber kicked and jabbed and prodded. They entered the winding, uncertain path of the catacombs, and Jacob's knees buckled beneath an ever-growing fear. He longed for the streetlamp and the rain and the wretched dampness that he had earlier cursed so vehemently.

"What are we doing down here?" he asked.

"I have received a pipe of what passes for Amontillado."

"Stop the Edgar Allan Poe nonsense, Marcus. Tell me the truth."

"Nonsense? Don't you dare call it nonsense. Did you know she loved it? Did you know she and I first met over that story? She asked if Fortunato deserved to die, and I said he did, and she called me a fool." He jabbed more. "But I was right. He did deserve to die, and he deserved the torture and the agony of his death. Just as you'll deserve yours."

They curved and wound and descended. Nothing existed beyond that tiny sphere of lantern light, just as nothing had existed beyond the bronze world beneath the streetlamp. The tempest raged, the winds howled, and these two men delved into the black underground where evil manifested itself most acutely in the form of isolation.

Soon they emerged into the open vault of the catacombs. McComber forced Jacob toward the small crevice where ten weeks earlier he had pinned Jacob against the wall and asked him to imagine being buried alive. As understanding began to inch up his spine, Jacob froze. McComber kicked him until he stumbled forward.

"Don't do it, Marcus. I'm innocent."

"How unfortunate this would be if that were true." McComber laughed. He shoved Jacob into the recess. The air was damp and heavy. Water trickled down the rock wall, glimmering in the lantern's light. "Sit down."

Jacob searched the crevice and prayed for a means of escape. There was none, so he sat.

"I didn't feel a need for restraints like those in the story. I suppose I could bind you with rope, but I expect you'll behave. Bold actions have never been part of your character, despite that silly adventure beneath the streetlamp."

"Marcus, listen to me. I didn't do it."

"It's time to accept death, dear Fortunato."

"I didn't even know her!"

"Ha!"

McComber grabbed a heavy stone block. He placed it in the opening, half way between Jacob and himself. He repeated the process two more times until a tiny wall stood between the two men. Six inches high, it might as well be a mountain range risen between Jacob and freedom. Next, McComber grabbed a bucket of water he must have stashed there on a previous visit. And now he produced a bag of concrete mix, which he poured into the bucket of water. He stirred the mortar, produced a trowel from some hidden niche, and slapped a fresh layer atop his new stone wall. Jacob felt a bit of awe at the premeditated nature of it all. His indifference to McComber's plotting proved itself a rather significant mistake, it would seem.

"I thought up lots of ways to kill," McComber said. "But this one has always been my favorite. And she would have liked it, given her fondness for Poe's macabre sense of justice."

"You don't know what you're doing, Marcus. Someone will find us down here. You'll have to explain."

"You know as well as I do that no one comes down here. And if they do, it won't matter. Once I'm finished, no one will know what lies behind this wall. Or should I say, 'Who'?"

For the first time, Jacob admitted to himself he was probably going to die. At best, he would have one chance to escape. Was he strong enough to take it? He would need to act soon. Every minute he delayed, his tomb grew deeper.

CHAPTER TWENTY-ONE

Three Weeks Ago

"Ahh," Marcus shouted, opening the tavern door, "my dear, dear Fortunato!"

He crossed the wooden threshold, all smiles, and ignored the watchful eyes of patrons who turned at his bellow. On a stool at the center of the bar, Jacob Lyons guzzled water from a pitcher, and it was he whom McComber had come to visit.

Angus Ferley broke from a patron's mindless whining to greet him. "Greetings, my dark, chipper friend."

"Since when does a bartender slander his patrons with words like chipper?"

The bartender growled. "Here I'm working my ass off to speak your language and all you do is criticize. How's this: What can I getcha, jackass?"

"Much more suiting. How about a draft of your best brandy?"

"Right away, you old devil."

Marcus sat down beside Jacob, eyes beaming, watching his old acquaintance with newfound insight. All this time, and he had never known. It would be a lie to say the thought never came to him. On a few occasions, as he listened to Jacob speak, as he heard the complaints Jacob lavished upon his doctor friend regarding life and marriage, he wondered if perhaps Jacob was the one. The idea seemed impossible even now, which explained why he so easily discounted it earlier. Now, he amused himself recounting all the times he sat here and essentially promised Jacob he would eventually kill him. Of course, neither of them had known the truth. His smile widened, remembering an adventure deep into the winding catacombs when he might have ended Jacob's life. He had been teasing then, ignorant of the truth, but how ironic that his chance had come and he had missed it.

Thankfully, he had learned long ago that life was full of second chances.

"Greetings," he said.

Jacob continued guzzling water.

"Thirsty?"

A nod.

Angus appeared with the brandy. "Drinking rich tonight, McComber. What's the occasion?"

"Isn't it always a woman?"

"I don't follow."

"Today, life returns to normal and the future is once again a spectacle worthy of beholding."

"You can stuff your riddles up your ass if you don't want to tell me."

McComber ignored the prodding, instead focusing on Jacob Lyons, the innocent, drunk, naïve husband. Fate continued to be kind.

When Jacob drained the pitcher and belched, Marcus said, "How is the writing coming along?"

The husband cocked his head and Marcus knew what he was thinking. Jacob had never told Marcus he was a writer. Jacob had never told Marcus much of anything, and Marcus had never cared enough to ask. That was the reason they had gone so long without the truth.

"The writing is fine." The words came slowly, cautiously, and he knew Jacob felt uncomfortable. That had been his intent.

"And your wife? How is she?" Jacob's head fell and he exhaled like a bull through his nose. McComber recognized the discontent and drew pleasure from it. Why not continue down the most painful paths, just for fun? "Well, my offer still stands. I could lend you my Goddess for a time, if you're capable of handling her."

"I don't need your imaginary minx, thank you."

"But Daniel tells me your marriage has suffered a few infidelities."

"Oh? What else has Daniel told you?"

"Only that he and Bree are close, and that he has visited her on occasion to discuss the situation."

"To discuss? Is that what he said?"

"He wore a wicked grin and winked when he said it, but it's not my place to make assumptions. If I were you, I'd watch him. He's already poked your wife in her most secretive places, and if he liked what he saw maybe he's up for a new sort of poking."

McComber knew it was crude, knew it was obnoxious and misleading, but that was the fun of it. The more time he spent in this quaint tavern, the more he felt certain it was populated with small-minded, inept morons who succumbed easily to manipulation.

"Ahh," he said, "Never mind. Daniel's your best friend. He would never do a thing like that." Jacob, he knew, would think otherwise. Planting the seeds of dissent provided such entertainment. "Besides, we have better things to celebrate."

"And what are those?"

"First, a most unfortunate situation has been remedied. And second, I have discovered an important secret."

"The suspense is numbing."

"Jest if you will, my dear Fortunato, but let me tell you the news before you judge it. At long last, I have discovered the identity of my Goddess's wretched husband."

Jacob raised his eyebrows. Of course he was interested. Jacob was a storyteller, and the identity of a man Marcus had promised to murder would be a tantalizing morsel. "Who is he?"

"And wouldn't you like to know? I won't say just yet. Let me bask in the knowledge myself before revealing it to another. You'll learn it soon enough, I'm sure."

"And will you kill him?"

"I don't know. I may not have to. His identity has offered new possibilities. With certainty, I can say I no longer have to fear him. Not that I ever did, but his likely efforts at revenge were always a consideration. I won't worry anymore. Besides, even without death, he will suffer enough, I think"

"If you do, what end did you decide on? Don't tell me you're going to bury him alive?"

McComber smiled at Jacob, who leaned away apprehensively. "If I decide to kill him," Marcus said, "You'll know the method before he dies. That I promise."

CHAPTER TWENTY-TWO

Three Weeks Ago

Bree spent a week in the hospital. The first five days she had been confined to a bed while organs healed and wounds mended. On the sixth day she learned the truth about what had befallen her, though the vague answers explained little.

Marcus had come and gone. During the first few days, while she had been drugged and incoherent, she knew he spent hours beside her bed. She remembered his reassuring presence like a happy childhood memory, emotion without detail. When she slept, which was often, she felt his fingers wrapped around her own.

The leather-bound Poe anthology he had given her sat on the table beside the bed. Whenever she read it, she remembered that night on the park bench when he'd surprised her with two gifts. They had yet to drink the aged bottle of Amontillado. Perhaps someday soon they would, she thought, now that the bitter corner of her brain reminded her she was no longer pregnant.

Daniel, too, was always near. He checked in several times an hour, bringing food or medicine. The nurses, he claimed, were the best, but he could never trust them with his most lovely patient. Other doctors checked on her as well, and she realized, because she was a patient in the intensive care ward, Daniel could not have been the doctor assigned to her. But he pretended to be, which made her happy, and he was the person, on the sixth day, to relate everything the doctors had thus far discovered.

"Pennyroyal," he said.

She sat up in her bed. The physical pain had become but a whisper compared to the emotional screams echoing through her mind every wakeful moment. "Pennyroyal?" she asked. "Isn't that tea?"

"Yes and no. It's an herb. A highly toxic herb."

"I don't understand."

"The herb can be used for making tea, but in very small quantities. There is also Pennyroyal oil, which is much more hazardous."

She had read about herbs before but remembered little. "I still don't understand."

"Pennyroyal, in some circles, is known as an abortifacient."

"A what?"

"Abortifacient. Any type of drug that, among other things, induces a miscarriage. Usually, it's self-induced. And self-ingested."

She saw doubt fill his eyes, and she suddenly understood his disturbed, disbelieving manner. "You're wrong," she said, "I didn't do this, Daniel. I wanted this baby."

He lowered his head.

"Are you kidding?" she asked. "Why would I? This is all I ever wanted. You know it. Why would I ruin my chances after all that effort?"

"I believe you. I really do. But I have to ask, for the record… And I'm sorry I must, Bree. But have you ever knowingly ingested any form of Pennyroyal?"

"No."

"Did you intentionally attempt to abort your pregnancy?"

"Absolutely not."

"Are you sure?"

"Daniel! How could you think that of me?"

He began to pace. "I'm sorry, I'm sorry. I'm not accusing you of anything. Really." He combed a hand through his hair. "It's just that, we found large traces of Pennyroyal toxins in your bloodstream, and the side effects match perfectly. The quantities of pennyroyal needed to induce abortion are so toxic they can also cause liver and kidney failure, bleeding, lots of bleeding, from any or all orifices. It's dangerous stuff, Bree. It's easier to kill yourself with the stuff than to actually abort a pregnancy. The other doctors think it was self-induced. I wasn't sure, and that's why I wanted to ask you about it."

"Never, Daniel."

"I know."

They stared at each other, and she asked, "But if I didn't do it intentionally, how did it happen?"

"Another good question."

"Are those toxins found anywhere else? Common foods? I've been so sick lately that I could only eat basics. Bread and eggs and juice and cereal."

"No, not in common food. But now I'm beginning to wonder about your illness."

"It was real."

"That's not what I meant. If somehow you've been ingesting the toxins over a period of time, they might have caused it, eventually resulting in trauma like what you experienced."

"But I haven't ingested much of anything. There's no way."

The two of them stared at each other for long moments. She could see that Daniel did not completely believe her story, but how could she offer proof to change his mind? Doctors' minds are too scientific, and they see everything as cause and effect, black and white. Here were these toxins and here was a sick woman with all the signs. Therefore, she must have drugged herself. But what did it mean if she hadn't? Well, it could only mean she was lying.

Then he changed direction, "Will you tell Jacob?"

"Why?" she asked without thinking.

"Because he was the father, and he should know."

Her first instinct was to laugh. At the irony, at the lie, at how easily

Daniel Jefferson had been deceived. It felt like madness, laughing in a hospital bed after a miscarriage, with the doctor accusing you of intentionally aborting the child of your lover and failing to tell your husband about any of it. Madness.

"I'll tell him," she said. "But not yet. I need time."

He nodded his understanding and sat back in his chair. An hour later, he had fallen asleep. She watched him for three hours, reliving the experiences they shared, reliving the turmoil of the past six months. Turmoil that had engulfed them both in ways neither could have predicted.

Admittedly, her thoughts were unclear. Life had recently exacted a grand toll on her and everyone she knew. And for a few brief moments, lying in bed, watching Daniel, she imagined life with Jacob as it had once been. Could they patch the wounds, fix the problems? Could she be happy? Could they try again to have children? Could everything that had been done be undone?

For whatever reason, when her thoughts turned toward Marcus, she felt somehow empty, if only a little, and emptiness was always disconcerting.

§

The hospital released her on the seventh day. Daniel brought her home. In the short time she was away, the house had grown dusty, smelling of mildew and littered with the shattered dreams of a lost child. She thanked him for being so kind, feeling some guilt for misleading him, and bid him farewell. He promised to be back, to check in, to arrive with flowers or candy or various other trite gifts aimed at lifting her spirits.

"One other thing," he said, standing on the front porch. "Be mindful of what you eat. I want you back at the office in a week, so we can monitor your levels and be certain that, wherever it came from, the pennyroyal is not reintroduced to your system. The effects could be devastating."

"I'll be there."

"And be mindful of Marcus McComber."

"Thank you, Daniel."

"I'm very serious."

"I know."

She closed the door and watched him through a drawn curtain. Squinting and frowning, he remained on the doorstep for too long. She saw worry on his face and confusion, but when he moseyed into the distance she let him fade from her thoughts. There would be many emotions to face now that she had returned home. She would quickly need to let her guard down, to battle through a series of painful memories, faded hopes, and overwhelming depression, always hopeful that better times waited beyond, fearful that better times had come and gone years earlier, never to be repeated. She would need to do all that, but not yet.

§

Marcus came to visit that night. Her eyes and forehead and cheeks ached from crying. She hoped he wouldn't notice.

"You look positively wretched," he said, coming in the front door, a smile on his face. She melted into his arms with a chuckle of her own. With charm like his, he could get away with anything.

"What's in the bag?" she asked.

"Brochures."

"For what?"

"You'll see."

He brought her to the sofa, where a mound of crumpled tissue acted as a white, snotty slipcover on the olive fabric. Preferring not to disturb her monument to depression, he maneuvered her onto a rocking chair and kneeled beside it.

"These are travel brochures," she said.

"I know."

"Are you taking a vacation?"

"No. We are."

"Oh?"

"An indefinite one."

She read the first brochure. "To the Bahamas?"

"Perhaps."

She flipped through the stack. "Florence, Morocco, Portugal, Belize, Jamaica. Zimbabwe?"

"It looks fascinating."

She laughed. "Where did you get these?"

"Pharmacy. The point is this: I still want us to leave this place. I know you're upset. So am I. But lingering here to wallow in our miseries and suffer the daily reminders of what might have been will be as devastating to our health as the event we mourn. There is no reason not to go. And I don't care if it's Zimbabwe or a fishing village in Iceland. The point is, I want to be with you, and I want us to start a new life away from here. Away from these memories. Surely you want the same?"

She stared at his anticipating eyes. It was as close to begging as she'd ever seen him. "Funny," she said. "I expected you to burst through that door with your clothes off, ready to dive into bed."

"We have eternity to make love, my dear. The only question is where we do it."

"I don't think it'll be in Zimbabwe."

"To be honest, I hope it's your bedroom in five minutes. But after that, I thought we might find someplace more in tune with your adventurous side. Away from this miserable cold and rain."

"But the rain suits me. Don't you remember? You said it yourself."

"Indeed I did. But a dark complexion, sun-bleached hair, and translucent gowns will suit you even better."

"How will I ever get you out of bed?"

"By getting out yourself." He stood and grinned, flaunting his masculinity. "If you can manage, that is."

"Oh, I'll manage."

They laughed together briefly, but Bree was exhausted. She didn't know what to think of Marcus's plan. As she watched him, as she examined his soft skin, his striking features, his unwrinkled face, his ever present smirk, she felt something amiss. Where was the aching in her bones? Where was the desire to strip off her clothes and feel his warmth penetrate into her darkest, most sensitive places? He sat at the kitchen table and flipped through the brochures, thoughtfully studying each one, as though any of them were viable possibilities. Had he picked any of them intentionally, or had he simply grabbed a handful from the nearest stacks? Did he know anything about Belize?

Perhaps she had undergone too much emotional distress to allow less painful feelings to surface. Perhaps the trauma and the loss of her child had once again brought the cruelties of the world to the forefront of her thoughts and reminded her that lust and sexual satisfaction were meaningless distractions to uncovering a true and open love between individuals.

Or perhaps she was tired. Too tired. Tired of the world and of pain and of regret. Tired of suffering. Perhaps getting away from the world she knew was her only means of escape. Like reading a good book, like getting lost in a new world of intrigue and mystery, perhaps living in a new city, with new surroundings and new people, would help fight back the sense of loss and produce a renewed optimism. Maybe she could start over. Maybe she and Marcus could truly begin a new life. Maybe they could have a child.

Maybe she could leave Jacob behind.

Was that what she wanted? To leave Jacob behind? And Daniel? And all the fascinating people she knew at the book store? The kind man who had been her mother's lover? Was that what she wanted? To leave her life behind?

Beset with guilt at the loss of her child, understanding she had not intentionally done anything wrong, Marcus's offer seemed the most logical.

"I don't know," she told him. "You have to give me some time."

"But I already have." When she furrowed her brow, he relented. "But I can give you more. I urge you, however, to hurry. Now is the time. Now, when wounds must be healed before they grow gangrenous, before they infect your entire mind and threaten to destroy your soul, now is when you must make the effort to change."

She remembered their first meeting at the bookstore, and the next, when she had called him a fool, and later when he arrived wearing a motley cape. Though the remark was made in jest, it had proven itself terribly wrong. Marcus was no fool, and he was no jester. He was serious and determined, and she knew, whether the passion returned or it did not, he would treat her well, care for her, and coddle her whims, whatever they happened to be. His attention focused itself on her alone, and that's more than any woman should hope for. At that moment, she realized she would never do better than Marcus McComber, so why resist him?

"Very well," she said.

He waited suspiciously. "Yes?"

"I will go. We'll have a new life. Together."

"Splendid. Where shall we go?"

"Anywhere, so long as it's far away from here."

He kissed her then, and lifted her in his arms. He carried her to the bedroom and made love to her. He was gentle but dominating. He made her feel safe and loved. She allowed herself to forget the world briefly, to succumb to his touch. At some point, the old passion emerged and filled her with a cold, dull incarnation of past ecstasy. For the moment at least, she felt happy.

The next morning, Jacob knocked on her door.

CHAPTER TWENTY-THREE

Three Weeks Ago

When he saw her face, when the door opened and allowed him to marvel at the beauty he had lost, when his throat tightened almost to the point of suffocation and two months of regret and pain and longing exploded in his chest like a canon fired from the deck of burning ship, Jacob managed one glorious word: "Hello."

They stood on the front porch of their house, him on the patio and her in the doorway. The season's first snowfall had slipped a thin veil of white across the trees and grasses to hide the decaying filth of autumn. Though the sidewalks were treacherous and dirty with slush, the yard and patio were serene, with the footprints from his hesitant approach marring an otherwise undisturbed landscape. He carried a copy of his completed manuscript in a leather satchel under his arm.

"Jacob," she said. He saw shock in her eyes, bitterness in her lips, and a flushed pink hue on her cheeks. She swallowed and stuttered before adding, "How are you?"

He had spent many hours debating with himself this very question. "Better," he said. "I've stopped drinking." It was a tiny lie, because he still had an occasional drink, but he doubted she would believe it anyway. "I'm staying at Daniel's place. Spare room. And I'm writing again."

"Good. I'm happy for you." She sounded surprisingly sincere.

"And you? How are you?"

"I'm okay. Tired, but okay."

More awkwardness settled in once they ran out of trivialities. When her shock at seeing him evaporated, Bree stared at the concrete patio. She looked as though she had stepped out of bed a moment earlier, wearing pajamas and no makeup. He wanted to hold her. He felt an unmistakable urge to run his finger down her cheek, to glide his hands up her back, to stroke her messy hair, to inhale the stale morning scent of her breath. Those were all privileges he had possessed but lost. To see her, unable to touch her, added a new level of tangibility to their separation. And a new level of pain. Still, he had come here with a purpose.

"I have something for you," he said. "It's not much, but—"

"I don't want your gifts," she said, interrupting.

"It's not a gift." Or maybe it was, but not the kind she meant. "I miss you," he said. "I didn't come here looking for reconciliation or forgiveness. I spent a lot of time thinking about what you said, and eventually, when I sobered up, I realized you were right. I was in a bad place. And I took you for granted. I know that now. I still love you, Bree. Always have. Always will." She responded by looking at a different section of patio. "Once I realized all that, I knew what I had to do. I had to find a way to prove my sincerity. I had to find a way to show you how I felt and to apologize. So I turned to the only thing I know."

He reached into the satchel and produced the heavy manuscript.

"What is that?" she asked.

"I wrote you a novel."

§

Bree did her best to wipe a silly expression from her face, feeling foolish and cruel at the same time.

"You wrote this?" she asked. The stack was thick. "When?"

"Over the past month. It's not polished, but the story's complete."

She reminisced briefly. "You always were a fast writer."

"Only for my muse."

She felt her heart sink a little. His eyes, glassy and wide, gazed achingly up at her, like those of a child who fell and scraped his knee and first discovered how painful life could be. The boy she had met ten years earlier beneath a Cyprus tree stood now on her doorstep, admiring her, and she saw how beautiful he was and how devoted. He loved her. And despite an understanding that she was destined to spend her life with Marcus McComber, she knew, as she had always known, that she loved him as well. The strength of such emotions, on top of all the other agonies, was almost too much to bear. He couldn't know what she'd been through. He couldn't know the suffering that had wreaked havoc upon her emotional welfare. But it wouldn't have made a difference. "I was your muse once," she said, breathless. Her eyes closed as she touched the manuscript, as she lifted it to her chest. It was heavy.

"You will always be my muse," he said. "I wrote that for you. When I sobered up, I went to work. You were my inspiration, and so I give it to you to read. I think you'll enjoy it."

She stared at the stranger who was her husband. How unexpected that he had come today. The night before, she had promised herself to Marcus forever. She had reluctantly agreed to life in another land. But now her past had returned, and she began to realize how difficult would be her decision to leave that past behind.

"Good bye," Jacob said suddenly. He twirled and began to retrace his footsteps in the snow.

She panicked. The moment was too short. She was still soaking it in. "Jacob!" she called. He spun to face her, anxious and nervous, like the day after they first met, when he recited a poem he'd written especially for her. She wondered if he had truly cleaned up. Had he reversed the downward spiral and emerged as the man she always thought he'd become? The idea tugged at her heart, as though some invisible puppeteer had strung a line to her chest and cut all the rest so she dangled by a single taught string. "I'll read it. I promise."

"Good," he said.

"Will you return?"

"In a couple weeks," he said confidently. Then he grinned, eyes twinkling with light reflected off the bright snow. She saw Marcus in that grin, but a very different Marcus. This one was bright and cheery and optimistic, but he shared the more exciting qualities. He possessed the mystery of an author, the aura of one who has built another world and knows all its secrets, one who can trick and mislead your emotions until you find yourself completely at his mercy. She had been attracted to him for that reason, had fallen in love with him because of it. Now, as he walked away, she noticed a bounce in his step she hadn't seen for years. Perhaps it was the joy of finishing a novel, or the satisfaction of turning his life around. Or perhaps it was simply the author in him, conscious of his decisions, knowing the effect his manuscript would have on her, understanding that he was in control now and soon she would fall in love with him once again. Whatever the reason, Bree knew she had to read the novel.

She closed the door and got comfortable on the sofa. With the same schoolgirl giddiness she felt when Marcus McComber had materialized with a rose and a kiss in the long tunnel of a darkened supermarket aisle, she began to read.

CHAPTER TWENTY-FOUR

Two Weeks Ago

Daniel had not been idle. From the moment he left Bree's front door, he'd been busy solving two obviously related riddles. Who was Marcus McComber? And how did Bree unknowingly ingest so vile a poison?

He suspected the second answer would come quickly after the first. Still, he had no idea where to start. He knew little of substance about McComber, and though Daniel had proven himself a worthy spy, he doubted his detective skills would be half as good. He'd chosen medicine over law primarily because he couldn't handle the intensive research and investigative work required to be a lawyer.

He asked everyone at the tavern what they knew about McComber. Like him, they knew almost nothing. Even Angus Ferley had very little to say, and that was a rarity.

"He's a loud, annoying, ridiculous man," Ferley said, "but he drinks by the barrel and pays his bills. He can spout all the fancy words and nonsense he sees fit, so long as he's got a beer in his hand and coin in his pocket."

The little they did know about him seemed voluminous compared to what they knew of his past. During the few conversations Daniel and McComber had shared, he learned McComber once had a wife who tried to kill him. But the motive, as McComber described it, made no sense. Was a desire not to have children any reason to kill a man? Why not just leave him? Or divorce him? Surely there was more to the story, but he had discovered nothing.

He went to the library with no plan. He found records for a great many McCombers but no Marcus. He became so desperate he broke into McComber's apartment, forcing himself through a half-open window, but found nothing of detail between the dull gray walls except a handful of travel brochures on a table and a ratty paperback version of an Edgar Allan Poe anthology tucked under a pillow.

After a week of no discoveries, he decided to change his tactics. Why not start with the Pennyroyal? He began calling the local pharmacies, asking about recent sales. He explained he was a doctor investigating a patient's illness, and, once they confirmed his story, most were eager to help. He had called nearly two dozen locations when he got lucky. A corner store on Whiskey Rd., not far from McBraidy Tavern, had sold significant quantities of the Pennyroyal herb to a tall man wearing black.

"I'll be right over," he told them.

In the shadows of taller buildings, the run-down pharmacy lurked like a tripped-out junk dealer in a crumbling, scantly-trodden corner of town. Medications and candy bars mingled haphazardly on shelves running the height and length of the cramped walls. A yellow tungsten light overhead flickered incessantly. Daniel's eye was immediately drawn to a door that seemed welded shut with a fifty cent condom dispenser hanging crooked above the broken knob.

Daniel hoped none of his patients filled their prescriptions here. Or purchased their contraceptives.

"Excuse me," he said. The fellow behind the counter, a scraggly, red-haired man with bread crumbs in his beard and a dull, gold incisor dug into his lower lip, was busy counting crisp hundred dollar bills between his dirty fingers.

"Yeah?"

Daniel smelled burning marijuana and the distinct odor of whiskey. "I called on the phone," he said. "About the Pennyroyal."

"Okay."

"Did I speak to you?"

"Doubt it."

Daniel's hope evaporated quickly. "Was someone else here I might have spoken with?"

"Maybe."

"Are they still here?"

"Dunno."

He wanted to growl, but the clerk continued counting the money, heedless of his interrogator, so Daniel began searching the shelves. Tucked behind a box of Pennyroyal tea bags and an empty prescription bottle of pain relievers belonging to Jon H. Doe, he found the cardboard remains of a shipping box stamped with the words, "Pennyroyal, See Manufacturer's Warning." He yanked a piece of black tape from the box lid. Beneath it were warning labels declaring the contents poisonous and toxic. Worst of all, the box was empty.

"Do you have any more of this?" he asked the clerk.

"Hell if I know, man."

He was ready to give up when the wall behind the clerk moved. Something creaked. And the movement became a door opening. The door was not hidden so much as disguised, with paper and mirrors and cigarette shelves mounted to it. Daniel hadn't noticed it at all, which he guessed was probably the point.

The gentleman who emerged wore a sleek gray Armani suit with his slick black mane pulled into a pony tail. As much as he should have, the newcomer failed to surprise Daniel. When dealing with a man like Marcus McComber, few things should surprise anyone, including McComber's associates. Still, Daniel felt like he'd stumbled onto a two-bit drug cartel, or worse yet, a thrilling, novelized version of an espionage ring. If he hadn't been genuinely uneasy, he might have laughed.

"May I help you?" the newcomer asked, ignoring the clerk.

Daniel recognized the voice. "Yes," he said. "We spoke on the phone."

"Ah, the Pennyroyal."

"You said you sold a large quantity to a man wearing black. Do you remember anything more?"

"Not much. It was rainy, dark, and he wore a hood."

"How long ago do you think that was? A few weeks?"

"Oh yes, probably more."

"But you can't describe him?"

"I'm sorry." The gentleman eyed Daniel suspiciously. "Are you a cop?" he asked.

"No. I'm a doctor." The man's concern didn't appear to lessen. "A patient of mine overdosed on Pennyroyal, and I think someone fed it to her. I'm trying to find out who."

"But you're not a cop?"

"Doctor."

"So you have no plans to bring the police into this?"

At first, Daniel wondered if this stranger might be covering for someone, for McComber even, but then he guessed otherwise. Likely, the bills behind the counter didn't come from legitimate sales, and this gentleman wanted to protect his supply chain. Normally, Daniel might call the authorities to report the store, as was his medical duty, but now he just wanted information. "No police," he said.

"Then I have one other bit of information for you. I don't think it will help much, primarily because of what it must mean. But the man you're looking for, the one wearing black, he's not a regular customer of mine. I've only seen him twice. Once, when he bought the herbs, and then again not long ago."

"Not sure how that helps me, unless you expect him back."

"No. I doubt he's coming back."

"Why is that?"

"He's leaving town. Last time he was here, he bought some travel brochures."

§

Breeana Lyons shivered, gliding through the yellow walls toward a room in Daniel Jefferson's office. She'd been home from the hospital an entire week and showed no signs of further poisoning. Her appetite had slowly returned, and the pain in her abdomen was nearly gone. New pains had taken its place, but they were emotional. Not of much interest, she guessed, to the nurse who had questioned her.

Once alone in the room, the lights blinding, the air artificially refreshed, she sat and took deep breaths, trying to calm a storm of emotions. She had only half finished Jacob's manuscript, but so far it was heart-wrenching and phenomenal. She kept the manuscript secret. Not sure why, she figured the situation could only be worsened if Marcus discovered it. As a result, she had difficulty finding time to read. Since she'd come home and promised to leave with him, Marcus had spent countless hours at her house and in her bed, pestering her daily to choose a destination. She let him grope and grab and penetrate, but she felt no passion, no love. Not that it didn't exist. She simply didn't feel it as before. Perhaps unfairly, her mind preoccupied itself with Jacob's lovelorn protagonist, whose suffering surely mirrored the turmoil she had inflicted upon the author. And though she felt no regret for their very necessary separation, still she felt the guilt of responsibility. She began to sympathize with the character, with his struggle, with his quest to change his life and win back his love. When lost in the pages of Jacob's book, Marcus McComber became an afterthought.

"How we feeling today?" Daniel said as he came through the door, scurrying about the small room staring at his clipboard or arranging supplies, edgy and apparently eager to avoid her gaze.

"Better. Physically."

"Emotionally?"

"How do you think?"

He turned toward her. His face flushed with concern. He had questions on his mind again, she could see, but she had to hear them to know what they were.

"You shouldn't be alone so much," he said. "Do you have family or friends you could talk to? Spend some time with?"

"I'm not alone."

He was obviously curious, but she doubted he had any idea how intimate she and Marcus had become. He returned to his clipboard, all business. "We'll take some blood. Screen for toxins. If they'd been reintroduced to your system so quickly, I'm certain you'd have felt the effects by now. So the news on that front is good. Have you given any more thought to how this happened?"

She could tell by his tone he had his own ideas. "I don't know," she said.

He washed his hands in the sink. They shook with tension. Daniel had never been this nervous around her, not even when she flirted with him.

"Daniel, is something wrong?"

"How well do you know Marcus McComber?" he asked.

"We've been through this."

"I need to know."

"No you don't."

"Obviously you know him better than you let on, or you wouldn't be stalling."

"Obviously, you don't know me very well."

"I've seen him at your apartment on several occasions. I know you're with him frequently."

"He's a friend." A realization struck her. "How many occasions?"

"Several," he said. Something about the way he said it made her question his honesty. "Most recently, he was with you when you became ill."

"He's in my book club. The group occasionally meets outside the bookstore."

"So you say. I've spoken to a couple people in your book clubs. They say he never attends anymore. They say you've been frequently absent as well. And yet you still entertain him. Why?"

"Dammit, Daniel." She tried to hide her anger, but these days her emotions were too raw to be disguised. "What does this have to do with my health? I came here because you asked me to. You say I'm recovering well. Everything is good. So can I go now?"

"You can leave any time you want, Bree. I'm not interrogating you. In case you've forgotten, you were dangerously ill and we don't know why. Don't you want to learn the truth?"

"Of course I do."

"Then tell me about Marcus McComber. How often are you with him?"

A growing sense of rage began to infiltrate her words. "I see him once or twice a week, if at all."

"And how well do you know him?"

"That's a ridiculous question. How well do you know me?"

"I'm your doctor."

"You know my anatomy. You don't know my thoughts. You don't know my world."

"I know why you were sick, and I think I know how. If not how, then who. And I suspect you can guess what I mean."

"You think Marcus poisoned me? That's absurd."

"What if I told you I had proof?"

"I'd say show it to me."

"I can't."

"That's not proof."

"A pharmacy," he said. "Nearby. They sold Marcus a large quantity of Pennyroyal."

"I don't believe you."

"I was there."

"How did they know it was Marcus?"

"Well…"

"They didn't, did they?"

"Not exactly. But they gave a description."

"Which was?"

He frowned. "A man wearing black."

"You're right, Daniel. That's got to be Marcus. No one else in the history of the world has ever worn black."

"It has to be," he pleaded.

She shook her head. "If there's one thing I learned the past few months, after suffering years of Jacob's disinterest, it's to speak my mind. Make myself heard. And this is what my mind is telling me now. You're Jacob's friend. You don't like Marcus. You think we have some romantic connection, and so you want to turn me against him. It's not going to happen. Yes, I want to know how I got sick. But no, I don't think Marcus is responsible. In fact, I know he's not. It's impossible. He doesn't cook, so he didn't poison my food. I usually pour the wine, so he didn't poison my drinks. He's never given me candy and he's never stuck a needle in me. Only you do that. So maybe you're the poisoner, Daniel. Maybe you did it."

"That's ridiculous."

"No more so than your accusations."

Daniel bowed his head, apparently exasperated. Bree didn't believe he had poisoned her, but it was the only way she could get her point across.

Once she knew that Daniel understood, she stormed out of the office, never intending to return.

§

Jacob watched Bree emerge and cross the street with a scowl on her face. That might be good news.

Seated on a plush sofa in a café across the street, with his face butted against the cold window pane, steamy breath condensing on the glass, he felt anger and hope at the same time. Anger that she had gone to see Daniel. Hope that his book convinced her to end the relationship. The scenario would explain her apparent mood, but he was not a fool enough to assume he guessed correctly.

Still, he thought maybe the tide was receding, maybe the dark moon was falling from the sky, maybe the autumn would end and spring would begin, because the winter of his discontent had already proven cold and everlasting.

Maybe she would love him again. Maybe his hope was justified. He would give her one more week and then all the maybes would be definite, for better or worse.

CHAPTER TWENTY-FIVE

One Week Ago

When they sat down to a late night meal, Bree suspected McComber's usual grin hid something new. She wondered why every time she looked at men these days she suspected them of harboring dark, damning secrets they planned to reveal only when she might be most inconvenienced. What wrong had she enacted upon them that they might all be out to harm her? None, so far as she could tell. Admittedly, the notion was silly, but as life continued to exploit her, to subject her to the whims of a handful of others, to let men like Marcus and Jacob and Daniel dictate her thoughts and her actions, she realized it would soon become necessary to take control of her own life. She thought she'd done so when she left Jacob, but in retrospect she understood what she did was leave the world of one man for the different but equally confining world of another. It wasn't bitterness she felt but a simple desire to control her own fate. She promised herself that when the opportunity came she would seize it.

Unfortunately, the time was not now. Her head ached, filled with questions and contradictions. Her emotions, sheltered behind a crumbling wall that threatened to collapse at any moment, were under siege by forces she could neither see nor manipulate. Life plodded along through turbulent waters. She felt alone on a rotting boat with white spray in the air and destructive rocks ahead. Would the boat rot and drown her before it could be destroyed upon the rocks, or would she starve to death, alone in the waters, besieged by forces she didn't understand? Could you even be under siege while at sea? With so many thoughts battling inside her head, she couldn't keep her metaphors aligned. That realization provoked a chuckle.

"What is it you find funny now?" Marcus asked with his normal smugness.

"I'd ask you the same," she said, "but you always have that silly grin on your face."

"Something always amuses me."

"What is it now?"

"Ah, the same question I asked you. I defer until you answer."

She stared across the table. Marcus sat with his back straight, a dignified posture that might imply a proper upbringing or, more likely, conceit. "I'm sorry," she said.

"For what?"

"I've been in a foul mood of late."

"I haven't noticed."

"Then you weren't paying attention."

"Perhaps it has something to do with Jacob's manuscript?"

She expected her nerves to quiver, her head to throb, her throat to tighten at the idea of Marcus's discovery, but none of that happened. She felt calm, almost relieved to be rid of the lie. "It has nothing to do with that," she said.

"Is it new?"

"What?"

"The manuscript. Is it new? Or do you feel the need to relive your youth?"

"It's new. He brought it here last week." She watched him for signs of insecurity. She saw none.

"How very nice of him. And have you read it?"

"Most of it."

"And?"

"It's marvelous. The best he's ever written."

"What's it about?"

"If you need to know, you can read it yourself."

"You'll allow it?"

"Of course."

"So is this Jacob's attempt to win you back? His attempt to seduce you back into his uneventful, unloving, unadventuresome world?"

"I guess."

"Is it working?"

She squeezed her fork, grinded her teeth. Again, Marcus seemed effortlessly able to read her thoughts, to force her to confront him before completely understanding her emotions. Too often that meant telling him the truth about something she might be better served keeping to herself. Allow a man to know everything about you, regardless of how much you love or despise him, and you have nothing left, no secrets of your own. And everyone needs a secret.

"No," she said. "It's not working."

"I wonder."

"And what is there to wonder about? Don't you believe me?"

"Perhaps you don't really know if it's working? Perhaps it is, and you're simply denying the truth to yourself."

The fork quivered in her hand. "Don't be ridiculous."

"Then why have you stalled? Why won't you decide on our new home? Do you regret the decision?"

"Of course not. I hated my life with Jacob. You know that. I don't want that back. And why shouldn't I take time to make a decision? It's not an easy one. Wouldn't be for you either. So I want to consider each possibility carefully. What's wrong with that?"

"No need to get defensive."

"I'm not being defensive. But you're being impatient. Especially considering the importance of my choice."

He pushed his chair away from the table, rising to take his empty plate to the kitchen. "I do apologize," he said, mockingly.

If she felt calm before, she felt agitated now.

"Marcus," she said. "Do you know what Pennyroyal is?"

He emerged from the kitchen, chin up, brows raised, eyes fixated beyond the ceiling. "Hmm. Tea, isn't it?"

She nearly laughed at his exaggerated mannerisms. "It is. It's also something more than that. Something worse. Any ideas?"

"I imagine it's an herb. Most teas are made from herbs. But that's simply a guess."

"It is an herb, yes. A dangerous herb. Toxic. And you know what it's sometimes used for?"

"I'm sure you'll tell me."

"To abort a pregnancy."

His acting quickly stopped and his muscles tensed. His feigned expressions suddenly bore the markings of sincere thought.

"Did you already know that?" she asked, confused.

"No," he said, walking towards her.

"The doctors found it in my blood when I lost the baby."

He maneuvered behind her, quiet and serious. She felt goose bumps ripple across her skin. His hands came to rest on her shoulders and he massaged them, strong fingers kneading the suddenly knotted fibers of muscle. She'd considered Daniel's accusation for days. She knew it wasn't true. It's couldn't be. Marcus couldn't have poisoned her without her knowing. It just wasn't possible.

"What is it, Marcus?" she asked. "What's wrong?"

She felt his lips near her ear, heard his quick, nasally breaths like the hiss of an old, powerful locomotive steam engine. And then she heard his voice, soft but commanding, gentle but firm, one contradiction after another, a whisper that at times had brought rapture or euphoria but now drew anxiety and unease. "I wish you hadn't mentioned Pennyroyal," he said. His fingers dug hard into her shoulders. His grasp grew stronger. His breathing whistled through her ear like a winter gale through a mountain pass, chilling and unforgiving.

"Why?" It was barely a whisper.

"This won't be easy for you to hear."

Her heart was the bead in a child's rattle, leaping and slamming against her insides with a deafening, interminable racket. Her muscles tensed further and Marcus kneaded harder. She felt pain but was too nervous to act, not that she could break free if she tried.

"What are you doing, Marcus?"

"I have to tell you," he said.

She was frightened, truly frightened, but she wouldn't believe he was a monster. "You're hurting me!"

And quickly he let go. He rubbed her shoulders where the kneading had been most intense. "I'm sorry," he said.

She felt the room spinning, saw her vision blur and refocus as Marcus walked around the table to sit across from her. Once she regained her breath, once the room's equilibrium returned to reality, she opened her eyes and spoke. "What won't be easy for me to hear?" she asked.

He tilted his head in obvious pity. She grew even more confused. "I didn't know," he said. "Why didn't you tell me they found Pennyroyal?"

"Why upset you?"

"You should've told me."

"Why?"

"Because I know where it came from."

Her face might have exhibited shock had it not already been overrun by bewilderment. "Where?"

"A few weeks ago, before you went to the hospital, I was at the tavern having a pleasant conversation with the bartender, a rather blunt, offensive fellow named Ferley. Anyway, a few stools down, Jacob and your doctor friend, Jefferson, they were deep in conversation. Old doc whipped out a prescription bottle. He slid it across the bar to your favorite little author. I didn't see what was in it, and until now I didn't think I understood any of their conversation. But when you mentioned the herb, I was struck by the realization that Pennyroyal was exactly the thing they'd been discussing."

He paused, watching her expression shift to disbelief.

"When you told me its use," he added, "and named it as the cause of your miscarriage, well, you understand my horror."

"What are you saying?"

He leaned back in his chair, no hint of a grin on his face. "I'm saying what you think I'm saying. The Pennyroyal came from your husband, who got it from your doctor. Daniel was simply a conspirator, I think." He stared squarely into her eyes. He said, "Jacob was the one. Jacob must have poisoned you."

CHAPTER TWENTY-SIX

Five Days Ago

Doubt infiltrated the tavern. It clung to the clothes, permeated the wood. It lurked at all the tables and claimed its own stool at the bar. Jacob felt it on his skin, clammy like perspiration, cold and sticky, uncomfortable. And he felt it polluting his brain. It was a black cloud of uncertainty defiling all his intentions and hopes. He doubted himself, he doubted others, he doubted everything.

"I'm sure it's fantastic," Daniel said.

"You've haven't read it."

"Nevertheless, I'm sure it's fantastic."

They shared a drink for the first time in a month.

"Being mocked doesn't help my confidence, you know," Jacob said.

"I wouldn't think so. But I'm not mocking you. In fact, I'd be happy to read it if you let me."

"It's not meant for you."

"So you say."

They sat at the bar, at the opposite end of the side entrance. A crowd of both sexes plagued the tavern tonight, grumpy patrons wet and cold from another storm, forced inside to drink away their misery. They ingested barrels of ale and kegs of beer, and with each empty mug they grew grumpier and more rambunctious. Their pantomimed whining and slurred tales of woe made it difficult for Jacob and Daniel to converse, and so they shared their drink in a silence broken only by an occasional criticism or sarcastic remark.

Jacob decided it was for the best. He had nothing to say to his friend. Nothing short of accusations or ridicule. He feigned cordiality, drinking his beer and minding his manners. This was neither the time nor the place to reveal his suspicions. Yet somehow, despite his efforts, the subject of Bree came up, and Daniel had asked about the novel.

"When will you see her again?" Daniel asked.

"Soon."

"Don't worry. She'll love it, I'm sure."

"You're guessing."

"Of course I am. But my guesses are based on probabilities. Consider her predicament, and consider her admiration of literature, and consider her words when you two split. I'm sure she'll love it."

"Your voice is not so confident."

"I suppose, if I'm honest, one might find reasons to doubt my guess, reasons other than the doubts of an author."

"What do you mean?"

"Authors, Jacob, like yourself, are inherently insecure about their writing, at least until they become wildly successful, so your doubts are a natural product of having written a novel and allowed another person to read it. In addition, that person happens to be your wife, your estranged wife, and you've placed a great deal of hope in the power of that novel. All these things create doubt."

"But that's not what you meant."

"I suppose." Daniel drained his mug. Jacob knew he was stalling.

"No no," Jacob pressed, "tell me what you meant. What other reasons exist to doubt she'll love it?"

"It might not be any good."

Jacob straightened his back, rolled his eyes. He wore his anger in the pocket of his coat: concealed, but easily produced. There were reasons Daniel hadn't mentioned, reasons involving Daniel himself, but he would let them slide until his current plan failed. He had seen Bree's face on that threshold, her pink cheeks backed by the inviting aromas of home and fronted by a soft blanket of snow, and he knew he'd made an impression. He knew by the way she let one ear drop, the way she exhaled through parted lips, the way her loosely clasped fingers dangled in front of her waist. She could not lie in such a relaxed, defenseless posture. He had managed to get his foot in the door, not literally but figuratively, and that was his goal. In another day or two he would return, this time with new goals. This time he would win back his wife back. This time he would steal her away from his old friend.

A clamor suddenly broke out at a nearby table. Both men turned to see the hefty Angus Ferley bear-hugging two gentleman who squealed as they rose into the air.

"It's bad enough you whine, bad enough you bicker," Angus shouted, "but when you refuse to pay, I'm afraid we're nearing odds." He bucked the two men toward the door, squeezing and constricting, slamming them into wooden beams, punishing them for attempted thievery. At the door, Angus motioned to a patron who then reached into each man's coat pockets fishing for coin. When he produced a handful of cash, Angus said, "I only want what they owe." He launched both men down the short stairs into the alley where they bounced and rolled and cried, and then he tossed their extra money after them.

A moment later, above the hushed murmurs that followed Angus back to the bar, Daniel said, "How well do you know Marcus McComber?"

Jacob laughed. Initially, he dismissed the question as irrelevant. Marcus McComber hadn't plucked his wife. Marcus McComber hadn't betrayed him. Marcus McComber was a sly but drunken rambler whose only true gift, other than a handsome profile, was a miraculous ability to spin nonsense into grand fiction. Who cared about Marcus McComber when the debaser of his spouse sat inches away?

"Will you answer me?" Daniel asked. "I need to know."

"Why?"

"Is it not enough that I ask, and that I, as your friend, expect an answer?"

Friend? Is that the punishment of a traitor? To be called friend? Or, he thought, is the traditional punishment more appropriate? Death. Execution. Both seem more adequate than friendly name calling.

"We have grown apart," Jacob said, concealing his anger only a touch. "Surely you've noticed. We may live beneath the same decrepit roof, and we may share a long history, but such circumstances are not exclusive to friendship."

Daniel's face crinkled with confusion. "Bitter today?"

Avoiding a nasty confrontation required all of Jacob's effort. "Not bitter, no. Hateful. Resentful. Sure. But not bitter. Bitterness is for the weak, for those who do nothing but cry over missed opportunities. By no means am I bitter."

Daniel perked up at Jacob's unusual demonstration of emotion. "What's gotten into you then? Who do you hate? McComber? Me?"

"I don't know." He wanted to demand an explanation. If only he could ask why. Why had Daniel done it? If the answer was loneliness and unbearable yearning, perhaps he could forgive. But if, as he suspected, the urge had long been brewing and Daniel had seized, or perhaps instigated, an opportunity, Jacob would want revenge. Unfortunately, he couldn't bring himself to ask. Not yet.

"If you don't know then you've got to relax. Bottled up emotions, when shaken, act just like bottled soda. The pressure builds on itself, until relief can only come in a sudden explosive outburst. You don't want that. I don't want that."

"I'm concerned. That's all."

"About the book?"

"Yes, the book."

"Ah, well, that's understandable. But forget it a minute and tell me what you know of Marcus McComber."

Jacob felt his anger quelled, but he could no longer sit. He stood and shoved his stool under the bar.

"What?" Daniel asked, standing. "Can't you tell me what you know?"

"Why? What does it matter? McComber's a storytelling drunk and half of what I know is mostly fiction while the other half is absolute lies. Why do you care and how can the little I know help you?"

"I don't trust him."

"Neither do I. So don't ask him to do you any favors, and don't let him talk you into getting any barrels of ale. You'll end up lost in his catacombs, and he'll teach you all you need to know about getting buried alive. I'm leaving."

"What's that supposed to mean?"

"Leaving? It means that in a few seconds I won't be here anymore. Quite rudimentary, but I see how one of your education might not grasp it."

"What catacombs?" Daniel asked.

"Beneath the tavern. He loves it down there. I'm sure he spends all night roaming those tunnels, concocting new stories and thinking up new ways to murder his lover's husband."

At that Daniel's face went limp. Jacob didn't understand or care to. McComber was a nuisance. Jacob admired his storytelling ability but it had grown lax, degenerating to a point where McComber could do nothing but relive redundant tales of sex and betrayal and exotic locales. Daniel, however, had become his nemesis, and if he didn't leave immediately, he might reveal his emotions in quite an inappropriate matter.

Fearing Angus's wrath, he happily paid his tab. Then he stormed out the exit, leaving Daniel lost in his own guilt. The time had come to learn the truth. The time had come for his last effort. He would go home and sleep, and in the morning he would set off on the final leg of a grand adventure. His destination would be Bree's front door.

CHAPTER TWENTY-SEVEN

Five Days Ago

For her part, Breeana Lyons finished Jacob's manuscript that afternoon. It was not a quick read, nor was it uneventful or cumbersome. The pace quickened gradually, culminating in an emotional demonstration of will by the protagonist as he fought for his life and his love. After reading the final words, after regaining her lost breath, after suffering the torture and agony of witnessing Jacob's obvious pain and turmoil, Bree set the pages on her nightstand and cried. The story hadn't really ended. With the battle won, with his energy renewed and life improved, the protagonist kneels at the feet of his beloved and takes her hand, strokes it, kisses it. He offers himself to her unconditionally. And as she is about to speak, as the typewriter must have itched to begin her quotation, a few blank lines interrupt the narrative and end with a solitary word. "Continued…" Jacob's metaphorical autobiography was unfinished, and the rest, as they say, was up to her.

But was she worthy of so grand a vision? Jacob had written his most important work, his best work, and knowing that her actions, her behavior, her life, would determine its resolution or fill the pages of its sequel struck her as intolerable. Had she not been so intimidated by its directness, by how it shifted accountability for their failed marriage from Jacob to her, she might have been offended that her life had been used so blatantly to fill the pages of a novel. The author had painted the protagonist in flawed colors, wrong hues, to illustrate his humanity and guilt and sorrow. But the female lead, the treasure of the protagonist's fantastical love, was perfect and pure, seduced by evil but not at fault, lured by lies and misdeeds into the lion's den. She was perfect, a flower whose petals had not yet been ravaged by sun and wind, a crystalline sky unmarred by storm clouds. Jacob had apologized for his own flaws by giving them to his main character, but he allowed hers to be forgotten. Bree's choices and decisions would now determine if those flaws materialized in the sequel. Sadly, she didn't know the ending herself.

She spent the afternoon in town. Her mind, however, was elsewhere. An infrequent rain came often enough to wet her hair and dampen her shoes. With her head down, eyes roaming the puddled concrete underfoot, she rarely noticed the gloomy skies or the absence of shadow around her. She walked the streets of uncertainty, a gray nothingness that provided no instruction as to how best she might purify her soul or make a decision.

The questions were no longer easy, and the details began to agitate. How genuine was Jacob's manuscript? How accurate was Marcus's warning that Jacob had poisoned her? How big a part did Daniel's friendship with Jacob influence his distrust of Marcus? And worst of all, how was she to possibly answer any of those questions? Who could she trust? How could she take control of her life without understanding all the forces tugging at her?

She passed the church where she and Marcus once spoke. In the gray afternoon light it seemed cold and terrifying.

She passed Café Noir, where several clandestine meetings with Marcus had led her to a new life of passion and adventure. Unfortunately, that passion and adventure had fizzled. Marcus seemed distant of late, more reserved, less exciting, certainly more secretive. Or maybe he seemed more distant because she herself had become more distant. She ignored his calls, avoided him, made excuses. She wanted to read Jacob's manuscript and Marcus was an obstacle. So here again it seemed she had instigated many of her own problems.

But that wasn't true, she thought. She wasn't the instigator. It was the men who loved or claimed to love her who created the dilemmas.

Eventually, as the sun fell from the sky beyond the clouds and colored the world a peculiar shade of orange, she found herself at the bookstore. It had been weeks since she last heard the bell toll at her entrance, an eternity since she last hosted a book club meeting. The old wood-framed corkboard sat near the curb. The parchment tacked to it read, in a script obviously not her own, "Tonight: *The Oval Portrait*, by Edgar Allan Poe." She knew the story, but not well, and could not recall when she had read it, whether in high school or college or sometime later. It was not a selection she would've made, and it was the selection itself which instilled in her a curiosity to know who had taken over responsibility for the book club in her absence. So she entered.

The bell tolled. She shook rain off her coat, pulled her matted hair back to keep it from her face. The familiar mustiness engulfed her, and the inviting aroma of brewing coffee elicited a relaxed, calming sensation that, for a short while, brought relief. At the bookstore, more than anywhere else, Breeana Lyons felt at home and at peace.

"My dear, dear Bree," cried a familiar voice. "Dear, child, how wonderful to see you!"

She rushed behind the counter to embrace her mother's former lover, the venerable Ellis Fitzgerald, owner of the bookstore. The casual observer would find their relationship strange, but not Bree. "Hello, Elly," she laughed. "I missed you."

"And I you."

Ellis Fitzgerald, who might have become her step-father, who, in a way, had indeed become her step-father, was her only link to a dead past. Always the nicest, most decent man, he now looked to her with pitiful eyes and a mournful face.

"How's business?" she asked, ignoring his gloom.

"Not great, but we'll survive."

"Why the slow down?"

He averted his gaze, apparently unsure how to answer. After a minute, he relented, "To be honest, which, I assume, is how you always want me to be, and oh, sweetheart, how gifted you are at bringing me to it. In fact, I don't care to be honest at all, don't desire it in the least, but, since this is you, and like I said, you bring out the best, I will be, as much as possible, as truthful as I can."

"I don't understand."

"Well, the slowdown, that's what you called it, not I, mind you… It is, well, and I don't mean this in any way you might construe as negative or bitter, it's because, and I suppose this may be speculation, but, well, wait, let me explain. As you know, my lovely child, our best days, those when our sales spike upward, well you know it happens only on those nights when everyone gathers for the book meetings. They come, they buy drinks, they buy books. They support us, you know, keep the ink black. I don't want to say this, especially not to you, my sweet dear, but we slowed down when the book meetings ended."

"Oh, Elly," she said, "it's my fault? Is it really? My goodness, but I'm so sorry."

"Don't be sorry, dear. Don't do that to yourself. You're not to blame, and we don't blame you."

"But it is my fault. And I'm sorry."

"It's not your fault. But, if you don't mind me asking, what kept you away?"

She couldn't tell him. Not a chance, especially with the guilt thumping her skull. She couldn't say she'd been out having an affair. He seemed to notice her unease, because he said, "Oh never mind, never mind. None of my business. You're a young lady with a busy life and no need to make excuses to an old curmudgeon like me."

"You are not a curmudgeon." She squeezed the old man in another embrace. "And I'm so sorry. But I do have one question."

"Which is?"

"You say the book meetings stopped. But what about the sign at the curb? *The Oval Portrait* by Poe, tonight? Is it an old sign? And if so, who put it there? I never suggested we read *The Oval Portrait*."

"Please understand, and don't be offended, because I don't mean it as an offense, but because of our decreased business, I've taken it upon myself to reinstitute the book clubs."

"You're leading them?"

"No, no, not me. I can't read fast enough to keep up with the younger folk."

"Who then?"

"Your friend, I think. Do you remember Gladys? She's always been a great customer. Friendly, polite. I adore her, and I offered her the job and she took it."

She remembered Gladys. The woman was friendly enough and had always teased her about the physical condition of her favorite Poe collection. "But when is the meeting?"

"Ahh, soon. Gladys prefers the early evening, whereas you entertained late at night. In fact, I'd guess they'll start in a few minutes. She's already in back with most of the group."

"Think they'd mind if I stopped by?"

"Not hardly. They'll be flabbergasted. Go right on back, go ahead now."

She hugged him. "Thank you, and again, I'm sorry."

"Ahh, never mind that now." His dentured grin was long and genuine, but the guilt she felt at letting him down had breathed new life into her other worries.

She navigated the maze of aisles, a feat she could accomplish with eyes closed, and found a crowd gathered on the sofas and chairs of the sitting area. The gray-haired, lanky Gladys sat perched on the center chair, conversing in whispers with another woman beside her. A few of the others she recognized, but the group had grown larger in her absence. Gladys must be a gifted leader, Bree thought, or she must have more friends. Bree hung back in the shadows, half-hiding behind several stacks of books waiting to be shelved. A moment later, she decided she was being ridiculous.

With her chin up, feigning confidence, she took a seat with the others.

Gladys saw her but made no effort to wave. Rather, she began flipping the pages of her book, shifting her eyes everywhere but toward Bree, asking a question of the woman beside her, and fidgeting however possible for the sole purpose, in Bree's opinion, of avoidance.

And so it went for several minutes. Bree felt awkward and uncomfortable with no book and no control in a place where she once ran everything. Like the ruler of a kingdom now the subject of a conquering power, she felt helpless, humiliated, deposed. The sensation grew worse once the session began.

"I hope everyone enjoyed the story," Gladys said, and a chorus of agreement followed. "It's brief, but in those few words Poe establishes a character every woman can identify with, perhaps a character every man might also identify with. For at its heart, this is a story about unrequited love, or the belief that love has gone unrequited, and the willingness to sacrifice one's existence, or, if you take the story as metaphor, to give up one's self, to put forth the ultimate effort, whether fatal or self-destructive, because of that love. There's no need for anyone to summarize, given the story's brevity, but for the few of you who haven't read it, let me give you the quick narrative. A man spends a night intrigued by a painting on the wall, an oval portrait of a young lady that, to the narrator, seems frighteningly life-like. In a book at his bedside, he finds a tale of the portrait. It seems the young woman who posed for the picture had married the artist and found herself competing against Art itself for the painter's affection. He so madly desired to paint her in the most life-like manner, was so excited by it and eager, she ultimately felt compelled to allow it. The arduous process, made worse by her jealousy, ultimately doomed her. And when the artist painted the last stroke, when he stepped back and marveled at the life imbued in his painting, he looked up to find the young woman, in her chair, still posing, but dead. There the story ends."

Bree paid little attention to the discussion, though she remembered the story. It was melancholic and disturbing. The poor woman became so threatened by the painter's love of art she died trying to overcome it, or perhaps to become it. If she became art itself, wouldn't he love her more? It was almost as disturbing as Gladys's refusal to acknowledge her, though she sat only three rows back.

"Anyone have any thoughts they'd like to discuss?" Gladys asked.

A sickly woman, or perhaps so thin as to appear languid, muttered, "Why did she care so much? Why not accept, like most of us eventually do, that men don't truly love any one thing, and when they do, it is generally something other than a woman? Isn't that right? Why should a woman sacrifice so much for a man? It's just so counterproductive, and no one can overcome nature. It's impossible. Art, like gambling or drinking, is her man's vice, and she ought to accept it."

"Well," Gladys said, "that's a whale of starter. Thank you, Lorraine. Anyone care to take a stab at it?" No one did. "Okay, well, while I don't know for sure and won't concede that most men don't love any single thing, or person, I would argue that it's possible to love two things equally and simultaneously. My guess is that, perhaps, this artist was better at expressing his love of art than his love for his bride. Being young, innocent, unwise, perhaps the girl couldn't understand, and so felt threatened. It would be a natural progression, to eventually grow to hate that which you are jealous of."

Bree realized Gladys was quite good at leading the discussion, and she might have been impressed if the subject of the talk had not struck a discordant note inside her head.

"Poe writes," Gladys said, preparing to quote from the story:

> *"She was a maiden of rarest beauty, and not more lovely than full of glee. And evil was the hour when she saw, and loved, and wedded the painter. He, passionate, studious, austere, and having already a bride in his Art; she a maiden of rarest beauty, and not more lovely than full of glee: all light and smiles, and frolicsome as the young fawn: loving and cherishing all things: hating only the Art which was her rival: dreading only the pallet and*

> *brushes and other untoward instruments which deprived her of the countenance of her lover."*

"Surely," Gladys continued, "the Artist loved both his work and his wife. These two loves need not be dichotomous. In fact, one will likely supplement the other. His love for Art heightens his sense of beauty, both physical and emotional, and that increased sensitivity strengthens his appreciation and love for his bride. Therefore, his wife is the fool. She is the more selfish. Rather than acknowledge his love of Art and encourage it, because doing so will strengthen his love of her, the young beauty hates it, detests the attention it garners, and ultimately, by desiring more attention for herself, lets it consume her."

"And the lesson here?" Lorraine asked, in obvious disagreement.

Gladys looked to Bree. Her stare, if not blank, displayed the tiniest shred of pity. Bree needed not hear a word to understand the lesson. It seemed Gladys paid more attention to Bree's life than Bree paid to it herself. For in that moment, Gladys delivered a harsh criticism, a painful critique on Bree's decision to leave Jacob for Marcus. "The lesson," she said, "is that what may appear, on the surface, to be something less than love, or even the love of something deemed lesser than oneself, may, in fact, be the truest, most selfless love of all. And though it may not be glamorous, though it may not be adventurous, it is honest, and it can be as exciting as one makes it. Human beings suffer endlessly, and those who still find enough love in their souls, who can love more than themselves, more than the person or persons with whom they copulate, they are the souls to treasure. They are the souls to love. To do otherwise is selfish and ignoble."

At that, Bree lunged to her feet. Her chair fell backwards and broke on the ceramic floor with a clutter that focused everyone's attention on her alone. Gladys remained seated.

"Is something wrong?" Gladys asked. Her smug grin stoked Bree's anger.

"How dare you," Bree said.

"If you don't mind, we're having a discussion here."

"This isn't a discussion. It's a sermon. Do you enjoy condemning me in front of the group?"

"I have no idea what—"

"You do so. You stared right at me when you said it. And who are you? Who are you to tell me how to run my life? How are you such an expert on love and adventure?"

"Bree, you obviously misunderstood. I was talking about the story. Don't make a scene."

"Why didn't you acknowledge me until just now? Why wait until just before your obvious critique of my life? Why look at that moment? Why, if not to criticize me, if not to demean me? Who are you to understand?"

"I'm sorry if I offended you. It wasn't intentional. I just noticed you there, and was happy to see you. Until now, that is."

But Bree refused to back down. She didn't care if the entire group stared at her. She looked like a lunatic out for unjustifiable revenge. So what? Gladys had no place to criticize her choices. She had good reasons for what she had done. Jacob loved her, yes, but he didn't show it. He spent all his time writing or drinking. He certainly didn't spend it with her, and he certainly didn't notice her suffering. She had no choice but to leave him, if only to make him aware. And Marcus… Marcus might love her, but she wasn't entirely sure. He said he did. Until recently, he showed it constantly. And he was dark and brooding and handsome, like some mysterious character from a book, the perfect man for her. It was the right thing to do, she knew. It must have been. Right? She had no other choices. It was unavoidable, unless she desired only misery. But why was it unavoidable? Why couldn't Jacob show her a little more love? Why did he put her to that decision in the first place? Why? And, though she didn't want to admit it, Bree knew this discussion had nothing to do with her situation. How could it? Gladys hadn't known Bree would be here. Bree herself didn't know she would be here. So the entire situation had been coincidental. But that story seemed to scream at her, to point its haunting finger and poke her in the chest. Poking, prodding, over and over and over…

Something struck her, an idea so obvious and yet so elusive, so dependent upon *The Oval Portrait* and Edgar Allan Poe she would never believe that being here tonight was simply a coincidence. "My God," she said, sighing.

"If you don't mind…" Gladys wanted to return to the discussion.

"You were right. I didn't see it."

"Excuse me?"

"About love and dichotomy. About a man's ability to love two things simultaneously. And yet, you were also wrong."

"You're interrupting. Please sit down."

"I know, but this is a discussion, right? You said, I think, that a man's love for one thing will supplement his love for another. Is that right? And in some cases, that may be true. But not always. Because if suddenly the relationship between a man and his passion becomes tumultuous, that stress, that turmoil, can cause strains in his relationship with a woman. Don't you see? If the Artist struggles with his Art, if he produces inferior works or loses his confidence, if he grows frustrated by his lack of success or lack of imagination, even if the lacking is psychological instead of real, his faith in himself will weaken. And when he feels uncertain of himself, he begins to question if others will see those same perceived faults and reject him. The Artist fears his bride will leave if he cannot overcome his problems. Still he cannot paint anything worthwhile, and his self-deprecation forces him to withdraw further into his pained little world. Every day he feels more insecure. He pulls back further and further, until he can no longer paint at all. He can no longer bear the knowing stare of his lover, who he believes must surely witness his pathetic flaws and must therefore find him weak and repulsive. Surely, he thinks, his bride considers him a failure. And so a struggle with one relationship, that of the Artist and his painting, rips through another relationship, that of the Artist and his wife. The two loves, in this case, may not be supplemental at all. Instead, they work in tandem, and each, ultimately, destroys the other."

Gladys stared for a long moment, but Bree was unmoved. She had found an insight into Jacob's mind, an answer why, for so long, his downward spiral continued unabated. His failures as a writer killed his confidence. He likely wasn't even aware. But he found an answer at the tavern, surrounded by other men who, like himself, had experienced recent failures. Daniel and his failed marriage were the most obvious examples. And though he occasionally attempted to show his love, he was embarrassed that she still loved him. And when she began to distance herself, because she felt unloved or unexcited, that only strengthened his belief in his own flaws. It wasn't until she left him that he was finally shocked out of his delirium. He gained confidence in his writing again because there was no longer anyone to answer to, no one to stare at him every day wondering if he would ever write anything meaningful. With Bree lost, he had nothing more to lose, and the restraints were removed. He wrote fervently, madly, understanding that no one expected anything of him. It was liberating, and, as a result, he produced his best work, a fantastic novel unresolved for one reason: to finish it, to make his protagonist's lover promise herself to him eternally, he would threaten his own confidence all over again. If she said yes, it would seem forced, it would seem impossibly contrived, serving only to inflate his ego and build his confidence further. If she said no, it might reinforce his own ideas of failure and shatter what confidence he had rebuilt while writing it. There was no way for him to finish without destroying himself. And so the ending he left up to her.

Now, for the first time, she knew how it would end.

"Thank you for your participation," Gladys said, then dismissed her. "Anyone else have any ideas? Anyone want to challenge Mrs. Lyons." She emphasized the name.

But Bree didn't wait for a challenger. Like a wind blowing through rustling autumn leaves, she breezed past rows of books, waved to Elly Fitzgerald behind the counter, and passed through the doorway so quickly she was gone before the bell tolled.

She felt invigorated, anxious, nervous, but her heart told her she must be right. The rains had stopped and the ceiling of clouds had broken. A starry night crowned the horizon, with a quarter moon shining on rooftops and trees. The world, usually so eerie and unforgiving, had been encrusted in silver, and she wondered if the future would be as rich as that night.

Now she would confront Marcus. She would explain to him that, while he provided her with exactly what she needed during a crucial, difficult period of time, her heart still belonged to Jacob, and it always would. Did she love Marcus? Perhaps. But Jacob was more than sex and adventure. In the morning, she would find him, and she would fall in love with him once again.

For the first time in weeks, she felt truly happy.

CHAPTER TWENTY-EIGHT

Five Days Ago

Sadly, Bree's happiness was short-lived. Marcus, once again, seemed to expect her arrival. Before she could offer a forceful knock on his apartment door, it swung open and he rushed her inside with a calm but grim face.

"We need to talk," she said.

He sat her down in the table's only chair, while he stood awkwardly beside her. She found it necessary to lift her chin to uncomfortable heights only to peer up his nostrils. But whatever mischievousness played in his mind, he seemed strangely content to listen first. "Very well."

"Is something wrong?" she asked.

"It is, yes, but you first."

And then she realized he was not content at all. He obviously had something he needed to say, and, though she didn't want to admit it to herself, he already had her so curious she couldn't possibly say what she wanted to say until hearing his story. Again she felt she was, if not helpless, certainly at Marcus's mercy. He could overcome any argument, withstand all scrutiny, and exude confidence and grace and grandeur with no apparent effort. All she could say to him, to that beautiful face, that dark complexion, that mysterious enigma named Marcus McComber, was, "I can wait. You say what you must."

He knelt beside her, on one knee but obviously without any nuptial intent. “Your husband,” he said, “I know what he did. And now, I know how he did it.”

“What are you talking about?”

“Our child,” he said, hushed, “he murdered our child.”

She felt her fingers tense, her back straighten. Her lips felt suddenly dry. “You’ve said that before, Marcus. You’ve made that claim before, and I didn’t like it then. What proof do you have now?”

“Damning evidence.”

“Really? Then let me see it.”

“Do you not believe me?”

“Of course I don’t. It’s an outlandish claim.”

“Tell me,” he said, “how else were you poisoned? Tell me the source. Tell me. I don’t think you can.”

“You know I can’t.” He was leading her, but she didn’t know where.

“What other explanation do you have?”

“None.”

He leaned toward her, pressed his lips to her ear. “Then believe me, because you must.”

When he pulled away, his hand reached into a pocket and produced a rolled cloth. He unwrapped it carefully, folding back the corners until the contents lay exposed in the palm of his hand.

She recognized them at once. “Those are vitamins,” she gasped.

“Yes.”

“Pre-natal vitamins?”

“Yes.” He was so calm, so serious, so assured.

“Are they?”

“Yes, the very brand prescribed to you by your doctor friend.”

“But I discarded what I had left, flushed them all. Where did you get these?”

He lifted her clenched fist with his one free hand, unfurled her tense fingers, and slipped a handful of pills into her palm. She straightened her elbow, offered them back, but he refused, and she held them there in her outstretched hand as if their mere proximity might kill her.

"How often did you take these?" he asked.

"Twice a day."

"Enough to poison."

"But no, these are pre-natal vitamins." She scanned them from a distance. "See the branding?"

"Indeed they are. And yet, they are more."

"Stop the riddles, Marcus."

"Very well." He stood, looking down on her, full of pity. "I brought them to the hospital to have them examined. Look closely. Your pills are white, very white. But these hold a yellowish tint. They are coated, a thin but potent coating of your herb, your Pennyroyal, and they are lethal."

Her limbs trembled, her teeth chattered. She squeezed her eyes shut, demanded unsuccessfully that her body settle down. "It can't be," she said. For several weeks she had struggled to forget the pain and heartbreak of losing her child. Now the emotions battled back, flooding her thoughts with an overwhelming foulness, festering in a pool of anxiety and sadness and anger.

"I'm afraid it can."

"But who? Who would do it?"

"Who could do it? That's the more appropriate question."

And she knew immediately. "Daniel." The name came quickly. The idea enraged her. Was he so capable of such anger? Willing to destroy her life by killing her unborn child? No wonder he spoke so vehemently about Marcus, no wonder his attempts to vilify came so often and were so severe. He hated that Marcus had stolen her from Jacob, hated that Marcus had stolen an opportunity. It was all so clear now, and yet she still couldn't believe it of Daniel.

"It was not the doctor," Marcus said, to her surprise. "He would have been my first guess had I not already known the truth. He may indeed have played some part obtaining the necessary items, may have even delivered them to your prescription bottle, but he was not the party ultimately responsible."

Bree closed her eyes, disbelief giving way to fear. She knew the accusation Marcus was about to make, and she didn't care to hear it, though she knew she must. "Who then?" she asked to fulfill her obligation. Anger forced her into a stiff, trembling paralysis.

"It was Jacob," he said. With her eyes clenched, Bree couldn't see his evil grin, but she knew it must be there, spread menacingly across his face.

"No," she said.

"I'm afraid so."

"How? I mean, how do you know? It might have been someone else."

"I was at the tavern. I saw him there. This cloth fell from his jacket pocket. I saw it, but no one else seemed to. Not even him. Once he left I picked it up, unwrapped it, and learned the truth."

Her head grew heavier, too heavy, but at the same time it felt lighter than air. The world became surreal. The gray walls upset her balance. The heavy bookshelf in the corner spun as she melted into vertigo. "That can't be, Marcus." Even so routine a task as breathing became difficult. The original intent of her visit flittered out of memory.

"I'm afraid it is," he said. I saw it myself."

She leapt to her feet then and nearly crashed into a wall. Her steps ran every way but straight. She slammed her fists into a kitchen counter, quite unintentionally and uncontrollably, crushed her knee into a cabinet, brushed her cheek against the hallway wall, and finally found the door. She flung it open with hopeless rage and plunged down the staircase, twisting her ankle on the landing, uttering a string of profanity she'd want no child to hear and no author to inscribe. A tornado of thoughts ransacked her brain and she found no shelter in that dark cellar of fear and anger. She bolted onto the street, stumbling like a sot from a tavern and no less dizzy. Her limbs burned. Her eyes stung. Her hair, long and flowing, lashed in the wind as she ran, waving like the auburn standard of a menacing army racing into battle. Had she possessed the ability to think rationally, still her efforts to describe such emotions would have failed.

She arrived home some time later, not certain how or by what path. Her brain focused, when it focused, on Jacob Lyons, and at him she directed all her pain. She could not sleep, but she could scream; she could not eat, but she could cry. Her face grew red and agitated, then redder still beneath a torrent of tears. Tissues, so soft and silky, felt coarse and steely, like a wire brush scraping at what little skin still remained on her cheeks and nostrils. Her breathing was ragged, and whenever she calmed enough to recognize it, she grew more bitter and angry at having lost control and broke into a new fit of rage.

She went downstairs. Jacob's office was just as he left it. Reams of blank paper collected dust near the typewriter. Unsharpened pencils filled an unused coffee mug. A few scattered articles clipped from the newspaper floated in the air, tacked to the corkboard wall, and several others lay upside down on the carpet, somehow torn and fallen from their perches. She glared at it all long enough to remember it always, and then she methodically, violently, and with much satisfaction, destroyed it. She overturned the typewriter and flung paper into the air. What books Jacob left on shelves along the wall she cast onto the floor, careless of their material or psychological worth. She stepped on them, kicked them. They landed in heaps, sometimes flat, sometimes open with their spines creased and pages bent. A presence inside her head winced at the site of her own sacrilege, at books scattered and wrecked upon the carpet, but that insignificant guilt had no voting privileges in the congress of her thoughts, and the dominant emotions easily relegated it to the darker chambers of irrelevance.

Marcus came to her door some time during the night. She told him to go away. She yelled at him to leave. She cried and she begged that he stop knocking and stop calling her name. She wanted only silence and to be alone with her fury. Eventually she let him in, unable even now to resist his urging, and he held her and spoke words of comfort that had no effect. He might as well be elsewhere for all the attention she paid him. She was lost in her own fiery world. He asked her to go away with him. He said it was the best way to escape, to put the past behind them. She scolded him for his worthless clichés and demanded he leave. Eventually, he did, but only after insisting she leave with him. They would vanish into their own Heaven, travel the world, from the careless tropics to historical Rome, from the snowy Appalachians to the darkest, loveliest bookshops of Germany. The world was theirs to explore. "But why are you so hurried to leave?" she asked.

"Eternity with you cannot begin soon enough," he said.

And she wouldn't remember if she gave him an answer, though he would insist she had agreed to go, and she wouldn't remember him leaving, but eventually, at some early hour when the skies lightened from a deep blue to darkened gray as dawn approached, Marcus was gone.

Again, her world had flip-flopped and imploded upon itself. Just when she had figured everything out, when ideas made sense and effects were married to their causes, life cast her back into the tangled web of betrayal and loss of control she had fought so hard to escape.

And the only question, the only damning phrase burning in her enraged mind, was nothing more than a plea for help. "What," she asked herself during those scant moments between violent fits, "What am I to do now?"

CHAPTER TWENTY-NINE

Four Days Ago

It was into this maelstrom of emotions that, when the morning finally broke, full and crisp and chill, Jacob Lyons plunged unexpectedly and irrevocably. He came for Bree's critique of his manuscript, and he came to win her back. As he made his way to the front door, to the threshold across which he once carried his bride, he marveled at how fate and circumstance had brought him here at this moment. He was not a believer in fate, but excessive coincidence often served to strengthen its case. Here he was, on the brink of a new life, awaiting a verdict that would influence both his marriage and his career, and it seemed far too coincidental that both paths hinged on the words of one woman.

Still, his confidence had strengthened. He read and reread his manuscript, searching for errors, questioning character motives and incentives, but he found not a single mistyped word or contrivance, no blatant authoring devices that might distract a reader. The characters were genuine. How could they not be? They were too grounded in reality. Bree would like it. She must.

It was well after she opened the door that he realized how mistaken he had been.

"Hello, Bree," he said, impaled by her bloodshot eyes, curious about her flaring nostrils and unkempt hair and raw cheeks.

She said nothing.

"I promised I would return," he said gallantly, though his enthusiasm and confidence were quickly waning, "and here I am."

A tear, obviously the last in a procession of many, tumbled down her cheek. She raised a finger, pointed it at him, and scowled so hard a dozen more tears burst forth.

"Was it that bad?" he asked, hoping to lift the mood.

"How?" she asked, and Jacob wondered if she would continue. She did. "How can you stand there? How can you come to this door, stand there in front of me, and utter anything but an apology? How dare you."

Unfortunately, Jacob hadn't a clue why he should do anything other than what he was doing. "Is there someplace else I should stand?" he asked jokingly.

Her icy palm connected with his cheek with a loud, fat smack. "Don't make jokes now. Don't you dare."

"I'm sorry," he said, chuckling somewhat at the sudden absurdity of his situation. In all his fantasized delusions about this moment, never had he imagined a scenario where she slapped him. His brain hadn't yet caught up. "I don't know what I've done, but I'm sorry."

"So meek, are we? So humble?"

"I assure you, I haven't a clue what you're talking about. I only came to see if you read the manuscript."

Her eyes blinked with momentary recognition, but her scowl never lessened. "I did. And it was fantastic."

His blood quickened. So many planned responses hurdled toward the tip of his tongue, but he had only questions. What about it was fantastic? The writing, the story, the imagery, the emotion? Never mind that the scowl on her face suggested, despite her praise, she was somehow displeased with him. Never mind the anger in her tone. She liked his book and he forgot all else. With questions aplenty rattling inside the boney cage of his skull, he said with grand delight and an intellectual air, "Really? You liked it?" So much for planning, he thought.

"I did. It was beautiful." Anger and sadness skewed her praise, however, and Jacob settled back down to the cold concrete of the front porch. "If only it hadn't been a lie."

"A what?"

"A lie. A wicked, horrible lie."

"Umm."

"You're neither a bumbling child nor a mindless idiot, so defend yourself with more than a garbled breath. Why did you do it, Jacob? How could you?"

"Do what?" he asked. "If you mean how did I write a book, well, then, stated simply, I used a typewriter."

"You're an ass and a fool. Don't you see? I loved your manuscript. It's the best I've read in years. And your best by far. But it's all fiction. Lying, twisted, deceitful fiction."

"As it was meant to be, to some extent."

"You just don't get it, do you?"

"No."

She howled with apparent rage. It was an expression of unbridled fury Jacob had never seen from her. She was normally so mild-mannered. If provoked, she grew witty or facetious or sardonic, but never enraged or incensed. But with that howl, Jacob knew, it was as if she had finally snapped, as if all the past months of separation had finally taken a toll.

"We're finished, Jacob." She said it calmly, having suppressed the trembling in her throat and fingers. "We're through."

"But didn't you see what I was trying to say?"

"I saw it. I saw the apology in your story, and I understood the question being asked, the forgiveness sought. I saw it all, Jacob, and I nearly fell victim to the charade."

"What charade? It wasn't a charade."

The tears returned, and she reached out to him from the doorway. She took his sweater's tight-knit wool into her clutching fists and twisted it, tightened it around his neck in an act of desperation. "It was. And I believed it. I was such a fool myself, such a sucker. The story was beautiful, Jacob, beautiful writing. A strong premise, a valiant protagonist, an evil villain. It's all there, but it's all a lie. And the ending, no ending, no resolution. But we know the ending, don't we?" She began to sound positively mad, almost insane. "We know the ending, Jacob, you and I. You tried to deceive me, to trick me, to charm me into forgiveness and forgetfulness, and you thought, you did, you thought I'd take you back because you changed, because you stopped drinking. But I know the truth now. I know you sacrificed one evil for another, one vice for another. You're no drunkard now, but damn it," she was screaming, "damn it all, Jacob, I know the truth, I know what you've done and we're through. You hear me! We're through!"

Jacob, for his part, did not cower or retreat from her outburst, but he did glance around to see if any neighbors poked their heads out to spot the disturbance. He was too confused, too angry by now, to understand or act. "I assure you," he said, "I didn't do anything but write a novel."

"You're a murderer!" Her eyes beamed with hatred. They were glassy and wide and red, and he doubted she had slept much recently. He said as much, and she grew madder still. "A murderer. How dare you? How could you? I'll call the police, have them here to arrest you, have them drag you away so you can spend eternity locked up in a cell, with no paper and no pen and certainly no typewriter." She calmed outwardly, but the anger still burned. "And no me," she said. "That's the ending, Jacob. The ending you didn't write, the one you feared but must have known was inevitable. That's the ending. The one where I leave you alone with yourself and your guilt and we never see each other again."

Still uncertain, and doubting her sincerity, he said, "Whatever I've done to upset you, I am truly sorry. But don't talk like this. Don't threaten me, please. You can't leave. You wouldn't. I love you."

She laughed. It was a loud, eerie, disturbing cackle, and it quickly reminded Jacob of Marcus McComber. "On the contrary," she said, "I can leave. And I will. But it won't matter to you, because even were I to stay, I would demand you never again come to this door. Never cross my path. Never enter my vision, even at night while I sleep, because even in my dreams I will not hesitate to turn you in. I will shout and scream and plead at anyone who will listen, and I will warn them of your treachery and your dishonesty. You are a murderer, and I will tell them so."

"But..."

She didn't let him finish. "We're through. No more words. Go, Jacob. Leave. I don't want to see you. Not ever again. Go."

"But I love you."

And then she paused, and with a cold, dead voice, she said, "I don't love you anymore, Jacob." The words stung, though he would never believe them. "I could never love anyone like you, knowing what you did. You're the vilest, wickedest, saddest man I've ever seen. And I never care to see you again. You wanted revenge, and you got it, and I hope you're happy."

"Revenge?"

"You ruined two people's lives, Jacob. You did know that, right?"

"I don't know what you mean."

"Whatever Daniel told you," she said, "it was a lie. The baby you killed... It wasn't yours."

She slammed the door and left Jacob dumbstruck on the porch. It took only a few minutes for him to comprehend her last statement, and when those minutes ended he grew fiery with his own rage. He flew from the house like a raven diving toward its prey, but his prey was human. He raged with two intertwined desires: to hunt down his best friend, the traitor, the impregnator, the bastard, and to kill him.

CHAPTER THIRTY

Four Days Ago

Daniel opened the heavy plank doors and descended into the tavern's cellar. He had been inclined to begin this adventure the previous night after speaking to Jacob, but he decided it best to wait until daytime, if not for his sanity then to assure himself he wouldn't accidentally encounter Marcus McComber, who, he expected, only visited the cellar at night to avoid the wrath of Angus Ferley. The prospect of encountering McComber below ground, in a location McComber knew intimately, was one he preferred not to think about.

He descended quickly, leaving the cold, damp, afternoon air for the dry, stagnant warmth of the cellar. When he pulled the planks shut behind him, he expected the darkness to be complete, but his expectations failed to match the absoluteness of reality. He crashed into what felt like a wall at the bottom of the stairs, stumbled blindly for indeterminable seconds, and then retraced his path backwards until he tripped and fell on the lowest step. He threw open the cellar doors, letting a bit of daylight illuminate his surroundings. When he finally noticed the lantern hanging from a rusty nail, he lit it first, then returned to close the cellar doors.

Once safely entombed in visible surroundings, his anticipation, which had grown all morning, abruptly faded. The cellar was a mess. Dust and debris littered the floor. The barrel racks appeared wobbly and ready to collapse if one more rat relieved itself on the rusty girders. Someone had thrown empty boxes into a mountainous heap in a corner, while another corner, cobwebbed and dark, bore a single footprint where some brave soul had considered exploring before wisely turning back.

Nevertheless, lacking a better alternative, he began a haphazard search. He expected to accomplish nothing. He focused his search in the most unlikely places, because Marcus McComber was not the type of man to hide anything where one might expect it to be hidden. He poked through boxes of glass mugs, behind what appeared to be an old bar stool, and he even stacked several boxes atop each other to peer over the uppermost girder of the barrel racks.

Whether conscious of it or not, he repeatedly glanced toward the cellar doors. He heard and saw no one.

After what must have been an hour of searching, he grew tired and short of breath. If his guess was accurate, that McComber kept a stash of Pennyroyal stowed somewhere in this cellar, Daniel ceded that he wasn't going to discover it without a bit of blind luck.

At that moment, he heard voices in the alley, and he heard footsteps near the cellar doors. He quickly extinguished the lantern and stumbled blindly toward the mountain of empty boxes. He tried to bury himself beneath them, but in the darkness it was impossible to know if he was actually hidden.

The cellar doors opened and a moment later the lantern flared to life.

"Odd," said a voice. He recognized it immediately as that of Angus Ferley. "Lantern feels warm."

"Why is that odd?" asked someone else. Daniel didn't recognize the voice, and that made him happy.

"Because I haven't been down here all day, and it only gets warm when it's been on."

"Let's just get the barrel and head back. You really oughtta get a lock for those doors, Angus."

"I've got one. Damn thing's a bitch to install, though, and I haven't found a need. A fool'd have to be crazy to try stealing one of these barrels. Ain't worth the effort. You'll see."

Daniel had to keep still for about ten minutes. Angus and his companion, presumably a tavern patron, had some difficulty heaving the barrel upstairs. "Told you it ain't worth the effort," Angus said to his struggling companion. Once they finished, Angus extinguished the lantern and disappeared into the alley, leaving Daniel alone.

The thought of Angus mounting a lock on the cellar doors and barricading him in the blackness was enough to convince Daniel to leave the cellar. While snuggled up under the mountain of cardboard, he had decided his best chance to learn the truth, though also perhaps his best chance at getting caught, was to surprise McComber in the cellar, to catch him in the act, whatever that act might be. He would wait until nightfall, wait for Marcus to descend, and then, when McComber was most vulnerable, Daniel would chase him into Hell.

So he stumbled through the darkness back to the stairwell, not without difficulty and not without masking his face in many layers of cobwebs. When he opened the cellar doors and poked his head through the opening, he was surprised to learn the sun had fallen and a cold, bitter dusk engulfed the world. He'd been buried belowground longer than planned.

He emerged into the alley and let the planks crash behind him. His skin hardened in the cold, but at least it wasn't raining. The stench of mold and wet things had been replaced by the generic stink of refuse. He surveyed the alley for a hiding spot, a niche where he might spy on McComber's comings and goings. Near the back of the alley, engulfed in shadow, he found a short well of steps leading down to one of the brothel's many doors. This one, presumably, allowed guests to enter or depart without the contemptuous scrutiny of pedestrians, but it also provided a concealed view of the entire alley.

Before he could hunker down for a long stay, however, a figure emerged at the far end of the alley. It was a backlit silhouette, but he knew the shape. He expected it to continue into the tavern, but it froze and stared down the alley. The outline of a long coat and old English cap and hunched shoulders belonged to his best friend, and it was speaking.

"Daniel!" Jacob called. "I know you're there. I saw you."

With no reason to hide, and excited by the prospect of having someone with whom to spend the long boring hours of observation, Daniel leapt from the stairwell. "Jacob! You are just in time. Come hide with me." But the face he saw, once he'd come close enough to peer beyond the shadows, was not the face of a friend. "What's the matter?"

"I believe you know."

"Then I believe you're wrong."

"She told me everything."

"Who?"

"Bree. I saw her today. I went to retrieve my manuscript. Instead, I learned what you didn't want me to know."

Despite himself, Daniel felt relief. "Ah, well, I suppose it's best that you know. I asked her often when she would tell you. 'When the time is right,' she said. Did she enjoy your book, then? Did she feel guilty at that point?"

"I can't say she did. In fact, I can't say she felt anything but anger, or hatred."

"Hatred? That's absurd. The book couldn't have been that bad."

"Toward me, Daniel, not toward the book. She screamed at me. I've never seen her so angry. I joked. Silly me, but I thought she was kidding."

"What didn't she like about it?"

"She loved it. Beautiful and brilliant, she said. And do you see? That's the perfect irony. After all these years, after so many ordeals, finally I write something worthy of my wife's admiration, the novel she always believed I could write, but it's too late. She's lost. She may be my wife by law and name, but her heart has found refuge elsewhere."

"Did she say that?" Daniel immediately thought of McComber.

"She didn't have to. She told me about the baby. What do you know about the baby, dear friend?"

"Only that we did our best, Jacob. Had I known earlier, had I diagnosed her illness correctly when she complained of stomach pains and nausea, had I known, we might have saved the pregnancy. Do you think a day goes by when I don't regret the mistake?"

Jacob's eyes shone wide and bright like two pale moons beneath the encroaching darkness. "What do I care about your mistakes as a doctor? I don't even care about your mistakes as a human begin. It's your mistakes as a friend I find insulting. Why did you lie to me?"

"I never lied, Jacob. I simply didn't tell you everything. That's not lying. But I'll tell you this. I hid the truth for two reasons. First, because I thought it best. You had plenty of obstacles to overcome to get your life together. You didn't need another. Second, and this was the primary reason, because Bree asked me to."

"Of course she did! In whose interest would it be to tell me of your affair?"

"Our what?"

"She told me, Daniel! She told me you lied about who the father was, though as you know, you never even mentioned a child to me. And she told me I was not the father. That leaves only one person, only one wicked, slimy person to sleep with my wife. That leaves only you, friend."

Daniel finally understood Jacob's anger. "But no," he pleaded. "No. It leaves many people, far too many, indeed. But I am not one of them."

"I know it was you. I saw you together. I followed her to your office. I followed you to her house. My house! Have you no decency? You took me in, for which I am forever grateful, but now I'm thinking you did it only to further your infatuation with my wife."

"But that's absurd, Jacob. Even had I desired Bree, she has no interest in me. To her, I am your drinking companion, an acquaintance of her drunken husband and nothing more."

"Why then was she at your office so frequently?"

"Because she was pregnant, and I know something about delivering babies."

"Why did you go to her house? I saw you. I watched you through the window. I saw it all, Daniel. You made love to her on my sofa!"

"I'm afraid your eyes see things that never happened, but you're right. I did see her at your house. She was ill with stomach pains, and she asked me, her doctor, to visit. I told you this already. I tried to isolate the pain. I failed, and she grew more ill, and subsequently, as you know, she lost the baby."

As much as Daniel reasoned with him, Jacob's anger would not be quelled.

"Tell me then," Jacob said, "tell me your version of events. Tell me, because without another explanation I must assume you are responsible, and at the moment I have every intention of inflicting harm."

Daniel laughed but regretted it when Jacob's lips and fists clenched. The notion of Jacob fighting him was amusing. Daniel was six inches taller with an extra fifty pounds of muscle, Jacob having long ago fallen out of shape as he spent his hours seated at a typewriter or bar, and the possibility of Jacob inflicting anything but a few glancing blows was slim at best. But he had no desire to infuriate his friend further.

"Very well," he said. "But I can only tell you what I know. And if you're asking why Bree suddenly lashed out at you, I can only speculate. As for the child, it was yours. Of that I am certain."

"She told me it wasn't, and I assume she knew best."

"Or perhaps she was lying because she was angry? Have you considered that? Perhaps she read your manuscript and understood you two were not meant to be together. She may have thought it best, may have thought it would be easiest if you got on with your life without thinking you had lost one of life's most precious treasures. She may have been trying to spare you the torment, Jacob."

"But it's been so long since she and I, you know, since we made love."

"I did the math. It was possible." Daniel recounted again the months since Bree and Jacob separated. It was indeed possible, and likely. Unless she slept with another man the very day she left Jacob, which seemed unlikely. He still wondered about McComber, but he suspected McComber of poisoning Bree, which would lend credibility to the idea of the child being Jacob's. Even Marcus McComber wouldn't kill his own child, would he?

"But we couldn't have a child," Jacob said. "We tried for years. You know we did."

"Miracles often take time, Jacob. It is, sadly, a very common thing."

Daniel explained his version of events to Jacob, who calmed considerably but kept that angry gleam in his eyes, hinting at further turmoil.

"What is it?" Daniel said. "What still bothers you?"

"Why were you hiding in the alley?"

"Waiting."

"For what?"

"For whom. But I can't say right now."

"Why?"

"I do not make accusations I cannot support with evidence."

"Accusations? Who are you accusing and of what are you accusing them?"

"I can't say."

"Hmm."

"What is it?"

"Bree accused me of something."

"What?"

"Poisoning the baby."

"Poison?"

"That's what she said. Is it true? That she was poisoned."

"We found large amounts of an herb in her bloodstream, a very toxic herb known to be quite effective at ending a pregnancy."

"And you think someone gave it to her intentionally?"

"I do."

"But who?"

"That I won't say. Not yet. But I'm close to discovering the truth."

"And you'll let me know as soon as you do?"

"Of course."

Jacob visibly relaxed. "You know," he said, "This entire situation is turning me into a lunatic. I don't know what to believe anymore. I came here intending to kill you."

"Well, to be honest, I can't say I blame you. I felt the same way when Alecia left me for someone else. And I'd kill him if I had any idea where they were. It's an understandable desire."

"But you're a better man than I," Jacob said.

"Why is that?"

Jacob placed his shaky hand on Daniel's shoulder. "Because you wait until you have proof before accusing someone. I didn't. And I apologize."

CHAPTER THIRTY-ONE

Three Days Ago

"You must have made up your mind by now. Surely you don't intend to stay here forever."

"And what if I do?" Bree asked. "What would you do?"

McComber watched her carefully. Her moods, of late, were unpredictable and fervent. The wrong phrase or question might send her careening down the halls in a blistering rage. He found it quite exciting, actually. "Whatever I must."

"What does that mean?"

"Simply this: if you stay, I will stay. But I don't desire to."

He cleared his plate from the table. In her somber mood, Bree had cooked dinner, and now that they had finished it was time for an answer. Her moods and fits had delayed them too long. He could not stay in this wretched town any longer. Not simply because he hated it, but because it was necessary to leave.

"I would expect," he added, "you don't desire to stay, either."

"What makes you say that?"

"How can you stay? If it were me, and my marriage had ended, and my husband had murdered my child, and his best friend helped him do it, I would leave. I couldn't stand the sight of such wretched, inhuman scum or the world that reminded me of them. I have a mind to kill

Jacob myself."

"Really?" She was all sarcasm now.

"Indeed. It was my child he killed, too."

"And so now we come back to it."

"To what?"

"Don't you remember?" She closed her eyes, drifting into a world of memory. "'There is something we must do,' you told me. We walked the streets of town, alone in the rain. You skipped beneath the moonlight. And you said, simply, 'We must kill your husband.' And here now you have the perfect motive." She opened her eyes and fixated her stare at the chair he had vacated. He knew, once upon a time, her husband occupied that seat. "Tell me," she said, "would you kill Jacob if I asked you to?"

"Absolutely," he said, without hesitation. It might have been too forceful, because she inhaled a startled breath, but he no longer cared. Breeana Lyons was under his control and she would go along with whatever he demanded or suggested. He had played a masterful hand, one few women could resist, and it was time to implement his endgame strategy. "What I mean is I would do anything you asked of me. If that meant killing your husband, he would be dead within the hour."

"Oh really? How would you do it?"

"How would you like it done?"

She chuckled a bit, obviously surprised and nervous about the unexpected conversation topic. "A bullet maybe?"

He laughed, having partaken in this same conversation once before. "Bullets are messy."

"Poison, then?"

"Or something worse."

"Something worse? What could be worse?"

"The rack maybe, or the guillotine."

"Yes," she laughed, "I suppose that would be worse." She finished the last of her food.

McComber returned to the table but did not sit. Instead, he knelt at her side. "Seriously," he said, "do you want me to kill Jacob?"

She contemplated for some time, long enough that his knees ached from squatting. He wondered if she contemplated murder or simply wondered if he would actually commit the crime. "No," she said. "I don't want you to kill him. He will suffer enough, I suppose."

"You're such a tease." He leapt to his feet and returned to his chair. "But if we have no murders to commit, no husbands to butcher, why then don't we leave this awful town? Let us go. Let us begin our adventure. You are healthy now, right?"

"I think so."

"Then what's stopping us? What keeps us here? Oh, yes, that's right. You. So let's get past this right now. Where, my dear, shall we go? Now's your chance. If you don't choose, I will make the decision for you, and I will gladly send us to a small, rural, Midwestern farm town with no bookstore. Call it spite for your inability to pick a paradise."

"You would die in a small town," she laughed.

"I will die here, most likely, because you continue to stall."

"I have no idea," she said anxiously.

"But you do want to go?"

"Yes." She touched the fingertips of one hand to the fingertips of another, stretching the tendons and bending the joints. "There is nothing for me here."

"Do you want me to make the choice?"

"Tell me your choice and I'll consider giving it my approval." He was about to speak, but she interrupted. "No Midwestern farm towns. I saw that grin. I know what you were thinking."

"Very well. How about Valencia."

"Italy?"

"I have always been fond of the Apps, and of the Apennines, and of the Mediterranean in general. We could venture throughout the peninsula, even to Rome. You would love Rome. All the mystery and romance and adventure you might imagine."

"And the Vatican?"

"You needn't go, but I must. Perhaps there I can cleanse my soul."

"Of what?"

"Foulness."

"You could just take a shower?"

"Only if you're naked beneath the stream waiting for me."

"Italy."

"I believe it would be best."

"Very well. To Italy."

McComber smiled. Finally, he had won. "We will be off soon then. No more than a few days."

"I have things to attend to. A house to sell. Furniture and belongings to ship."

"But you'll have no need of them. We will start fresh, new, with nothing."

"What will we do for money?"

"I have money. Never fear. And it will be enough to support whatever we decide to do."

"I can't just leave all my things behind."

He knew she was thinking of her books. Her eyes darted toward the study. But he also knew the idea of adventure had finally begun to take hold. She must have felt the pangs of excitement, the breathless anticipation of a new world, the faint hope that her old world could really be forgotten. "Certainly you can. The adventure will be that much more exciting."

She paused for just a moment. "So be it."

After months of scheming and lying, and not to mention murder, he had convinced her to go. It had always been inevitable, but he still felt a warm satisfaction at how well his conniving had worked in the end. "I shall make the necessary preparations," he said. "And a few days from now, we shall begin our adventure."

She smiled back, sipped tea from a mug, and closed her eyes.

§

They schemed and planned much of the evening. At times, as they flushed out their itinerary, Bree felt exhilaration coursing through her cold veins. They would leave in three days, at night, travel by bus to the sea, and rent a sailing vessel of grand design to carry them across the Atlantic. Of course, neither knew anything about sailing they hadn't learned from Joseph Conrad or Patrick O'Brian, authors who wrote of days long past and techniques quite outdated, and so they would hire a Captain and a crew, and they would travel the ocean at leisure, free to read or make love or gaze in silent contemplation across the vast expanse of empty horizon.

At other times, however, she felt nervous and distant. Marcus found an atlas among Jacob's books, and he charted routes and waypoints, islands to visit, sites to behold. He spoke quickly, pointedly, almost as if his route had been preordained by fate and he had known for years where it would lead him. He spoke as though a madness had consumed his mind. She drew back. She tried to observe him as objectively as possible, to decide which was more irrational: his behavior or her worries. After hours of study, she was no nearer a conclusion. Something in Marcus's sudden anxiety to leave, in his preparedness, rubbed her in a way she decided was quite irritating. Still, she could think of no better way to spend her life than adventuring with Marcus throughout the world. What sights might she see?

By midnight, after a quick, dispassionate, routine bout of sex in bed, Marcus had gone. There was planning to do, he told her, and he was, besides, far too excited to sleep. She felt the same.

The house was cold, and she pulled tight on her robe. In the middle of their naked foray, Marcus had suddenly withdrawn himself and rushed to open a window. Sweat poured down his chest and back and buttocks, and she had laughed watching him struggle to open the window because, though perspiring and naked, his breathing was still calm and his hair was undisturbed. Such was Marcus McComber.

She closed the window and went downstairs. She built a fire in the hearth and warmed a delicious blend of black tea and cinnamon. A few minutes later, she cozied into the cold birch rocking chair with her tea mug cupped between her icy hands, and she watched the warm flames ravage the same dead, blackened logs that fueled their strength.

If she possessed tears still waiting to be shed, now would have been the time for them. But she was dry. A well surrounded by endless desert. Besides, she had no desire to cry, no sense of sadness. Instead, her mind whirled and danced, like the flames in the hearth, and her heart was akin to the blackened log, eaten and torn, withering into a dead stump incapable of feeling. Events had left her stripped and barren. The sensation was so great she set her mug down and pulled her robe tight against her skin, hoping to remove the sense of nakedness, of vulnerability. The past months had been a whirlwind, and she had felt helpless through most of it. All she desired was control. Some control. Any control. What more could she hope for? Certainly, she no longer expected happiness.

And so she decided, perhaps because her options were so few, that her eagerness to go with Marcus had more to do with escaping what had come before than with the excitement of what was still to come. The past must vanish. Her past, the anguish and loneliness, must disappear. Deep inside, a voice whispered to her of experiences neither painful nor unpleasant, insisting not all of her past should be forgotten, but that voice cried out with weak determination, and so it was easily dismissed.

She stood from the rocking chair and located the hefty stack of Jacob's manuscript in the cabinet of an end table. The pages screamed at her, begged her to reconsider, understanding her intent before she knew it herself. It was such a sad tale, so dark and brooding. It was everything she loved. Unfortunately, in so many ways, it was worthless fiction. And so she cast the entire manuscript into the fireplace.

It erupted in flame. Shreds of fiery paper soared into the chimney. Entire sections melted into ash. Days and weeks and months of writing were swept away as quickly as a whisper carried aloft by the wind. She felt no sorrow.

A moment later she turned from the flames and traversed the cold ceramic tiles to the den. On the desk, glaring back at her as if daring her to subject it to the same fate, was the Edgar Allan Poe anthology Jacob had given her so many years ago. It was creased and bent, with pages torn or earmarked. Usage and time had massacred it just as they had her marriage. The volume was testament to the destruction enforced by stress and aging. And worst of all, it was a symbol of a past she must forget.

So she cast it, too, into the flames. This time, the sense of loss burned much fiercer. But she was resolved to end the agony. Let the past burn itself out of memory. The future was all that mattered now. She had much to do, and many relics to burn, before she could embark on Marcus' adventure. But she was determined to let nothing block her path, nothing keep her from gaining control, not even the regret eating away at her mind as Edgar Allan Poe burned in the hearth.

CHAPTER THIRTY-TWO

Two Days Ago

It was an open air market, which to Daniel Jefferson made it all the more surprising that crowds of people walked the sidewalks and peered through storefront windows. The weather had gone foul overnight. A howling wind ripped through the shopping lanes. The gales sent raindrops slicing through the crowd of shoppers, who, though wet and cold and tired, huddled together and rebuked the storm with their laughing and singing. It was, after all, the season of holidays.

But celebration was furthest from his mind as he watched Bree in the busy market. Inside a leather maker's quaint showroom, Mrs. Lyons surveyed an exquisite, matching suede set of travel luggage. He wondered where she planned to travel and when, but at the moment the thought was irrelevant. He had only one purpose this afternoon.

Jacob was at home, confused and, for lack of a more appropriate word, lonely. Daniel warned him to occupy himself with a book or with a lengthy bout of writing. Idleness would only exacerbate his turmoil. But no man could be told how to grieve, and he knew Jacob would eventually discover his own method of recuperation. In the meantime, Daniel must persuade Bree that Jacob was innocent, and, even more difficult, convince her that Marcus McComber poisoned her, though as of yet he had nothing but circumstantial evidence to support either argument.

After a nightlong stakeout in the alley, where rats and felines and whores gathered but Marcus McComber never appeared, Daniel had gone to find her. Perhaps she knew another haunt of McComber's, another location where the Pennyroyal might be hidden. He had reached her block as she was leaving the house, and, unsure how best to approach, trailed her to the market where he now sat ready to pounce.

With her purchase complete, Bree wheeled onto the sidewalk a brown suede handbag atop a matching leather suitcase. Daniel marveled at the sight of her. Even draped in wet clothes, with her hair in a ponytail and her eyeglasses dripping raindrops down her cheek, she was a marvel of anatomical beauty. He continued to question, to that very day, how he had neglected to notice her attributes when she had been strictly a patient. The excuses were many, but the truth, he knew, was simple. Indeed he had noticed. He had simply refused to admit it to himself, and that refusal was, perhaps, for the best.

"Bree," he called, afraid the throng of caroling shopgoers might overpower his voice. He ran the necessary distance to block her path. "Hello," he said. "What a coincidence we should meet in so busy a place. What could the odds be?"

"Better than expected," she answered. "As they normally are when one person follows another. Or do you always stroll the market in the rain?"

"I have something to ask you," he said.

"Go ahead, but please be quick. Time is short."

"It is?" Indicating the luggage, he said, "Are you planning to travel?"

"Is that your question? It's a bad one. If you can't tell I have travel plans, given the suitcases and such, you don't really deserve permission to ask a question. I thought you were smarter than that. Now I must go."

"To be honest, I'm afraid that wasn't my question. Though, admittedly, your response disturbs me. If you're planning to travel, is it possible you chose the destination from a handful of brochures?"

The startled way her eyebrows arched across her forehead proved answer enough.

"You see," he said. "I know things, Bree. I know you, I know your husband, and I know where your travel brochures came from. What I don't know, or who rather, is Marcus McComber."

"There is nothing you need to know. We've discussed it before, and I have nothing to add."

"Don't worry. I'm not here this time to warn you away from him, though I admit it would be in your best interest. Today I just need information."

"And that would be?"

"I often see Marcus at the tavern. But where else does he spend his time when he's not at home? Do you know? Can you help?"

"I see no reason to."

"For a friend?"

"A friend? Is that what you call yourself? My friend?"

"Am I not?"

"I know the truth, Daniel. I know how the baby died. I've seen proof. And I know it was Jacob. He had reason and motivation. The only thing he didn't have was the knowledge of how best to accomplish it. But he did have you, didn't he? And who was it that told me about Pennyroyal? Who was it that constantly tried to blame Marcus? Who was it that called himself my friend?"

"Bree, I assure you, I had nothing to do with it. And neither did Jacob. He came to find me last night after talking to you, and he wanted to pummel my face into the pavement. I've never seen him so enraged. He would never harm you. Not intentionally."

"You needn't continue. I know the truth."

"Then you know it was Marcus who poisoned you?"

"That is not the truth. It was Marcus who saved me, Marcus who offered comfort and love. He gave me proof, Daniel. He showed me the evidence. You… You offer accusations, but Marcus offers proof. I honestly hope we never meet again, Daniel. Neither you nor Jacob deserves to spend another night on this earth. So good day."

She pushed through him, and, as he was unprepared, he stumbled backward into another cart filled with candies and decorations belonging to a barrel of a woman wearing too much makeup and a frightening scowl. As he hefted himself off the cart and onto his feet, apologizing endlessly, Bree disappeared into the rain, and he knew it would be pointless to follow. Until he had proof of McComber's crime, he would get no help from Breeana Lyons, nor could he offer any.

Without more information from Bree, his only hope of discovering proof seemed to hide in the cellar beneath McBraidy Tavern. Unfortunately, that meant more days of stakeout. But now he feared Bree and McComber might flee to wherever they planned to go before he could learn the truth. Suddenly a clock was ticking. Its hands and face were hidden from him, but in his head the swaying of its pendulum roared with ferocious importance.

CHAPTER THIRTY-THREE

YESTERDAY

Jacob bit his nails. He twiddled his thumbs. He lit an entire matchbook one match at a time, watching as the flame first consumed the match itself and then burned down between his thumb and forefinger creating all manners of pain, each one equally as unbearable as the previous. His fingers blackened, then became red, then began to blister and peel. Oddly, he didn't very much care. His entire arm could burn to ash, scattered by the wind, and he wouldn't care. If he believed everything Daniel told him, nothing in the world mattered anymore.

For whatever reason, however, he didn't believe everything Daniel told him. He couldn't. What was worse: thinking your best friend had impregnated your wife, or knowing your own child, your own son perhaps, had been destined for this world but stolen away? Both possibilities proved difficult to digest. Neither was especially inspiring. Of course, if the child was indeed Jacob's, Daniel couldn't be the father, but the idea wouldn't leave willingly.

For two days he tried busying himself, at Daniel's suggestion, by reading books or writing. In light of the melodramatic tendencies his life had acquired, reading fiction failed to capture his attention for any lengthy period. When he sat down at his desk to write, if the words came at all, they were ranting and bitter and incoherent. He went for walks, but they bored him. He went to a coffee-house for a drink and to observe people, but instead he found himself staring out the window into an empty sky. Alone in Daniel's apartment, he spoke aloud, first deriding himself and then his roommate. He rehearsed everything he ever wanted to say to Daniel or to Bree or, even, to Marcus McComber. But he knew, all too well, when the opportunity came to say anything, his lips would betray him and remain tightly sealed.

Eventually, when he discovered himself asleep on the bathroom floor, a roll of toilet paper beneath his head as a pillow, a small towel across his knee as a blanket, he decided nothing could be worse than so much suffering while sober.

He picked himself up off the floor, miraculously remembered to pull a pair of pants over his legs, and made for the tavern.

Marcus McComber sat upon a barstool, conversing with no one and offering his dazzlingly wicked smile to anyone who looked his way. His eyes lifted when Jacob arrived. "My dear Fortunato," McComber howled, "how fantastic to see you."

Not in the mood for conversation, Jacob nodded, took the stool beside Marcus, and waved to Angus Ferley.

"What'll it be, Lord Tennyson?" Angus always teased Jacob about being a writer. Angus seemed to consider the occupation a small part mystery and an enormous part nonsense. He often said, "Sitting on your ass all day making up stories ain't work. You want some real work, try carrying one of those ale barrels up from the cellar." Well, Jacob had tried it, and he didn't care to 'work' anymore.

"Bourbon. Dry and full."

"Any special occasion?"

"Finished a novel."

"I would think congratulations might be in order, but you don't seem happy at the occasion."

"I'd rather not talk about it."

"Why?" Angus was puzzled. He hadn't read a book since, well, ever. "Ain't it any good?"

"Not good enough, apparently."

McComber chimed in, "Nonsense. You demean yourself. I'm sure it was fabulous."

"You wouldn't know, now would you?"

"I don't reckon I understand," said Angus. "Good enough for what?"

"I wrote it to impress my wife and to win her back," Jacob said. "And, while it may have impressed her, it certainly didn't win her back. In fact, it would seem I may have made things worse."

"At least you gave it a shot, lad. Can't fault you for that." Angus reached his bulky arm across the bartop and gave Jacob a friendly whack on the shoulder. "More than most men'll do."

Once Angus had poured the drink and disappeared to attend to other activities, McComber spoke up. "Don't be too hard on yourself. I'm sure your book was fantastic enough. If your wife didn't like it, as you say, she probably had other reasons."

"Like?"

"I don't pretend to know. Not I. But perhaps some outside influence poisoned her against you. Perhaps something else, or someone else, convinced her you had ill intentions. It's something to consider."

"Who would do that? Who has that much influence with her?"

McComber smiled. "I haven't the faintest notion. Can't you think of anyone?"

In fact, Jacob certainly could think of someone. The very someone with whom he shared an apartment. And it all made sense, too. "Daniel," he whispered.

Marcus heard him and smiled wider. "No. You don't suppose, do you? Not your doctor friend. He seems far too decent for such a nasty deception."

"Indeed he does."

"Not that he couldn't have done it. The cruelest people inside often seem kindest on the outside."

"What are you saying?"

"Nothing. Nothing at all. I'm certainly not making accusations, only suggesting there might be reasons your wife disliked your novel other than its lack of merit."

Jacob eyed McComber long and with a bit of apprehension. Why did it always seem Marcus McComber worked from a secret agenda? "No," he said. "I can't believe Daniel would do something so sinister. If I believed it, I would be forced to believe too many other horrible things I have no desire to believe."

"Quite understandable."

Jacob gulped his bourbon and called for another. When he finished his second and third and sixth, McComber said, "We won't be seeing much more of each other."

Having trouble making sentences, Jacob asked, "And why is what? This. That. Why is that?"

"I'm going away."

"To when? Uh… Where?"

"Italy. A sailing cruise across the Atlantic. Picturesque views, sweet salty sea air, and a stacked bosom with which to busy myself whenever I grow tired of the rest."

Jacob drunkenly twisted his neck and peered at McComber's chest. "I don't see any breasts on you." Spittle erupted from his mouth as he slurred the word "breasts."

"Not mine, you fool. Those of my Goddess."

"Ahh. The mythic heroine come down to earth to eat, drink, and be sexed by Marcus McComber. The pitiful damsel ought to have bypassed Earth and dove right into Hell. I dare say it couldn't be worse than you." He laughed loud enough to draw many eyes toward his exaggerated, clumsy movements. He was aware of their disdain, just as he was aware that his saliva sprayed on anything within a few feet of him, but, upon both accounts, he dismissed everything as irrelevant. All that mattered now was that Angus Ferley kept his tumbler full. "To where shall you go?"

"I already told you, you fool. To Italy. To Rome."

"I'll be saddened to see you go, my friend."

"I dare say you will. Who else will buy you so many free drinks?"

"I don't drink anymore." Jacob belched.

Angus refilled his glass, and Jacob downed another bourbon. "What then," he said, "did you decide to, did you decide to, did you, umm, yes, decide to..." He belched again. "What did you decide to do about her husband? Or is he already dead?"

"He is quite alive, I assure you. As for his fate, I'm afraid he will likely live."

"But what of your grand plans? Do you need a gun? Angus might lend you one."

"I don't need a gun, even were I planning to shoot him, which I'm not. No, I had a much more fitting death in mind. And everything is ready for it, too. All the necessary pieces are gathered, waiting in their preordained spots, anxious to be used for so malicious a purpose. I dare say they will be disappointed."

"But why?"

"My Goddess asked me to spare him."

"And you're obeying?"

"Most likely. I expect, unless something unforeseen threatens our plans, he will live to discover her absence. And it could be supposed that such torment is worse than death."

"Unless it was a long, slow, agonizing death."

McComber smiled. "Oh, indeed it would be."

Some time later Jacob was on his way home, utterly drunk, stumbling down a cobblestone street. His conversation with McComber was but a faint memory lost in the ocean of bourbon flooding his skull. Because his plan was to return to Daniel's apartment, he was rather surprised when he found himself on the sidewalk in front of his old house. Evening had come quickly, and the cold skies were black and moonless, and no stars reflected in the house's dark windows. Even to his drunken eyes, it appeared no one was home.

What he saw next might have astonished a sober man. It had only temporary effects on Jacob.

A sign, at least head-high, stood in the yard like a sentry guarding the front door against intruders. Its purpose was bold and clear even through his blurry vision. The house, Bree's house, his house, was for sale. Bree was moving.

He should have wondered where she was moving to. He should have remembered his conversation with Marcus McComber and linked the two items together. He should have questioned how she might sell the house with his name on the mortgage. Instead, he laughed, and he thought to himself, "I hope she gets a terrible offer."

When he woke the next morning, he couldn't recall much from the night before, but, for whatever reason, he felt decidedly unsettled.

CHAPTER THIRTY-FOUR

Yesterday

Hiding deep in the alleyway, Daniel Jefferson twitched with anticipation. He had spent all day chasing phantoms, unable to locate the elusive Marcus McComber until two hours earlier when he found the man carousing with a whore near the tavern's back wall. For the next two hours, Daniel had waited outside in a sunken stairwell across from the side entrance, hoping McComber would emerge and lead him to the Pennyroyal.

His trembling increased when McComber appeared in the doorway and, instead of vanishing down the street, turned toward Daniel's hiding spot. A cold gust of wind swirled debris into the air. Even without a barometer he sensed a ferocious tempest barreling toward the city.

It was an unusual bit of luck when McComber suddenly threw open the cellar doors. Not one for loitering, the man vanished down the dark steps and pulled the wooden planks tightly shut. Daniel waited no less than a heartbeat. He leapt from his concealment and dashed toward the cellar, listening and watching for any other patrons who might stumble drunkenly from the tavern door.

The cellar planks were heavier than he remembered, perhaps because the last time he threw them open he wasn't concerned with silence. The glow of a lantern drifted through the tiny crack, so he opened it slowly, fearing to reveal himself.

The light waned. He froze with the doors half open, the wind swirling around him. Had he been discovered? Instead of growing brighter, however, the flickering faded. It was not the fading he might associate with the lantern being extinguished. Rather, the flame seemed to move into the distance. He opened the doors further and dropped his head inside. The light grew fainter still. He felt a rush of air, as though the underground chamber had been exposed on both ends and the pressure tried to equalize itself. Still the light grew fainter.

Certain McComber was disappearing into some secret cove or tunnel, Daniel slinked down the staircase, allowing the plank doors to close noiselessly behind him. Where he stood was dark and draped in shadow. The lantern's glow continued to fade, the path of its radiance slimming into a narrow beam. He peered around the corner and cursed himself.

Light seeped from an open door at the back of the cellar. Behind it, a tunnel of sorts descended into the earth. How had he not discovered that door while searching the room? The answer, unsurprisingly, was the stack of boxes several feet from the wall. Disturbed dust on the floor around them told him they had been pushed aside. The lantern, and presumably Marcus McComber, drilled deeper into the tunnel.

With a quick breath and a quicker step, he bounded through the doorway.

He stayed as far back as possible. On the fringes of shadow, with the lantern always barely visible in the distance, he crept across the stony path as cautiously as he could. He traced his fingers along the damp tunnel walls and imagined his warm bed, a cozy fire, and a good book. Some excitement was best experienced in the pages of a novel.

The light vanished around a corner ahead of him. He increased his speed, fearful of getting lost in the void. He should be able to find his way back by retracing his steps and fingering the cold walls, because he hadn't made any turns. Nevertheless, he would rather not get lost at all, thereby eliminating the need to retrace anything.

He came to a dead end of sorts, in a chamber that felt quite large and open. Without the lantern's light to expose it, the ceiling of the chamber concealed itself in a cloak of nothingness. To his left, faint in the distance, the lantern's flickering flame shone brightly on the rock walls.

He chased it, quicker now but still cautious.

Soon he was in an open chamber where the tunnel diverged into many. The lantern had stopped moving. He saw it on a table near a wall, along with a smaller candle lamp. McComber sat at the table and appeared to be writing.

Suddenly, a voice shouted from behind Daniel's hiding spot. "What devil enters my cellar? Be rid of you and be damned!" The voice was distant but hoarse and deep, as if the ancient rock itself sprung to life and demanded an answer for the intrusion. "I know you're there. And I'll find you, sooner or later."

Daniel crouched frozen behind the low wall, his eyes on McComber. He believed the voice belonged to Angus Ferley, who must have ventured into the cellar and pieced together signs of trespassing. Marcus went about his writing without a care or an acknowledgement of the threat. A moment later, the man dropped his pen, closed the book, extinguished the table lamp, grabbed his lantern and began the journey back to the cellar.

Daniel waited. He waited long, interminable moments. McComber had departed empty-handed. That meant any evidence present when he arrived was still there. This was his chance. Here he might discover some tantalizing secret about Marcus McComber that would set things right between Jacob and Bree, something that might hasten McComber's demise. He would make things right, and he would save a friend's marriage. Perhaps it was penance for having failed to save his own.

He emerged from his hiding spot and stumbled through the darkness to where he expected the table to be. He found the candle lamp and flipped it on. A tiny flame flared behind the pale glass.

In that instant, everything became clear. Several vials of liquid filled one corner of the desk. In bold, block, black letters against a white label, the bottles screamed to the world of their contents. Pennyroyal.

Beside them, a bowl, perhaps for mixing ingredients, and a pestle, for crushing pills into powder, lingered like instruments of death. Half a dozen prescription bottles lay scattered across the desk. All but one was empty. They were vitamin bottles. And Daniel had his proof.

What surprised him most, however, was not the poison or the pills, not the confirmation of all his fears, but the leather journal on the desk. Curiosity impelled him to sneak a glance. The pages were dated. The earliest entries were several years old, but the ink was black and flowing. McComber had a fantastic penmanship. He flipped to the back of the journal. Only a few blank pages remained. He found the entry McComber had written moments earlier.

> *"We leave tomorrow. Everything is in place. I will return anon for the necessities, but the rest shall remain, hidden, until again I have need. Never one knows when the tools and instruments of death might come in handy."*

Daniel felt his bones grow brittle, as though the shudder running up his spine might shatter them all into fragments. He flipped backwards through McComber's world, searching for information, skimming random pages, astounded by what the man would commit to writing.

Four months ago:

> *"I met my Goddess tonight. And she met me. Dare I say she was impressed? Of course I dare. She is married, but such trivial matters are unimportant, and I will do what I can to stake a claim. Hopefully it won't take long, because I can't linger in this wretched city forever."*

He flipped further back in time. A year, and then two. At three years ago, he read:

> *"They follow me everywhere. It matters not. I am un-*

touchable. Even were that bald-faced incompetent one to grab hold and rein me in, still they have no proof to offer the courts. The woman has nothing on me, either, the whore. I should like to kill her. To wrangle her neck between my forefingers and watch every last breath pierce her fat lips until she can only whisper my name and beg forgiveness. She knows I did it. She knows of the herb. But she has no proof. And I only run because I enjoy it. Perhaps someday I will find a new woman. Of course, I'm sure I'll find many, and I'll enjoy many. But someday I shall find one, and we will, together, disappear. Someday I will find love."

Daniel hung on the last word. He could hear McComber's voice loud inside his head, predicting many years earlier all that would transpire over the past few months. Suddenly he felt terrified and gratified together. He had proof to show Bree. The killer's own writing. But he feared what McComber would do if he found out. After a heartbeat of indecision, he scooped up a bottle of Pennyroyal and dropped it in his coat pocket. Then he heard a voice behind him. The scribbles in the journal had come to life.

"So," said Marcus McComber. "I see we have another Fortunato."

Daniel didn't turn. His breath came in quick bursts and he fought to control himself.

"What do you say, doc? Just out for a stroll?"

Daniel stared at the journal still in his hands. McComber stood directly behind him, holding a lantern of his own, and it was unlikely the man could see the book. If Daniel were to escape alive, he decided, it would be best to escape with evidence, because it won't be here after tonight and returning with a thousand officers won't help. He slipped the journal inside his jacket and under his shirt, trying not to be obvious.

"Turn around, Doc. Let me see the trespasser's face."

"If I am an intruder," Daniel said, turning, "it is Angus Ferley who ought be offended. He, at least, may have some claim to these tunnels. You have none."

The two men faced each other now. The lanterns flickered. The shadows danced.

"I have claim to the entire world," McComber said. "For the world is at my mercy."

"You have claim to nothing, save a giant ego."

"Ahh. I see. But could mine possibly match that of my accuser? For certainly, Doctor, everyone knows which profession boasts the grandest egomania."

"At least I have a profession. What is yours but murder and adultery?"

McComber laughed his wicked laugh. "So we come to it. What harebrained idea have you concocted now? And what, if I might ask, have I ever done to earn such scorn?"

"The proof is in this room, Mr. McComber. Everything you've done, all your connivances. Fitting because where better to study death and murder than in a place surrounded by it?"

"Do not speak ill of these catacombs!" McComber chided. "This is my office." He inched forward. "You work in a hospital, right?"

"Occasionally."

"Aren't you then, also, surrounded by death and dying. If my crimes, as you call them, are evidenced here, so are they in a hospital. And therefore, my dear Fortunato, any implication of me in those crimes, because of what is here, is also an implication of you, because of what is there. Do you see your conundrum?"

Daniel inhaled deeply. He must remain calm. McComber was trying to confuse him, to deceive him, and he mustn't fall victim to the man's taunting. "I did not kill an unborn child," he said, hoping the accusation would put McComber on the defensive.

"Nor did I."

"You lie. And you know it. I've seen the proof. The Pennyroyal. Bree ingested so much it nearly killed her, and the child had no chance. It was your doing."

"Again, I must disagree. Mrs. Lyons, as you ought refer to your best friend's wife, took her pills voluntarily. I did not ask her to. Actually, I believe you did that. So you're as responsible as anyone."

"Stop playing games. We both know the truth."

McComber laughed. He was, ever so slowly, approaching Daniel. But he was also sidestepping, flanking to his left, trying to circle around. The mystery of his reasoning was as unnerving as his laugh. "As there is no one else here, I suppose we can dispense with the air of innocence. What can it harm me now, your knowing? You've known for quite some time, haven't you? And still I'm victorious. That bothers you, doesn't it? That I should walk away arm-in-arm with a treasure you covet. How wonderful."

"I do not covet Bree. She is, as you pointed out, the wife of my friend, and I won't have you interfering with their lives."

"As you have?"

"Pardon me?"

"Don't lie to me, Doc. Wasn't it you who felt glee at their separation? Was it not a dream of yours, or rather, a fantasy, to spend an evening in bed, naked, with your friend's wife?"

"It was nothing of the sort!"

"You love that bosom, don't you, Doc? Let me tell you about it, about how firm it is, about how erect those nipples get while she screams orgasmic ecstasy. Isn't that what you want to hear? Isn't that what you want to experience? I can tell you all about it. You can live through me."

"Why did you do it?"

"Did I fail to mention her bosom?"

"Why did you kill the child? Or were you trying to kill her as well? Are you just a failure?"

"Why would I spoil such a bountiful fruit? Of course it was the child." McComber paused, realizing what he said but quickly deciding the revelation didn't matter. "Children are impediments to freedom. And they are nuisances. Especially in matters of lust."

"You might try closing a door. Or waiting until they're asleep."

"Ha! And what would you know about it, Doctor? Have you and your wife born any children of late? Oh, wait, I remember. My condolences. Seems Mrs. Lyons isn't the only woman to seek in another man what she cannot get from her husband."

By now, McComber had circled all the way around Daniel, but they still faced each other. Daniel didn't know why McComber wanted to skirt around him, but none of the answers he gave himself were at all reassuring. "So that's it?" he asked. "You killed her child because it would be a nuisance? Because it might interfere with your frolicking?"

"It's not as simple as your simple mind makes it. Children have no place in my plans."

"And what plans are those? To ruin more marriages?"

"This marriage was ruined before I arrived."

"But it might have survived. The child…"

"Is that what you think?"

"Bree and Jacob love each other. A child might have reminded them of it."

"Apparently you don't follow up too often with your patients. But anyway, I don't imagine this child would have benefited their marriage. Not on any terms."

"We'll never know because of you."

"Trust me, my friend, some of us already know."

"Then what plans do you have? What's so important?"

"I'm off on an adventure."

"With Bree?"

"You're quick. Congratulate yourself."

"To where?"

"The ends of the earth."

"The earth has no ends."

"Ahh, because it is round, eh? You're too smart for me, Doc. I was obfuscating, dissembling. I apologize."

"Then tell me."

"It wouldn't be fair."

"To whom?"

"To you. You might want to follow us, to take revenge. That can't happen. No. I would much rather you be here, alone with Jacob, knowing that my goddess and I will spend eternity together, and that you are incapable of preventing it. At least you will have no turmoil inside, wondering if you should seek revenge or not. It would be better for both of us this way. I only desire what is in your best interests, my friend."

"You're a conniving bastard, Mr. McComber, if you don't mind my ingratitude."

"Not at all."

McComber was now only five paces from him. They stood almost at opposite ends of the table. McComber eyed the writing surface frequently, perhaps scanning for his journal, or perhaps for something else. Daniel didn't want to find out. He was about to turn and run as fast as he could down the tunnel when McComber spoke.

"Have you ever killed someone?"

Daniel was so taken aback his knees locked in place. "Can't say that I have."

"Jacob once told me a woman died on your table giving birth, that you were her doctor and you couldn't save her."

"That's true."

"He told me, and this is his choice of words, not mine, that you goofed."

"I misjudged."

"You induced labor too soon, is that not correct? And then you called for surgery because something was wrong, and when you sewed her up you forgot to close an incision. She bled to death. Isn't that right? The blood gushed through the very same passageway that moments earlier flowed with a new life. Do you remember?"

"It's not the same."

"You killed that woman, Doc. Do you think God will treat you differently than He will me?"

"It was an accident."

"It was a mistake. And you killed her. So do not pretend to be better than me."

"I needn't pretend. God will know the difference."

"Wrong. You won't admit that you're at fault. Whereas I admit it regularly. And I have begged His forgiveness for years now. You beg for nothing, and so we shall see who is forgiven and who is not."

"For years?" he asked. "Are you saying you've done this before? You've killed before? But wait, you spoke of betrayal, of your wife's betrayal. I remember now. You said she tried to have you killed!"

"You have a decent memory." McComber stepped forward.

"She wanted you dead because you didn't want children. But that wasn't the reason, was it?"

"It was. I didn't want children."

"The Herb. Pennyroyal. You killed her unborn child, too, didn't you."

"God will forgive me, my dear Fortunato."

"You evil, smug, maniacal son of a bitch. That's why you're on the run. That's why you want to take Bree away. You've got the police after you. Tell me, did you murder your wife as well?"

McComber smiled. "I couldn't very well let her live, could I? She would crave revenge in much the same way you do. You're really not as bright as I thought, Doc."

"I will tell Bree."

"She won't believe you."

"I'll tell Jacob. Wait until he finds out."

"I'm giddy with anticipation."

Then McComber lunged at the table. In a moment of panic, Daniel grabbed the lantern from the desk and swung it. The two lanterns smashed into each other. McComber's flew from his grasp, but Daniel held onto his. McComber reached for a shiny object suddenly spinning on the table, and Daniel knew he must run.

He ran as quickly as his shaky knees allowed. He followed the tunnel back toward the open vault of the catacombs. Once there, he extinguished the light and paused to listen for the footsteps of pursuit. None came. He continued up the tunnel without relighting the lantern. After traversing the many twisting inclines, he burst through the wooden door into the cellar and slammed it shut behind him. To his dismay, he found it had no lock. Without hesitating, always afraid of McComber's pursuit, he ran quickly to the stairwell and smashed the lantern against the wall.

When he emerged into the rank, putrid alley air, he inhaled the cleanest, most heavenly breath he had ever taken.

§

Alone in the underworld, Marcus McComber laughed. He laughed at the doctor's terror. He laughed at Jacob's innocence. He laughed at the easily manipulated Breeana Lyons. And he laughed at himself. After so long on the run, finally it would all come to an end.

He stepped two feet to his right, bent down, and lifted the lantern from where he knew it had fallen. When its yellow light flared into being, he lifted his other hand to reveal the object he had sought on the desk. He marveled at the beauty of his weapon. The metallic shine, the symmetrical engravings. He purchased it from a street peddler two years earlier and paid a tenth of its true value. So far, he had never used it. The Doctor was nearly its first victim. Perhaps he still would be.

Marcus slipped the weapon into the pocket of his coat and examined the disarray atop his table. He had fumbled blindly for his gun while the doctor ran off, and as a result nothing was where he had left it. Judging quickly, he noticed only one thing missing. His journal. The Doctor must have stolen it. No matter. There wouldn't be enough time to make use of it. In twenty-four hours, he and Bree would be gone. Daniel and Jacob could read the journal together and marvel at their own stupidity.

McComber thought for a moment about Jacob. Part of him still considered revealing the truth to the ignorant sot. What could it matter? And what would be Jacob's reaction? The poor bastard would probably want to write a story about it, but he never would. Ambition was a quality neither Jacob nor the Doctor possessed.

No, he wouldn't tell Jacob. Let the idiot discover it for himself. The realization would be torture enough. No good toying with Divine Will. Tomorrow, he would say goodbye to Jacob and and every moron at that infernal tavern. He and Breeana would be gone forever.

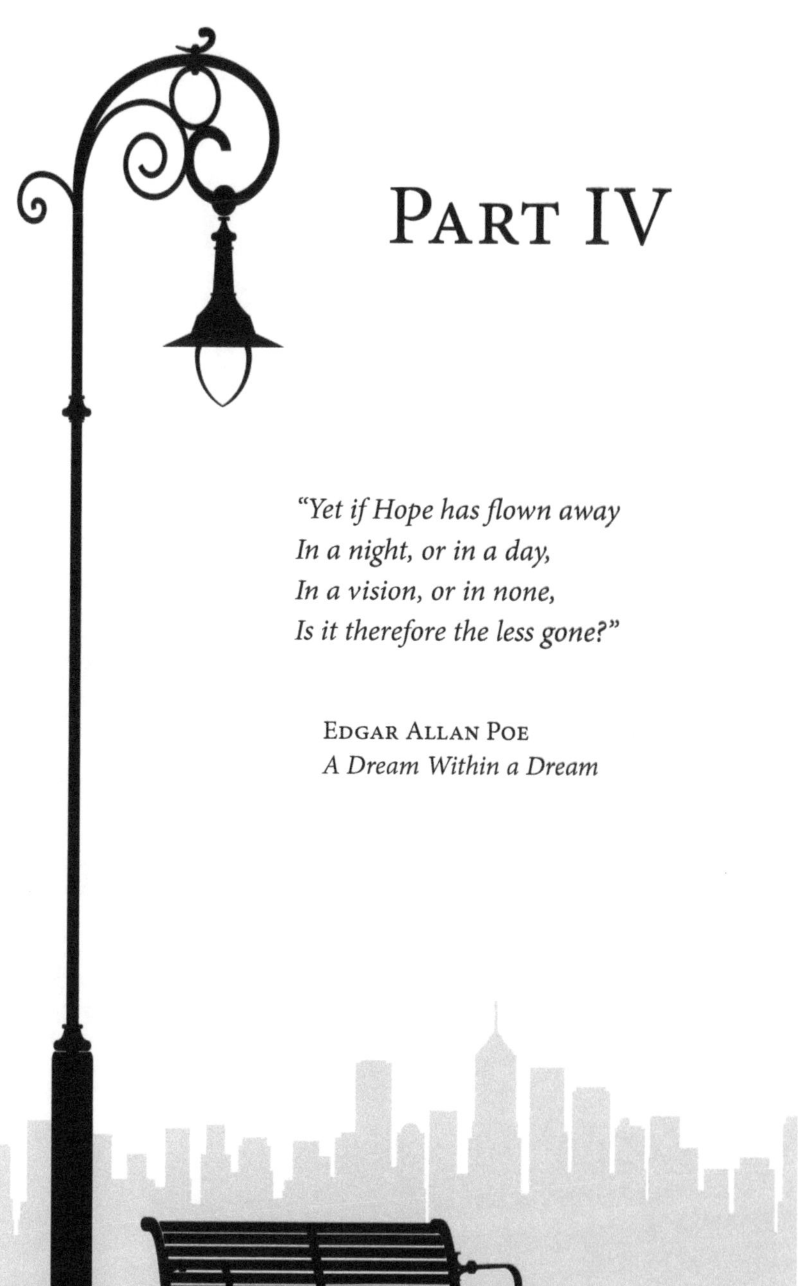

Part IV

"Yet if Hope has flown away
In a night, or in a day,
In a vision, or in none,
Is it therefore the less gone?"

Edgar Allan Poe
A Dream Within a Dream

CHAPTER THIRTY-FIVE

9:00 PM

Years pass, but such things as brick and earth, even hatred, often seem as immutable as time itself. To be imprisoned by these steadfast monuments to eternity is to welcome death. For in death the soul is free to pass beyond earthly confinements, to transcend the mundane reality of a limited world and be welcomed into the boundless realms of Heaven, where peace and harmony and virtue dominate, where vice and hatred are forbidden. Of course, if the imprisoned fellow does not believe in God or Heaven, his soul may welcome death with somewhat less enthusiasm. Still, the black depths of nonbeing are utterly preferable to the moldy, wet, heavy air of entombment. Or so thought Jacob Lyons.

The brick wall had already grown to three feet tall. At this current pace, it would reach the ceiling within an hour. With one hand, in an untiring demonstration of will, McComber laid brick upon mortar upon brick, burying Jacob alive in the tiny crevice of the catacombs. McComber's other hand pointed a silver revolver at Jacob's face. Occasionally, when the strain of exertion overwhelmed him, McComber unleashed torrents of sweat. He coughed and wheezed. Blood sprayed into the air. When he smiled his wicked smile, his teeth gleamed like the red fangs of a satiated vampire.

"Will you never listen?" Jacob pleaded. His cap had fallen to the dirt floor, his hair wet with rain and sweat. He had long ago stopped fretting over urination.

"I listen to those who speak the truth."

"Then listen to me. I didn't do it."

"I will say again what I recently said to your doctor friend, not far from this very spot. We are alone here. What harm will it do to dispense with the air of innocence? Why not confess to your crimes and beg forgiveness, not from me but from Him?"

"If I have anything for which to beg forgiveness, it is my weakness for liquor. What other disease might condemn me to befriending a man like you?"

"One way or another, Jacob, your fate was sealed the night I met my Goddess."

"What does she have to do with me? I told you, I've never met her. And I didn't kill her."

"Lies, my dear Fortunato. Lies."

The wall grew by another layer of bricks and still another. McComber coughed louder. This time blood spat on his hands and his coat sleeves. He ignored it.

Jacob watched, defeated, his thoughts swirling into storm clouds of fear. There seemed no way out. When McComber coughed and fell to knees and hands, Jacob failed to act. When McComber set his gun on the floor to wipe blood from his mouth, Jacob failed to act. He was lost to the nightmares of certain doom, already conceding to the terrors of starvation, suffocation, confinement. He almost felt lackadaisical, resigned. His mind began to play silly tricks. His eyes began to tease. And though he recognized his delirium, he felt powerless to stop it. The bricks around him morphed into new shapes. They became novels. They became all the manuscripts he would never finish. They became all the pages he had previously typed and discarded. They became faces, a hundred tiny faces, every face the same, every face Breeana. She smiled at him, and cried, until her eyes became glowing orbs of rage and bitterness. She screamed, and a hundred tiny faces screamed, but they screamed in silence. And they scolded him, and the hundred became a thousand, and the thousand Breeanas became a thousand Jacobs, and he stared at himself, at a thousand selves, and they closed their eyes and screamed their muted screams and dug clenched fists into thumping temples. And they became McComber. One McComber. And he laid another brick atop the rising wall. His smile, broken by blood on his lips and teeth, was wide and vengeful, and he spat and belched and vomited all sorts of foulness, but always he smiled, as if tonight was the culmination of a fantasy, and the night would end as a story ended, with his Fortunato entombed and all the years of life left to prosper and gloat at so literary an accomplishment.

But Jacob was no Fortunato. At least, he didn't want to be.

He ran his palms across the dirt floor, searching for a tool or weapon, trying to snap himself out of a hopelessness. The wall had not grown so high as to hide McComber's face, nor had it risen to a height that prevented Jacob from leaping over it. If only he could find strength and courage. If only McComber would give him another chance.

Thankfully, he did. And McComber did.

It began as a low, guttural moan that quickly became a grunt. McComber's chin buried itself into his chest, and beneath his wet clothes all the muscles of his body quivered and tautened. Next came blood. Red and black and viscous, it clung to his chin and lips, and he coughed, and chunks of fleshy tissue splattered against the brick. He fell to his side, fetal, writhing in pain. The revolver fell to the ground with a slow, echoing clank.

Jacob had one last chance. This time, he took it.

He launched himself at McComber, up and over the growing wall. His foot caught on the uppermost brick. His face smacked the cold, damp floor and his breath flushed from his lungs like air from a bellows. He struggled to his knees and gasped. McComber's body lay still beside him, the writhing and the moaning ceased. Jacob tried to stand. His legs buckled. His left ankle felt swollen. Dirt caked his hands and his face and, when he finally inhaled, his lungs burned with a fresh coat of brown filth.

He cautioned a last glance toward McComber. The man, the devil, did not move. So Jacob tried again to stand. His ankle supported him, but he knew he could never run on it. He made for the lantern but knew McComber would follow its light. He had no desire to find his way in the dark, but he seemed to have no other choice. Then he saw the cold metal of the revolver on the ground. He could grab it and shoot the man. If anyone discovered the crime, he could claim self-defense. Or perhaps he could toss McComber into the crevice and finish constructing the wall. How ironic that would be, he thought. But he knew he couldn't do it, even to McComber. The weapon, however, could help him escape, and if McComber confronted him again it would be on different terms.

He stepped cautiously to McComber's side. He reached a shivering hand toward the weapon. He clasped it, lifted it, and stared at it. He aimed it at McComber's lifeless head, at those haunting, upturned lips and bloody teeth. But he could not fire.

The next moments became a blur of dust and rock. He grabbed the lantern, less afraid of McComber's pursuit than any chance of getting lost in the black tunnels, and he struggled down the bleak road toward freedom. The lantern's radiance glistened on the muddy walls. At moments, suffering from nervous exhaustion and a few lingering symptoms of earlier drunkenness, he feared he had lost his way, that somehow he had spun round and was, with each haphazard step, returning to the bleak future of eternity in McComber's makeshift tomb. Then he would see a familiar landmark, often nothing more than a strange protrusion of rock worn and bent at awkward angles by time and elements, and he would grow increasingly confident of escape. His ankle throbbed. His entire body began to ache. A lifetime of stress and tension, suffered cumulatively in the short span of one evening, had rendered his limbs sore and his muscles weak. But most of the pain was drowned by an ocean of adrenaline, and in this anxious, pained condition, he strode ever upward, through black tunnel and over damp earth, climbing, as it were, toward a cellar.

Moments became hours. Hours became ages. He felt lost, but knew he was not. He felt tired, and cursed himself for drinking. He pictured McComber behind him, perhaps dead on the chamber floor, but thankfully not from Jacob's bullet. He would sleep better that night, he knew, if ever he reached his bed.

As he rounded another curve, as he sensed freedom, as he somehow felt the fresh, putrid air of a distant alley winnowing his sweat-soaked locks, the sudden clapping of footsteps grew loud, louder, and quickly louder, and the force of a raging bull slammed into him from behind. The lantern flew from his fingers, and it crashed forward, twirling and spinning and tossing its light in myriad directions, until a strobing effect overtook the underworld and begged Father Time to saunter for a bit. Jacob fell to the ground. He somehow managed to retain the revolver. The weight of his attacker flattened atop him and stole his breath.

As the lantern spun, he was flipped onto his back, and a flash of light zipped across the cold, evil, bloody face of Marcus McComber. The light moved on and McComber rained a blow on Jacob's left cheekbone. Then another. Jacob grabbed McComber's neck with his free hand and squeezed. With his other hand, he slammed the butt of the revolver against McComber's chest. Nothing had any effect. McComber continued to pound his face. He grew dizzy, faint. He wanted to vomit. Curiously, he felt somehow apologetic, ashamed for laughing at McComber's bloody teeth, because surely his beaten face was now a mirror image.

He lashed out again with the gun, striking McComber's left cheekbone. The crack was audible, perhaps a broken jaw, and McComber grimaced but never let go. The lantern continued to spin on the floor. Light crossed McComber's face as he pulled his arm back for another blow, and everything went black as the light passed. Then he felt the crunch on his cheek and the crack in his lip. The light spun back and McComber was smiling, laughing even, but Jacob heard no laughter and saw no reason to smile. He felt himself falling, losing his grip on the world. How rotten to come this close to freedom. What would happen if he gave in? What would happen if he closed his eyes? McComber would no doubt return him to the catacombs and bury him alive. And for what? A misunderstanding?

Jacob didn't want to play McComber's drunken games. And no amount of facial pulverizing would convince him being buried alive was a satisfactory remedy. Romantic and tragic perhaps. A fitting end for a failed writer. But it was an end he didn't like, nevertheless.

With one last deep breath, he gathered all his strength and struck McComber with the revolver just behind the ear. The man crumpled sideways. Jacob was free.

He tried to stand, but McComber, still conscious and unwilling to concede, knocked him down. He dropped the revolver and it skittered sideways. He and Marcus both lunged for it. They wrestled, each pulling the other's hand away from the weapon. In the corner, the lantern's twirling began to slow, the imaginary flashes of lightning calming before the storm had passed. Jacob's fingertips touched the barrel. It was still out of reach. McComber grabbed the trigger, but the weapon only spun away. They tore at each other's clothing. They inhaled each other's breath. At one point, Jacob even tousled McComber's hair and managed to laugh, wishing he could see the result, wondering if it had ever been ruffled before.

A sharp, nauseating pain overcame him and he curled up, unable to think. By the time he realized McComber had kneed him in the groin, it was too late. Then he felt the revolver hit his face.

The only sound he heard above his own ragged breathing was the unforgettable, haunting, debonair chuckle of Marcus McComber. The lantern spun round again and came to a slow and steady rest, its light shining on McComber's sweaty, sickened face. He stood above Jacob, who lay on the floor, and he held the revolver outstretched in his hand. It was pointed at Jacob's head.

"A valiant effort," McComber said, his voice laced with sarcasm. "Do you know your mistake?"

Jacob didn't answer.

"The lantern, you fool. Did you assume I would be unconscious forever? Or did you plan to shoot me if I came close? No. Obviously you had no plans of murder, or you would have shot me when I was helpless on the floor, crumpled into a worthless heap as you are now. Why didn't you kill me?"

Still nothing. He felt too numb, too broken.

"You did put a crimp in my plans with that silly stunt, but never fear. I was to be off tonight with my love, escaping to freedom and paradise, but now that you've killed her I have nowhere to go and am in no such hurry. That gives me two possibilities. Either I march you back to your new home behind the brick wall or I kill you now. Each has its drawbacks, mind you. If I let you live, you might again try, and fail, to escape. Can't really have a repeat of this little incident, can we? But if I kill you now there's that wretched burden of carrying your lifeless carcass back down this miserably dark sewer. What to do."

"Kill me," Jacob finally managed to say. "Kill me and stop playing your games. I have done no wrong, committed no crime, and so it is your soul that will be held up for final judgment, not mine. I will die and won't even know I'm dead. But when you die, you'll suffer a thousand years of torture, humiliation, pain and misery."

"That may be true, my dear Fortunato, but it won't be because I killed a liar like you."

"Kill me."

"In a rush, are we?"

"What good will it do to prolong the inevitable? You've proven you'll never believe me."

"With good reason. Who else might have done it?"

"I haven't a clue. Perhaps she did it to herself."

"Never."

"Why not? If I had given myself and my body to you, I'd kill myself."

"But she wasn't you, Fortunato. She was strong and defiant."

"You had broken her. Isn't that right? Isn't that what you told me every night on the barstool, that you, Marcus McComber, had overcome all her trepidations and seduced her to your will?"

Ever boastful, McComber laughed. "Of course I said it. And it was true."

"Then perhaps she learned who the true Marcus McComber was. Perhaps she saw this side of you. Perhaps she realized which devil had shared her bed, and she couldn't bear it."

McComber stared at Jacob, enraged. His finger tightened on the revolver's trigger. Jacob stared into the barrel, watching it tremble, expecting at any moment for it and everything else to disappear forever. McComber squeezed harder, trembled faster, ground his teeth. Before the gun went off, Jacob realized he could see McComber's disheveled hair, and he laughed. He laughed loud, and he felt it in his chest and heard it rattling off the stone walls. His lungs burned. His cheeks and jaw ached from the movement. But still he laughed.

And McComber fired. The gunshot pierced the air and reverberated up and down the tunnel.

Strangely, Jacob felt deaf, and it was a marvelous sensation. It meant he wasn't dead. He looked up and saw McComber standing with the revolver at his side. He had fired wide perhaps. Missed on purpose. But why?

"You didn't kill me," Jacob whispered.

McComber's grin had vanished. Jacob saw an emotion in that blankness he had never seen before on the man. It looked like fear. Realization. Terror.

Marcus coughed and convulsed. Blood sprayed on Jacob's face. It was hot and wet and chunky.

"There is no reason to kill you now," McComber groaned. "I suppose you'll be haunted enough by death in the coming hours. No need to hasten your own."

"I don't understand."

"The Amontillado," McComber said, barely audible.

"What about it?"

"I had none to share with you. Such was Fortunato's fate. But I shared it with another."

"Amontillado?"

"Such a tragic tale, that one. A pipe of Amontillado. But the narrator had doubts." McComber sunk into himself, deflated. He seemed lost in another world. "I no longer have any doubts."

"What on earth are you talking about, Marcus?"

"Amontillado, my dear Fortunato. Amontillado."

With that, McComber spun away and vanished into the distance. Jacob closed his eyes, felt blood on his face, smelled kerosene burning in the lantern and urine creeping down his leg. He wanted to leap to his feet and run, but instead he lay motionless. One word kept repeating itself inside his head. Amontillado. He heard McComber's voice repeating it. He saw the terrified look in McComber's eyes. Amontillado. It had something to do with the story, that Edgar Allan Poe story, but it made no sense. Nothing McComber ever said or did made any sense. He was an anomaly. Now he was gone. And with Amontillado flooding his mind, Jacob finally felt relieved. On the cold, earthen floor of the tunnels, he lost consciousness.

CHAPTER THIRTY-SIX

Present

"And then what?"

"That's it."

"What do you mean that's it?"

"I mean that's it. There's nothing more to tell."

Ruben is angry again. I had never met a Detective before tonight, but now I believe they are lonely, suffering, bitter souls with short tempers and no patience.

"So McComber left you there, unconscious on the tunnel floor? Is that your story?"

"It is."

"And you woke up? When?"

"Don't know. Some time later, but not too much. The lantern had burned through its kerosene, so the tunnel was dark. I assume, based on the smell, most of the kerosene spilled when McComber knocked me down."

"What did you do then, in the dark?"

"I ran my fingers along the wall, certain to continue upward. Eventually I found the cellar, and from there the alley. Then I walked home."

Ruben is up and pacing again. He strokes the coarse hairs of fur knotted beneath his chin. Seated across from me, silent, is Detective

Burrows. His eyes drop to the table then lift toward Ruben then drift back and forth and back and forth, as if anticipating some lofty proclamation from his messianic partner before deciding to beat me senseless.

Hanging behind the detective is Jesus Christ, eternally tacked to his cherry-stained particle board crucifix. He laughs at me and my fear, but no glory or praise will be found in my death, no martyrdom achieved for a destitute writer killed at the foot of a madman, so he can laugh all he wants. I see no reason to die. I just want to see my Bree again, to hold her, to explain myself. Have I not confessed my sins? Did my novel not apologize tenfold for every wrong I inflicted upon her? If that foot high Jesus tacked to the interrogation room wall was any sort of witness to the power of honesty and confession, it surely saw me speak the truth to these detectives, and it surely sent a message skyward to remind the Almighty of forgiveness. But my biggest fear, though I do not believe in God or his son, is that right now, at the gates of Heaven, Marcus McComber is charming his way into the Lord's graces. Just as he manipulates everyone else, McComber will connive his way into paradise and convince God to forsake me. I will be the last fish plucked from the ocean, unwanted, beyond the limit, and so they will toss me back into the sea, lips torn and bloody, gut wrenched and intestines knotted, unable to survive. It will be a Hell, of sorts. Thanks to Marcus McComber.

"Did you encounter anyone else on your walk home?" Ruben asks.

"No."

"Events? Occurrences? Anything unusual happen?"

"Occurrences? No. Although, at some point, while on the tunnel floor, I thought, and this is just a guess, because I've never heard the sound before, I thought I heard a gunshot."

"A gunshot?" Ruben doesn't believe me.

"A gunshot. Yes."

"From where?"

"I don't know. It was dull, far off. Either that or my eardrums had drowned in blood. A definite possibility. It came from above. That's all

I know. But then, I was on my back so every noise came from above."

"Not very helpful."

I don't care if Ruben's soul is lonely and suffering, I still hate him.

He returns to his seat and kneads his temples with thick knuckles. Poor fellow. How awful to bear the discomfort of an aching head. Perhaps we might switch places. I'll gladly suffer the stress for him if he agrees to a beating and three accusations of murder. Hell, I'd trade places with Jesus on that cross for a few hours. At least he knew he would die sooner or later from his wounds. Me, on the other hand, I may endure this name-calling forever, and it'll only get worse if they imprison me.

How McComber must be howling in Hell, bemused with the irony of my predicament. His entire goal had been to bury me alive, to jail me in my own tomb until death plucked me from the black seas of that macabre prison. Sadly, I escaped one fate only to find it again, this time cloaked by an air of legality and authority. Now, if convicted of the guilt leveled upon me by Ruben and Burrows and half a dozen more violent protectors-of-the-peace, I face eternity in an aesthetically different but functionally equivalent jail cell. Either one would kill me. At least McComber's vision would have succeeded with its murderous intentions on a much quicker scale.

"Do you understand the significance of your testimony, Mr. Lyons?"

"Not exactly."

"Let me enlighten you." He stroked his beard, as someone might who was deep in thought, contemplating loftier ideals than the best way to remind a murderer of his crimes. "We have three dead bodies here. To be honest, right now, I think you killed them all."

"You're wrong."

"Number one! Marcus McComber. Witnesses at McBraidy Tavern say you and he knew each other and that you conversed regularly. Another witness watched you and McComber argue tonight on a street corner. You admit he tried to kill you and you were angry and scared. Now he's dead. The evidence may be circumstantial, but it fits. Number two: Daniel Jefferson."

"Daniel was my friend."

"And you thought he was fucking your wife."

"But he wasn't."

"So you say. Now. But perhaps your thinking was different earlier, when you were drunk at the tavern, high after the rush of killing Marcus McComber."

"I didn't kill him."

"I believe you did. And so we get to number three."

Here he pauses and tries to goad me with a wrinkled forehead. But it's no use. I never knew the name of McComber's lover. I never cared. And I still don't.

"Breeana Lyons," he says.

"What about her?"

"Number three."

Time does not stop here, nor does life. If either did, it would be less shocking than Ruben's most recent revelation. Denial surfaces quickly, as it should, but already a pressurized volume of anger is building deep inside. I feel it rising, steadily, but there are some moments left before I erupt.

"Bree is dead?" I ask. "I don't believe it."

Finally, Burrows demonstrates his purpose. He reaches into a folder on the table and produces a photograph. Before he slides it across the table, I know what it must show. I try not to look. I try to deny everything. I fail.

She is beautiful even in death. Beneath an ocean of blood and vomit is a red silk nightgown I bought for our last anniversary. On an exposed ankle, I see the tattoo she demanded in college. A raven, dark and mysterious. How she loved reading. How she loved me. If only I had lived up to her dreams. If only I had been as interesting to her as all those dead authors.

The shattered remains of a wine glass draw blood from her left hand. Wine soils the silk bed sheets. I don't understand. I don't know what's happened. Or maybe I do. But I don't believe she ever slept with Marcus

McComber.

The one thing that makes me smile, even as the emotions continue to build and agony threatens to overpower anger, is the ring on her finger. It's the diamond I bought for our wedding, and it's set on the platinum band that was her fifth anniversary present. The last time I saw her, she hadn't worn it. Now, for whatever reason, she did. It was little solace in a sea of pain, but it was solace nonetheless.

Ruben fails to feign sympathy. "So your wife fucked your best friend and McComber. Reason enough, as I see it, to kill all three. That's why you're here. That's what you have to explain. Tell me how it happened if you didn't do it? Tell me. That's all I'm asking. Tell me what happened, and if you're as innocent as you say, we'll gladly let you go."

I stare at him. I want to kill him. I want to scream and cry and bury myself in McComber's catacombs. But all I can do is say, "I don't know how it happened."

"Tell me."

"I don't know."

"Tell me!"

I jump to my unsteady feet, kicking over the chair and pounding my fists on the wobbly table. "I don't fucking know, damn it! I don't fucking know." And I begin to cry.

CHAPTER THIRTY-SEVEN

Tonight

6:30 PM

Daniel Jefferson gave up. It was not an easy decision. He had ventured across the city all day, through alleyways and across bridges, from her home to the tavern to McComber's apartment, but he never caught sight of Breeana Lyons. He encountered Jacob at the tavern, but he said nothing. Bree should be the first to know what he discovered. The decisions that needed to be made were hers alone, and Daniel wanted to be certain she made those decisions with all the information possible. His only fear was that Bree and Marcus had already vanished.

Being much less fit than he would have guessed, he could only search for so long. Now he found himself at the bookstore, his last hope, almost too exhausted to enter. If she wasn't here, he was finished. A storm had begun blowing in from the west, and dusk had already given way to night. The clouds of the approaching tempest were gray against an empty backdrop, like crosshatched chalk sketches on an artist's black canvas. A fitting backdrop, he knew.

When he entered the bookstore, a bell tolled. An elderly man behind the register greeted him with a smile. "Can I help you, sir?"

"Do you know Breeana Lyons?"

"Of course. But who might you be?"

"A friend of her husband and her doctor. My name is Daniel. Is she here?"

"Can't say as she is. Haven't seen her since she stormed out 'bout a week ago."

"Stormed out?"

"Fell into a tiff over the meaning of a story. You know how these young ladies get. Ask me, they're far too emotional. I love books as much as the next fellow, but they're still just books. I'm too damn old to understand, I guess."

"So you haven't seen her recently?"

"Can't say as I have."

Daniel noticed a woman to his left. Occasionally pretending to examine a shelf of books, she spent most of her time staring in his direction. "Why did she storm out?" he asked.

"Argument of some sort with somebody or other. I don't really know. She's a good kid. Bit fiery at times, and mischievous, but that's to be expected."

The woman pretending to look at books spoke up. "It was me," she said. "She argued with me."

Daniel watched her approach. He didn't think they'd ever met before.

"I'm Gladys," she said, extending her hand.

"You know Bree?"

"Pleasure to meet you, too."

"Sorry. I'm Daniel. But this is somewhat important."

"What is?"

"That I find Bree."

"She was here fifteen minutes ago. You were close. Why are you looking?"

"She was here?" He turned to Ellis Fitzgerald. "You said she hasn't been here."

"I never saw her."

"She was outside," Gladys explained. "We met in front of the building.

Well, we didn't so much meet as bump into each other. She apologized."

"For what?"

"I tried to explain that it wasn't her fault, that it wasn't even an argument, just heated criticism, but she insisted. Said she wanted to apologize before she left, that she was going somewhere. Don't know where, but it sounded rather long term. And she gave me some books to sell, because they were too heavy to take with her. Do you know where she's going?"

"This was fifteen minutes ago?"

"Yes."

"Did she say where she was going?"

"I just asked you that."

"Not long term, not that. Did she say where she was going immediately, right after she left you?"

"Oh, sure. She was on her way home to pack."

"Thank you."

A minute later he galloped down a cobblestone street, the red brick dangerous and slippery beneath a soft rain that foreshadowed a grand storm, like the first crackles of kindling in a fireplace before flames engulf the entire log. The streets emptied quickly. Aside from a group of theatergoers and several teens no doubt instigating trouble, he saw no one.

When he arrived at the Lyons' household, a light shone beyond the front doorway. His nerves lurched to a higher gear, resulting in more twitching and giddiness, but he had no time for second guessing. Bree had to know what Marcus McComber did to her. When she knew, she would never leave with him, and perhaps Jacob would get another chance. More importantly, McComber wouldn't win.

When she opened the door, in an elegant robe of ruby silk that draped across her clavicles and hung loose enough to reveal her navel and barely hide those erect nipples, his goal was quickly forgotten.

"Daniel," she said, startled, but made no effort to cover herself.

"I'm glad you're home." He very much meant it. He could have said, "I'm glad you're almost naked," and he would have meant that also.

"Why are you here?"

"Uh."

There! She caught him! His eyes had followed that red silk cascading and clinging to her wet skin down to where it ended at the smooth, bronze flesh of her thigh. He followed those thighs down to her tiny ankles and bare feet, and when as he realized how cold she must be , he looked up to see her smug face smiling at him.

"It's not going to happen, Daniel. Not ever."

"I beg your pardon?"

"You can ogle all you like. It won't do any good."

"I assure you… Bree, I promise you, I was only fretting over the temperature. Aren't you cold?"

"Always clever, Daniel. Always quick. I applaud your creativity." She cinched her robe. "What do you want?"

He wondered which was colder: the rainy weather outside or the lady in red at the door.

"I have something for you."

"I told you, Daniel, it isn't going to happen."

"Not like that. I have proof, Bree. Proof that explains how and why you fell sick, how and why you lost your baby. Proof that explains everything."

Her eyes dipped to the items he pulled from his jacket. "I told you, I already know the truth." She said it with far less confidence than the last time he'd heard it.

"This bottle," he said, "do I have to tell you where I found it?"

"At Marcus' house?"

"In a tunnel, actually. The long tunnels beneath McBraidy Tavern, beyond the old catacombs. I found it on a table with a dozen others, all empty. It's Pennyroyal, Bree. And it sat beside a handful of your prenatal vitamins."

"So Jacob has taken to living underground, has he? How fitting."

"It wasn't Jacob's table. It belonged to Marcus McComber."

"I'm sure it did. How exactly did you discover it?"

"I followed him there."

"When?"

"Last night. And I searched for you all day."

"To show me some random bottle of liquid that doesn't prove anything?"

"Actually, I meant to show you this." He handed her McComber's journal. "It accompanied the bottles."

"What is it?"

"Read it. Read it soon. You'll learn many things."

Her fingers traced the journal's aged leather surface, and as they did so, her expression morphed from dismissive to concerned. "Why do you care so much?" she asked.

"Just read it, Bree. I beg you. Then you'll understand, and you'll know what to do."

With that, he turned and started off toward the tavern. He had done what he could. Now it was up to Bree. He was determined to keep what he had discovered secret from Jacob. Though he assumed Bree would make the right choices, he refused to kindle Jacob's hope. Sometimes, no matter how obvious the right choice was, a person could be entirely unpredictable. Alecia had been that way. It seemed, at least to Daniel Jefferson, that capriciousness was God's gift to women. Perhaps that explained why he was none too happy with God these days.

§

7:00PM

Across town, at McBraidy Tavern, Jacob rocked back and forth on his feet, occasionally pissing on the bathroom wall. His eyes couldn't focus on the pendulum-like urinal, and, in his drunken confusion, he blasphemed the contraption's inventor, whoever it may be. Never mind that the walls and dividers between stalls rocked with the urinal, all moving independently of him. Never mind that the entire world spun and swayed, producing a rather intense sensation of vertigo to accompany his nausea. He did manage to convince himself it would be best to limit his drinking for the rest of the night. He wasn't too drunk to know that if he sobered up he'd have better aim.

Once finished with the wall, he returned to the bar, his seat still warm. Angus had a full, frothy mug of thick ale waiting for him. "This is my last for a while," he told the bartender.

"Sure it is," Angus laughed.

"I'm serious. I wouldn't stumble, sample, uhh… Say it! I wouldn't say it if it weren't true."

"Is that right?"

"Indeed."

"My friend. Should I tell you then that, on your three previous trips to piss on my wall, you also returned to declare you were finished?

"First, I would never believe such nonsense. I could not forget something so important as asking you to cut me off. Second, I have never pissed on your wall, and if I had, which I have not, it would be your fault, because only someone who desired piss on his wall would install spinning, dancing, teeter-totter toilets. And third, if, as you say, I asked you to stop, why do you insist on serving me?"

"Because if I don't, you start whining about your wife, and, quite frankly, none of these fellas want to hear more of that. So I got three options. Kick everyone else out so you can moan. Kick you out. Or keep serving you."

"You've chosen wisely."

"Let me know when you want another."

"You're a riot tonight, Angus Ferley."

"And you're a miserable wretch!"

For his part, Jacob did what he could to slow his drinking. He slid the mug as far from himself as possible without tipping it off the bartop. It was a difficult thing to do given the liquor's effect on his vision.

The Tavern's door blew open, as it frequently did, and the man who pulled it closed quickly displayed his meteorological skills, as though he were some farmer conveniently dropped down in the middle of their sprawling metropolis to read the weather for incapable city dwellers. "Wind coming in north by northwest," he howled. How he knew that, Jacob wasn't sure. With the Tavern situated, as it was, in the alley, every breeze blew east or west. If the air moved in any other direction, it generally originated at either end of a patron's digestive system.

The crowd of several hours earlier had become the crowd of right now, same size but peopled with a new, and equally outrageous, cast of characters. Buddy Millen, loud and obnoxious, sat a few stools down. In a back corner, seated with six or seven finely dressed ladies, was Julius Andersatten, rumored to be the mysterious owner of the brothel next door. He was a prosperous, well-respected businessman, and the stories say he inherited the brothel from some great great uncle. He couldn't sell it, the rumor went, because the bill of sale would become public and, he feared, if everyone knew he owned a brothel, the respect he enjoyed throughout town would be diminished. Of course, everyone already knew, they simply kept the knowledge secret from Andersatten.

Jacob thought he caught glimpses of Marcus McComber in every corner of the bar. He knew it likely his intoxicated mind was playing games, but those games were nevertheless disconcerting. Still, if McComber had been present, no doubt he would plop down next to Jacob for a conversation about murder or adultery or some other heathen ritual.

With no plans and not a soul with whom to converse, Jacob lifted his mug and drained it. It would be another boring, lifeless evening. Same as the one before, same as the ones to come. It was a depressing thought, made easier, as all things were, by a bottomless supply of ale.

§

7:15PM

Bree hyperventilated. She vomited. She cried and she screamed, she stomped her feet like a child, kicked the wall and pounded a door with the flat side of her fists. She launched a book at a window, but when the glass failed to break, she stomped toward it, grabbed a chair, and with one swing transformed the solid pane into shimmering glass islands scattered across an ocean of ceramic tile.

Rain and cold became unwelcome but tolerated guests, gushing in through the shattered window. She stormed from one chilly room to the next, eyes wet and red, mind a whirlwind of conflicting emotions. McComber's journal sat on the kitchen table. She hadn't read it all, but she had read enough. Disturbing and sick and violent and hateful, it was a collection of the most vile thoughts imaginable. It was a trove of horror stories, but no bookstore would stock it. Schools would burn it. And worst of all, it would never sit on a fiction shelf, because it was all too true. With every word, Marcus's voice seethed like some omnipotent god, tugging the strings of her life as if she was a puppet whose fate had been hijacked by the devil.

But how had she been deceived? A million times she relived the past months, searching for clues, demanding answers, ransacking every memory for any trace of McComber's treachery. To her rather significant dismay, there was no shortage of evidence. He had swooped in and taken control from the start. She had been his device, his toy, his stimulant. He had scripted a part and she had performed it with a hint of predictability and a heap of pure zeal. From that first appearance in the bookstore, he had acted selfishly, recklessly, and quite intently. He surprised her with charm and wit, romanced her with gifts and sherry, sexed her with knowledge and debonair masculinity, and she enjoyed every lustful moment. But it was all a lie.

Soon she found herself in the front den, staring and reminiscing at a name written in gold-leaf on the leather binding of a magnificent tome. Edgar Allan Poe. Her hands trembled when she grasped it. It felt wonderful, perfect, as all books should feel. She traced the golden letters with her pinky, fingered several thick pages. She opened it to where the ribboned bookmark split the binding. A tear dripped from her chin and stained the heavy page beside the story's title. *The Cask of Amontillado*. "I must not only punish," the page said, in Poe's eerie, unmistakable style, "but punish with impunity."

The book was a gift from Marcus. It reminded her of him, of Amontillado, of a night in the park, of a kiss beneath a lamp post, of an affair in which she was the adulterer. With a howl and a shriek, she flung it at another window. This time the glass shattered immediately. The book lay open, pages up, at the feet of a growing tempest. Winds teased and tickled the pages. Rain pelted the ink, staining and soaking each page until the entire volume became a giant glob of muddled, clumping paper. She laughed hysterically.

Soon the laughter deteriorated into more tears. She didn't know what do but pace and scream. Her life had become a tumultuous lie. She had sought emotion and adventure in Marcus McComber. Passion and mystery. She had found it. She had found everything. But his journal bared all and destroyed the allure. It was cold and calculating, a million words shy of passionate. She had given up her life and her marriage for a murderer, and now she couldn't get them back. Her husband had written her a novel, a beautiful, apologetic masterpiece, and she rejected it, along with him, based on misinformed, hasty reasoning. Now she didn't know if he'd want her back.

And so what? Did she think life with Jacob would solve her problems? Wasn't it life with Jacob that first propelled her into this mess? If he hadn't been so depressed, so self-involved, so insecure and distant, she wouldn't have left him. Perhaps he had truly changed in the past months, but it didn't matter. She had called him a murderer, and she had believed it. That alone placed an impassible chasm between them. The idea saddened her more than she expected, and a replenished well of tears began to pour down her cheek.

She shook and she trembled. As the frustration and despair built, adrenaline pumped through her veins. She felt it. She smelled it. She let it pulse in her ears, thump in her chest, and seep from her wide-open but blind eyes.

"I must not only punish," she thought to herself, "but punish with impunity."

The thought intrigued her.

Suddenly it was not sadness and despair she felt most, but rage and an unfettered desire for vengeance. Time and again she had let others determine her fate, but she didn't believe in fate, now did she? She believed in free will, the ability to make one's own choices. Marcus McComber had manipulated her, set her course, aimed her in a single direction and kept her from straying. To say she felt used would be an understated cliché.

What hurt more than all the manipulation, what stung with far greater ferociousness, was that Marcus McComber had murdered her child. Then, once successful, he manipulated her further into thinking Jacob and Daniel had done it. How very clever of him. How very evil.

She went to the kitchen for a tissue and rubbed the tears from her cheek. She wondered how the tale would play out, how her existence would continue from this point. She imagined herself in one of Poe's stories. How would she react as a tragic character in a gothic tale? How would she suffer the humiliation and anger and betrayal? Could she ever gain some measure of control over the events in her life? Could she free herself from the manipulation? Could she be like the Narrator in *The Cask of Amontillado* and bury Marcus alive in the dark recesses of an underground tunnel?

A memory struck her then. She opened a cabinet above the stove where she kept the liquor. Behind a nearly empty bottle of scotch, she found the amber bottle of Amontillado Marcus had given her so many months earlier. With a damp rag she wiped dust, thick and gray, from its label, brown and gold, and stared into the swirling bottle of memory. She saw park benches, gifts, roses, supermarket aisles, kitchen tables, beds, pillows, hospitals and hallways, all in a swirl of Amontillado. She saw closets, hearths, countertops and candle shops, bookstores, cafes, carpet and tile, blanket and dirt, all the places her and Marcus had made love.

She saw Jacob in that bottle, too, beneath the broad Cyprus tree on a college campus that served as an umbrella protecting creative souls from the harsh reality of their futures. He kissed her over pizza. He wrote her a poem. He gave her stories and coffee and cocoa, and they cuddled in bed in a cramped dorm room, with radios blasting through concrete walls, with sighs and moans and a creaking bed on the floor above, and they lost themselves in those stories and each other. He read Tolkien like everyone else while she read Shakespeare and Marlowe, Hemingway and Hawthorne, Flannery O'Connor and Edgar Allan Poe. His stories were epic, hers were short. His were lofty and melodramatic, hers were simple, painful, and true.

Except for Poe. Poe was different. He was twisted, dark, mysterious. And she loved him. And as she grew more in love with Poe's stories, as her life became his book, she grew more distant from Jacob. And when Marcus McComber arrived, dark and drunk and twisted like Edgar Allan Poe, she had fallen for his mystery, been lulled by his everything. Her entire life changed, her path diverged, her sanity and her health vanished into the netherworlds of an invisible backstage, and she was lost, frightened, consumed by overpowering forces intent on bending her will.

She laughed, but it was a heartless laugh. Cold. Afraid. She feared she would never find her way back to anything approaching happiness. Never. Never to a place she understood, never to the world she once despised, never to the life she began with Marcus, never to the lives Marcus had destroyed. She laughed again as her thoughts began to chant in her head. The rhythm matched the pounding in her chest. Never, she knew. Never would end the madness, never the pain, never the anger and bitterness and hatred and sorrow. Never the fear, never the torture, never the anxiety of a different tomorrow. "Of 'Never—Nevermore." Never Shelley or Frost, never Paradise Lost. To quothe the Raven, "Nevermore." Never happiness. Never lust. Never joy and never love. "And my soul from out that shadow that lies floating on the floor / Shall be lifted—nevermore!"

Her life, every memory, rose from the bottle like a ghastly, garish ghoul, and those memories stung until her knees began to buckle and she fell to the floor, unable or unwilling to breathe, hateful of – or indifferent to – all the tragedies of the world. She pulled herself onto a chair. The view was dreamy and washed away behind a layer of tears. The pendulum of a clock above the mantle rocked back and forth and forward and back, but the pendulum itself traveled as several fluid parts, none ever together at the same point, as though time itself, and the world and her life and the very essences of being, began to twist and contort, and what once had meaning or importance became incoherent or trivial. Solid objects became abstract pieces of melted clay once molded into reasonable things but now fallen and forgotten, and these ruins of her life developed voices of their own, and as they twisted and collapsed they screamed with wretched pitches for her to save them, to forsake herself in hopes of reviving the world and reshaping it into definable form. They screamed and they beckoned, but she refused to listen. She had no strength to help them, nor the will. She could help no one any longer, because no one would help her. They would break her, deceive her, feign caring and sincerity while blinding her to their true nature, that of devils and demons, with vengeance and evil as their driving forces.

Such thoughts, such crazy thoughts. She held that bottle of Amontillado in her hand. She wanted to throw it at the wall, to throw it at Jacob, to beat Marcus over the head with it, to slam it against the voices.

She grew distrustful of herself, of her own thoughts. The screaming, melting objects whined and begged, and she thought maybe, just maybe, they needed her, but no, they couldn't. They weren't melting and they weren't shouting her name. They weren't demons or furious gods. They weren't her responsibility. Nothing was her responsibility. She had given herself time and again in search of love and excitement and a life worth living, and she had learned only one painful lesson. Those things do not and will not exist. Not ever. Quothe that awful Raven, "Nevermore!"

She felt a million swirling emotions, swirling like Amontillado in a bottle, and in her sadness, her bitterness, her pain, her madness, she hatched a plan. A plan to end it all. A plan to finally take control of her life. A plan to answer all her questions. A plan of retribution and vengeance, of apology and forgiveness. Best of all, it was a plan that fit the situation. A plan even Edgar Allan Poe would admire. She must punish everyone responsible for the events in her life. Everyone. She must punish, and punish with impunity. And she knew how.

CHAPTER THIRTY-EIGHT

Tonight

7:30PM

Daniel, sprinting and winded, failed to escape the tempest's early ranting. With McBraidy Tavern a growing settlement on a crowded horizon, and no stars or moon visible in a blackened sky, he felt the storm clouds begin to shiver and perspire above him. First came a few drops, cold and hard, and then millions, thumping and freezing the world, until a veil of glistening rain obscured the city and secluded him inside a tiny bubble of vision. He passed beneath a street lamp at full stride, through its bronze cone of wetness, toward the alley outside the tavern.

The door swung open easily, but closing it became a challenge. A hail of moans roared until he managed to secure it against the wind. Not surprisingly, the whines of the patronage took several minutes to subside. Daniel ignored them.

He found Jacob at the bar, seated on the same worn stool he'd been on five hours earlier when Daniel stopped by.

"How's the weather, Doc?" shouted Angus.

"Refreshing."

Angus, as was his custom, whether he found a patron's joke humorous or not, bellowed jovially. Daniel asked for a glass of water, and Angus obliged with apparent reluctance. It was understandable. No profit to be made freely distributing water.

Drink in hand, Daniel took a stool beside Jacob. Red cheeked and narrow eyed, Jacob wobbled on his stool and failed to acknowledge Daniel's existence. As for himself, Daniel felt rather uncomfortable, both because of his wet clothes and because of the knowledge he lugged around like some leaden lock box that no one else could be permitted to open, or even to carry. It was a definite burden. Hopefully, Bree was reading McComber's journal that very moment, and soon she would come to her senses.

Of course, there was the frightening possibility she would dismiss the validity of the journal, assuming it a forgery or hoax intended to frame McComber. She and Marcus might still disappear together that very night, never to be seen again. How awful that would be for Jacob, he thought.

"What's on your mind?" Jacob finally asked.

"If only I could say."

"And what exactly can't you say?"

"Many things, but this especially. You'll learn of it someday, I'm sure, but not from me."

Thankfully, Jacob didn't press further. Instead, he shouted to Angus, "How about another?"

The bartender arrived to fill Jacob's glass. "How easily we forget, Jacob. I knew you'd want another. Do keep out of my bathroom the rest of the night, would you please?"

Daniel didn't understand the reference. Perhaps it had something to do with Jacob's tendency to miss the toilet while inebriated.

Angus turned toward Daniel, consternation clear on his face. "How about you, Doc? Seems to me you need something with a bit more kick than tap water."

"I'm fine."

Angus pointed to a table at the back of the bar. "See that table? Why don't you drink your medicine over there? Make some room at the bar for real men."

"I said I'm fine." Daniel had been through too much the past couple days to feel intimidated by an oversized bartender.

Angus heaved his shoulders, resisted the urge to argue, much to Daniel's delight, and released his breath in a long, frustrated blow. After he calmed a bit, he grabbed a soaking mug from the sink and began to knead the glass with a dry rag. While he wiped, he said to Jacob, "So where were we before the doc arrived? Ah yes, Elouise Finghold. Have I told you about her?"

"As a matter of fact, yes," said Jacob smiling.

"Ahh, Jacob, that woman was spectacular. Of course, she did all the doing, and she did it splendidly. Wish I had married that one."

Jacob sighed. "I haven't made love to my wife for months."

A few stools down, Buddy Millen shouted, "I fucked her last week! You ain't missing a thing." Laughter percolated around them.

But Daniel was still stuck on Jacob's comment. Something in the way Jacob said it implied a quantity of time greater than Daniel would have expected. Mainly out of detached curiosity, he asked, "How many months?"

"Not as many as you, Danny boy," shouted Buddy Millen. "You hold the record."

Daniel might have punched him if he hadn't been so distracted. "How many months?"

"Why?"

"How many?"

"I don't know. Haven't actually counted. Since before we separated, obviously. Six or seven months, maybe. Why? You got a prescription for me?"

The laughter came again, and this time Angus' hefty bellow joined the throng. Daniel didn't find it funny. Everything suddenly made sense. He had been too naïve, too accepting, too trusting. After all the scheming, after all the dreaming, he finely saw his mistake, and he understood the tragic implications.

"Jacob," he said, "Did you and Bree have dinner any time after you separated?"

"Dinner?"

"Dinner and drinks? Did you meet at all between the day you moved out and the day you gave her your manuscript? Think."

"No."

"Think hard. Could it have happened? Could you have been too drunk to remember?"

"Of course not."

"Don't you see then, Jacob?"

"Apparently not."

"It wasn't you. It couldn't have been you. The timing is off. She lied to me. They both lied to me."

"Angus," Jacob laughed, "you sure there's nothing but water in his cup?" More confused laughter.

But it wasn't funny. Daniel saw no humor in his own idiocy, or Jacob's drunkenness, or Bree's treachery, or McComber's despicableness. The world was a garbled mass of confusion. Laughter burst from Jacob's drooling lips, and Daniel saw, in slow motion, a stupid, ignorant, fool of a man chortling and snorting like a moronic buffoon, joking at his own expense, unaware of all the events surrounding him. All Daniel had ever wanted was to help his friend. If Marcus McComber was the father of Bree's never-to-be-born child, he feared it was too late for Jacob and Bree, regardless of Bree's ultimate decision.

"Go home, Jacob. Go home and talk to her. Please."

And a fit of anger stole into his heart, and rage melted into his veins. Jacob's poor, skinny, plastered expression of heedless ignorance, with his lips curled into a smirk, an eyebrow raised, nostrils stretching, only instilled more ferocity. How had Marcus McComber caused so much pain?

Without a word, he leapt from his chair and shuffled through the tavern crowd toward the exit. He remembered Alecia at that moment. He remembered her treachery, and he imagined all the things he might say to her, or to the man who stole her away. He knew that chance would never come. But Marcus McComber had done the same to Daniel's only friend. Perhaps this was Daniel's chance to say everything he desired to say, to close a chapter in an otherwise unending story of suffering. Perhaps this was his chance to prove his strength, to beat McComber's bloody face into a wall, all while imagining he was another man, the unknown figure who had ruined his life and stolen his lover. Perhaps this was Daniel's chance at retribution.

§

7:45 PM

Marcus McComber emerged from the bathroom and saw the fine doctor disappearing out the door. The poor fellow would miss McComber's farewell. How tragic. Perhaps they could meet up later, and McComber could introduce the doctor to the revolver tucked into his coat. Wouldn't that be pleasant? The man had, after all, stolen his journal.

"I do believe," Marcus told a group of whores seated near the back, "that somebody has pissed all over the bathroom wall. Steer clear of him. If he can't aim the pisser in there, imagine what he'd do to you in the bedroom!"

The sots seated nearest the ladies fell into uproarious laughter. Marcus, ever the showman, swiped one of their fullest mugs, hefted it skyward, and led them all in a chorus to a song he didn't know the words to. Then he fixated on Jacob Lyons.

"Ah," he shouted, "my dear Fortunato." It was true that, because he no longer maintained any intention to kill Jacob, the name Fortunato had lost its significance. But he still enjoyed saying it, and it reminded him of the night they first met, the night he met his Goddess. "I hoped you'd be here. Another drink, perhaps? On me, of course." It was the least he could do for the man whose wife he had stolen.

"No, Marcus, but thank you. I'm fine. It appears, however, that you've had a few too many."

"Nonsense, nonsense. This is but my first. I am legitimately joyful this evening, traversing the brink of a new life."

An idiot at the far end of the bar shouted, "Damn it, man, do us all a favor and speak English!" Laughter followed, but Marcus had never taken this raggedy group of alcoholics too seriously.

"Poke fun," he said, "my poor, miserable, pathetic fellows. But hear this, and allow a moment of pleasure to creep into your wretched, pointless existences." He lifted his mug into the air for sport. "Tonight… Tonight shall be the last you see of me. Once I depart, never again will you set your eyes upon Marcus McComber."

The assembled morons began a sardonic slapping of applause.

"Hallelujah," Jacob said.

The bartender asked, "But Marcus, lad, how will we manage without our loudest patron?"

"Jest if you will, gentlemen. But tonight, the cellar is cold and the Amontillado tasty. Tonight, we usher in the unknown, and we embrace it. Life, for some, begins anew."

"So it is farewell to you then?" Jacob asked, extending his hand.

"No, Jacob. It is farewell to you. You've been a marvelous listener, though never listened enough, I suppose." Marcus couldn't help but smile at the fool's ignorance. He took one last swallow of his ale, and said, "Never forget, Jacob. A writer is first and always an observer, and the most important aspect of observation is listening. If only you would have listened."

The speech made him laugh. He laughed all the way out the door and most of the way to Bree's house.

§

8:00 PM

For Breeana Lyons, the end could not come soon enough. In order for events to transpire as they must, however, she needed a little time to get everything in order. Marcus was to arrive within the hour, and she had promised to be ready for him. She would be ready, but not in the manner he expected.

She began her preparations with the infamous bottle of aged Amontillado. It truly was beautiful, with its clouded, amber glass, its thin, steeply curved neck, a gold leaf foil label pronouncing the bottle's Spanish heritage, and, screwed deeply into its mouth, a cylindrical cork imprinted with the distiller's insignia. Part of her wished to enjoy it under different circumstances. Another part of her realized circumstances couldn't be more appropriate. Somewhere in her kitchen she had a corkscrew, but it had gone long unused. She searched for several minutes before discovering it deep inside a drawer beneath the liquor cabinet.

Next she found two white wine glasses, a pen, and a sheet of flat parchment Jacob had always kept around the house for scribbling. Centered on the foyer tiles was a table normally shoved against a wall. She had situated it directly in front of the doorway in the hope it wouldn't go unnoticed. She set the bottle, glasses and parchment on the table beside McComber's journal. She did the same with the bottle of Pennyroyal Daniel had found in McComber's catacombs. She worked the cork from the sherry bottle and filled both glasses half way.

Her heart began to leap in her chest. The first swirls of doubt lurked in those glasses of Amontillado, twisting like wraiths through the amber liquid, waiting for the correct moment to burst forth and wrap their slimy tentacles around her face and throat, suffocating her will.

The Pennyroyal bottle was small but full of a thick, dark, oily liquid. The bottle itself displayed three separate warning labels and instructions not to ingest more than the recommended dose. When she opened it, the aroma shot upwards, and she grew lightheaded. The minty smell was foreign and altogether harmless, but it carried with it a million fragrances of agony and sadness, all the memories of sickness, of abortion, of adultery, and of a traitorous lover. They were memories she didn't want to live with any longer. She poured half the Pennyroyal into one wine glass, then emptied the bottle into the other. Both lethal doses.

She topped off each glass with more Amontillado and took a long breath. The room, normally warm and cozy, sucked in air through the shattered windows. The air felt icy, haunting, intimidating, even disapproving. She ignored it. She ignored everything but her tasks, trying not to think at all.

On the sheet of parchment she scribbled a quick note. Her hand was shaky, her penmanship poor. She folded the paper in half, top to bottom, to conceal her message, and she wrote Marcus's name on the visible side. She set it carefully at the front of the table, so that when Marcus entered, if he entered, the first thing he would see was his name on that sheet of parchment. Behind it went the bottle of Amontillado and one of the full glasses. Amontillado, she had read on the label, could be served at room temperature, chilled, or on the rocks. Room temperature suited her plans well.

Afraid the door might lock, by whatever magical means, and prevent Marcus from entering, she opened it a crack and twisted the dead bolt out of concealment.

She surveyed the foyer for a brief minute, taking in the sight and the smell, remembering better times, happier days, and far too many troubling moments. She remembered Jacob carrying her across the threshold the day they were married. It was corny and cliché, but he had been a true romantic in those days, and often she would have sacrificed everything to relive them. Now, because reliving them was impossible, she would sacrifice everything anyway. She had always been a fan of irony.

With a quivering hand she lifted one of the Amontillado glasses to her lips. Her tongue tasted it without tasting it, and the expectation of drops down her throat brought forth images of Marcus standing over a table, painting poison on her vitamins. He had taken control. Now it was her turn.

But it wasn't time yet. She carried the glass, the pen, and McComber's journal down the hallway into her bedroom. Despite the cold, she rummaged through her armoire and produced a silky, red nightgown. It had been a gift from Jacob on their anniversary, and she had worn it to bed with Marcus McComber. Few things could better symbolize the reason for her actions, save for the Amontillado and the Pennyroyal. Perhaps the worn out collection of Edgar Allan Poe stories or the thick manuscript Jacob had written her might be equally symbolic, but she had destroyed both in the fireplace and did not have their ashes handy.

She slipped into the nightgown, savoring the texture of the silk against her skin, marveling at the ecstasy at which it hinted and the pleasure it often preceded. She didn't expect such ecstasy now. She expected pain. Self-induced pain. She was in control. For the first time, and likely the last, she felt pride and confidence in determination. No one would caress her or manipulate her. She would have the final say, and it would be a tragic, magnificent statement. Perhaps someday, if he ever understood, Jacob would tell of it in his next manuscript. She had, in fact, concocted the perfect ending to his novel, or perhaps the basis for its sequel. He had left that task to her from the beginning, and she no longer worried about failing him.

She lay down in bed. Her glass of Amontillado rested stoically on the nightstand. She flipped open Marcus' journal to the page where he wrote of their first meeting, some four months earlier. How long ago it seemed. Dreams of a past life. "I met my Goddess tonight," he wrote. "And she met me. Dare I say she was impressed? Of course I dare. She is married, but such trivial matters are unimportant, and I will do what I can to stake a claim. Hopefully it won't take long, because I can't linger in this wretched city forever. Time is almost up already."

Indeed it was. Marcus would arrive at any moment. Time was definitely up.

She reached for the glass of Amontillado and raised it to her lips. It hung there, its rim trembling against her tongue, cold and yet hot as the embers of a blistering inferno, much like her heart, beating with the remorseless calculation of a woman determined to right a past wrong yet raging like a hellish conflagration, searing her insides and burning her memories to ash. She raised that glass all the way. It tipped into her mouth. The poisoned liquid splashed on her tongue and crashed against her cheeks. She swirled it around her gums and her teeth, her nerves twitching, her throat resisting, gagging, her body working toward one last effort to prevent this traitor from stealing its life. And she swallowed. One perverse gulp that left droplets of amber clinging to her lips and dribbling down her chin. She thought of Marcus McComber, and she breathed deeply, and she smiled. A sense of peace overcame her, and all thoughts of malice departed.

She let the glass fall to the bed. Amontillado dripped onto the bed sheets. Her heart slowed, her eyes closed. She might have slept.

Her eyes opened again when she coughed. It was a hoarse cough, a painful cough. She clutched her stomach and tried to swallow the pain from her throat. Her body felt numb, exhausted, heavy. Remembering, she reached for Marcus' journal beside her. On the last page, a blank one, she scribbled a message for Marcus. She wondered if he would ever see it but knew it didn't matter. Still, it made her feel better to write it, so she did.

A minute later she coughed again, and then again. She clutched the journal to her chest. With each increasingly painful fit, pride and anxiety were shoved aside as a greater portion of her emotions was lost to fear. The next cough produced a dribble of blood that leaked off her chin onto her nightgown. She had worn red for exactly that reason, but now, as planning was replaced with the reality of execution, she wondered if she had made the right choice. She grew frantic. She coughed again, and chunks of bloody phlegm splattered across her bed sheets. She began to regret the choice. Another cough. More blood. Pain. Her heart was a wave crashing against rocks, tumbling and thumping and churning.

And she remembered a story by Edgar Allan Poe. A famous story. The Tell-Tale Heart. Where one man is haunted by the ghostly heartbeat of another man he buried beneath the wooden planks of his floor. Despite the bile in her throat, the blood on her lips, she grinned. This was the ending she wanted. If Marcus had his catacombs and wanted to bury her alive like some ignorant Fortunato, she had other ideas. And so far, everything proceeded as she imagined, and no amount of pain could overshadow all the torture and torment she endured during the past few years. Especially during the past few weeks.

For so long, she craved the mystery and adventure of an Edgar Allan Poe tale, the darkness and the macabre. Finally, at her end, on her deathbed, she had found what she so long desired. Mystery, happiness, and adventure.

The coughing increased, as did the blood. She wretched and vomited. Blood and bloody organic tissue. She choked and suffocated, bled to death and vomited her stomach onto her nightgown. But despite it all, Breeana Lyons died with a smile on her face.

§

8:45 pm

Marcus McComber knocked on Bree's front door, causing it to open slightly.

"Bree?" he asked, but he got no response.

He pushed the door open further and slipped inside. No lights were on. Several candles burned on a table in front of him. Normally that table was against the wall. Why was it in the center of the foyer?

"Bree?" Still no response. A light shone from her bedroom doorway down the hall.

He immediately noticed the bottle of Amontillado and the wine glass. Then he saw his name inscribed on a piece of paper. "Dear Marcus," it said, in Bree's elegant script, "tonight we begin our life together. Thought we might celebrate. Have a drink. I'll be out in a minute."

McComber smiled. Finally, God saw things his way and offered the ultimate reward. Eternity in paradise with a beautiful woman. Of course, Italy wasn't exactly paradise to Marcus McComber, but so long as Bree's silky thighs and ample bosom accompanied him, he would have all the paradise he needed.

He eyed the bottle of Amontillado, remembering the night he bought it. Actually, it was an expensive bottle. Amontillado was dangerously hard to find in this city, and he visited four separate liquor stores to acquire it. Perhaps he understood why Fortunato got so excited by the prospect of an entire cask of the stuff.

He grinned, then lifted the glass to his nose. The liquor smelled nutty, with a hint of mint. He had never tried Amontillado until that moment.

He sipped it at first, swirled it in his mouth, experimenting with its flavor. He paced as he drank, waiting for Bree to emerge from the bedroom. The minutes grew long and he grew curious about her delay. In the meantime, he finished his glass of Amontillado and poured another.

"Bree?" he called down the hall, but he was met with silence. Impatient, he approached her bedroom, eager to surprise her but fearful of terrifying her. He knocked on the door. Nothing happened. The light inside flickered. Candlelight. Was she, perhaps, expecting him to enter? He imagined her waiting for him naked in bed, so they might kick off their adventure with a rollicking bout of candlelit sex. How magnificent.

He pushed open the door, stepped into the room, and dropped his wine glass. Amontillado splattered onto the carpet.

A grotesque nightmare awaited him. He stared at it for long moments, unable to comprehend the significance. Breeana was dead. Not simply dead, but mutilated, bloodied, tortured. It was a scene of violence and anger. Her entire face was bloody, her hands and clothes bloody. He nearly vomited himself, and that angered him.

Beneath a blanket of blood, he saw his journal resting on her stomach, and, as if time hadn't already stopped, time stopped. He reached for it, doing his best not to touch her body. He knew immediately that Daniel Jefferson had given it to her. He thought he had enough time to avoid that, but apparently he had been wrong. It was a strange feeling to be wrong, one he was not particularly accustomed to.

A pen sat inside the back cover, and he opened the journal to that last page. Bree had written him a message. "I have not read all this, Marcus," it said. "But I've read enough to know how you truly feel about me. And we shall still spend eternity together, my dear Fortunato."

His heart lifted. He understood what happened. She obviously hadn't read the most damning parts, or she had and didn't care. Either way, she still wanted them to be together.

But now she was dead. Why? How? Who would want her dead? He remembered Jacob's manuscript, his failed attempt to win back his wife. She must have rejected him finally, and he couldn't bare it.

Jacob Lyons, the innocent drunk, had murdered his own wife. If Marcus wasn't so enraged he might have laughed at the irony.

Perhaps he still would, but not until he killed the murderer. All his plans were suddenly ruined, and Jacob was responsible. Jacob would pay. Marcus would at least get some enjoyment out of the situation. He stuffed the journal into his coat pocket, allowed his rage to carry him out the door and down the street, heading for McBraidy Tavern.

When he stumbled upon Jacob Lyons moping down a barren street beneath a horrendous downfall of rain and dead, dampened leaves, he approached quietly. As Jacob stepped into the bronze light of a street lamp, Marcus emerged from the shadows like a wraith. His hood was tossed back and rain cascaded down his forehead. Jacob halted, startled. McComber struggled not to attack him then and there. He had other plans.

"Tell me," Marcus said to Jacob Lyons. "From the beginning, from the outset, spin me the tale of your treachery, my dear Fortunato, and then I will kill you."

§

9:30 PM

Daniel Jefferson pounded on McComber's apartment door. He beat it repeatedly. "Come out, McComber. I know what you did. Show yourself, you lying bastard."

No one answered. He went around back and beat on the window. There was no light inside. A neighbor emerged from a doorway and demanded he leave or she would call the cops. He almost told her to go ahead, that the cops would be needed eventually anyway. "Your neighbor is a murderer," he almost said. Instead, he accepted that Marcus wasn't home and decided to search for him back at the tavern. He wanted an answer for how the man could kill his own child.

He ran most of the way, stopping periodically to catch his breath. Hadn't he been running all day? He felt fatigued and groggy, but he knew it wasn't quite time to give up. Too much mattered.

Eventually, he reached the tavern. McComber wasn't there.

"He's gone forever," Angus said.

"What do you mean?"

"Weren't you in here when he left? Thought you were. Anyways, he said we ain't never gonna see him again. Then he whispered something nonsensical to Jacob and laughed himself silly right out the door."

"Where's Jacob?"

"Don't know. He left some time ago. You can't have missed either of them by much more than about an hour."

"Thank you, Angus."

The tempest raged outside. Daniel pulled his hood up and stepped into the rain. He hurried down the street, a bit uncertain where to go. He decided the Lyons' house was his best option, but he stopped hurrying when he heard the clunk of wooden planks slamming shut behind him. It was a sound he knew, that of the tavern's cellar doors closing. He turned quickly, and through the haze of the torrential downpour, he saw Marcus McComber's black figure emerge from the alley and disappear around a corner. What had he been doing in those tunnels?

Daniel chased after him, quickly gaining ground. Marcus had no idea someone followed. As they neared the Clarkston Bridge, Daniel called out. McComber didn't look back. He broke into a run. Daniel lunged forward, diving at McComber's legs. As he grabbed on, he caught a glimpse of something metallic and silver in McComber's hand.

They fell in a tangle of limbs. Both men pushed, pulled and jabbed at each other. Punches flew. They cursed and squirmed and wrestled. Daniel realized McComber was covered in blood. McComber coughed then and sprayed a hot bloody mess onto Daniel's face. He felt sick and struggled to get atop the man. At that moment, as he rolled onto McComber's stomach, pulling on the man's coat, he heard a sudden thud, a muffled band, and he felt a stinging pain in his stomach. He couldn't swallow, and he felt numb. He laid his head on McComber's chest, wondering what had happened.

McComber shoved him sideways, and Daniel rolled onto his back. The pavement felt cold and wet. He looked down and saw blood spilling from his gut. He watched McComber stand up, a revolver in his hand. It still took several minutes to understand what had happened.

"This is all your fault, Doc. You deserved that. You shouldn't have stolen my journal. You should have kept it all to yourself." McComber smiled, but it was broken by a ragged, bloody cough.

Daniel attempted to swallow as McComber vanished into the distance, but his throat tightened. His body stopped working. He cried to Bree and Jacob that he had failed them. He cried to Alecia, apologizing for everything, missing her now more than ever. He begged forgiveness from everyone, wondering why his body wouldn't let him stand or move, wondering why he no longer felt the rain, wondering what he had been doing that day, wondering how he had ended up alone on the pavement with a hole in his stomach. Love and friendship and loss pressed in from all sides, mixing joy with pain, until suddenly the sky grew brighter and the weight of his failures lessened.

At the very instant he realized he had been shot, Daniel Jefferson closed his eyes and died.

§

9:45 PM

McComber felt wretched and weak. Wrestling with the doctor had hastened the onset of the poison. He understood exactly what Bree had done. He realized it while standing over Jacob in the darkness. Somehow, some way, she had poisoned the Amontillado. He guessed, based on the symptoms, she had uncovered the Pennyroyal and used it in the sherry before drinking it herself. That frightened him more than anything.

He stumbled across the Clarkston Bridge, tossing his revolver and his journal into the quick moving water below. If he was going to die, he would not leave behind proof of his deeds.

But he wasn't going to die. He had enough time. He could return home, get his bags, which were already packed, and drive to a town where he knew he might find an antidote. An old doctor acquaintance lived there. Of course, the acquaintance wanted McComber dead. He happened to be the husband of the last woman Marcus had impregnated, and so Marcus would likely need to kill the man to get at his remedies. But that prospect didn't concern him.

He reached home and grabbed his bags, but bent over to suffer through another fit of coughing and bleeding. This one was the strongest yet, and he vomited. When he opened his eyes, he saw bits of what must be organ tissue on the floor. Then he remembered Bree dead in her nightgown, the same repugnant filth blanketing her bedsheets.

He fell to his knees. Stood back up. Stumbled. Fell on his face. Rolled onto his back. He remembered Bree's message in his journal. "And we shall still spend eternity together, my dear Fortunato."

As he choked up more blood, as it filled his throat and lungs and suffocated him, he realized she meant an eternity together in Hell. Clever to the end, she had turned him into a Fortunato. She had killed him, but he hadn't seen it coming. Now it was inevitable, and he realized he had been correct that night they first met. Ignorance of impending death is fortunate when death is inevitable. If only he could let her know. He would smile that smug smile and tell her, "I was right."

And Marcus McComber, the anomaly, the antagonist, the vile worm whose hook so many innocent fish had chewed, died with that wicked, mischievous, debonair grin spread wide across his face.

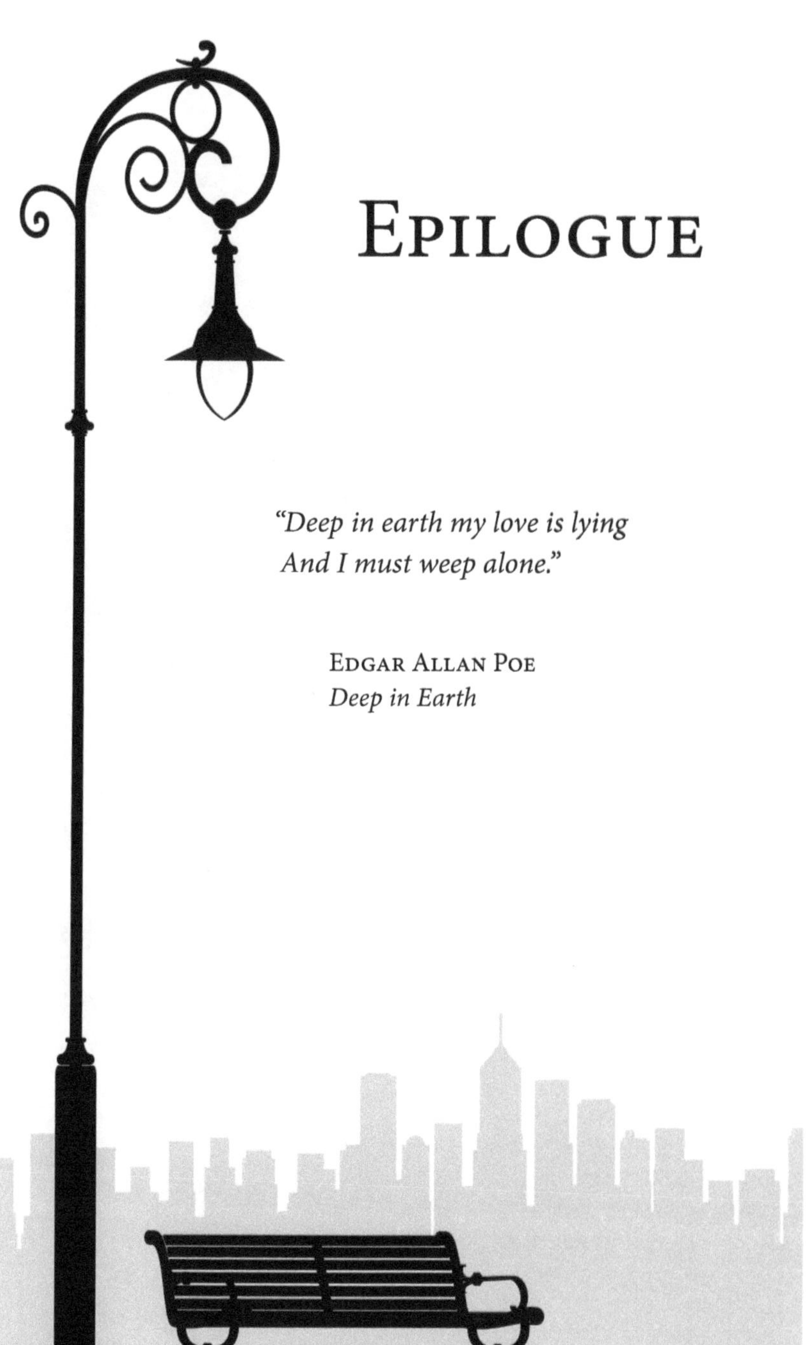

Epilogue

"Deep in earth my love is lying
And I must weep alone."

Edgar Allan Poe
Deep in Earth

CHAPTER THIRTY-NINE

Present

Imagine, if you will, just for a moment, that dying fish. Imagine it leaping off the fishmonger's table, flapping in the air as it clings to life, wiggling its lips, trying to explain to fishermen who can't understand and don't care to that it doesn't deserve to die. That is my life. These detectives are those vile fishermen, searching the black waters of uncertainty for any clue to explain the deaths of three people. They yanked my unexpecting soul from those harsh waters, alone, innocent, scavenging for my own survival. And they use their fancy lures and hidden nets until I give only the answers they want to hear. It's a trap I can't avoid, a death I can't escape.

The strength of ignorance has failed me. The most important people in my life are gone. My wife is dead. Murdered. As is my best friend. I know nothing of how or why they died, except to guess that Marcus McComber was somehow involved. But he is dead, too, and there is no one left to answer the unaswerables, to explain the unexplainables. That's the way Marcus would have wanted it. Leave no evidence, no trace of wrongdoing. If he had buried me alive in those catacombs, who might ever have searched for me there? And if someone had, how would they have discovered my hidden tomb? Marcus McComber knew how to keep secrets, and he knew how to mold fascinating and disturbing tales.

In combination, those skills do not lend themselves to hard answers or concrete evidence. That is why I have no chance. Such is Marcus McComber.

"Jacob Moses Lyons," says the detective, the fisherman, Andrew Ruben, "you are under arrest." He's reading me my rights now, but I don't hear him. I only stare at the ignorant face of authority. He has no concern for me. He cares only about closing this case and returning home to sleep in a warm bed. His wife, if he has one, is not dead. His best friend will call him the next day for lunch.

Me? I have no one but myself. And what a sad friend I make. A drunk, unsuccessful author, wet and shivering, reeking of beer and urine.

Ruben stands me up now. How my legs ache. Burrows claps handcuffs on my wrists. They don't believe me. They figure I'm a writer, which, in their minds, means I'm creative. And they say I've concocted this entire narrative. I tried to explain that I'm too drunk to be creative, too miserable. I explain that I've never been very creative. In fact, I've written only one creative thing in the past ten years. A novel for my wife. My muse. But she is dead, and any inkling of creativity still swirling in the shadows of my mind has since been whisked into oblivion by death and despair.

In the tunnels beneath McBraidy Tavern, Marcus McComber said to me, "I suppose you'll be haunted enough by death in the coming hours. No need to hasten your own." He was right. And now I see that he has his revenge. A hasty death would've been the best thing for me. Now, my death might stretch out over decades, and it will be ten times more painful that Bree is gone. The days will be spent either in solitary or with a handful of convicted felons behind steel bars.

I try not to feel sorry for myself, but, as with most of my endeavors, I fail.

Burrows leads me out of the dungeon. That crucified Jesus Christ waves to me on the way out. Perhaps he's jealous of the fact I'm allowed to leave that dismal chamber. Or perhaps he's wishing me well on my way to earthly Hell.

Now we're in a cold, long, barren corridor, and I see only a stairwell at its end. A stairwell leading downward. And I imagine that I am a dying fish, trapped in the web of a fisherman's net. My only desire, my dying wish, is one more plunge deep into the black depths of the ocean, a return to life as it existed before a treacherous worm named Marcus McComber arrived for ale. I thrash in the fisherman's arms, my eyes closed, imagining one last glimpse of home, back when Breeana loved me. And I quote her a sonnet, and she smiles, and we sing a song, staring out across the sea. We melt into each other's embrace, there beneath a cloudless sky of moon and stars and eternity, and we make love beneath a giant Cypress, and our love is infinite and unyielding. Imagine it. You must, because it will never happen. I am but a fading memory at the bottom of an empty bottle. A dying fish in a tangled net.

Acknowledgements

This tale's journey is long and complex for no good reason. It began as a short story in college, then became a screenplay, then became a novel. The twists and cliffs and obstacles of life did their best to halt its progress at each phase, but a lot of great people along the way offered the encouragement that always brought me back to it. It's to all of them who I would like to say thanks, even if I forget a name or two.

Thanks to my parents, who may still be trying to figure out why a college kid would abandon Architecture for Creative Writing. They really only gave me grief about it for seven years, so I equate the punishment with swallowing a piece of gum or breaking a mirror, but I don't regret it, and I suspect they're proud of me despite the occasional questionable decision.

Thanks to the members of my critique group, who suffered through long bouts of my procrastination and non-productivity to help me rework and rework and rework the first part of a confusing manuscript. Thank you Randy Richardson, Lynn Voedisch, Paul G. Neilan, and Gregg Garmisa. I couldn't have done it without you.

Thanks to everyone who has read and commented on the manuscript in various forms. Kara Henson, Peggy Koperski, Kacy Koperski, Diane Tarshis, Libbie Dollinger, Gary Dollinger, Brian Dean, Erik Gloor, Brad

Panozzo, Tina Haas Kress, Linda Drummond, Pauline Lifton, Judy Newman, Jennifer Rossi. I know I'm forgetting someone. Forgive me.

Thanks to Josh Wiemer for editorial guidance, and a bit of ego-massaging. To Angela Edgerton for mystery, musings, and inspiration. To everyone who has followed this Amontillado saga over the years and kept it alive online dating back to the MySpace days.

Thanks to my daughters, Lexi and Rory, who think it's pretty cool that Daddy wrote a book, even if it's a book they're not yet allowed to read.

Thanks to author Tad Williams, who long ago told me the most important part of writing is finishing what you start. Well, I started this particular novel a long time ago under very different circumstances, but I'm happy to say, "Tad, I finished the damn thing! Thanks!"

And lastly, thanks to Rebecca Lynn. Once upon a time, when I considered turning a short story into a screenplay into a novel, she offered the encouragement I needed to give it a try. Writing is a lonely endeavor, often made tolerable by the support of the people we care about during the journey. Life moves on, worlds change, but those moments of encouragement can last lifetimes, and their importance deserves acknowledgement.

About the Author

Kevin Koperski is an entrepreneur, web designer, programmer, filmmaker, history buff, and technology enthusiast, but his first passion lands squarely in the realm of books. He's lived on both coasts of the United States, from Seattle to Jersey, and visited many a bookstore along the way. He currently lives in the Chicago area with his two daughters. Amontillado is his first novel.

www.ingramcontent.com/pod-product-compliance
Lightning Source LLC
Chambersburg PA
CBHW030525310726
48979CB00010B/1810/J

* 9 7 8 0 9 8 8 4 5 1 6 0 5 *